W9-CHY-908

Miami:
A Saga

Also by Evelyn Wilde Mayerson
in Thorndike Large Print ®

Well and Truly

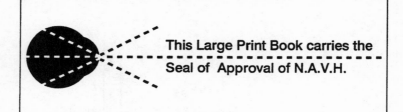

This Large Print Book carries the
Seal of Approval of N.A.V.H.

Miami:
A Saga

Evelyn Wilde Mayerson

Thorndike Press • Thorndike, Maine

Copyright © Evelyn Wilde Mayerson, 1994

All rights reserved.

Published in 1994 by arrangement with Dutton Signet, a division of Penquin Books USA Inc.

This is a work of fiction. Names, characters, places, and incidents either are the products of the author's imagination or are used fictitiously, and any resemblance to actual persons, living or dead, events, or locales is entirely coincidental.

Thorndike Large Print ® Basic Series.

The tree indicium is a trademark of Thorndike Press.

The text of this Large Print edition is unabridged.
Other aspects of the book may vary from the original edition.

Set in 16 pt. News Plantin by Minnie B. Raven.

Printed in the United States on acid-free paper.

Library of Congress Cataloging in Publication Data

Mayerson, Evelyn Wilde, 1934–
   Miami : a saga / Evelyn Wilde Mayerson.
    p.   cm.
   ISBN 0-7862-0267-X (alk. paper : lg. print)
   1. Large type books. I. Title.
  [PS3563.A9554M53   1994]
  813'.54—dc20   94-17035

*To James Michener,
who encouraged me to try
a broad canvas*

Acknowledgments

I am indebted to scores of scholars and writers, travelers and plain folk whose books and articles, journals and letters did the spadework for me. I am also indebted to dozens of native Miamians for their memories and their photographs.

My sincere thanks to Marjorie Stoneman Douglas; Helen Muir; Thelma Peters, Ph.D.; Thelma Gibson; Dorothy Jenkins Fields; Patsy West; Buffalo Tiger; Dorothy Downs; Mark Derr; Julia Morton; Rebecca A. Smith; Dawn Hugh; Sam Boldrick; William E. Brown, Jr.; Gladys Ramos; Ivan Rodriguez; William Straight, M.D.; Jerry Stolzenberg, M.D.; Elinor Backman; Henry Green, Ph.D.; Atlee W. Wampler III; Carroll Shuster D.D.; Don Gayer; Jerry Coleman; Ileano Bravo; Erica Rauzin; and Howard Kleinberg.

I am especially grateful to historian Arvah Moore Parks, who provided me with a road map, and to my wonderful editor Donna Cullen-Dolce, who helped me make sense out of a manuscript that spanned over one hundred years.

Above all, I thank my husband, Don, who solved the glitches of my computer and who survived three years pillow-talking about plot.

While their information has been invaluable, none of my sources is responsible for an author's interpretation of a community and its history or for invented characters and situations used to further a work of fiction.

The Coombs Family

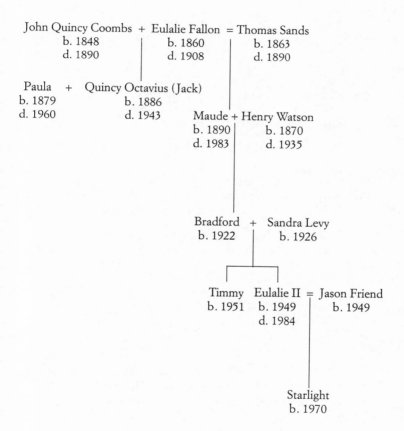

John Quincy Coombs + Eulalie Fallon = Thomas Sands
    b. 1848   b. 1860   b. 1863
    d. 1890   d. 1908   d. 1890

Paula + Quincy Octavius (Jack)
b. 1879   b. 1886
d. 1960   d. 1943   Maude + Henry Watson
                        b. 1890 b. 1870
                        d. 1983 d. 1935

Bradford + Sandra Levy
b. 1922   b. 1926

Timmy Eulalie II = Jason Friend
b. 1951 b. 1949   b. 1949
        d. 1984

Starlight
b. 1970

The Sands-McCloud Family

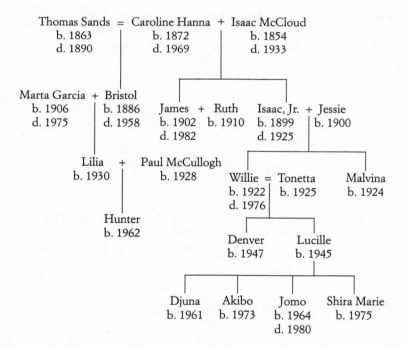

The Garcia-Alvarez Family

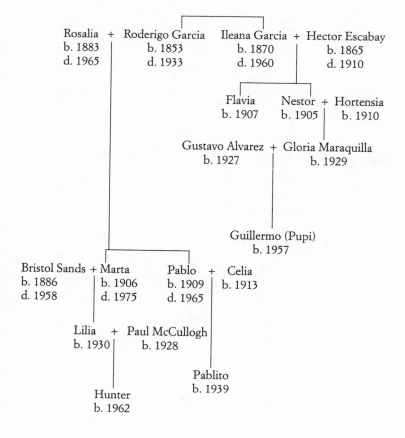

Rosalia + Roderigo Garcia   Ileana Garcia + Hector Escabay
b. 1883   b. 1853   b. 1870   b. 1865
d. 1965   d. 1933   d. 1960   d. 1910

Flavia   Nestor + Hortensia
b. 1907   b. 1905   b. 1910

Gustavo Alvarez + Gloria Maraquilla
b. 1927   b. 1929

Guillermo (Pupi)
b. 1957

Bristol Sands + Marta   Pablo + Celia
b. 1886   b. 1906   b. 1909   b. 1913
d. 1958   d. 1975   d. 1965

Lilia + Paul McCullogh
b. 1930   b. 1928

Pablito
b. 1939

Hunter
b. 1962

The Levy Family

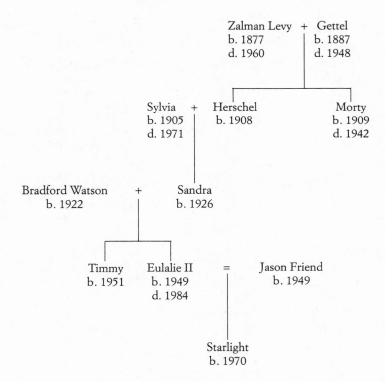

Zalman Levy + Gettel
b. 1877   b. 1887
d. 1960   d. 1948

Sylvia + Herschel   Morty
b. 1905   b. 1908   b. 1909
d. 1971   d. 1942

Bradford Watson +   Sandra
b. 1922   b. 1926

Timmy   Eulalie II   =   Jason Friend
b. 1951   b. 1949   b. 1949
          d. 1984

Starlight
b. 1970

The Doctor-Cypress Family

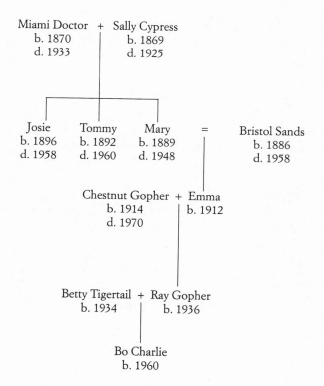

Miami Doctor + Sally Cypress
b. 1870   b. 1869
d. 1933   d. 1925

Josie   Tommy   Mary   =   Bristol Sands
b. 1896   b. 1892   b. 1889   b. 1886
d. 1958   d. 1960   d. 1948   d. 1958

Chestnut Gopher + Emma
b. 1914   b. 1912
d. 1970

Betty Tigertail + Ray Gopher
b. 1934   b. 1936

Bo Charlie
b. 1960

Prologue

The day was sunny and eerily calm, the absence of any air current creating a collective hush like a giant intake of breath. It was hard for Starlight to believe that a little puff of hot air spawned in the summer sky over Africa had become a category four hurricane chewing its way across the Atlantic toward the coast of Florida.

She ran her right hand through the crop of curly, taffy-colored hair cut to the nape of her neck, and with her left, steered her open Jeep north on Old Cutler Road, her broad, tanned cheekbones gleaming in the midday sun.

Cars with plywood strapped to their roofs zipped in and out of line, while a newscaster on the radio advised listeners to gather a first aid kit, a battery-powered radio, a flashlight, candles, matches, canned food, bottled drinking water, sterno, and a manual can opener in preparation for the hurricane ahead. Pregnant women were informed that since extreme low barometric pressure induced labor, hospitals were admitting those in their last trimester. Starlight was glad that pregnancy was not her problem; nor would it likely be in the foreseeable future now that she and Pupi had called off the wedding.

She reached her destination, a street behind the coral rock bluff on Bayshore Drive. The board and batten-pine house that her great-great grandparents had built stood half-hidden in overgrown vegetation, dwarfed by the property around it, almost defiant in its antiquity. She parked in the driveway beneath the shelter of the banyan, atop the buttress of horizontal roots that spread like fingers on the ground. Her eye was caught by a raccoon's nest above, that trembled and fluttered in the shelter of the tree's hollow crook. She noticed that the banyan had attached itself to the cedar shingles of the roof, and was growing through the cracks.

Starlight regarded the house with a curious affection despite its hanging front porch, its rough-hewn stone chimney that ran up the side like a squirrel. Other than the loss of all the copper gutters and downspouts, and a few exterior shutters stripped away by the salvagers, the pine cottage was the same as when she had seen it last.

Her grandfather had not understood her fierce protectiveness toward the house, especially her plans to secure it before the hurricane struck. "The house is not a living thing, Starlight," he had said. "We haven't even closed on it yet, which means that legally it's not yours. If anything, the property is still the responsibility of its present owner."

Starlight had kissed her grandfather on his handsome, weathered face.

"You know he doesn't give two hoots. He would have bulldozed it to the ground if you hadn't made the offer to buy it. Besides, you're talking like a lawyer. It doesn't matter who has the deed. The house belongs to me. It's as much mine as my nose or the color of my hair."

Starlight picked her way through overgrown pink-petaled oleander and rotten avocados that littered the yard. From nearby villas, she heard the whine of chain saws trimming tree limbs and excessive canopies whose weight might cause their trunks to topple in the storm.

The kitchen door, flanked by sweet-smelling acacia, was unlocked. Starlight stepped across its splintered threshold as someone yelled to someone else in the shrubbery-shrouded cottage next door to fill the bathtub so they would have water to flush the toilets.

The floor dipped and buckled and creaked beneath her feet. Cobwebs shrouded the exposed rafters while from every corner drifted the spicy odor of pine intermingled with a faint, lingering aroma that Starlight could not identify. In addition, the pungent smell of vegetation, lush and overripe and threatening to reclaim the hammock and all that intruded upon it, permeated the air.

She noticed angrily that despite the restraining order that her grandfather had obtained, the salvagers and their crowbars had stripped away the ceiling moldings, a hand-painted panel that had covered one wall of the dining room, the fireplace mantel, the glass-fronted kitchen cabinets, and the banister from the narrow rickety staircase, leaving broken balusters to sag against the steps.

Disgusted, Starlight rolled up the sleeves of Pupi's plaid shirt and ran outside to check the shutters, managing to fasten those on the first floor with rusty hooks that scraped into place. A sound truck blared from the street, advising everyone east of U.S.1 to evacuate immediately, bringing whatever medicines they needed and securing their pets as best they could as the shelters would not accept them. Starlight remembered the duct tape that she carried in her pocket, and ripped off long strips with which she crisscrossed the two uncovered kitchen windows to prevent their glass from shattering.

She cut through a tangle of foliage to ask a woman in the house next door if she could borrow a ladder to close the shutters on the second floor. The woman said she was using the ladder, but if Starlight was willing to wait, she could have it in an hour.

By the time Starlight had done all she could on the outside, the wind had picked up to a salty breeze. She took one last look at the pine house that connected her to her history. Her grandfather had said that Hurricane Andrew could become a force five hurricane with winds over one hundred sixty miles per hour. But that such a storm was rare, an event that occurred only once a century. Incredibly, thought Starlight, the modest frame dwelling before her had withstood the ravages of a hundred years of storms. She hoped it was a sign that it would likely survive this one as well.

Satisfied that there was no more she could do, Starlight climbed into the Jeep, headed south on Bayshore Drive, and switched on the radio. While the announcer reported that Miami Beach and Key Biscayne were closed and that most of the shelters were filled, Starlight was aware that the scent of the yellow-flowered acacia was still in her nose. She suddenly swung around, executing a hairpin U-turn that she had been advised by her grandfather never to make in the Jeep, and returned to the pine frame house. This was where she would wait out the storm. She knew the idea that this house needed her was irrational, yet its pull was as insistent as the acacia.

Starlight checked her backpack to make sure she still carried a flashlight, a liter bottle of Evian water, a package of Fritos, and a jar of pistachio nuts. Then she called her grandparents on her cellular phone and left a message on their answering machine to say that she would be staying with Pupi, careful to explain that this was not to be interpreted as a reconciliation, only that his apartment on Brickell was closer

19

than their home in Gables Estates.

The night seemed to come in great blankets of purple sky. Starlight sat eating pistachio nuts on the living room floor with the beam from her flashlight for her only illumination.

Outside the kitchen window, limbs on the poinciana rose and fell like swaying tentacles as the growling wind grew stronger. One of the shutters began to bang on its hinges. She put on her Walkman and turned to station Y-100 to listen to meteorologist Bryan Norcross advising everyone that the hurricane was heading straight for Miami, and that it was over warm water, which meant that it would likely pick up speed.

Suddenly, beyond the swaying poinciana, Starlight noticed that the nighttime glow from downtown Miami had disappeared, and in its place an unfamiliar blackness, as fathomless as the ocean at night. The electricity had failed, plunging the city, like the pine house, into darkness.

Starlight dozed on the floor with her head on the emptied backpack and dreamed that her mother was still alive, then she woke to pistachio shells floating in a pool of brackish water that trickled from beneath the front door. She ran upstairs to seek shelter in a bathroom until the tub rattled away from the wall and water poured in around the medicine chest. When the wind began to howl from the attic, she flung open the bathroom door and dashed down the creaking staircase to the safety of a closet in the narrow hall below.

The smell of mildew was overpowering. Starlight trained her flashlight on the darkness. Scattered about were mothballs and wire hangers, along with a sepia photograph of a fair-haired woman squinting in the sun while standing stiffly beside a little boy in a dress.

Some of the floorboards had sprung. Starlight examined the floor more closely, wondering if it was her great-great grandfather who had nailed down the planks of wood wider than the span of her hand. Something glinted beneath a board in the corner. She pried up the lifted end with her sandal. There in the rocky dirt lay a rusted tin box. It opened with a raspy sound. Inside the box was a frayed leather-bound book eaten with mildew.

Starlight flipped the book open, unmindful of the muffled jangle of a dozen car alarms, the sounds of shattering glass, of metal scraping across the pavement, of crashing coconuts and garbage cans. She tried to read the faded brown ink under the beam of the flashlight. The book appeared to be a diary written in an old-fashioned, meticulously crafted script. But the entries were too faint to make out in the dimly lit closet. Only the cover page was legible, revealing that the journal belonged to Eulalie Coombs and that its contents were private.

The diary's owner, Starlight realized, must have been the first Eulalie, her great-great

21

grandmother, the woman for whom her own mother was named. She was wondering if the first Eulalie was the woman in the sepia photograph when she became aware that something had changed.

She felt it before she heard it: the house groaning on its foundation as though trying to wrest itself from the coral rock that anchored it in place. Starlight set the diary aside to listen, to wait, to hold her breath, and huddle in the creaking dark.

Part One

1886–1898

Chapter One

MIAMI DOCTOR

My uncle, Willie Tiger, spent the first three years of his life in silence, buried to his neck with only a palmetto leaf to shield his tiny head from rain, sun, and mosquito.

Willie Tiger survived because my grandmother Ocelopee, hiding in scrub palmetto by day, came out by night to feed him. He had been planted like other little ones, to avoid detection by white soldiers charged to drag those among us who spoke English back to slavery, and those of us who spoke Seminole to Arkansas, there to join the Creeks, who hate us because of the fork that divides our paths.

The experience has marked my mother's brother, the Tustenugge of our clan. To this day, he sits with his shoulders hooked to his ears, as if he is still neck deep in sand, as if he still expects a rattlesnake to coil about his baby forehead. While deciding if Crop-ear Tommie is to be steamed for lying, he sits as if waiting for my grandmother to come at night and feed him sofke dripping from a wooden spoon that, of course, she cannot since her ghost has long since gone up north, over the curving shelf of the night.

Because of his ability to wait and listen, my uncle, as a youth, was the first in our camp to hide Billy Sunshine from the slave catchers, and the first, as an elder, to notice that the white settler was not only coming closer, but in greater numbers.

"They come," he said, "like angry wasps with lies in their mouths seeking the Indian's lands."

At first no one believed him. Not because Willie Tiger told untruths but because the idea was like the black muck, unfathomable. We did not choose to live in the Pahahokee, the waving grass prairie that is in reality a shallow river flowing south to meet the sea. We were driven into its marshy depths in our flight from the white man, who wanted us gone from the long land he calls Florida, whose pinelands and hammocks he knotted with forts to wage his rope of war. Why would the white man become willing food for the mosquito and the deer fly unless he too was a fugitive, and how could so many be fugitives on land they claimed as their own?

My uncle insisted. He knew by certain telltale signs, the way he always knew, for example, from the bloom on the sawgrass that a great wind was coming. "Do you think I am like a bat that hangs by its claws in the cypress that I see nothing of what is going on around me?

They're getting closer," he said, "the half-baked ones," allowing a smile to slip out of the corner of his mouth at the common joke that, while the black man was overbaked and the white man underbaked, the red man was done to a turn by the giver of breath.

"Are slave catchers among them?" asked my mother, her neck encased shoulder to chin in string upon string of blue glass beads the weight of two turkeys. She asked this knowing that the matter of slave catching had been settled before the time of my birth when the white man went to war against himself. She also knew, as did everyone else, that the white man paid little attention to treaties, even those made with his own brother, and so was not the least surprised if the half-baked ones persisted in tracking down and placing in irons the runaway property of his grandfathers.

My uncle didn't answer. He believed that talk with women was like trying to hide from mosquitoes, a wasted effort. Like the wasted effort spent with the agent who arrived in a folding canvas canoe and wearing a canvas hunting coat to tell us that Washington had put aside money to buy us homesteads. Take advantage of this law, the agent had said, while Billy Sunshine's fourth wife treated the jagged gashes of the sawgrass on the agent's hands and face with the stems of wild grape. Willie Tiger agreed. The agent said he would inquire at the land office. When he returned, this time wearing deerskin gloves, he told us that no public lands could be found. "Lies in their mouths," said Willie Tiger when the agent had left.

Now my uncle turned to me and said that he had seen feeble wisps of smoke over the horizon, not the choking clouds of black from peat fires that burn in the swamp, but pallid curls from the direction of the burnt-out cabin, made by some new white man unable to kindle swamp wood. More disturbing, my uncle suspected that this same white man had desecrated the mound.

While the hillock's birth is beyond anyone's recall, its veneration has been handed down, the way Tony Bowlegs' medicine bundle has been passed from one withered fist to the next. We know that the mound people were not people of our fire because they buried their dead in refuse piled high with shells instead of on a proper scaffold. Nevertheless, we always walk softly about these ancient spirits so as not to awaken them, thereby causing them to wander restlessly and bring misfortune to the living.

Our fathers tell us that after the white man dragged mound people north into slavery, those of their descendents who escaped their bondage returned to the long land seeking refuge with the Seminole. Billy Sunshine, renowned for his garments taken long ago from a caravan of whites who chanted like medicine men, is such a person. He is a red man, yet his softened nose speaks of a black grandmother. We ask him to explain the meaning of the mound, but he can't remember, not even when he is sense-gathering.

I was sent with Jimmy Jumper to hide our cattle and our hogs. We poled east through sawgrass as wiry as whips, an impenetrable barrier to the white man, who is often lost and starving in its maze, through soft black muck, past tiny streams blocked by sawgrass curtains, following the trail of half-submerged alligators as steering currents rushed our dugout past mangroves with roots as twisted as the white man's words. Each of us wore deerskin leggings with a fringe of thongs, many necker-chiefs, a medicine dress belted with a bright sash, and a buckskin belt from which hung a hunting knife, revolver, and ammunition pouch. Our heads were wrapped in cloth wound around a frame of bark. Jimmy Jumper's headdress, with egret plumes and silver clasps, was par-ticularly awe-inspiring, especially since he is taller than most whites to begin with.

At the edge of the Pahahokee, where the wind whistles over the stiff beard of the pines, we came to a narrow pass through which shore-to-shore fish pushed to return from the river. Alligators so tightly packed, it would have been easy to walk the rest of the way on their heads, were gobbling up the fish, squeezing them in their jaws while the tails of the trout flapped about the alligators' eyes.

We pulled our dugout ashore while a lizard slipped over a wrinkled root that had buried itself like a finger in the sand. Turkey buzzards wheeled overhead on motionless wings. The white people made no move to conceal their tracks, and we spotted them at once. This particular white man was meager, scrawny, with a body as narrow as a plank. His squaw, his dog, his ox, and his pig were as gaunt as he. His dim, sad face was as pale as any I have seen, with skin the color of maggots. We think it is the sow belly and grits that keeps them this light. His hair was bleached as white as bones, yet he was not old, for even at a distance I could see that his light blue eyes were unclouded.

At first his squaw's face and hair were hidden in her hat. It appeared that like Sally Cypress, whose half-white child had been left for the buzzards to eat, the women of this white woman's clan had punished her too, pulling each of her hairs out one by one, but when she turned in my direction, bits of hair that poked like straw from beneath her bonnet told me that this was not so. Her face, burned and flaking from the sun, was pinched, as if she had sucked a kumquat for the first time. Her eyes were narrowed into slits. Later I learned that she did not squint to see in the distance, but because the sun was particularly vengeful

on clear eyes. I judged her to be not in her first youth, at least twenty-five. She cried so continually we thought she might be a captive.

I was disappointed that we did not spy him covering her, as it is said that the white man's way is different. How can that be, I asked, when there is only one gate? My uncle laughed. My nephew cannot count, he said. When he explained that it was not the gate but the approach, that white women lie on their backs like upended turtles, I was glad that I did not see it.

We might have had a good visit, a squat and eyeball meeting with maybe a bottle or two of whiskey thrown in. Unfortunately, she saw us before he did and began to scream, a bloodcurdling yip as good as any I have ever heard, which made the dog bare his teeth and the man run for his rifle. The woman ducked beneath their tattered shelter, a lean-to propped against the mound while the man spat tobacco juice and cocked his rifle.

"You shouldn't sneak up on folks," he said. "It's not friendly."

Jimmy Jumper, who speaks the white man's tongue, told him that we didn't sneak up. We are taught to walk softly, at one with the land, at one with our mothers and fathers, toe, heel, along the side of the foot, like a gliding snake, a drifting plume of fog. If we are noiseless, it is because that is our custom.

Then Jimmy Jumper offered the white man a string pouch filled with venison and encouraged him not to disturb the mound any more than he already had. It was necessary that he understood that spirits, when violated, are always angry, as would be anyone who woke to find that he lay buried in a heap of cowrie shells.

The white man interrupted. "I don't know what the hell ghosts you're talking about, and I don't much care what pieces you'all carry on your belts. I catch you creeping around here again, you're going to get sure-shot right between the eyes." Then he put his hand into the tent and pulled his woman out. I would never drag my own woman in that manner even if I had one. Besides the possibility that she might be carrying a child, there is the greater likelihood of injuring her firewood and cooking arm, but the white man did not seem to know that, just as he did not know that he had disturbed the spirits of the ancient ones.

"Don't let them see you afraid," he said.

The woman didn't scream, but just stared at us with the wide, unseeing eyes of a dead person. Then the man pointed at us with his rifle, took the venison and sweet potatoes, and spoke through his teeth, "You'all just turn around, get back to that canoe of yours before I plug it full of holes. Go on, hightail it out of here."

That signaled the end of our visit, which was a pity since the woman looked as if she might be going into a sense-gathering trance.

We returned to the smells of my mother's pumpkin bread and venison stew. She had already begun to give away her beads, yet she could still cook. A small tent of thatch had been erected near the cooking chickee. My uncle, Billy Sunshine, and Jimmy Jumper's grandfather were preparing to steam Crop-ear Tommie.

We told them as the heated stones sizzled in the water-filled hole that settlers on the south side of the Mayami River had hollowed out a portion of the mound to make their lean-to. Jimmy Jumper's grandfather shook his head and said he longed for the days of bringing in the hair. Not that he wished to wage war; we all knew that the war days were over, even though we had signed no treaty. It was just that he wished, as he wished so desperately every night with his fourth wife, to be able to prove his own power once again. No one thought that bringing in hair was a good idea, in any case. Now that we've moved deeper into the swamp, there's no place to put it. Hair must be strung and properly dried; otherwise it does no good at all.

Later that night we all felt it, even Crop-ear Tommie, leeched out and weakened from his ordeal. It wasn't the screams of the panthers or the hoots of the owls. It was the fire suddenly going out, an unfamiliar breath upon one's face, a scalp crawling away from the skull beneath. The spirits were loose, which meant that now nobody would get any sleep.

Chapter Two

My dear Thomas,

I shall skip pleasantries and get to the matter at hand, which is the plantation. You must know that the conversion from pineapple to the production of sisal, while promising, is no simple task. If you care nothing for me or for our holdings, then consider your mother, who pines for you.

You call yourself a wrecker and tell me that it is within the law. Piracy, in its heyday, was a weapon against the Spaniards. It was a noble calling, if not a bloodthirsty one. Many a ruined colonist found his way into its number, your great-uncle Jeremy among them. When these privateers took up arms against the Spaniards, they were avenging outraged humanity, considering it no crime to deprive that hateful nation

34

of its ill-gotten treasures obtained from the mines of the new world with a terrible sacrifice of human life. Similarly, while I was not a blockade runner during the war between the states, I funded such operations. That too was a noble cause, to wit, striking a blow against the Union. On the other hand, what you are calling legal is nothing more than plunder, and if you continue to reap its rewards, then you are no better than the worst buccaneer.

I cannot understand why you choose a barbarian existence in such a godforsaken place as the village they call Miami. Your grandfather, as you have been told, fled South Carolina following the colonial insurrection. And while he sought sanctuary in St. Augustine, his selection was not engendered by any love of Florida, but rather because of British rule. He soon fled for his life, as you might remember, when Florida was ceded to the Spaniards, finding not only sanctuary in the Bahamas, but a land grant from the Earl of Dunsmore, then governor.

What you may not know is that the silver mace which is now in use in the House of Assembly, once used in the assembly in the province of South Carolina, was conveyed to the Bahamas by your grandfather. In contrast, the iron body cage that you once uncovered and which you attribute to his use against his slaves, seems hardly the sort of thing that would interest a man who risked his life for a badge of office.

The point being, he was driven from his home, his estates confiscated by former friends and neighbors. When hostilities ceased, the Whigs committed a great crime by manifesting a spirit determined to place your grandfather and other humbled loyalists beneath their boots. Because of it, I still cherish the most intense hatred toward the United States and its people, and would hope that you did the same.

I know that among your grievances, other than a restless spirit which I attribute to youth, is the colonial policy of bestowing the principal posts of emolument and honor to persons sent out from England, and that many of these posts are closed to Bahamians. As one who has lived into his sixth decade, I can tell you that all of these things will change, but it will take time, of which, I might add, you have a surfeit.

As to the young lady in question, I have handled the affair as I have the previous two, a chore I found as tedious and as wearisome as the constant sighing of your mother, due to the persistence of the young lady's father. It is time you learned, Thomas, not to make a pledge you cannot keep. In the other matter, I have settled upon the woman Caroline the five pounds which you sent, a sum adequate for her immediate needs and those of her child. I have seen the boy, and while his skin is dusky as one might expect, his hair is almost blonde and lightly curled, as yours, and his eyes likewise an uncommon green. It will be interesting to see him about the island from time to time, watch him grow, and become, while not a grandchild in the purest sense, a bête noire of sorts of yourself.

I turn your attention back to the most pressing matter at hand. I must say that I am very encouraged. Sisal requires very little outlay of capital and in contrast to pineapple, very little labor. The price of the fiber is £ 34 a ton, yet its cost of production is only £ 12. An acre of land will produce a yearly crop of about half a ton of fiber, and the sisal plants last up to fifteen years. Since they are planted in rows with young ones coming up between them, the crop is practically self-renewing. In my opinion, the fiber industry, with which we have recently cast our lot, will be the future great staple of the colony. Come home to Eleuthera and join with me in making this so.

Your loving father who supplicates for your swift and safe return,
Edward Sands

Caroline's skin was mahogany, a deep, maroon black that glinted like port in the sun, the pupils of her wide eyes the color of chocolate. Papa Hanna told her that she had the same comeliness as her great-grandmother, the African, undiminished by servitude in the Bahamas or the lust of a colonial forbear. Her beauty, however, could not help her now and, in fact, was the source of her trouble, for Caroline knew that the Obeah was upon her even before she spied the rusty knife suspended at the front door of her cottage, or found the chicken bones in the pocket of her cotton shift. She put her fingers to her head, touching the tight, crinkly braids done up with ribbon, the vulnerable back of her small, slender neck, as she searched the cabin for a tiny niche, a meager cranny that would admit the serpent Diablesse. Her eyes darted over the tattered screen pasted with newsprint, the patchwork quilt that covered the narrow iron bed, the chair with crochet armrests, the paper-covered window, the boarded daylight-crazed walls. Praying that Obeahman had not gotten her footprints or the footprints of the child, she hurried outside to sprinkle rice around her cabin so that he would have to count every grain before he could enter.

That night she walked barefoot with the boy on her back, through myrtle- and jasmine-scented shadows to escape the earlier heat of the day and the watchful eye of Obeahman, within sight of foaming, moonlit breakers, her cotton frock frilled at the neck and arms, tucked up in a bunch about her waist so that her free, elastic stride might not be impeded. Since the age of nine, she had worked on a sugar estate, carrying the canes, carting away the trash in the scorching sun. Now, at fifteen, she was lithe and strong, and the journey to the Mamadjou on the other side of the island, past white misses taking tea on moonlit verandas, was effortless.

It was midnight when Caroline stood among the moving shadows before the rude stone altar, her skin glowing in the light of the candles as the Mamadjou, dressed in scarlet robe and red turban, droned an ancient chant, and a naked drummer, his body painted to look like a skeleton, held his drum between his knees and beat it with the tips of his fingers. Someone shook a tambourine, and Bristol stirred in Caroline's arms.

Then, to the beat of the quickening drum and the jingling slivers of the tambourine, the Mamadjou, quivering with each beat of the drum, sipped from a bottle of rum, picked up a glittering machete, and with the other hand grabbed a black rooster, whirled the bird around her head until feathers flew in all directions, and with one swift, violent stroke severed its head from its body. Only when the priestess pressed the bleeding neck of the fowl to her lips to suck its squirting blood that filled her mouth faster than she could swallow, and the silent worshipers burst into shouts, did the boy wake and begin to cry.

Caroline returned at daybreak thinking herself wrapped in the protection of the Mamadjou, and therefore not minding the rain that was turning the lanes into mud. When she found the coconut

39

stuffed with charcoal beneath her front step, she fled in terror to her grandfather's hut.

At first they sat in silence while the palmetto fans dripped like gutters. Papa Hanna had gone blind when still a slave from raking salt in brilliant, white-lit flats. He stared beyond her as if he were still squinting from the light.

"Perhaps I did not give her enough money," she said.

"It is not the money," the old man replied. He broke apart a dark green melon with an inside like cotton sopped in sugar, and brought it to his lips. "Has the Obeahman ever honored you?" he asked.

Caroline shivered at the thought of the specter who carried everywhere a skin bag of feathers, rags, bones, and bits of earth from graves. He lived in a windowless, wattled hut where he sat at a bench before a burning shark oil lamp. Many times he had beckoned her to come inside. She told her grandfather how the month before she had stood in the doorway and had seen on the bench the shriveled head of a cat, a waxy hand cut off at the wrist, and the tiny figure of a man with the head of a cock.

"Let the yellow-haired child wait outside," Obeahman had commanded. Something about his voice filled her with terror, or perhaps it was the severed hand with which she was afraid he might touch her. She had picked up Bristol and run for her life.

Caroline's grandfather now regarded her with

40

clouded eyes that looked as if they could be peeled. He thought of the cholera that had taken his wife and sons, remembering the deserted wharf where ships with unfurled sails lay at anchor while villagers brought out their dead, and the camphor bag that his wife had worn around her neck.

"Obeahman can't work his curse if you're not here," he finally said.

"Where do I go, Papa Hanna?" she asked. "Nassau?"

"No," replied the old man sadly. "Not Nassau. Not even Bimini. You must leave the islands. Take the boy and sail with the spongers. Don't go to Key West. It is too well traveled. You'd be found. Go to the place they call Miami."

"What if there is no work?"

He reminded her that she could carry a basket of firewood on her head, pound any garment clean, and plant limes on coral rock and make them grow. "If you remain," he warned, "you and the boy will surely die."

"How soon must I leave?" she asked.

"Now," he replied. "Before the rain turns to steam."

Caroline clutched her son by the hand and wondered if Sands had gotten another woman. Probably. He was too much like the sea he loved, with the same sudden shifts, the same restless energy, the same imperious surges to be satisfied with one.

The night was alive with fireflies, and the child tried to grab them in his tiny fist. Scattered on the deck behind them were heaps of onions and coconuts, a basin full of limes, kegs of flour, barrels of hominy, dried fish, and sponges lying in strings, while washing hung from the boom and from the yards above.

With little wind to stir the oil-like water, the sponging schooner slipped across the harbor softly with all the sails unfurled while a steerman set his course by the stars and by a compass set between his feet. Now and then a wave swept the deck, depositing the dried fish from one corner of the two-masted vessel to the other.

By noon the next day, they had left the shield of the islands, and the wind blew in gusts that shook the sails with sounds like cannon shots.

"Rigging's bust," called a boatman while two of his crewmates clung to the edge of the vessel with their toes, leaning out over the water to catch the frayed end of the slashing rope. "All fast," they cried when the sheet was tied again.

"Nothing to fear," said the captain, but soon the ship hurled about like a cork, reminding Caroline of a storm two years before, when she had run toward the beach after hearing the signal guns of distress. She had stood with other onlookers as wind-whipped salt water stung her face, watching a skiff bound toward a brig with broken masts and sails that flew apart like threads. Caroline had recognized the markings of the skiff and tried to contain her pride when Thomas pulled alongside the plunging brig, handed down the survivors of the foundering vessel, then struggled with the angry waves with the same desperate energy with which he shared her iron cot. They had been together the week before, and the memory of his hands and mouth had stirred her on the windswept beach as it stirred her now.

Caroline turned her attention back toward the lookout who clung to the rigging, his ragged garments fluttering in the wind, while waves hurled on deck with a deafening noise. "More squalls ahead," he shouted as rain poured in blinding sheets and the boatmen tore at the ropes to pull in the mainsail.

She ran to huddle in the water-drenched hold with the boy in her arms. "What is happening?" she shouted to a boatman who had run below for an ax.

"No man can tell you that," he replied, "can't do no more now except try to keep this boat from capsizing and trust in the Lord. That's the onliest thing we can do."

She heard them chopping down a mast and wondered if the coconut that she thought she saw rolling on the deck was really a withered cat head. She also wondered if Jesus with the pale gentle hands and the same golden hair as her son had any power over Obeahman.

Dear Father,

I trust this letter finds both you and Mother well and hope you will understand why I cannot accede to your continued request. It does not mean that I do not wish you great success. Sisal is a useful crop and I am confident that you will do well in its production. Perhaps you might see it my way if I point out that just as it is necessary to separate sisal pulp from its fiber, so it was necessary for me to leave the plantation.

I prefer the sea, Father. I need to pit my vessel against weather and reef. I particularly relish the challenge of coming upon some poor stranded wretch of a captain, rescuing him, his crew, and his cargo, and earning money in the bargain. Only last week, for example, I salvaged a mahogany piano, a Pleyel of French manufacture, a pianino really, in the design of a secretaire console out of Marseilles. Brickell, a local trader, assures me that once it is dry and tuned, it will sound almost new, except for the lowest octave, which is hardly ever used.

Think of my preference the result of a difference in temperament. You, for example, are a proponent of the deep keel craft. I, on the other hand, have come to prefer the centerboard, *an innovation well suited to the shoal waters of Florida where a sailor places a premium on an extreme light draft, on a vessel quick to lift at the impact of a wave, unlike the deep boat, which is held down by the inertia of the keel.*

If you are still of the mind that I have no head for business, you will be pleased to learn that I have just acquired dry pine land that I believe will ultimately be worth a great deal of money because of its suitability to cattle raising. It had been homesteaded by a man with no head for farming, other than a sparse patch of pineapples which seems to thrive no matter what we do to it. The man in question did not fulfill the requirements of the law, namely to post his intentions in a newspaper for six weeks running. Since I have no intention of living inland, it is being managed by a chap named Tatum who lives on the adjacent homestead, to whom I have promised one third the proceeds, who seems to understand something about ranching and who is not afraid to try something new. For example, we are experimenting with the use of water hyacinths as fodder. As a matter of interest, one cannot work the scrub palmettoes with lariats as they do in the American west; instead, local cowmen use catch dogs who hold the cattle by the nose until they can be branded. You may be amused by my brand, an S with a twist at the end, like sisal rope.

You ask why I no longer reside in Key West. Frankly, I am not sorry to be quit of Cubans and their cigar trade which has taken over the island, although I have kept my warehouse. What is now called Coconut Grove, by contrast, is open, unfinished, sparsely settled, although there is talk of a railroad, perhaps five or ten years in the future. Then, of course, all this will change.

There are two distinct classes who seldom mix. First there are the settlers, louts for the most part, although able and hardy, except for their women, who shrivel like starfish. Then there are the winter visitors, a likely sort, who regard themselves as "polite society." While many of them consider me something of a Jean LaFitte, the fact that I was educated in England oddly accounts for my invitation to enter their regatta on the occasion of George Washington's birthday, in itself an irony and something I thought you might find amusing.

Of course there are the Indians who often outnumber the whites and who bring provisions to trade and who make fine hunting guides. One grand old fellow wears velvet doublets straight out of Shakespeare. I wonder how he came upon it. Plundered costume from some unfortunate actor, no doubt.

Incidentally, Caroline has settled here, although not at my invitation. She is employed at the hotel and has the boy with her. I see him on occasion, a sprightly child, who resembles

46

me in that smoky way that your foreman, Hugh, resembles you.

> *Your devoted, if not dutiful son,*
> *Thomas*

Chapter Three

John Quincy Coombs erected a sailcloth tent beneath the shelter of a mammoth banyan, cleaned his nails with a bowie knife, and said that he had no more stomach for homesteading.

"We're not going to do it hardscrabble anymore, Eulalie," he declared. "We're gonna squat right here on the bay. Plunk ourselves down just like that. After a spell if no one claims it, it's ours. Once in a while, a fellow gets lucky."

His wife, Eulalie, who was trying to tend a feverish child, considered the hot, sticky, mosquito-filled shelter one more trial from the Lord. Despite the floppy bonnet she always wore, her sunburnt nose continued to peel like an onion. "We never would have lost our homestead if you had put notices in the Key West newspaper the way you were supposed to," she said.

Her husband stabbed at a chameleon. It wriggled pinioned at the end of his knife, its dewflap billowing a bright scarlet. "You don't know nothing. The land office never meant for us to have that property in the first place."

Eulalie glanced at her husband. She had first laid eyes on him at a revival meeting. His hanging hair and drooping hat reminded her of the Spanish moss that clung to the cypress, and she thought he was handsome. When he told her that he was fixing to leave Palatka, quit his job wheeling flannel-wrapped Yankee consumptives, and move south to Dade County, where fruit was ripe for picking and where fish were so thick a man could blow them right out of the water, he was the answer to a prayer.

Now John Quincy was just something else to be borne, like the blue-tailed flies the size of bees, the brush fires set by the cattlemen that kept the sky awash in a silver haze, the heavy rains that drowned the seedlings of anything they tried to grow in saucer-like prairies, the capricious decision to move from the piney woods to the colony on the bay.

Eulalie listened to the occasional sounds that came from the settlement: the yelp of a dog, the crow of a rooster, a sail luffing in the salty breeze. She wondered about the other unseen shacks and tents that nestled nearby in an aroma of fish and tobacco, between sabal palm and yellow pine growing from rock encrusted with skeletons of marine life long extinct.

When John Quincy pointed his knife at all the guava waiting to be picked, Eulalie prayed for grace enough not to tell him a thing or two and focused her attention on coaxing two-year-old Jack to take a dose of quinine mixed in coffee, a fever remedy she had learned from her mother.

"Met a fellow with a skiff," he said, his voice a slow, wheedling drawl. "Knows everything there is to know about the water. He can take off the top of a pelican's head with a derringer, and steer with one hand on one spoke of the wheel. Sands, that's this fellow's name, Sands told me that if I knew anything about sailing, he would take me to the reef where we can board legal any ship that's run aground and take what we want. The richest cargo in the world, Eulalie. Laces, silks, wines, silver knives and forks." He looked sideways, trying to flush out a look of respect. "Sometimes if a man knows what he's about, he doesn't even have to wait for a wreck."

"What does that mean?"

"Ever hear of decoy lights?"

She stood before the open fire, wilting collard greens to make a poultice. "Sounds like thieving to me."

He regarded her as if she were simple while she wrapped the collard poultice about the boy's forehead and bound it with a rag.

"After this next baby gets itself born, Eulalie,

49

I heard of a way for a woman not to get gone up."

Eulalie folded her arms across the shelf of her abdomen and replied that if he was talking about a sponge soaked with vinegar and quinine, she would have nothing to do with it.

"I'm the one puts it on," he said. "It's some kind of rubber thing."

"That's a sorry idea if I ever heard one. What if it gets lost, then where would we be?"

"I could break you of your arguing ways, Eulalie, but I don't have the time." He reached for the short-handled grub hoe and swung it down angrily against the coral rock.

While her husband hacked a clearing beneath shafts of white, unrelenting sunlight, Eulalie took the child inside the lean-to to sort out her meager belongings: a diary bound with empty vellum pages, a flat iron, a sewing machine with a foot treadle, a crate of Sweet China orange plants, a daguerreotype of her father, Octavius, in his Confederate uniform, and a trunk filled with clothing, most of it her mother's in the style of twenty years before, with panniers and godets and voluminous skirts meant to swing over hoops.

She was about to unlock the trunk when the boy called from his pallet for his toys. Eulalie felt in her apron pockets for the dry, dusty objects that John Quincy had pecked with his bowie knife from the strange mound in the piney woods, pottery shards faintly traced with ochre in the pattern of a diamondback snake, a mortar and pestle, a bone in the shape of an oversized fish hook, and a string of beads made from some unfamiliar shiny black stone.

Eulalie bent beneath the mosquito netting of the boy's pallet to lay the ancient relics at his side. Despite his fever, his translucent skin was as pearly to her as the gates of heaven. "Someday," she said, "you'll wear a vest with a watch fob just like your grandfather Octavius."

John Quincy opened the flap of the lean-to, admitting the fragrances of custard apple and jasmine. "You through filling his head with hogwash?" he said, then pulled her beneath the cheesecloth canopy of their bed.

She lay on her side so that the weight of the baby was borne by the thin mattress, while he whispered through the sweet smell of whiskey that after the baby was born, he wanted her to put on her corsets like she used to do, and lace them up real, real tight. He put his hands on her tender, swollen breasts. "Real tight, Eulalie, so that your titties stand out like this."

When he thrust himself inside her, she edged herself as far back as she could so that his thumping would not make the unborn child senseless, and decided that it was not nearly so awful as the time in the piney woods when he had her on the ground within sight of sleek black vultures perched on a scrub oak.

Eulalie tried to forget the homestead that

was almost theirs. Loss, in her experience, was something one both expected and accepted. The alternative was to wither in grief, like her widowed mother, Lavinia, who lived in a brother's attic between a marble and marquetried accumulation of three generations of Georgian revival. It was a luxury Eulalie could not afford, like smelling salts or shoes for Jack, or those new cellulose pads a woman could buy to absorb her monthly flow, if and when she ever got another one.

She told herself that none of it mattered, that she still burned out stumps, still watched for rattlers, still cooked outdoors over an open fire, still took turns with John Quincy swinging down the grub hoe to ring against the porous rocks or thud against the roots of the palmettoes. And if the occasional woman who came bearing an egg, a jar of guava jelly, treated her with the mild disdain they might hold for any squatter, she knew they were as lonely, as work weary as she.

Eulalie was stripping hot, wet feathers from the carcass of a chicken when a stranger appeared with a cigar clamped between his teeth, pushing his way through the ferns and orchid-draped, twisted gumbo limbo, then stepping carelessly over a smudge of burning coconut husks. He smelled of sweat and bay rum and tobacco, an aroma as arrogant as his stance.

Eulalie guessed that he had come to tell them

to get off his property. She dropped the chicken into a pot of water and wiped her hands on her apron while the stranger whisked sand spurs from his boots with his straw hat.

"Here's where you've hidden yourself," he said. "I knew I'd find you sooner or later."

John Quincy seemed to know him, for he smiled, hooked his thumbs beneath his galluses, and snapped them over his shirt. "This here is Tom Sands," he said, then nodded toward Eulalie. "My missus."

Sands lifted his straw hat and regarded the spare, work-worn woman before him with a practiced eye. Wearing mitts of old lisle stockings crosshatched with a dozen darnings, she was younger than he had expected if her teeth and the sway of her breasts were any indication, although her eyes were already creased into slits from the sun. Her mouth, he decided, was her best feature, lush even, if she would only not gather her lips like a purse string. He decided that if she were out of the sun for a month, no longer pregnant, dressed in the right clothes, her wheat blonde hair arranged and pomaded, a drop of perfume behind her ears and knees, in the crease of her elbows and the valley between her breasts, she might even be lovely.

Eulalie had expected Thomas Sands to be less polished, less well favored, someone rough and ready with unkempt beard and missing teeth, someone like John Quincy. Masking her surprise, she responded to the tip of his hat with seldom used etiquette, her antebellum lineage evident in the graceful lift of her torn and smudged calico skirts as she dipped a knee in curtsy.

When she lifted her head, she noticed that Sands' hair and skin were a muted bisque, like oatmeal or almonds, or the shelly beach at dusk. "I am pleased to meet you, Mrs. Coombs," he said in a lilting cadence neither the soft, trailing drawl of southern folk nor the nasal twang of the Yankee.

It was his eyes from which she averted her gaze, intense and rusty green like the bronzes that her father, Octavius, pawned for taxes.

"You can call her Eulalie," said John Quincy, upending a barrel for Sands to sit on. "That's her Christian name."

Eulalie knew that Sands, like her father, was a gentleman, despite his callused hands. It wasn't because he didn't chew tobacco or spit, or because he used fancy words like those in their homestead papers that they couldn't understand. It was the way he moved, like water pouring from a spout, easy, smooth, as if everything were his to drench, mildew, spill over, or drown. John Quincy had said he wasn't married. Eulalie knew that too, the moment she laid eyes on him. It was his chancy, eager glance, as if he were ticking off possibilities with all the time in the world to pursue them.

Jack regarded the stranger with solemn, trusting, child-round eyes while Eulalie dangled the fowl by its yellow feet and singed it with a flaming piece of paper. When the flame went out, Sands struck a long match against the heel of his boot and rekindled the paper.

"Allow me, ma'am," he said.

Eulalie avoided his eyes, which he held as steady as the flame. It was difficult enough getting all the hairs off the chicken to have to contend with intimate attentions more appropriate to suitors or dimly remembered servants smelling of rose water and permanganate. It was not his attentions that made her uneasy so much as her own illicit pleasure at being noticed.

Eulalie made herself busy. After the fowl had been dumped into the boiling cooking pot, she led Jack to the tin washtub. "Fine-looking woman," said Sands. He placed a board on the ground and opened a wooden box. "Muggins or sniff," he asked. He stayed for a jug of whiskey, a handful of cigars, and a game of dominoes, in which John Quincy, whose head had begun to buzz like a hive, had difficulty standing the blocks on end.

"I'm taking out the sloop tomorrow," Sands said as he left. "You coming?"

John Quincy drew himself upright. "Count on me," he replied.

"Good man," said Sands with a tip of his hat to Eulalie, who was drying Jack with a yellowed, moth-eaten, lace-trimmed dressing sacque that had belonged to her mother.

"What does he want with you?" Eulalie asked when Sands had disappeared through the foliage. Her tone was sharp, disapproving, as nettled as the acacia.

John Quincy broke off a twig of chinaberry the width of his thumb. "I can beat you with this," he said. "Anytime I like. It's the law in Florida."

Eulalie didn't need to hold up the lantern to see that his eyes were red from drink. She ignored his threat and continued to dress the barefoot child in a nainsook dress that had once been hers. The boy stamped his foot and said he wanted britches. "You don't need britches," she said. "Britches are hard to take off when you want to sit on the pot. Besides, it's just like the long shirts the Indians wear."

John Quincy broke the twig in half. "I saw you sashaying this way and that, picking up your skirt, trying to attract his attention."

"I was doing no such thing, John Quincy. I was seeing to the stew and to the boy."

"You can't do that to a man," he said. "No sir. A man gets bottled up, he gets sick. Can't do that. Get inside the tent."

Eulalie sighed. "Quincy Octavius," she said.

"Don't worry about Jack." He secured the child with a length of rope to the upright root of a banyan, then led Eulalie into the tent, where he pushed her facedown on the bed, pulled her up on her knees, and thought that

56

for once he would like to see her with all her clothes off. She in turn prayed to Jesus that it would soon be over and wondered how old a man got before he stopped having such thoughts. The only solace for her, a summer that was only months away, bringing with it another bout of dengue fever for John Quincy, which would leave him unable to do anything but search for his breath.

The tethered child's protests and Eulalie's attempts to wriggle out from under caused John Quincy to become once more erect, and he grabbed her hips to hold her still, thinking that despite her round belly, her haunches felt the same as those of his first wife, bones really, nothing like the plump behinds of the ladies in the postcards, who posed agreeably with coy, wanton smiles and mounds of pinchable, squeezable, accommodating fat.

Eulalie was slicing soap into the boiling wash pot when Seminoles materialized through the palm fronds, wearing long shirts and turbans as big as buckets, fastened with silver gorgets.

There had been talk at Brickell's trading post of another uprising, a possibility more terrifying than an uprising of Negroes, since southern Florida had few of the latter and no one knew how many Indians hid in the 'Glades.

She grabbed Jack's hand and ran clumsily to stand behind John Quincy, her heart beating in her throat until she noticed the barefoot women carrying pots and slings of food, turning in their feet as they walked to kick their long, trailing skirts before them.

"What do they want?" she whispered while the women set their cooking logs like spokes in a wheel.

"It looks like they're fixing to set up camp. I recognize two of them bucks for sure. That one there with the cypress poles calls himself Miami Doctor. I don't recollect the tall one's name, but the old fellow in the red satin breeches, that's Billy Sunshine. I've seen him at Brickell's trading post."

One young squaw with tufts of hair that wisped about her head like smoke hung back from the cook fire as solitary as a pine. Like the other women who were preparing a gruel of coontie root and corn, she wore a cape to the waist. When she raised her arms to hang a bucket from an oak branch, Eulalie noticed the faint scars that the girl bore from shoulder to wrist.

Eulalie left the shield of her husband's back for a closer inspection. She approached the squaw with slow, measured steps, as if she were gentling one of the wild, emaciated ponies that wandered through the piney woods. An arm's length away, she looked into the girl's eyes, as black and as shiny as the thong of beads that she kept for Jack in her apron pocket. Then she pointed to the scars and raised her eyebrows in question. "How did that happen?"

The young squaw shook her head and put up her hand, a gesture to stay away while John Quincy shouted to Eulalie to stop running off half-cocked.

That night the Indians passed around a quart bottle, then buried land turtles in the coals of the cookfire while Billy Sunshine, with iron gray hair that straggled over a bandanna, spoke of the deeds of Osceola and of all who were forced to go to Arkansas on the big walk.

John Quincy sat on an upended barrel sucking a turtle leg. "This Osceola you put so much stock in, he was half white. His real name was Powell."

The tallest brave who the others called Jimmy Jumper drew himself to his feet. He wore no turban. His glossy black hair shone in the moonlight. "Osceola stick knife in treaty," he said. "Osceola all Indian."

A panther screamed somewhere in the brush. Left to themselves, the women, all with top-knotted hair cut in bangs, smiled at Eulalie and patted her belly. Billy Sunshine's fourth squaw judged Eulalie's time to be the season of big winds. She asked, through words and gestures, where Eulalie would put the baby house, the place where she would remain in isolation for four moons after the baby was born. When Eulalie made it known that there was none, they shook their heads sadly.

Then Eulalie asked why the squaw with the scars on her arms stood apart from the others, half-hidden by the moss-hung oaks. From their shrugs and words, she gathered that babies and baby houses were of no more interest to Sally Cypress, who had no husband and whose job it was to drain the dugouts.

"That means that she had a baby," Eulalie said. "Did it die?"

"Sally Cypress holowagus. Baby holowagus," said Billy Sunshine's fourth wife.

When the Indians broke camp the next morning, Eulalie, in a sudden, impulsive afterthought, ran to place one of her mother's frocks in the arms of Sally Cypress, a mildewed coral crepe de chine with a torn overskirt of rose pink gauze and blue silk rosettes, the gown her mother had worn when Jefferson Davis visited Palatka.

"What'd you do that for?" asked John Quincy after the calicoed band had disappeared into the hammock. "Give your clothes away to a squaw."

Eulalie didn't know either. Maybe it was the awful loneliness in the Seminole woman's eyes, a glimpse of the utter solitude that she herself so keenly felt, in which a body could hear the course of her own biles and humors, her unstable, shifting female organs, her heartbeat unlearn its rhythms, against which blue rosettes might provide remedy. "I can't wear that anyplace I know of," she replied.

"Well, if you can't, it's for damn sure she can't either." He put her foolhardy generosity down to the fact that she was gone up. Women in that condition did such things, if his first wife, whose face he could scarcely recall, was any example.

The next morning, John Quincy left to crew for Sands. He stayed away a week while Eulalie put her home in order — wrapping the uneven table legs in kerosene-soaked rags to keep the bugs away from the tins of brown sugar and flour, stuffing pillows with pine straw, grafting sweet china buds onto wild sour-orange trees with pieces of muslin dipped in beeswax. When her chores were done and the boy asleep, she crafted careful diary entries in the fine Spenserian hand that she had been taught by her mother.

The next day, Sally Cypress showed up unexpectedly, kicking before her a skirt of pink gauze-covered crepe de chine, with hair grown out in a ruff so black, it caught the purple of the water hyacinth, the blue of the pickerelweed.

Eulalie scurried across the width of the clearing, her skirts scooped up in her hands.

"Miami Doctor say husband leave you to die," said Sally Cypress. "I say she not dead. Owl not hoot." She carried a grinder made of shoe peg nails with which, she said, she would teach Eulalie to make starch from coontie root.

"As you can plainly see, I'm still alive. How long can you stay? How many days?"

"No days. Till sun goes down. You too skinny for baby. Too much bones. Not good. Baby need cushion to sleep on. You eat sofke. You make plenty cushion."

Eulalie put her arms around Sally Cypress, who stood motionless and unsmiling in the white woman's embrace, her pleasure revealed only in the way she glanced shyly at the sky, the scrub palmetto, the vines that tumbled coiling from the canopy of the treetops.

They worked in silence, digging up the coontie with its leathery green fronds, grinding the roots to a pulp, stirring the mass in a bucket, waiting until the starch settled, then dumping out the tannin-colored water and spreading the starch on a strip of cloth to dry.

The sun was high overhead. Coots with wings half-spread skittered above the ground, looking to hide themselves in the grass.

"What happened to your baby?" Eulalie finally asked.

"Baby die." Sally Cypress stood and helped her pregnant friend to her feet. "Baby holowagus. No good."

"You mean the baby was sick?"

"Baby like a snake with wings."

"You mean a half-breed?"

Sally Cypress closed her eyes in a deep, shuddering sigh that revealed that she was naked beneath her waist-length cape. Then she brushed a cocklebur from a blue silk rosette, rinsed out her shoe-peg grinder in the rain barrel, told Eulalie to use cobwebs to stop any bleeding, and closed the subject of babies the way Eulalie hooked up her high-button shoes.

When Jack was talking in sentences and chasing lizards through the scrub, Eulalie's pains began. John Quincy ran to the inn for Mrs. Peacock, the innkeeper's wife. The ample-bosomed woman did her best to hasten the delivery, including preparing a tea made of sassafras and lime, blowing pepper in Eulalie's face, and putting an ax beneath the bed to cut the pain.

The baby girl was born at sunup. In the clear lemon yellow light of early morning, Eulalie inspected her child, relieved that, like Jack, she did not have the webbed toes of two of Eulalie's cousins. While Mrs. Peacock read from Ezekiel to stanch the bleeding, Eulalie tried to tell her to use cobwebs but was too weak to get her words out.

Eulalie named the baby Lavinia after her mother. The infant lived a month, then, fever-bright and parched, died of a claylike diarrhea that no remedy would stop, neither a powder made from one grain of rhubarb, nor ten drops of the tincture of Kino mixed with sugar and water in a spoon.

By the time Eulalie's milk dried up and she unwrapped the bindings from her breasts, she realized that she had not seen Sally Cypress in months. She missed the tandem movements of their working silences, free of white women's silly chatter and forced, nervous smiles, and she longed to see her.

She heard nothing more of her friend until the hollow call of a conch shell brought the settlement scurrying through thickets to the long, skinny dock of the Bayview Hotel, where a flotilla of flat-bottomed dugouts bobbed in the shimmering water.

Eulalie scanned the brightly calicoed Seminoles. Her eye was caught by a headdress wound with torn pink gauze and blue silk rosettes, and she hurried with the boy on her hip to Miami Doctor, who stood in a dugout beside Jimmy Jumper, unloading fox skins and cabbages.

"Where is Sally Cypress?" she asked.

Miami Doctor ignored her question. He offered instead a sling of dried pumpkin strips tied to the deep fringe of his deerskin cape while Jimmy Jumper, wearing a derby hat over his plaited scalp lock, bound bundles of egret feathers with sawgrass.

"Why isn't she with everyone else?" Eulalie insisted. "Don't make out like you don't understand me. You're wearing something that belonged to my mother. Something I gave to Sally Cypress. She's the only one you could have gotten it from."

Miami Doctor handed Jack a baby alligator, showed him how to hold its jaw closed while telling him to be careful of its many teeth, then turned to Eulalie. "Sally Cypress my wife."

"Why didn't you say so in the first place? Is she in the baby house?"

"No," he replied. "Sally Cypress stay in camp. Learn to sew."

"She knows how to sew. I'm the one who taught her."

John Quincy's boots resounded on the wooden dock. He strode toward Miami Doctor's dugout, then turned to Jimmy Jumper, who stood in the prow with a handful of egret feathers bound in sawgrass. "Will you look at that?" he said. "Wearing a white man's hat. Go get him your mirror, Eulalie, so he can see how foolish he looks. I hear tell, Jimmy, that you're pretty sweet on John Barleycorn."

Jimmy Jumper's eyes flashed, but he said nothing as he continued to lay out his goods on the wooden dock.

"That Brickell ought to be ashamed of hisself selling liquor to Indians. None of you can hold it worth a damn."

The tall Indian drew himself erect, his hands held hard at his thighs. He spoke in cold, even tones. "Strangers are on your land," he said, "sleeping in your cabin, drinking from your well, eating your tomatoes, trampling your pineapples with their cattle."

Miami Doctor interrupted. "Not know about cows. Feeding them flowers," he added with a shake of his head.

"What do Indians know about cows?" challenged John Quincy.

"Enough to keep them hidden from the white man," replied Jimmy Jumper.

John Quincy's cheek began to twitch. "It doesn't mean a hill of beans to me," he said. "None of it. You got what you came for, Eulalie?"

"I expect so."

"Then let's git." He led his wife and child up the dock to the two-story inn. "You so bad off for company all you can think of is that squaw?"

"We used to pass the time of day. I miss that."

"There's white women here to pass the time of day with. There's one right over there, and I know a fellow named Frow has himself a wife."

There was no point in trying to explain to a man how a particular friend, even a savage, could dovetail into a woman's soul. "Why do you suppose Sally Cypress can't leave the camp?" she asked.

"Indians have peculiar ways. You need another baby is what's wrong with you."

They passed the veranda, where guests sat rocking in creaking monotony, a man with his shirt gartered above his elbows, the women in elaborate straw hats trimmed with feathers and yellow tulle and black velvet primroses. The man stopped his rocking to lean over the railing and call to a young black woman whose hair was covered with a bandanna. "My shirts need more starch, missy. I expect my linen to gleam. Shirt fronts, collars, cuffs, all of it needs to be as stiff as a board."

The laundress nodded, then picked up a basket and placed it on her small, well-shaped head and walked away as Peacock, the inn's proprietor, hurried up the steps with a basketful of venison. Peacock seemed to recognize John Quincy and gave him a passing nod.

"Cracker women are so awfully thin," whispered a woman behind a twirling parasol.

"Pitiful," replied another. "I understand it's the oranges they eat."

Eulalie fingered her bonnet strings and realized that they were referring to her, using a word her mother had applied often to shiftless, bone-thin, dirt-eating tenant farmers with cracks in the corners of their mouths, who, it was whispered, impregnated their own daughters, and to whom one brought bountiful baskets at Thanksgiving and at Christmas. She had never seen her mother deliver such gifts, but they sounded copious, generous, given from the luxury of excess. She wanted to tell the tourists on the veranda that her father had once owned one of the finest groves in Putnam County. Her mother was right. A lady should never go about without a corset. Eulalie would put hers on tomorrow, even in the stifling heat, even if the whalebone stays gave her a fainting spell, even if John Quincy had to lace her up.

★ ★ ★

John Quincy returned from a wreck with a sling of oysters and three casks of French Madiera, and announced that he had decided to build Eulalie a house.

"It was Sands' idea," he said, "being as how the law favors squatters and there's no stakes anywhere that anyone can see. Sands says to use timbers washed ashore for corner posts and beams, and the pine around us for the frame."

Used to foolish talk that came to nothing, Eulalie pulled her laundry from the branches of a pigeon plum, the trunk of which still bore the winter claw marks of raccoons, and folded it rough dry.

"Sands says pine wood is hell on a saw, but good against rot and termites," John Quincy added, with the winded sigh of a man who has come to realize how hard it is to live in a tent with a woman who treats him like poison.

"I'm tired of hearing the man's name," she said. "And I'm tired of setting wash to dry on bushes. I need a clothesline. And I need to stop hearing about Thomas Sands, like he's someone important when you and I both know that if he's Bahamian" — she dropped her voice — "he's probably got some Negro blood in him. Can't you see that?"

"What I see," he replied, "is a woman getting meaner by the day."

"Look at the moons of his nails if you don't believe me. Except you won't be able to because

68

he keeps his hands in his pockets."

To Eulalie's surprise, the house was begun when the winter people and their yachts left the settlement, and John Quincy arranged to swap Ned Pent two kegs of Madiera in exchange for hand-hewn planks.

Eulalie heard the clamor of hammers, axes, and rasping ripsaws, and at first refused to watch John Quincy drive the corner posts into the ground over the limestone rock, or Pent plane the tops of the posts with a long crosscut timber saw. When John Quincy ducked into the tent to announce that he was going to build her a real wooden floor and erect a partition to give her two rooms, she put on her persnickety, eyebrow-locked, concentrating face and dotted her son's insect bites with turpentine.

It was to herself, to the warm, sweaty folds at the back of Jack's neck, and to Sally Cypress through whispers floated westward on the down of thistles that Eulalie confided her joy at the possibility of having windows to look out of, walls to hang pictures on, doors that could be bolted.

With the sometime help of Pent's younger brother John and a man named Carney, who tended the yacht of a rich man from New York, the house was framed in a week, joists, windows, floor, studs, and rafters — standing spindly and skeleton-like, as clean as laundry soap, spice-scented like the woods, a timbered hull that rose before Eulalie like a vow.

Each man worked when he could, hammering flat nails into wide vertical boards with narrow batten in between, while Ned Pent complained that the saw was getting so gummed up from pine resin, he had to keep dipping it in turpentine. They thatched the roof with palmetto, fitted the windows with wooden shutters held open with sticks and leather straps, crafted a door with a leather hinge fastened by a board lifted by a rawhide latch string, and built a latrine and privy behind the glossy, stiff-leaved sapodilla.

Sands stopped by on a blazing afternoon as dark clouds rolled in from the west. He wore white flannel trousers and a white rowing jersey buttoned to the neck, his broad-brimmed straw hat askew as he strolled about the frame with hands clasped behind his back to offer advice. The grain of the floorboards didn't match, the studs for the window openings were not plumb, no one took into account the prevailing breezes, where were the porch supports, the beams of the loft should have been notched, and they needed to pick up their pace if they wanted to finish the loft before the rain.

Sands left an angry Pent muttering that it didn't matter if the window studs were not plumb since you always needed to allow an inch for clearance and that prevailing breezes didn't mean shit when it was hot. The Bahamian found Eulalie outside the tent pressing a shirt-waist with a sizzling flat iron. "I thought you'd

70

be watching it go up," he said, slipping Jack a two-cent copper piece.

Eulalie pinched her mouth shut before she spoke, determined not to reveal to Sands her feelings about the house. "I expect he'll raise that shack with or without me."

"A man needs comfort in his woman, Mrs. Coombs. John might like to know that you appreciate his labor. It makes the dangerous work at sea worthwhile."

"No one here has asked him to risk his life for foolishness," she replied, wetting her finger and touching it to the sizzling iron. "Not ever."

"It seems to me that you don't approve."

"I don't."

Sands fanned himself with his hat. "There's money in wreckage."

"I haven't seen any," she replied.

"I have, Mama," said Jack.

While Eulalie scowled at the boy, Sands opened the top button of his jersey, pushing its sleeves to his elbows. The scent of bay rum and sweat drifted from his opened shirt. "It's hot," he said. "Too hot to be ironing."

"It's what I do," Eulalie replied, feeling the heat of the day flaming her face, the tips of her earlobes.

The air seemed to have stopped. Even the flock of purple martins that had been picking beetles from the bark of an oak now sought the shelter of its crown. The only motion was the flutter of a monarch butterfly feeding on

71

a vine. Jack chased it with cupped hands while Eulalie glanced overhead at a sky that appeared cleft, one half a brittle blue, the other, now billowing toward them from the west, as black as squid ink.

She touched a finger to the iron. It had lost its sizzle. She was going to place it over the cookfire when the air became sweet with ozone. Sands put out his cigar and left just as fat drops of rain suddenly spattered the clearing, raising puffs of sand and limestone dust the size of silver dollars. Despite the heat she shivered. Someone was walking over her grave.

With the odor of cigar and bay rum still in her nostrils, Eulalie thrust the shirtwaist and the iron inside the tent, gathered her skirts above her shoe tops, and ran through the raindrops to inspect the new house. John Quincy seemed pleased to see her. He said to take a look at the kitchen shed they were building behind the pigeon plum, with window frames made of salt-pork boxes, screened to keep out sand flies. She spoke aloud, to no one in particular, that the house looked like the ribs of a carcass. Where were the finished, smooth-plastered walls, she asked, like the kind in her uncle's house that you could hang paper on, or the dimly remembered walls of her childhood upon which hung portraits of aunts and uncles long deceased? The men, including John Quincy, searched one another for answers until Pent explained that sheathing was necessary only in colder climates. Eulalie had to remember that she was in the tropics now, where walls were just something to trap rats in.

John Quincy wiped his forehead on his sleeve, determined to have a wife who would put her arms around his neck at night instead of looking everywhichaway as if she were watching for a snake. "It's still not finished, Eulalie," he said, "I'm fixing to build you a front porch just for setting."

"Whose idea is that?"

"Mine," he said. "Sands said not to do it, said that a porch could pull the rest of the house down with it, but Pent here says unless everyone in the village comes to stand on it, it'll hold."

Eulalie unpursed her mouth. Her teeth were still good, and they glinted like shells as she thought of how a body could sit on a porch and teach a child Scripture. "Could you fix it to wrap around the house? And maybe get me a rocker like they have over to the hotel?"

"Never can satisfy a woman," he replied, "and that's the truth."

When John Quincy went off on another wrecking expedition, Eulalie looked at herself in the half-eaten mirror and decided that she was not mean-looking at all. In fact, out of the blinding sun, where she could open her eyes all the way, with her poke bonnet off and her hair smoothed into a bun, and if her nose ever stopped peeling, she might even be perky. She considered carrying her mother's parasol against the sun, only to find that its silken folds had become pitted like the skin of an orange.

With the boy to care for as well as the house, she had more than a body could hope for. The boy was becoming a companion, asking her questions, believing her answers, satisfied to play with bits of nothing — wood chips, seed pods that rattled when he ran, lizards, the pot shards, the mortar and pestle, the string of beads and the bone fishhook that had spilled from the mound in the piney woods.

While the boy was delight, the house was contentment, refuge. Perhaps it was the spicy scent of the wood, the high, cool ceilings, or the loft, where possessions could be stored out of the way. Perhaps it was the way her high-topped shoes click-clacked on the wooden floor, the front windows that looked out over the banyan and chinaberry and orchid-draped gumbo limbo, or the porch, where she could sit and rock and catch soft, salty breezes perfumed with orange blossoms, pink-petaled oleander, and strong coffee brewing over a dozen cookfires.

Eulalie peeled off her stocking gloves, now shredded beyond repair, to plant a garden. She grubbed roots and raked away small rocks that she piled into stiles, while Jack funneled kerosene into the hearts of young palmettoes. Then, while the boy carried a bucket of water to drench each slip, she rooted croton clippings and planted a bed of phlox with a border of periwinkles.

When the croton clippings took root, Jack appeared at the open door with a little boy at his side. Each child clutched a seed pod in his hand. The boy's curly hair was golden, his eyes a greenish bronze, his skin the color of the quinine and coffee that Eulalie had given to Jack to bring down his fever.

She was on her knees scouring her floor with sand and lye soap. "Who does he belong to?" she asked, "and don't either one of you step on my floor."

"Name Bristol," the child said.

"Who's your mama, Bristol?"

"Caroline."

"Does she do laundry?"

"Yes, ma'am."

"I think I've seen her at the hotel."

Eulalie finished drying the floor with a croker sack, then took each child by the hand in search of the servants' quarters, which she found shrouded in lines of drying laundry behind the Bayview Inn. The shack smelled of verbena, bacon fat, and bay rum. Its floor was covered with overlapping corn shuck mattresses, its walls draped with peg-hung garments, some of which had the crisp, shiny look of Sunday best.

The woman named Caroline sat on a ladder-back chair in a corner mending sheets. In the shadow behind her, a man sat pulling on his boots. "You his mama?" asked Eulalie.

"Yes, ma'am," replied Caroline, standing, laying her sewing aside.

"Your boy and my son here have been playing."

"Bristol won't bother you again."

"He's no bother," replied Eulalie. "He can visit anytime he likes."

When Jack pulled away from her hand and smiled into the shadows, Eulalie peered more closely and saw that the man in the corner was Sands. This meant that John Quincy was back and would be messing up her floor and mashing her plants and God knows what all. She glanced down at her shoe tops while Sands tucked his shirt into his pants. "I didn't know you were back," she said. "Where's John Quincy? Is he seeing to the sloop?"

He smiled slowly. "John is still out, Mrs. Coombs."

Eulalie felt foolish, needing answers, having to fish them out like scorpions. "He's supposed to be wrecking with you."

"He's wrecking," he replied, "but not with me, as you can see." He stepped closer, rolling up his sleeves over his wrists. His eyes were heavy with the torpor of late afternoon. "John Quincy took the sloop out himself. Your man's becoming a capital sailor. Absolutely fearless."

Doubting that John Quincy was much good at anything, Eulalie suddenly realized that Sands was Bristol's father, just as her own father had begot darkies the spit of him. It was a fact of life. There was one's children and then one's offspring, the two not necessarily the same.

John Quincy returned with a rocking chair, a keg of flour that was dry on the inside, and ten dollars in his pocket. He pulled his dog from under the porch by its ears, thumped Jack's head in gruff, heavy-handed affection, then smiled and said that Eulalie had made the house homey. He was so agreeable and the rocker so snappy and bright, she didn't mention anything about the mud that he tracked over her floor.

"Things are going to be different, Eulalie," he said, pulling off his water-soaked brogans. "I know it in my bones."

That night, with Jack asleep in the loft, she was receptive to his attentions, even agreeing, with the kerosene lantern out and the shutters tightly closed, to take off her shift like the plump woman in the postcard that John Quincy carried in his pocket next to his tobacco plug. The one concession she refused was to pose with her chin resting on her hand.

When she closed her eyes, she was startled that it was Sands' handsome, arrogant face she imagined in the indigo velvet behind her lids, it was Sands poised above her, cleaving her body in half.

"That's it," said John Quincy, "move your

77

hips. Show me how glad you are to see me."

The next day, John Quincy promised that when the rains let up, he would see about replacing the palmetto thatch with cypress shingles. They were sitting on their front porch in a miasma of coconut smudge and jasmine, the dog asleep in the shadows beneath them, when Sheriff Mettair strode through the clearing. Eulalie got up from her rocker and offered the sheriff a glass of iced tea, a nicety borrowed from Matilda Pent. The sheriff nodded his thanks, downed the tea, then wiped his mouth with the back of his hand and informed John Quincy that he was under arrest.

John Quincy drew himself up from the step. "What the hell for?"

"Wrecking without a license. Causing the wreck to happen in the first place with decoy lights. Setting fire to the ship to destroy evidence. The warrant's in my pocket. Have to take you to Key West to stand trial."

Eulalie moved to her husband's side. "Why aren't you arresting Sands? He's the one you want to take to Key West. John Quincy just works for him. Does what he tells him to. He doesn't even own the boat. It belongs to Sands."

"Sands wasn't involved in this, ma'am. Your husband broke the law on his own. Him and two other fellows."

Eulalie found herself shaking. "No one can tell me it's not that man's fault. All of it."

John Quincy brushed off his brown jeans.

"Don't go mouthing off on something you don't know beans about, Eulalie," he said. "Anything good came from that man, including this house, and don't you forget it."

"You ready?" asked Mettair.

John Quincy placed his hat on his head, cocked it, and pinched off a plug of tobacco. "As ready as I'll ever be with a government that interferes with a man's legitimate business. How is a fellow going to live?"

Eulalie felt her throat close. She turned to Mettair. "When will he be back?"

"That depends," replied the sheriff, who prided himself on keeping order without ever having to notch his gun, "on the judge."

Chapter Four

MIAMI DOCTOR

It was my uncle, Willie Tiger, and the mother of Sally Cypress, whose idea it was for me to take Sally Cypress as my wife. She cannot be entirely blamed, my uncle said, that she had become a white man's squaw. What can you expect of an unmarried girl whose midwife at her birth forgot to bury her navel string? Marry the woman, he said, undo what has been done, and enjoy the comforts that a man is entitled to.

Why not Jimmy Jumper? I argued, having no taste for this woman, older than me by at least ten fire seasons, who not only has hair as sparse as that on a buttonwood leaf, but who is as skinny as the white woman, with nothing of the sturdy rump we all admire. My uncle drew his neck even deeper into his shoulders. Jimmy Jumper spends too much time with his head on his chest. As for you, young men are expected to marry older women. It is bad for man and wife to be the same age. Too much grabbing. Such things are not right. She is a good cook, he argued. And she does not talk too much. He did not mention, although I knew it put her in his favor, that she had cured his slow leak with an infusion of milkweed. Keep the woman confined and she will fatten, your own mother agrees with me, and that was that.

So I left the hammock of my mother for that of my wife's mother, joining Sally Cypress under her mother's chickee until our own sleeping chickee could be built, bringing blankets, cookware, and beads in exchange for a new shirt made by my wife's relatives.

I think that to have made such a match, my uncle must have been buried as a baby not only up to his neck, but to the top of his head as well, for this woman who I call wife has made my life a place of bad dreams. The difference between those of day and those of night is that those in the sunlight go on longer.

You would think she would be grateful, but she was not. Even before her hair was washed for the Night-Chant that would purify her, Sally Cypress complained that she has less beads than any woman in the camp. She wanted to be covered from shoulder to chin. And although she would not say it outright, she blamed me for the death of her half-white child when she knew that it was the women who decided that it be tied to the frond of a palm, that I was only the one they sent scrambling up the trunk.

Sally Cypress claimed she still heard it crying in the night. I didn't believe her. If the thing's spirit had made any noise, I would have heard it. I am certain this is the reason she rushes nightly into the sweet water, submerging herself to her beads, dissolving my essence into the clear, swirling eddies, probably causing me to father five-fingered alligators who I will never see.

Jimmy Jumper suggested that white men are larger in their parts. Sally Cypress, he said, might be comparing me to Clarke. Billy Bow-legs had a remedy for this, the slimy sap of the spiderwort, which causes the parts of the user to swell. Even though I consider myself more than adequate, I tried the sap of the spiderwort. I even tried the white man's way, rolling her on her back and entering her from above, the feeling, like that of splitting a mango in half. Because I saw her hands rip the mosquito netting from our chickee, I thought at first she felt my heat, but it was not so. Rather than please her, it seemed to anger her even more, and we resumed the natural ways, from the rear, and my own favored way, from the side, which allows me to see the woman's eyes.

First I threatened to return to my mother's camp. This didn't move her. What is it you want? I asked while she sat defiantly at her sewing, refusing to create flaws in a cape but insisting on the perfection of the Great Spirit.

Later that night as we lay side by side beneath separate mosquito nets, the time of her monthly flux, she whispered that she wanted to leave camp to see the white woman whom she has taught to make sofke, and who has taught her in turn to use turpentine for throat on fire.

Even a great horned owl hooted.

"Aren't there enough women of our fire nearby?" I asked. "Why do you need to see a white woman who hides her head in a hat?"

"She doesn't look through me as if searching for a fish in the water," she replied.

I told her that the woman's husband has been taken in handcuffs to the white man's court in Key West. Jimmy Jumper saw the whole thing from the dock. Jimmy Jumper also said that he heard someone say that John Quincy was another man's "dupe." He repeated this with an unsteady tongue, so I do not know if he heard this word right. Since we are not

82

sure of the meaning other than to know that it is not a good thing, we are waiting to ask Billy Sunshine, when we see him, to interpret.

It is a story familiar to our people. While others raise cattle on land that was once his, John Quincy sits imprisoned. By now his woman has probably returned to her mother's camp. Sally Cypress believed this last the least, since white people belong to the camp of their father's people and Oolalee's father's people were gone.

After a few months, in the season of soggy air, when the Pahahokee had overflowed into the prairie, I struck a bargain. If Sally Cypress refrained from purging herself nightly in the sweet water, I would take her to find the white woman, Oolalee, when I went to trade at Brickell's post.

By the time the wet air turned to heavy winds that howled mournfully through our roof and we awoke each morning to a pool around our chickee, she agreed. Willie Tiger warned me that the bloom was on the sawgrass and to wait before traveling out of the Pahahokee, but I didn't want Sally Cypress to change her mind. Since the white man is easily alarmed if he sees the red man at night, we went by day, poling through shortcuts, openings in the sawgrass that the white man knows nothing about. We glided past our old camping grounds and our abandoned chickees, now overgrown with palmetto, past the big wire fence thirty of the white man's miles. The land that it enclosed did not belong to the white man who fenced it in. Yet his custom allowed him to fence off for his own use as much land as he needed to graze his cattle. We knew why he wanted this place where the grass is fine and tender. Our own cattle, when we still had them, liked to graze there. Jimmy Jumper wanted to fight the white man who put up this fence but could not, just as he cannot battle the band of whites who raid our cattle and our hogs. We are only a handful, and the white man numbers in the thousands. The fight has reached inside my friend, burrowing like a mole so that now Jimmy Jumper fights only himself.

We found Oolalee in a new house of pine with its floor elevated like our sleeping platforms off the ground. The white woman's hair was more yellow than before, threaded with golden lights that I thought came from the sun, but that Sally Cypress said came from camomile and many, many lemons. Beside her was the boy, now as high as her hip, holding a spinning toy in his hand, and on her other side, the curly-haired straw-hat man leaning toward her like a tree in the wind. I thought he had become a suitor, but Sally Cypress shook her head. The woman, Oolalee, had not oiled her hair.

They were all regarding a large wooden box with two pistols stuck into its bottom when straw-hat man caught us peering through the open window. "That looks like Clarke's squaw," he said. "I suppose you'll have to let them in."

Since it is forbidden for our women to speak to the white man, Sally Cypress made no response. We entered the house. "This my wife," I said, putting my woman behind me as one might adjust a shadow.

Oolalee hugged Sally Cypress like a bear. I knew this was out of gladness and that my woman had the same glad feelings. Except that she, in the custom of our people, hid such thoughts from her face. We handed over sweet potatoes and venison while straw-hat man looked at us as though we were mosquitoes that he might, at any moment, swat away.

The boy put the spinning toy in a corner next to objects that I recognized as belonging to the people of the mounds, a broken vessel patterned like the diamondback, beads of obsidian, a mortar and pestle, a bone shaped like a fishhook. I could not find the water to swallow, for I knew that the owners of these implements would not rest until they were buried once more beside them. While I was collecting words to reveal this calamity, straw-hat man sat on a bench before the thing with the pistols at its feet that we soon learned was a white man's music box, not as large as a dugout, yet taking as much wood and probably the same six moons to fashion.

"It's missing an octave," he said, striking

pieces of bone with his fingers. "Actually, it has a nice sound if you keep to the upper range."

It felt to our ears like the squealing of pigs, but naturally we said nothing while the woman Oolalee, smelling of orange blossom, smoothed her hair back with her palms. "I'm grateful for the whirligig you brought my boy, but you had no call to move in that piano while I was out. I don't cotton to folks taking liberties with my house when I'm not home for say-so, and I particularly don't like it when folks bring in all kinds of things without first asking me if I want them."

No wonder Sally Cypress likes this white woman. Except for the difference in their tanning, they are cut from the same hide.

"If it wasn't missing an octave or two, this would be a valuable instrument," he insisted. "It came all the way from France." He took her hand and guided it over the bones. "Try it for yourself."

She pulled her hand away and turned color. White people do that easily. It is an interesting thing to watch. When they are excited or angry, the color enters their face. When they are frightened, it leaves, making them even more drained, if that is possible.

"My daddy had one that was as big as a bed draped with a fringed, silk shawl the color of midnight," she said. "This old thing can go back to France for all I care. I don't want anything from you. Not your money. Not this pile of junk."

Straw-hat man stood and twirled his hat by its brim. "You won't take money. You won't take this piano. What can I do to repay John for his loyalty?"

"It's his loyalty that's got us in this awful mess. It's his loyalty that got him put in jail while you're as free as a bird."

Straw-hat man's words were like oil. "I wasn't with him, as you well know. He acted on his own. I was never even charged. I'm doing all I can, ma'am, to get him out."

The boy climbed up on the bench with the sly grin of a fox, then picked at the bones, fearless, as are his older white brothers, of dead things, which is not surprising considering his other toys.

Oolalee folded her arms across her meager chest. Despite the awful noises that he made, she regarded her child with a mother's soft eye. "The keys are stuck," she said.

"They're just damp," straw-hat man replied. "If you place the kerosene lamp on the floor beside it, the heat will rise and dry it out."

"Can we keep it, Mama?"

We stood by silently, I with an eye on the ancient objects in the corner, straw-hat man leaning his elbow on the music box, while Oolalee made up her mind.

She spoke with a frown to show her strength and to deny her interest in this man that rose from her like the heat from the kerosene lamp, which she carried to place beside the box. "I guess I can let you leave it here until my husband returns," she said, "but if he says it goes back, it goes back."

"You strike a hard bargain," replied straw-hat man, swinging the boy off the bench and into the air. Then he put the boy down and looked at the mother in the way that a man looks at a woman when he finds her comely.

Her eyes opened wider than I have ever seen. I used to think they were the color of water. Now I thought they were like the mid-morning sky, and from the way straw-hat man studied their depths as he said goodbye, I knew he was thinking the same thing.

"Straw hat man holowagus," said Sally Cypress.

"I don't want to talk about Thomas," said Oolalee, her hand tenderly on my wife's shoulder. "I want to hear all about you. I want you to tell me everything. Don't leave anything out."

And because the storyteller's way is to tell only of the distant past, my wife had to imagine herself as if already dead so that she could accommodate her friend. "It was many fire seasons, many moons past," she began, "when Woven Grass of the Bird clan took Coiling Snake of the Wind clan to the fire of her mother." As I listened in surprise to Sally Cypress reveal our Indian names to a white woman,

88

I hoped she wouldn't also reveal the times she dissolved my essence nightly in the waters of the Pahahokee, or when I tried to enlarge my parts with the sap of spiderwort.

We stayed for three days, sleeping on the porch at night, while by day I went to trade skins and whistles that Willie Tiger made from alligator teeth. Sally Cypress stayed behind with Oolalee, sealing guava jelly jars with beeswax and pine resin, and talking woman things of which I know nothing about. Oolalee gave my wife small boards as richly colored as tree snails that she called Bible cards. Some had very good pictures of white people in soft robes with spikes around their heads, some sort of torture, no doubt. One with hair as yellow as straw-hat man she said was the greatest spirit of all. I doubted this since his robe came to his feet, forcing him to walk with toes turned in like a woman. He might be the same white spirit that the missionary women chatter about. It is hard to know.

The visit turned out not to be entirely fruit-less. Besides trading all my goods, I learned of white men at the hotel who needed guides. They want to hunt plume birds, but I switch them to otter. I have seen enough strewn nests and broken eggs and birds lying with plumes ripped from their backs as if they had been scalped. Once, Willie Tiger said, plume birds filled the skies like rainbows, nesting so thickly that white hunters had to kick a path through them. I think I remember such a time, but I don't know if it is my own memory or that of my people.

This not good time for plume birds, I said. Better time for otter. Since my people are the only ones who know the secret ways of the Pahahokee, there is silver to be made. I will discuss this with Jimmy Jumper when he is not confusing himself with the white man's drink. It is a way to buy enough beads in which to wrap Sally Cypress from head to toe and, if she continues to cooperate, a necklace of silver coins.

That we remained even after the big wind was the white woman's fault. Our delay began when Oolalee saw a snake hanging from the thatch to catch the palmetto bugs that glide on stiffened wings. The angry sea had already washed over the beach, and a raft of men with their arms lashed about one another leaned into the gusts to secure their boats. Still Sally Cypress would not leave until she helped Oolalee kill the snake, even though our grandfathers tell us that in so doing she will likely make herself lame. By the time she coaxed the creature down, the wind began to tear through the trees.

When the water rushed over the limestone ridge, Oolalee beckoned us inside and closed tight her shutters. The house began to groan in the storm like someone sick. The boy gathered his toys, Oolalee dragged her mattress, I carried the sewing machine, Sally Cypress carried the dog and the picture cards, and we climbed the ladder to the loft. There we stayed through the night, smelling dog and white people, watching them watch us with round, unblinking eyes, while the creaking house was pelted with coral and driftwood.

Once Oolalee finally began a steady, sleeping breath, I tried to take the fishhook and the clay vessel from the boy, but I was not quick enough, for just as I reached them, the dog slicked back its ears and growled, and Oolalee woke. "Harm my boy," she whispered, "and John Quincy will kill you." It was no use. She could not be made to understand, and I did not try.

In the morning, we climbed down to find that the wind and the water had left ankle-deep mud in the house and had shredded the land the way one tears apart the husk of a coconut. Branches and shacks were down, broken and twisted with the white man's shoes and cooking pots. Tree roots had been upended in huge, rock-grasping claws. The hut that stood at the rear of Oolalee's house, where white people hid to fertilize their soil, had been smashed to bits, and the latrine it covered now overflowed its margins. Some things had blown overhead, like a man who hung by his trousers from the limb of a tree. A woman came running to shout that the wind had even swept a baby from its mother's arms, but she did not know who or where, and when Oolalee held her by her shoulders to seize her mind, she had forgotten her own name as well.

With the scattering of the white men's possessions and the blurring of his boundaries, I thought that it was time to leave the place we call little hunting grounds. I was certain when straw-hat man returned to help Oolalee put to rights her house and I saw him take her hand and say that he was worried about her, and when she pulled her own away, it was slowly, as one attempts to attract a fish. He is her suitor, I said to Sally Cypress, and I do not care if her hair is oiled or not.

Sally Cypress and I poled up the Mayami River through dead fish, choked by the storm-stirred mud, now floating like leaves alongside my dugout. I watched anxiously to see if my wife would go lame from killing the snake, then reasoned that perhaps the storm had been her punishment. I would ask Willie Tiger. A white man lay broken on the bank with his fist still caught in his fishing net, his ears and nose eaten by crabs. He reminded me of Tommy Otter, whose clan sliced off a piece of his ear for lying. What lies had this man told, I wondered, and how did his Great Spirit find out?

Then, as if a veil of moss had been peeled from my eyes, I understood, in the sudden understanding I once had after I spent ten days with Billy Bowlegs and his medicine bundle, eating only herbs. The storm had been the punishment of the mound people, who scattered the possessions of the white man because their own possessions had been so carelessly strewn.

Chapter Five

The afternoon began as others before it. Thomas Sands brought a loop of licorice for the boy, a length of yard goods for Eulalie, then sat on her humpbacked green-fringed settee and smoked a cigar while telling of sweeping through the waters close-hauled to the wind to rescue a ship that had run aground.

Everything was damp from a molten rain that left the glistening foliage laden with moisture and that brought the spicy aroma of the hammock indoors. Wearing a cameo brooch fastened beneath the collar of her dress, Eulalie sat primly and listened to her guest, her ankles crossed, her hands folded in her lap.

Sands offered to tack wax paper over Eulalie's open windows, a contrivance that would let in light yet keep out insects. When she replied that she needed open windows to keep an eye on the boy, he reached his hand out to touch her cheek with the tips of his fingers, a soft grazing caress, and promised to bring her face cream from New York.

Eulalie looked down at her folded hands. "There's things we need a whole lot worse than face cream."

"I don't agree," he said. "You have an obligation to yourself. I mean to see you keep it."

Eulalie tried to catch her breath. The room felt stuffy, airless, as if he had already sealed the windows. He fixed her in a steady, narrowed gaze, but made no other move. She did it all, leaning toward his bay rum and his salt spray, closing her eyes to receive his kiss, pulling the pins from her hair that she let ripple over her face and neck like a child, like an old woman who had taken leave of her senses, like a harlot, like a woman who experienced for the first time the lust of the flesh that she had read about in 1 John 2:16.

"Stay," she whispered.

"You mean till supper?"

"Till I put the boy to bed."

When it was dark and the boy asleep, he led her into the bedroom, where he flung his hat on the corner post.

"I haven't ever done this before," she said.

"I know," he replied.

At first she thought the trembling in her knees was another visit of the Holy Spirit, and her heart gladdened, although in wonder how the Lord picked his own time and place. Then she forgot about the Lord and, working with dozens of hooks and tapes, took off her

94

dress and lay breathless in her shift, filled with carnal thoughts that she had kept from her own marriage bed, from herself, wanting the man who stripped off his boots and breeches, spreading her knees for him, unlike with John Quincy, when they had to be forced apart.

He knew her better than she knew herself, where to touch her, where to press his lips, when to pull her fiercely toward him, then roll beneath her so that she sat astride, a position she had never taken with John Quincy, stroking her long hair while she rode to a jolting, shuddering, convulsive climax that left her wondering if something had split apart, had shifted, had broken inside.

Afterward, she moved to sit on the edge of the bed, but he pulled her back to lie beside him in a lingering embrace, tracing the outlines of her jaw, her cheeks, her lips, pushing a finger between her lips to touch her teeth, telling her she smelled of sandalwood. He seemed to have all the time in the world, even when she had to get up to tend to Jack, who cried out from some evil, alligator-chasing, taffy-footed dream.

When she returned to shyly fit her body into the hollows of his own, he took her hand and kissed her palm. "There's no turning back even if you wanted to, Eulalie. You're mine now," he said. "Never forget that."

And despite the impossibility of his words, she believed him and promised that she never would forget his claim, until he began to lick the spaces between her fingers and she thought no more of hopeless contradictions.

In the weeks that followed, Eulalie knew for certain that she was condemned to eternal hell fire. The Lord had seen it all, right through the dense, vine-covered canopy of the hammock. Had seen the wanton, fevered, adulterous embraces in which she gasped for breath, unlike the times when the cabin was shuttered and sweltering, instead panting, chasing after air with her eyes fluttering and her mouth opened like a fish. The Lord had even heard her, with her hips lifted to meet Thomas poised above, beg for more. Never again would she be graced to speak in tongues, nor would she ever understand the holy babel of another.

She could not claim that Sands had forced her, nor could she say, being as how she was temperance, that she had succumbed because of strong drink. She could not even say that it had happened once, but that having seen the error of her ways, she had set about, repentant, to mend them. It was, rather, as if she had sunk into a pit, as deep as the pit, according to Proverbs 22:14, that was the mouth of an adulteress, from which she could not, and would not rise.

Eulalie was unprepared for a sin that fed itself, that begat its own perpetuity.

Desire for his tanned and handsome face,

the faint bay rum odor of his body, his long, tapering fingers and rock-hard thighs took over, clouding her mind, weakening her resolve, dissolving her virtue like the strangler fig that wrapped around its host until the captive tree rotted away, leaving only a ghostly, circular embrace.

Sometimes after a long absence, her passion buried in a never-ending round of daily chores, banked by candlelit nights entering recipes and remedies in her diary, bolting door and windows against the panthers that prowled the settlement, she was determined to put an end to her iniquity. Then he returned, immaculate in a clean white rowing jersey and white flannel trousers, tentative, restrained, seeming to sense her resolve.

They sat in the parlor, where she served him ginger wine that she made with yeast that was thick and fresh. He gave her a pair of green-tinted sun spectacles that came all the way from Paris and high-topped shoes for Jack. They discussed the weather, chilly even for February, how fast Jack was growing, the yacht club's Washington's Birthday regatta to which he, not she, had been invited, the winter people, no longer content to vacation at the Peacock Inn for ten dollars a week, building cottages and costly mansions, one with coral domes like Turkish minarets.

He said very little else. "I expect I didn't put enough raisins in the ginger wine," she said. "The recipe calls for two pounds. I could only get but one."

"The wine is adequate," he replied.

After a supper of corn bread, stone crabs, and sweet potatoes baked with honey, it was she who finally broached the subject. "You left no word," she said.

"There is no proper way to get word to you, Eulalie, without arousing suspicion. With whom could I send such a message?"

The smell of jasmine came in through the cracks in the walls, the floor. "You could tell me before you sail. At least I would know."

"I can't do that, dear heart, because I never know myself. When the call comes that a ship has run aground, I'm off. It's as simple as that."

Eulalie thought about the Negress Caroline and of Thomas looming in the shadows of her cabin, of the boy Bristol, who had his eyes. "Is there someone else?"

"That's nonsense. You know every woman in the village. Who else could it be?"

"The laundress. At the inn."

He folded his napkin and stood. "Your comments are unseemly, Eulalie. Unbecoming at the least."

"You're telling me that boy of hers isn't the spittin' image of you?"

"You demean yourself."

Then he stepped close enough just to graze her body with his own, as if accidentally, thanked her for supper, and left. As soon as the door closed behind him, the longing set in, twisted with uncertainty, with a wracking jealousy that took away appetite and resolve.

Two days later he was back, leaning against the porch railing while Eulalie bathed Jack in a tin tub with a bar of Fels Naphtha that would not suds, carrying the child to bed on his shoulders, telling him stories of pirates while Eulalie dumped the tub into a clump of oleander bushes. Then, inside, with no explanation of where he had been, he opened the buttons at her neck, and dipped his hand into the front of her dampened dress, caressing her nipples, which quickly became hard nubs, kissing the base of her throat, until her knees buckled and she leaned against his chest. "Do you want me to go?" he asked.

"No," she whispered, "I need you near me always."

He pushed his knee between her legs. "Always," he said.

Eulalie decided that she would make an effort to be once more a lady, more like the women Thomas was used to. She exchanged her bonnet for a straw hat with flowers, attempted a blancmange with bitter almonds and isinglass which didn't mold because she had no cream, covered her Vaselined hands at night with gloves, and practiced speaking as he did, saying *thing* instead of *thang*, *iron* instead of *arn*. Because he liked the color of her hair, she rinsed it with camomile and lemon juice and let it bleach out golden in the sun.

In April, when the air was acrid with fires from the 'Glades, she styled her hair after a picture she found in an old copy of Godey's Lady's Book, an elaborate approximation with wires and puffs that took a box of hairpins and hours to arrange.

More annoyed than pleased, Thomas had been put off. "What the devil did you do to yourself?" he asked, frowning in disapproval.

Eulalie put her hands to the mound of curls and puffs, brushing back stray wisps that feathered her forehead and temples and the back of her neck. "I thought you would like it."

"If I want haut monde, Eulalie, I would pursue someone who knew that the rat's nest you've put on top of your head is five years out of date. Wash it out."

Eulalie, who had had to sleep with her head supported on two pillows for a week, tried to keep back the tears, but they fell in spite of her efforts. "There's no call to be ugly. I just wanted to please you."

"Well, you didn't. It's out of place. It goes with satin slippers and filmy frocks designed to show shoulders as white as snow. Wash it out, Eulalie. If you please."

She pulled out the hairpins, one by one, biting her lip to keep from crying and went outside. He followed her to the rain barrel, where she rolled up her sleeves, then dipped her head in the water. While she soaped her hair, he put one hand firmly on the back of her neck, and with the other raised her skirts. Surprised, she picked her head up and tried to turn around, her sopping hair dripping on her dress, but he pushed her head forward, her body against the wooden staves, and entered her.

His voice was husky. "The point is," he said, "to take the lady as close to drowning as you can, to make her think she's going to die. They do this in the Orient, or so I've been told."

He plunged her head in again, only deeper, submerging it completely so that she could not breathe, driving into her body while she struggled beneath his hands, before his lunging thighs.

He allowed her to come up for air, and while she sputtered and fought to free herself, he whispered hoarsely, "Thrash, Eulalie, gasp for breath . . .", then pushed her down again.

When it was over, and she, bedraggled, bewildered, began to sob, he held her close and comforted her.

"I couldn't breathe. You knew I couldn't breathe, but you held my head down anyways."

"You want to please me, don't you?"

She pulled away and stared into the night. "I don't know. Yes," she whispered.

"And you did," he said, kissing her eyelids. "You were my good girl. You didn't think I would really let you drown, did you?"

"No," she lied.

Then to reward her, he dried her hair with his shirt and led her to bed. He was gentle, tender, spending what seemed like hours stroking her, murmuring words of love into her ear, delaying her orgasm so that when she finally climaxed it was with a chain of linking spasms that never seemed to stop. There was no talk of what he had done to her at the rain barrel, no talk of John Quincy, no talk that she was as much a prisoner as her husband in jail in Key West.

Eulalie stuffed moss and mud into the cracks of the house to keep out mosquitoes and the smell of jasmine and prayed that the eyes full of adultery mentioned in James 2:11 did not apply to her own. With Quincy Octavius beside her on the porch copying his letters backwards on a piece of tarpaper, she flipped through her Bible for guidance, picking random verses and hoping for a sign, but nothing made sense and she concluded that her ability to interpret the Holy Writ was lost along with her ability to speak in tongues.

The only thing that would make it right was marriage. Eulalie allowed herself to think of how Thomas would take her and Jack to the Bahamas to meet his family. She would introduce the boy as Quincy Octavius, tell his people that her father, for whom the boy was named, once had the biggest groves in Palatka, and they would smile and say, "His breeding shows."

The question was how and when such a marriage would take place. Even in John Quincy's worst moments, Eulalie would never wish her husband dead. She had heard of divorce, knew that it was a great scandal that one whispered about like cancer or dark-hued babies born to white women, but she never knew anyone who had been divorced. Neither did she know how people went about getting a divorce, nor was there anyone to ask. Thomas would know. She reasoned that his reluctance to discuss the matter was due to his sense of decorum, of propriety. He was waiting for her to bring the subject up.

Eulalie did so one sunny afternoon when he took them sailing on a flat-bottomed skiff, skimming through channels cut by the current to show Jack how sponges were caught. His fatherly attention to her son prompted her petition.

She waited until the skiff bobbed at anchor. Thomas had brought along a glass-bottomed bucket, but they didn't need it. The bay was smooth and they were able to see without it through the clear water to the marly bottom.

Jack said the sponges looked like frosted cakes.

Thomas laughed while he held a long three-pronged pole over the side. "You guide it," he said to Jack. "I'll help you hold it."

The only sounds were the screeching seagulls, the lap of the waves, and the luffing sail. "Where will we live?" she asked.

"We? What are you talking about, Eulalie?"

"When we . . . are free to marry. Where will we go?"

"You're already married." He poked the pole farther out in the water. "You have to insert the hook under the sponge, Jack, to detach it from the rocks."

Eulalie persisted. "People get divorced."

"Other people divorce. People with means, people who can afford barristers. Women with a family of standing to cushion them against the repercussions of such an action."

He helped Jack swing a sponge on board. Eulalie stepped back from the foul-smelling creature. "It's alive," he said to the boy. "If we were spongers, we'd be bringing this and a score like it to some krall for the tides to wash it clean, then we'd hang it up to dry."

Eulalie's voice took on the peevish edge that she heard only in invalids and Yankees. Nevertheless, she continued to press her argument, paying no attention to Jack, who stared at her solemn and wide-eyed. "You told me never to forget that I was yours. What did you mean if not marriage?"

"People say things in the heat of the moment. I thought you understood. You have said things to me that I know you could not mean under the circumstances."

A waterspout appeared, a long, sinuous flume, twisted and bent by the wind as it sped along the surface of the water. Thomas pulled up anchor and they set sail for the docks.

"What circumstances?" she asked.

"You have responsibilities. I have responsibilities."

"I know what mine are," she said. "What are yours?"

He sighed while he tightened the jib. "To my family."

"What do you mean?"

"I don't wish to wound you, but you insist. Eulalie, darling, try to understand. Someday I will inherit my father's estates. I'm expected to marry someone of my own class, preferably a Bahamian, someone who understands crown and station, someone who will be an asset."

"I do understand. I understand how cruel you are."

"I love you, Eulalie. How is that cruel?"

They slipped over waving seagrass where turtles fed in the pale green shallows beneath, then reached the dock, where nearby sloops and skiffs lay scattered on the narrow beach. Jack scrambled over the side to secure the lines while Eulalie gathered her skirts in her hand.

"You treat me like I was a cracker," she said. "I'm not a cracker and neither is my son. We came upon hard times is all, and maybe my clothes aren't the latest fashion and my hair's not fixed right, maybe my hands are rough and my nose is peeling, but I am well bred, as were my parents before me and their

105

parents before them. My father was an important man in Putnam County."

Sands steadied his craft, then handed Eulalie onto the narrow quay, his eye focused on some distant spot beyond. "Of course he was. I was thoughtless to suggest otherwise."

Certain that he would change his mind, Eulalie waited for Sands each day as did the boy, her chin tucked to her chest as she commenced her chores, grubbing coontie from the whorls and crevices of the limestone, boiling guava into jelly, then skimming the hot jelly into glass jars with a metal spoon. Sometimes a week, two or three, would go by, and fearful that she might never see him again, she prayed for a fainting spell that would help her forget, for just a little while. She could not even convince herself that her sinful affection sprang from Sands' efforts to get John Quincy released from prison, for in her heart of hearts she did not care if John Quincy came out in six months or six years.

Once, frantic, she ran to search for Sands' sloop, scarcely noticing the man who was measuring out the land behind her with long, giant steps, or his companion who looked through something on a tripod.

It was the first full moon in May, a season when villagers waited on the beach to catch the migrating turtles. Eulalie took off her shoes at the water's edge and waded over the flats,

106

staring past the indigo blue rollers of the Gulf Stream, trying to see all the way to the crystal blue-green waters of the reef, while silt sucked at her ankles like quicksand and Jack played among the mangrove roots, making elevated catwalks of flotsam that floated in the tide.

Then, because there were people about and she needed a reason to be on the beach, she searched the sand for deep white holes in which turtles had deposited their eggs. Later, when she smeared turtle eggs with avocado oil and packed them for storage in sawdust, she imagined the curling blonde hairs on the back of Thomas's knowing hands, then forced herself to think of how John Quincy must be suffering in prison, and knew that the devil had gotten her soul for sure when she realized that she had forgotten the color of her husband's eyes.

When the waiting became interminable, Eulalie trudged to Peacock's with John Quincy's dog following behind her. Jack and Bristol were riding pine saplings, bending them back to spring through the air in joyous shouts. Jack stopped, expecting his mother to scold him for getting pine resin on his new britches, but she walked by him without a glance. Eulalie found Caroline at the steaming wash house next to the hotel's kitchen, where linens lay soaking in tubs, some containers filled with lye, others with unslaked lime. The black woman moved from tub to tub, working with paddles and a corrugated washboard. She was pretty, despite the sweat that beaded her face and stained scimitars beneath her arms, despite the bandanna that covered up her hair. Eulalie ignored the stab of jealousy at the sight of the woman with whom Thomas had shared a bed and handed her a tinful of powdered coontie. "I brought you some starch."

Caroline noticed that white skin had no secrets. The flush that spread through Eulalie's face and neck was as telling as the laundry flags that fluttered from the yachts. Feeling contempt for the white woman's vulnerability, for her lack of pride, she lifted her eyebrows in disdain. "What you give it to me for? Best give it to Peacock. He'll pay you for it."

Eulalie released the strings of her bonnet. "Have you seen him?" she asked.

"Who?" replied the laundress, brushing the sweat from her brow with her forearm.

"Thomas Sands."

"What you want with him?"

"My husband works for him."

"Not now he don't. Your husband in jail. He been in jail for months."

"I was hoping you would know where he is. I just want to speak to him."

"Probably he on the water, doing his business. Ask at the hotel. That where he stay."

Lavinia would never have tolerated such out-and-out insolence from a Negro, thought

108

Eulalie. She reeled in anger as she retied her bonnet strings in a smart bow. "What I can't abide," she said, "is a darky who doesn't know her place."

"I know one thing," said Caroline. "My place better than your place. I'm not looking every which way for some man not my husband."

When Eulalie thought she might be gone up, she sent away to Brickell for Bradfield's female regulator but was told that anything from Atlanta would take months. When Eulalie was sure, she sent a message with Jimmy Jumper to Sally Cypress, who knew more about stopping babies than Aunt Bella Peacock, whose skill extended only to delivering them. Eulalie was afraid that the message would not reach its destination, since the Cypress Indian was drunk when he stuffed the diaper inside his big shirt. Within days, however, Miami Doctor returned with a deerskin bundle. Sally Cypress was in the baby house, but she sent dried leaves and twigs with instructions to parch them first over a fire until they were deep brown. Eulalie boiled the infusion until it became the dark liquid that Miami Doctor called black drink. When it cooled, she sipped it in deep drafts, then vomited through the day and night. In the morning, when nothing happened, no bleeding, no cramps, no pain to herald a miscarriage, she searched frantically through the undergrowth for John the Conqueror roots, looking for the yellow petals and reddish dots that were the blood of the beheaded John the Baptist, despairing when she realized that even if she found them, the roots would do no good, as this was only May, and the root was best used on June 24, which was St. John's birthday.

With no choices left, Eulalie pierced the unquickened child with a knitting needle dipped in turpentine, threading the sharp instrument somewhere deep inside her secret place that she knew nothing about. It was bloody and excruciatingly painful. She bit on a spoon to keep from fainting, gasped; then when the blood began to flow, stopped, pulled out the instrument and packed her torn body with spiderwebs and moss, grateful to have brought about something she had heard of only in whispers.

Chapter Six

Thomas Sands was back in Caroline's bed even before John Quincy Coombs returned from prison. There were no recriminations, no entreaties not to discard her again when he found someone new. Caroline was content to have her mattress smell once more of bay rum and sweat. Not that she ever felt the heart-chewing jealousy she had felt in the island, the kind that eats at your heart and leaves you as hollow as a gourd. The girl that Thomas had courted in Eleuthera had been beautiful, had fanned herself on her veranda with slender, lily-white arms, had worn her sleek, glossy curls high on the back of her head with a gardenia tucked between them. Despite her yellow hair and glass blue eyes, this Coombs woman was stringy and would soon be old, already fixed with a permanent squint that poor whites got when they carried no parasol. Besides, Thomas had long since tired of her, for when he learned that the white woman had come looking for him, he told Caroline to tell her he was at sea. What if she sees your craft? she asked. Tell her I'm on another, he replied. What if she goes to the inn? She won't do that, he said.

The baby was a girl. Caroline didn't have to see it to know that it was his. No early baby could be that big. But more telling, it looked like Bristol, only paler, as if the tiny thing had had a terrible fright. Caroline saw the infant named Maude when she came to bring its mother a pot of fish head soup made with curry powder and thyme that she carried on her head. The white women had talked in front of her as white people did, believing that somehow she did not hear or understand. Mrs. Peacock said she had heard of ten-month babies, even eleven- and twelve-month babies. The Pent woman said she had heard of a husband's seed lying dormant in his wife for years, a case in point the baby girl born to Martha Delaney, whose husband, Samuel, had died three years before and who was so mean-spirited, wearing her husband's boots and hat, that no man went near. No, corrected Mrs. Peacock. It is possible for a girl child, she explained, to carry the seed of her own father from the time she was conceived. The Frow woman did not believe any of it and said so.

Sands asked about the baby only once. "You went to see it?" he asked. She said she had. "Who does it look like?" he asked.

"The child favors Bristol," she replied, "only lighter." He smiled and asked if she would make fish with orange sauce. He hadn't had that since he left the islands.

When a paler, thinner Coombs was finally released, Caroline knew that his woman had her hands full keeping him from tearing up the place. When he wasn't punching through the wax paper windows or getting drunk with Jimmy Jumper, he was worrying the guests at the hotel, looking everywhere for Thomas Sands, including bawling outside Caroline's shack and scaring Bristol half to death as he shouted, "I know you're in there, you coon-loving son of a bitch!"

Caroline was glad when public school began in the Sunday school building for children of the settlement, even though Bristol was told

112

to sit in the back because of the three-year-old state law that mandated separate school facilities for Negroes and white. Bristol was allowed on sufferance only because there was no other facility for Negro children and because Caroline threatened to leave the inn if he could not attend. There was a slate for almost everyone, a potbelly stove in the corner with a teakettle, and a warning from the teacher, Miss MacFarlane, that people who went barefoot got worms.

Thomas Sands supplied Bristol with a slate and Caroline a straw hat with an apple green ribbon, telling her not to wear bandannas on her head anymore unless she was in the steam house. He promised to bring gloves from Key West to match the ribbon. The next morning, when his boot marks were nowhere to be seen in the damp marl, Caroline shivered at the awful possibility that somehow Obeahman had gotten his footprints.

For the first few months, after most of the winter people had sailed north, she lit candles for her lover's safety, praying that he was on the water, perhaps gone back to Eleuthera, and watching in terror in the darkness of her cabin for the fiery eyes of the rolling calf that would tell her that he had not.

On her half day off, to fill her pocket and to occupy thoughts that might otherwise turn to fretful, worrisome doubts, Caroline took in laundry from a wealthy couple from Staten Island who were building a home with a staircase that led in two directions. Bristol told her that John Quincy, with Pent and Carney to help him, had added sheathing to the inside of his house with pine boards laid diagonally over the studs and braces, and tacked behind, to keep out crawling things, sheathing paper filched from the Staten Island people's construction site. As it was not her concern, she went about her business and said nothing to her new employers, yet with every passing week, the water made by her bowels, the heartbeat hammering in her ears, and once the sight of carmine eyes glowing in the night told her that something terrible had happened to her lover.

Eleuthera, Bahamas
August, 1890

Dear Mr. Peacock,

Since you confirm my worst suspicions, I will be sailing for Coconut Grove as soon as my gout enables me to get on my feet. My wife will not be joining me in this difficult journey. As you can imagine, the uncertainty has been particularly hard on her; consequently, I will require accommodations for only one. Any room will do. I have no interest in view or prevailing breeze.

You have assured me that my son's room has been kept exactly as he left it. Would

114

you be so kind as to maintain this vigilance until my arrival so that I may be able to search through his possessions in the hope of finding some clue as to what has happened to him?

It might be helpful if you told no one of my visit or of my reasons for coming. I do not wish to give undue advantage should there be those with need to conceal. I am sure you understand the necessity for confidentiality.

With all gratitude, I remain, sir,
Yours most sincerely,
Edward Sands

Caroline learned that Sands' father had come to the Peacock Inn when she was asked to carry his portmanteau up to his room. After a long conversation with Peacock behind closed doors, the white-haired planter visited Caroline's cabin, waiting patiently outside the tightly closed door until the boy brought her out. "I am looking for my son," he said. "I had hoped perhaps you could tell me something that might help me in my search."

He looked older than the last time she had seen him, more portly, his blue eyes milky as if their color were dissolving. Caroline thought about the footprints that had been stolen by Obeahman, but decided not to mention this. When white folks heard of such things, they tended to smile at you as if you were

115

simple. "Man work for him," she said. "Name Coombs."

"I had heard that," he said. "Can you show me where this Coombs fellow lives?"

"Bristol, he can."

The elder Sands looked down at the boy who was probably his grandson, who, under other circumstances, would be off to boarding school in Sussex. He pressed a coin into Bristol's hand. "Bristol, is it? Lead the way, Bristol, but slowly if you please."

Caroline sent Bristol with a lantern. Later that night, as Caroline worked over a basket of stained linen, rubbing spots with yellow soap over the back of a spoon, Bristol returned to tell her that the old man had asked one question after another — how long they had lived there, what had brought them to the settlement, how well had they known his son.

"We didn't know him hardly at all," Coombs had said. "From time to time I'd sign on. That was about it." Coombs spoke of dangerous work on the water, of ships foundering and sinking on the treacherous reef. Did they find his sloop? No? Well, that should tell you something.

"Indeed it does," replied the elder Sands. "You've spent some time in prison, I understand."

Here was where, by Bristol's account, Coombs got whiskey-mean and nasty. "What I spent," he said, "is all the time with you I've a mind to."

116

The old man didn't blink an eye. "How about you, ma'am?"

"It's as my husband says. We didn't know him too well."

The baby cried. The Coombs woman went to get it. The old man looked at it real interested, pulled back its swaddling wrap. "A beautiful child, ma'am. Favors you, I suppose, except around the eyes." Then he turned to the piano. "How did you come by this?"

"I rescued it," said Coombs. "At the reef."

The elder Sands ran his fingers over the keys. That's when Jack decided to speak. "We put a kerosene lamp by its side, like Mr. Sands told us to, and it dried it out some, 'cept you still hear only thumping from that end."

Bristol said that when they left, John Quincy whipped the boy good. He didn't even wait until they were out of earshot, but began to wear out Jack as soon as they had reached the edge of the clearing.

It was clear that they knew something about Thomas' disappearance. At least Coombs did. Caroline wondered if the Coombs woman knew as well.

Caroline filled a coconut shell with charcoal and a plug of John Quincy's chewing tobacco. She did this even before the sheriff looked into the Coombs' latrine, a likely place for a body whose decomposition would not be noticed, or asked her if she had some buck who was sweet on her.

The investigation of Sands' disappearance came to a halt when Peacock learned that Key West would soon be under quarantine. With four cases of yellow fever, thought to be brought by two vessels from Havana, the Monroe County health officer was going to institute a pass-card system. Anyone who could prove that they had survived an attack of yellow fever and all Negroes, who for some reason seemed to be immune, would be issued pass cards. Anyone else who could not provide such cards to the quarantine officer were confined at the least to their village, at the most to their homes. If the Bahamian planter intended to sail for Eleuthera, it had to be now. In a day or two, there would be no ships going in or out, possibly for months.

"I hear," said Peacock, "that at the county line there are men with shotguns demanding yellow fever passes. If a fellow doesn't have one, they won't let him cross." He added that in Key West they were firing cannons into the air to hammer the airborne yellow fever germs.

The elder Sands left, as did the remaining winter people, who quickly paid their bills and fled north. Streets were cleared of refuse and offal, privies were covered with lime. People were cautioned not to pull up weeds, or cut down trees, or turn the earth, for it was known that the summer sun acting on the newly ex-posed earth would create the fever-bearing miasma, and since yellow fever was acquired at night, everyone was told to stay in after dark. Those planning to buy groceries at Brickell's were advised not to leave home until after sunup, and to return before sundown.

When John Quincy took to his bed with what he believed to be a return of breakbone, Eulalie sponged his drenching sweats and recalled the first few weeks of his return. She had been able to conceal the bulge of her belly beneath a pinafore, knowing that it was only a matter of time before he found out.

She thought of the afternoon she hurried to corner Jack outside the wooden schoolhouse. "I'm not asking you to lie, you understand?"

"I think so, Mama."

"Remember when we didn't have coffee and we used chicory instead? We did without. What I'm asking you to do is to do without some of the truth. You think you could do that for me?"

"Yes, ma'am. Like what?"

"Don't talk about Thomas around your father. Don't say that he was over to the house, that he came to visit, that he brought you presents."

"He brought you presents too."

Eulalie sighed. "That's what I want you to forget."

"Yes, Mama. Can I go now?" He turned toward Bristol, who was waiting patiently in the shade of an oak.

"You going off with him again?" she asked.

"We're going to catch crabs. Bristol has a trick for getting them to come out of their holes."

Eulalie squinted against the light, the green-tinted spectacles long since tossed in the bay along with the straw hat with flowers and face cream from New York. "I want to see you with white friends. You can't learn anything from a darky."

"Yes, I can. Bristol's smart. He can read better than me."

"You can teach a monkey to dance, but that doesn't mean you want him for a partner."

It was during the first cold snap when Eulalie was running around covering her seedlings with newspaper that John Quincy realized that she was pregnant. "I thought you was getting thick in the middle," he said. "You're gone up. I make you out to be six, seven months."

"No," she said, "the baby is about due, nine months to the day you were gone."

He smiled a lopsided grin. He had lost more teeth, and the spaces made him seem vulnerable, somehow, older. "Why didn't you say anything?"

"I didn't want to worry you, what with you coming out of jail and all."

"Is that so?"

"We was alone all the time," said Jack.

"Were," said Eulalie, "not was."

Her diversion did not work. John Quincy came to stand unsteadily before the boy, looming over him toe to toe. "You got something to tell me?"

Jack stared at the floor. "No, sir."

"I think you do. I think you're a liar. You know what happens to liars?"

The boy began to tremble, "No, sir."

"They get found out and then they get the tar whupped out of them."

Eulalie stepped between them. "Don't, John Quincy. He's been a good boy, helped me out a lot when you were gone. If it wasn't for Jack, I don't know what I would have done."

"It's him or it's you, Eulalie. One of you is gonna get a hiding. Take your pick. Some man's had my wife. There's payment to be made."

Eulalie wrapped her arms around her son. "He had us both, John Quincy. Thomas Sands. He had you too. You were the one behind bars. Not him. You're the one's got nothing to show for all that time in jail while he's got a warehouse filled to the ceiling."

His face turned as dark as cane syrup. Then, without a word, he lay on the bed, where he stared at the ceiling until night. Three days later the baby was born. John Quincy took one look at the child and stormed out of the house while Eulalie lay with her face to the wall, refusing to look at the infant crying in its cradle, who, despite its baldness, resembled Thomas Sands.

Existence with John Quincy was a daily battle to keep herself and the boy out of his way.

When she heard rumors that Thomas Sands had gone, leaving an unpaid bill at Peacock's, she was relieved. Without his sloop at anchor, the occasional sight of him in the village to remind her, it was as if what had happened between them had never been. Then John Quincy came home with a bundle that smelled like Thomas, made her go outside while he hid it somewhere inside. Eulalie came back into a familiar aroma of bay rum and cigars.

"That's to remind you," he said. "That's so you'll never forget the evil thing you did."

And because she was afraid of his answer, afraid that he would take his anger out again on the boy, she didn't ask him how he got the garments. She lived in silence with the smell of Thomas, the anger of John Quincy, the demands of a selfish baby who could not be satisfied, and the shame of dissembling to a courteous, heartbroken old man looking for his son. If she noticed the barrels of tar that burned in the narrow, weed-choked lanes, creating in the hot, heavy air a pall of smoke by day, and an eerie glow at night, it was only a warrant that hell was possible on earth.

Eulalie put down her basin and lit a lamp, then saw the yellow jaundice and knew that their house would soon be placed under quarantine with a yellow flag nailed to their front door. She gave her husband hot mustard baths, painted his genitals with tincture of iodine to stimulate his water, and spooned into his fever-parched mouth infusions of orange leaves and powdered watermelon seeds. When he began to spew the fatal black vomit over everything, including his pine needle pillow and mattress, she cut out paper crosses and placed them on the soiled bed cover, then opened a fumigated letter from her mother that smelled of brimstone and hellfire.

On instructions from his mother, Bristol hid behind the fat fan-shaped leaves of a sea grape to watch Pent hammering a coffin in the clearing while a mattress and pillow burned in a refuse pile. He ran home after he peeked in the window and saw John Quincy's stiffening body wrapped in a winding sheet as Eulalie fumigated the house with vinegar and tar.

The charm had worked as she knew it would. Wearing her apple green banded straw hat and her hair fixed in a bun, Caroline went to offer to take the baby back for the rest of the afternoon. An exhausted and grief-numbed Eulalie agreed. With the door of her cabin tightly locked and the crannies packed with sand against Obeahman, Caroline gave Sands' daughter doses of calomel, sponged her with whiskey and quinine water, rubbed her with melted tallow candle in which a rusty nail had been dipped, put plasters of red pepper and earth at the nape of her small, baby neck. She gave the baby conch stew with a few small eggs and prayed for the survival of the child who looked like

Bristol, who looked like him.

With the baby protected and memories of Thomas Sands locked safely away beside those of Papa Hanna, Caroline moved with Bristol into a narrow cottage. Servant quarters had been hastily built to house the dozens of laborers and housemaids arriving every month, most from the Bahamas, a few from Jamaica, some from Georgia or the Carolinas. One of several packed tightly together, the dwelling was called a shotgun house because all three of its rooms were laid out in a straight line. Caroline and Bristol were to share it with an older, gray-haired man, a former slave and spy for the Confederacy named Galilee, who would occupy the back room, and who wore beneath his clothes a leather strap that held his bulging intestines in place.

"This not bad," he said to Caroline, setting his bedroll against a wall. "You too young to recollect slave houses. Besides, you from the Bahamas. Might be they do things different there. This place have windows, doors, a water pump outside. Where they kept us, just a dirt floor. The beds were straw and old rags, thrown down in a corner and boxed in with boards." He set down two hobnail drinking glasses and a Bible. "Got to make a table," he said. "Can't have these things setting on the floor."

"It's your room," said Caroline. "I guess you can do what you like." She searched the walls for cracks.

"Can you read it?" asked Bristol.

"I used to be able to read it better, son, but the words is getting too small. Now I can only make out a word there, a word here. My mind fills in the rest."

Galilee followed Caroline to the front porch and watched as she sprinkled rice around the house. "I didn't know," he said, "that anyone did that old-timey stuff anymore."

She continued to work her spell in silence. He said he would try not to get in the way and to look after the boy when he could.

"I don't want Bristol knowing about slave huts and such," she said. "He thinks too much on it, he wind up with his head bent same as you. He too young to have his mind filled with suffering."

"Lots of ways to suffer," Galilee replied. "Some folks suffer longer than they has to."

"What you talking about?"

"If hard times be over, they be over. Sorrow is supposed to curl itself up and shrivel like a navel string so that the thing it attached to be broken."

"I still don't know what you saying, old man."

He took a handful of rice and sprinkled it before the front door. "I'm saying if a man be gone, girl, let him be gone."

Caroline paid little attention to Galilee's chatter until one afternoon he mentioned that when he was cutting back sea grape with his machete, Eulalie Coombs came to see the Commodore, the white-bearded rich Yankee who paid his wages. Someone told widow Coombs that she had two months to get off her land. That the property that her house stood on belonged to the Commodore. She offered to buy three acres, promised to pay it off with money from her coontie starch and guava jelly.

"What he want for it?" asked Caroline.

The Commodore's price was one hundred and fifty dollars. At first Galilee didn't think the Commodore would pay her much mind, considering as how he refused to cut a road to the Negro section while he knew that all his workers had to stumble through the hammock in the dark.

The widow Coombs held her ground, the baby on her hip, the boy at her side, not moving an inch while the Commodore asked her if she knew that Ponce de Leon stood right where they were standing in 1523.

She allowed as how she didn't know that. Then the Commodore led her to the deep well hewn into the limestone near his boathouse, where he climbed down halfway, resting on an outcropping of rock. "This could have been dug by Ponce de Leon searching for his fountain of youth," he said.

She shifted the baby to her other hip while he climbed out of the well. Galilee thought he would have to help him up, but the Commodore was pretty spry and got out himself.

"Where would you get all that money?" the

Commodore asked.

"I can pay you a little at a time."

"A man," he said, wiping the sweat off his brow with his sleeve, "can dig five or six barrels of roots a day. How many barrels of roots do you need to get a barrel of starch?"

"Eight," she said.

"How much do you get for a barrel?"

She followed him to his boathouse. "Nine dollars."

"How many barrels can you dig a day?"

"One, maybe two."

"Tell you what," the Commodore said. "Order an apple mill from the catalogue at Brickell's. Help you grind faster. That way you can pay me off quicker. Hire yourself a hand. Galilee, over there, he can help you grub when he's through working for me. Pay him a dollar a day. He'd be glad for the work. The only problem is, you need collateral."

"What's that?" she asked, failing in the test that rich white folks give to everyone else.

"Something of value."

Now the Commodore, explained Galilee, he knew she had nothing of value. None of these grubby whites had much of anything a body could speak of. This woman belonged to the class of used-to-was, but he asked her just the same.

Eulalie offered him the sewing machine and the walnut headboard that she had brought from Palatka. The Commodore said that these things were of no interest to him. Then she told him about the piano that played, although not all over.

The baby began to cry. I think, said Galilee, it put the Commodore in mind of his own baby girl who died. "I guess the piano will have to do," he said.

"How the Coombs child look?" asked Caroline.

"She's a pretty little thing. Except she's as quiet as one of them Indian young ones come around here every once in a while. You ever hear one of them speak? I never did."

"That woman is a fool. And the man you work for is no better, refusing to cut us a path when he have the tools."

Galilee smiled. His tongue poked around in his mouth like something live. "We has the tools, too," he said. He warned Bristol to stay awake because later that night, after the colored folks had assembled all the lanterns, pickaxes, mules, carts, and shovels they could lay their hands on, they were going to cut themselves a road right through the hammock, pave it with coral rock, and even give it a name. They were going to call it Charles Avenue. "The Lord helps those," he said, "who help themselves. And you getting to be a good-sized boy, Bristol. We can use your help for sure."

Chapter Seven

The new household for whom Caroline worked outfitted her in dove gray uniforms with white collars and cuffs that could be starched until they shined and allowed her to tote home all the leftover food and cast-off clothing she could carry. She was charged with the responsibility of the laundry and the upstairs, in a household of three, an easy job compared to the constant steam of her first position, or the unwanted attentions of the husband of the second, a man from Staten Island who said he heard that she liked white men.

She no longer had to boil soap from lye and grease but was encouraged to order packaged goods like Octagon soap and Gold Dust Powder from Brickell's. And when she stood flat irons on their heels in front of the fire to heat them — triangular irons, oval irons, a hollow box iron heated by a red-hot iron inserted into the box, and a hollow tube raised on a slender pedestal, an Italian iron used for ironing frills — no two were alike.

She was able to lay aside eight dollars at the end of each month, kept safely buried by Galilee in a tin box. The price she paid in return was to spend her days in the refurbished plantation house and her nights in the old, crumbling, ivy-covered rock building that had once been Fort Dallas barracks, returning to Evangelist Street only on Sunday afternoons.

Her new mistress, a middle-aged Cleveland widow who always wore black, had first seen Caroline serving at the home of the Staten Island couple. She liked the way Caroline steadied a platter, even when the man of the house slipped an importunate hand along the serving woman's thigh.

Although Julia Tuttle brought a maid and manservant from Cleveland, she needed someone else who knew how to keep house in the tropics, someone who knew to sprinkle cucumber peelings on the kitchen floor to attract and kill roaches, who knew to keep ants out of a sugar bowl with a piece of gum camphor the size of an almond wrapped in linen, who knew how to keep ice under straw, and how to restore black silk by sponging it with gin.

Unlike most of the other white women, like Eulalie Coombs, with freckles on their noses and calluses on their reddened hands from doing their own work, the widow was, to Caroline, a fine lady whose skirts whispered as she did, who arranged alamanders with wires and served genuine Java coffee, who had a corset just for morning and a fork just for fish.

Caroline's Sunday conversations on Evangelist Street began to feature matters that related to her new mistress, divulged with an earnest intensity as if they were happening to her. At a meeting of the Sons and Daughters of Samaria, Caroline disclosed that Mrs. Tuttle had asked a man named Flagler to extend his railroad down the Florida peninsula all the way to Miami.

Smelling of verbena and lime, the Sunday-dressed porters and day laborers, maids and cooks, listened politely while the stiff rustle of palm fronds came through the open window.

"Mrs. Tuttle says," continued Caroline softly, "that someday someone will build a railroad to Miami, and that she will give that person half her property for a town site."

"I worked on railroads fifteen years of my life," said Jesse Jones, said to have graduated from Amherst College somewhere up North. "No one offered me half their property. And I would have made it an anything-they-wanted site."

Caroline put a napkin on Bristol's lap, slapping it on his knee as if it were a poultice, determined to rein in the conversation where it belonged. "Mrs. Tuttle writes one letter after another to that man. She's made up her mind to have a railroad, and there's no stopping her."

Mariah Brown was a large, imposing woman who had spent that morning cleaning the grates of two fireplaces, sifting cinders so that only ashes were thrown away, then black-leading the grates with a mixture of asphaltum, linseed oil, and turpentine that she had prepared the night before. "She playing at business," she said. "Like she a man."

"She's not playing at anything," replied Caroline. "You see her living on her daddy's homestead? I don't. She bought this land herself from the Biscayne Bay company. That should tell you something."

Mariah Brown fanned herself with a palmetto leaf. "It tells me she have money to burn, and it tells me you putting too much store in what she do and what she say. You know what happens when you do that with white folks."

"Who is Flagler?" asked Bristol, trying to keep cake crumbs from spilling off his napkin.

"He a partner, son, of John D. Rockefeller," replied Galilee. "Flagler and Rockefeller some of the richest men in the world."

Jesse Jones said that rich men put their pants on one leg at a time like everyone else. Then he spoke of settlers coming in so fast that Brickell was beginning to ask five hundred dollars an acre. "This is a good time to invest in land," he said.

"Where you going to get five hundred or even one hundred dollars, Brother Jesse?" asked Mariah.

"There's ways to buy land," he replied, "without having a whole lot of money. Best way is to find someone who borrowed from a bank to buy his land. You come to him, you say, I'm here to bail you out. Depending on how hard up he is, you can offer him break-even money, he doesn't lose, you don't lose because you've got a contract to use of the land for twenty, thirty years, with an option to buy."

Isaac McCloud was somewhere in his middle years, thick and solid, wearing a starched and shiny wing collar that threatened to unsnap. He cleared his throat to speak, with a sideways glance, as always, on Caroline.

"I go to some white man," he said, "tell him I'm there to bail him out, he'll tell me to get my black nigger behind off his front porch and that be the end of it. Isn't that so, Miss Caroline?"

"I expect so," she replied.

Caroline's thoughts were elsewhere, on the conversation she had overheard the night before when Mr. Flagler said that if he brought the railroad, there would be no place for Indians in the new Miami. The railroad brings people, he explained. People buy the railroad's goods. People need land. How do you propose to do this? Mrs. Tuttle asked. I doubt that they'll leave voluntarily. Our strategy, replied Flagler, is quite simple. We will drain the Everglades.

"We here to talk of something else," said Mariah Brown, who had had enough of Caroline's chitchat when there was only three hours of daylight left. "We here to discuss getting a church of our own. Being able to sing and shout, and praise Jesus, that's what this all about. Not hold back like we been doing when we worship with the white folks."

133

"No one says we has to hold back," said Galilee.

"But you do," said Isaac McCloud. "That's the point. You ever once clap your hands, stamp your feet in Union Chapel? Jump? All Mrs. Peacock has to do is turn and give one of those flat-faced looks of hers, and you shut up pretty quick. We tried to fit our ways to theirs. That was all right when there was just a handful of us. Now we're more than fifty. It didn't work. It's time to be thinking of our own church and our own pastor."

The last drops of coffee were poured, the few remaining stale petit fours that Caroline toted home were packed in a tin. Shirtwaists were smoothed, vests buttoned, gloves pulled on finger by finger, bowlers tipped and angled, reticules snapped closed.

Mariah Brown asked Galilee how he liked boiling guava jelly for the Coombs woman. "She got you working in that house of hers besides."

"She pay me extra."

"What she have you to do in there?"

Galilee had just finished plastering the walls at the Coombs place, where he had felt the presence of a ghost watching him at work from somewhere in the room that smelled of bay rum. He knew a ghost was there, being as there were two ways to tell the presence of ghosts, cold spots and smells. He had never met Sands, but he was sure it was the white man's bay rum smell that had filled the loft.

Sands was probably watching over his child. Galilee had decided not to tell Caroline. If she got riled up, she'd be making charms, sprinkling chicken blood everywhere. It was better, he reasoned, to let sleeping dogs lie.

"Set in window glass" was all he said. "Plaster over her walls."

"Why she want you to plaster her walls?"

"They was too rough to suit her taste. She wants them smooth. I think she has in mind to put up wallpaper."

"Might be she have money, but it's a shame the way she treat that child," said Ma Edie.

"How do she treat her? She whip her?" asked Caroline.

"No," said Mariah Brown. "She just never puts her eyes on her. Like she's not there."

"Everyone in this room knows how that feels," said Jesse Jones.

"Eulalie Coombs not so bad," said Galilee. "She just have her ways is all."

"Seems like someone else around here has their ways, too," said Caroline. "You got to keep that kerosene heater turned down, Galilee. You got the walls and ceiling in the house smoked so bad it's going to take me the next five Sundays to get things right."

Galilee rubbed his chin while others exchanged glances as if they were passing illegal coin. Isaac McCloud clapped him on the shoulder. "Brother Galilee, when you were crossing Union lines, why did you come back?"

Galilee smiled. "I brought them Confederates bad news. I was glad to do it."

Before Caroline took the cart back through the darkening hammock, she handed Bristol a bit of folded dark green ribbon, frayed at the ends, to give to the little Coombs girl.

"You made Galilee feel bad," said Bristol.

"Never mind about that. Galilee can take care of himself. The child can't. She don't have to know who this came from. Tell Maude it's for her hair."

"She gonna know that."

"Not if no one's looked at her long enough to tell her."

"What if she's hiding under the house, Mama? That's where she go sometimes."

"Then you go in and get her out."

"There's chicken slime under there."

"You can wash off chicken slime. Some things you can't wash off no matter what."

"That girl my sister?"

"What makes you talk so crazy?"

"I heard you tell Galilee she's my sister."

"She a white child. Are you a white child?"

"No'm."

"Then how can she be your sister?"

Chapter Eight

In the twelve years since she had followed John Quincy to Dade County, Eulalie had grown taut and lean, her face tanned and crinkled around the eyes, hardened around the jaw. She kept her skirts hemmed above her ankles, her sun-bleached hair no longer in a bun but worn down her back in a single braid tied at the end with rawhide. She had long since discarded the sun bonnet for a hat of plaited palmetto strips, bleached almost the color of her hair.

Many times she felt she would not survive. When her second baby, Lavinia, shriveled like a leaf, when they lost their homestead, when she thought she could not live without Thomas Sands, when the Holy Spirit abandoned her, when, despite her agonizing efforts, Sands' child was born, and again when John Quincy breathed his last and she was left alone with Jack and the baby, she thought she would die. Once, with sagging shoulders and labored, shallow breath, she prayed that the Lord would take her in her sleep, and was surprised to wake up in the morning and find that He had not.

In time feelings had sifted like flour. Nagging

fears like whether she should take her two children and return to her uncle's home in Palatka, whether John Quincy had really done away with her lover or only frightened him off, and if the latter were true, why he had stuffed Thomas' garments behind a wall, no longer woke her up in the middle of the night. John Quincy did what he had to do, just as she did what she had to do, which was to get from one day to the next, to keep the land beneath their house. She had hated begging for what was rightfully hers, standing with a child on her hip while that old man dragged her all over his property, climbing down some fool well to tell her of some long ago Spanish fellow, knowing that she would follow him to hell and back with both children on her hips to get him to say yes.

Tenderness had been caught like rocks in a sieve. What had shaken through was endurance. If she allowed herself to get soft, if she allowed herself to think, she knew she would dissolve like the gelatin she added to the boiling guava.

She had no time for Peacock's new bathing casino, much less for the silly bathing costumes or the black cotton stockings that some women wore with their calico dresses. She was uncomfortable with the newly arrived Yankee wives from eastern drawing rooms with their cucumber sandwiches, twangy voices, and smooth, unbroken nails. When she attended a meeting of the Housekeepers' Club, it was only because the schoolteacher who organized the club invited her. As far as she was concerned, most of the members were Johnny-come-latelies who made fun of crackers when they thought she wasn't listening, asking her if she took snuff, while they shifted insinuating eyebrows. They imitated the Indians, declaring that they would never permit them to camp on their property. Adelaide Frow confirmed that Jimmy Jumper had been found dead drunk in her backyard. "Not in a manner of speaking, mind you. I mean drunk himself to death. Miami Doctor had to carry his body back to the 'Glades."

A Staten Island matron known for weak lungs and columns of palm trunks supporting her front porch begged Eulalie to tell them how she carried her son into the Everglades to cure his snake-bitten leg. Eulalie clutched the reticule she held in her lap and refused to discuss the terrifying afternoon she had found Jack collapsed on the porch, his leg reddened, swollen, slashed in a crisscross where he had tried to suck out the poison.

The memory of his personal trial was not one to share, least of all with these prying, self-righteous ninnies, most of whom had men to care for them, all of whom still whispered of Thomas Sands and of the child who looked just like him, and of his sudden and suspicious disappearance. Only her dead mother and the Lord knew how she had given Jack doses of echinacia through the night. When he seemed near death toward morning, she entrusted Maude to Galilee, put the feverish boy in the oxcart and drove through the hammock to Brickell's, where a dozen dugouts lay tied to the dock. There she met the stately Emathla, who ferried them deep into the Everglades.

The events of the next ten days seemed mottled, like the bark of a gumbo limbo — the pen of logs covered with palmetto leaves that shielded Jimmy Jumper's body from the wild, his widow's long black tresses covering her face, giving her a forsaken, pitiable appearance, Sally Cypress holding an infant in the smoke of a burning bird's nest (her third baby, the second one had died, she told Eulalie, because its nails were cut before the fourth moon), Sally Cypress treating Jack's blackening leg with wormseed taken from the east side of the plant, the side of greatest potency from the sun.

While Eulalie sat anxiously beside her soporous son, she learned that the Indians were bad off. Their previous camp had been lost when whites claiming the cultivated plots as their own were granted a homestead on its boundaries. Game was not as plentiful as before. White men had stolen most of their hogs and all of their cattle. Because the camp was temporary, their chickees were not as well braced against the wind, their palmetto thatches loosely laid, causing leaks in the rain. Miami Doctor said that Major Duncan, the Indian inspector, had come to inspect the swamp to see if it belonged to the state.

"State and Washington same but not same," said Miami Doctor. "Like two nations. State wants to give us Long Key. Does Washington say this, too? we ask. Jimmy Jumper stands up, tall, taller than white man. We got go there, he says. It worthless island. Storm tide come, everything under water." Miami Doctor shook his head. "White man no good," he said. "Lie too much."

"What did they do? It must have been terribly frightening. Where did you sleep? Tell us," the women asked between sips of tea.

"They cured him," Eulalie replied.

"We know that, but how?" insisted the Staten Island matron.

Eulalie sighed and put down her cup of tea. "They lay Jack in a chickee. He was burning up with fever. His leg was black as soot. I was afeared that we was going to have to cut off the black parts, but an Indian woman covered them with herbs."

"What kind of herbs?" asked Adelaide Frow.

"Elder flower water and wormseed mostly," replied Eulalie. "I don't know what all else she used. Then she packed his leg with moss."

"You're saying a squaw cured your boy," said the Staten Island matron, "and not a medicine man?"

"Sally Cypress knows as much about healing as any medicine man."

141

"I don't know how you stood their smell so close up," said a woman in a straw hat. "How much did you have to pay her?"

Eulalie stood. "Sally Cypress is my friend. She would never ask for payment. And she bathes every day, which is more than any of us do. If there was a smell, it came from Jack's leg. The stink was awful, but no one turned up his nose the way you're all doing now."

After she left, the members of the House-keepers' Club went on to discuss the railroad and the town that was springing up overnight, the suggestion that an oyster supper was the way to raise $4.70 for a globe with mountains you could feel, and the new state law that allowed Flagler to divorce his second wife. When Eulalie left, they voted on her membership. Flora MacFarland seemed disappointed to see two black beans in a pile of white. "I like to see all the mothers attend," she said.

Eulalie's interest remained on her house and yard and the three acres around it where, from early dawn past nightfall, sometimes with a kerosene lamp, she ground coontie starch and labored in the guava shack with the foul-smelling rinds and boiling pots of fruit. That she could not bear to look at the girl was not her fault. She tried. But it was Thomas' face she saw beneath the mop of curly blonde hair, Thomas' bronze-green eyes in the child's sullen face. She did what she had to, dressed the girl, fed

142

her, kept her safe in the clearing, tied by her waist to a banyan tree until Jack came home from school, away from the debris of the newly finished quarried limestone house, with its colonnade, parapet, and piped-in water.

Eulalie had little concern that Jack at twelve was still in the chart class at school, the level for children for whom reading was a struggle. It was his conduct that shamed her, particularly when the teacher had to rap his knuckles with a ruler for crawling beneath the schoolhouse and thumping the floor with his head, or putting live coals in frogs to watch them turn up, when he had been told to spend recess pulling weeds.

"You're supposed to do me proud," she said, handing him a lard bucket filled with a boiled sweet potato and a sandwich of tomato preserves. "When's that going to happen?"

She was convinced that his school troubles and his failure to obey such simple rules as carrying his shoes when it rained were the result of his friendship with Bristol, and she was glad when the Negro children were put into a separate school, which was, after all, the law.

If the boy did not delight her as he once had, the house offered solace of another kind. There was wallpaper patterned with ivy creepers on the smoothly plastered walls, and a new feather mattress shaken to a puff every morning. Galilee and a man named Jesse Jones were building a roofed breezeway between the house and the kitchen with a shelf to hold a wash basin, water bucket, and towel. After they were finished, Eulalie planned for them to build a platform as well so she could walk from one structure to the other in the rain and not step into mud.

Even her garden was a source of pride. The freezes of the winter of 1894 and 1895 that almost wiped out the citrus industry of Florida never reached below Palm Beach, consequently never touched her orange plants, now growing, not in the damp ground, but cut into the limestone rock, where Galilee said they liked to keep their feet dry.

In a settlement with few women and a passable widow still in her childbearing years, with a home of her own and a little money put by, Eulalie had suitors. She looked for their flaws the way she candled eggs. Only once, with a locomotive engineer from Pennsylvania, whose powerful hand controlled the throttle of a shrieking, steam-belching train that thundered down the silver tracks, did she feel a hint of the desire that had bound her to Sands. But the man's Yankee speech, too quick, too glib, forced through his nose instead of resonating from his chest, put her off.

"Is it the children?" he asked one Sunday afternoon, rocking beside her on her front porch, his hair slicked to either side of his head with maccasar oil. "You know I'd be good to them."

144

"No," she replied, a glance into the yard, where Jack lifted Maude from the hollow of a banyan. "I just can't see my way clear."

"If I had the chance, I guess I could change your mind."

"How do you plan to do that?"

He smiled. "That's for me to know and you to find out. Don't you want more children, Eulalie? To care for you in your old age?"

"I pray the good Lord has given me my last."

He reached across to pat her knee. "I bet there's life in the old gal yet."

Eulalie flung his hand away and brought her rocker to a standstill, a signal that the visit was at an end. "Don't darest touch me again without my say-so, which you'll have to wait till hell freezes over to get."

The locomotive engineer, used to a hero's adoration, slammed his hat on his head. "Don't get swell-headed, Eulalie. You're getting long in the tooth. Main thing you're good for these days is the roof over your head. I wouldn't have stayed very long anyway."

With his mother's suitor out of the yard, Jack sprinted up the steps with Maude chasing after him, her little legs pumping to keep up. "Is he coming around again, Mama?"

"I expect not."

"I didn't like him a whole lot."

"I guess you didn't like the way he treated your mama."

"No, ma'am. He was peculiar, is all."

"Peculiar how? Speak your mind, boy. I've got things to do."

Jack swallowed, then decided not to tell his mother that the engineer had asked him if there was any place men could swim in the buff, the way nature intended, and not be bothered with women.

Eulalie's suitor was just one of many men that the railroad had brought to the settlement, the effect not unlike the one the gold rush had on Sutter's Creek. They pitched tents and shacks, anchored boats or upturned them at the water's edge, tried to rent rooms wherever they could find them, emptied Brickell's and every other trading post of goods, looked for women, and finding none, slapped at mosquitoes, talked of all the money they were going to make, badgered the Indians, and scrapped among themselves.

Mostly young, they came from all over to clear away the dense hammock and pineland, drain the swamp, lay track, and build the luxury hotel around which the new town would be laid out, Negroes from Florida, Georgia, and Alabama, drifters from California, immigrants from Ireland, Italy, and Sweden, Cubans, West Indians, leased convicts, shanghaied Bowery bums impressed by Flagler's men, and poor whites from the piney woods.

One afternoon after Galilee and Jack carried a cartful of guava jelly to Brickell's, they took

146

the barge across the river and learned that the railroad men were laying sewer pipe and dynamiting everything that could not be hacked away, blowing up ironwood trees, and burning out the poisonous manchineel, whose sap caused skin to fester. They were clearing streets and paving them with glaring, dusty coral rock, then erecting on either side rude, hastily constructed storefronts that would include a shoe store, a bank, a men's furnishings store, a tailor, a jewelry store, an ice cream shop, a Chinese laundry, a livery stable, pool rooms, soft drink stands, an insurance company, an ice company, an electric company, and a box car designated as a jail. A man with a gold watch chain told them that the Fort Dallas land company was asking fifty to a thousand dollars a lot. Terms were a quarter in cash, the balance in three annual payments, with eight percent interest. Brickell was mad, he confided, because Flagler wasn't making improvements on his side of the river. Jack later told Eulalie that the man said that some of the shopkeepers were Jews.

She had soured milk in a wide, shallow pan, and was dipping a saucer into the custard that had formed at the top. "Probably the banker," she said. "Did you find out if there's going to be a grocery?"

Jack admitted that he had not.

"That's what I needed to know," she said. "I was going to pour molasses on your clabber. Now I don't know if you rightly deserve it. Next time find out. And if you see one, give the owner a jar of jelly."

"You going to give some clabber to Maude?"

"I didn't see her standing there," said Eulalie. "Who untied her? I didn't tell you to untie her."

"She must have done it herself," said Jack.

Eulalie glanced at her small daughter, wearing Jack's cast-off shoes three sizes too big. The child could not keep tidy, no matter how hard she tried. Yet despite her unkempt hair and the dirt that smudged her face, the child was as pretty as a valentine cupid. There was no denying. Eulalie reached across and gave her a casual slap across the face, more from habit than anger, borne of an abiding conviction that a child who had survived a knitting needle and a gallon of emetic to grow defiantly in Thomas Sands' image was wicked to the core.

"Where'd you get that hair bow? I better not hear that it was Bristol again."

The child stepped back, one small fist clutching the ribbon on her head. "I want it," she said.

Eulalie turned away from her as if she were no longer of interest. "It's time that pickaninny played with his own kind," she said, "commencing right now."

"Bristol is my friend," said Jack.

"It's all right to play with darkies when you're a child. You're almost twelve. Get her washed. And try to get that rag off her head."

148

Jack took his sister by the hand. "You know Jesse Jones who was helping Galilee build that walkway? They found him in the Miami River. Galilee told me his neck was broken and there was a rope around it. They said it was accidental drowning."

"Then he couldn't have had a rope around his neck. Accidental drowning means you can't swim. Galilee has sand where his sense is supposed to be."

Not long after a man came to the front porch while Eulalie and Galilee were replacing the worn-out valve on the pitcher pump with leather from an old shoe. The stranger didn't look Eulalie in the eye. Instead he looked down and sideways, holding his felt hat in his hands, fingering the brim. He was small, puny, not much bigger than Jack and gave his name as Virgil Lolly. He said he was working on the railroad and asked if he could sleep in the guava shack. There was something else about him. Eulalie studied Virgil Lolly, then realized what it was. His thumbs were long.

"He been hung up," whispered Galilee.

"Hung up? Where?"

"All kinds of places that happen. Could be anywhere."

Eulalie didn't know if she wanted a stranger on her property with thumbs that looked like they were still growing.

"He ain't going to bother you," said Galilee. "That man's bothering days is over."

Eulalie warned the man that if he couldn't find a mule cart ride, he had to walk seven miles each way. He said he didn't mind. She asked him what he expected to earn. He told her two dollars, maybe three dollars a day. She charged him fifty cents a night.

He cleared his throat. "Does that include breakfast, ma'am?" he asked.

"You don't look biggity, but you sure sound it. It includes coffee." Eulalie turned to Galilee, her back to Virgil Lolly. "The Bible says to show hospitality to a stranger, but I don't know."

"You think you entertaining an angel without knowing it?" asked Galilee. "He too beat down to be an angel. Too beat down to be a devil neither."

She glanced over her shoulder. "You can stay. But be out of my way in the morning. I don't want you under my foot when I commence my work. And don't mess with any of those jars."

Virgil Lolly's word was good. He left in the early morning and kept out of her way when he returned at night. Every week he gave her three dollars and fifty cents, called her ma'am, and thanked her. He always took off his hat in her presence, didn't chew tobacco, and didn't drink. He did, however, cough into the night, and she heard him all the way from the guava shack. He seemed to never have enough breath. "If you expect to work," she said, "you need

150

a tonic." She sent Jack with a concoction of one teaspoon of lime juice, two teaspoons of sugar mixed in a glass of water with an iron nail in it. When Jack returned to the house, he said that Virgil Lolly stuffed newspapers under his clothes to keep away the mosquitoes.

Gradually Eulalie added breakfast to Virgil Lolly's coffee, starting with a biscuit and red-eyed gravy, adding next a piece of bacon, later a bowl of grits. In September he offered to change her roof from thatch to tin. Eulalie said that if she had her druthers, which she did since she owned the house, she preferred cypress shingles. Virgil said that wood shingles shrank in the dry season, and let in rain in the wet season. He knew where to get tin cheap. He worked in the late evening with a miner's lamp attached to his forehead.

"Don't go falling off," she warned. "I'm not about to set any broken bones."

"I know the name of the new doctor," said Jack. "In case he does."

"I'm not fixing to fall off, son."

"It's Jackson," said the boy. "Mr. Flagler sent for him, and his wife is coming, too."

After Virgil Lolly finished the roof, he painted the house with creosote that cost ten cents a gallon, saying the creosote would keep out moisture and insects. It began as a nutty brown color that faded silver before the year was out. With Galilee's help he dug a deeper privy, laid a foundation of cement, built a bench with two holes, and added an old Montgomery Ward catalogue for paper.

He was the quietest man Eulalie ever knew. He never asked for anything and seldom spoke unless it was to thank her, to apologize for the noise of the rain beating on the tin, or to suggest something that needed fixing. When he said he could put in dormer windows that would give her more head room in the loft, breakfast soon included supper and long evenings rocking on the front porch in a scent of citronella and jasmine.

In April, Jack took Maude in the oxcart to see the first train drawn by a wood-burning, smoke-spouting locomotive puff into the station on wobbly tracks. They went without Galilee because of the new city code which specified that Negroes, unless they were employed in the soon-to-be incorporated area, had to keep to the other side of the railroad tracks. Jack carried his sister on his shoulders as they stood among a cheering crowd of three hundred, a few of whom they knew, including Virgil Lolly, talking to some man whose vest glinted in the sunlight. Jack didn't recognize their boarder at first because his felt hat was pulled so far down over his face. It was Maude who pointed him out. They called to him, but he pulled his hat down even farther and scurried through a line of porters pulling luggage carts.

Later Jack told Eulalie that maybe the reason

Virgil didn't wave back was that he couldn't see them through his hat.

"When a man's busy working," she replied, "he has no time for waving."

"It didn't look like he was working."

"You'll find out that there's a whole lot of work that men folks do that you don't know anything about. Your grandfather Octavius, for one. Did you know that he owned one of the biggest groves in Putnam County?"

"Was he rich?"

"He was very prosperous."

"Are we?"

"We get by. Times change. But Yankees don't. Remember that and never trust a one."

When Virgil used his day off to help out in the guava shack, refusing to take money or a reduction on his room and board, Eulalie thought it was time to set him straight. "Don't go getting ideas about me," she said. "I been married once and that's enough to last me for a lifetime."

"No disrespect, ma'am," he replied, "but I don't aim to marry anyone."

Eulalie wiped the sweat from her brow with the back of her arm. "You saying I'm not good enough for you?"

"No, ma'am. Nothing to do with you at all. It's me. I'm just not the husband type."

One day he brought home a human skull and gave it to Jack. He explained that he was part of a crew that had leveled the Indian mound that stood at the mouth of the Miami River. They had to make way for a veranda for the new Royal Palm Hotel. The mound, he said, was one hundred feet long and seventy-five feet high. Nothing was wasted. They screened the soil for a lawn bed, and used the shells and shards as road material. There were skeletons in the center, fifty or sixty, they were coming out too fast to count. They hauled the bones away in wheelbarrows. There was a skeleton on top, more recent than the others because it still had fragments of flesh clinging to the bones. It was probably a white man because it was taller and not laid out all curled up like the others, but sort of lying this way and that.

"The mound people aren't the same as the Cypress Indians," said Jack. "The mound people left with the Spanish."

"How do you know that?" asked Eulalie.

"Billy Bowlegs told me. When I got bit by the snake."

Eulalie's words were soft, almost inaudible. "Were there any clothes on the white man? Could you tell the color of his hair?"

Virgil took her hand. "Don't fret yourself, Eulalie, over some stranger dead and long gone. Whoever he is, he's probably right now resting with the angels."

Jack announced, while sifting flour through cheesecloth, that he was tired of writing maxims in his copybook like *A Stitch in Time Saves*

154

Nine, A Watched Pot Never Boils. He had to write those foolish things fifty times each, he said. He wanted to quit school and get a job dynamiting or laying pipe. Eulalie objected, not to quitting school, but to wanting to work for someone else.

Virgil brought in a block of ice and asked if he could put in his two cents although he might have to go around the barn to do it. He said some boss man got an idea that there was an underground stream running from the Everglades to the ocean. They dug this excavation ten foot square and five feet deep, he said, but then struck solid rock. Didn't hardly make an inch all day, just drilling all the time until they got this pipe down fifty, sixty feet. Then, with no warning, the roof of the river caved in, the water rushed through the pipe so fast it drowned two men. One of them was on lease from the state.

"When a leased convict gets killed in this work," Virgil explained, "his body gets covered up with the railroad fill. A man who works for wages, he's lucky if someone carts his body away. What I'm saying, son, is that clearing a city is mighty dangerous work. Men get killed everyday, especially with all the dynamiting and people setting fuses every which way who don't know their right hand from their left. You best stay in school, help your momma, take care of your little sister."

"That couldn't happen to me," said Jack. "I

155

know how to swim." He looked to Eulalie for her final answer.

"Keep sifting," she said. "I still see weevils."

The next day, Eulalie told Virgil Lolly that he had her leave to move from the guava shack to the loft, provided that there was no cigar smoking and no drinking.

"Your husband, he sure did like bay rum," said Virgil, carrying his meager belongings up the ladder.

Eulalie watched him climb, then found herself thinking of Thomas and how his aroma lingered, although more faintly than before, diminishing with the memory and the pain.

That night, Eulalie listened to the ceiling creak beneath his footsteps. She hoped she hadn't made a mistake. With some men you might as well give them the mile because they were going to try to take it anyway. She unbraided her hair and brushed it through, pulling from the brush a clump of blonde and silver strands. Soon she would be all gray, according to Proverbs 16:31, her head a crown of glory. Then she would have her change. Women got crazy with the change, or sick with tumors and such. They went to the bed, as if nature was saying, you did your part, now mosey on and give someone else the room. She braided her hair and tied off the end with a leather thong. At least she didn't need glasses to read and she could follow a wheeling hawk all the way into the 'Glades, pick a weevil out of flour with one eye shut, notice the evil in her own daughter's eyes.

When the creaking stopped, Eulalie tiptoed past her sleeping children, climbed the ladder to the loft, and crawled beneath Virgil's mosquito net. "Don't ask me to take down my hair," she said, dropping to his side. "And I never take off my nightdress."

"That's okay, ma'am. I look the same standing up or laying down myself."

The light of the moon cast the loft in silver. From outside came the night shrills of mockingbirds and crickets and the smell of burning smudge. "You never ask about my husband," she said.

"He must have been a fine man to get you for a wife," he replied.

"John Quincy never did take hold. Seems like everything just slipped away from him."

"I know all about what that feels like," he said. "Like a person's got butterfingers on life."

He told her about the election held in the pool hall that made Miami an official city. He didn't vote because a fellow had to register to vote. Flagler saw to it that his men were registered. Flagler's men, they were mostly Negroes. He heard the first person who signed the charter was a Negro, but he didn't know if he believed it. Some of them wanted to call the city Flagler, but they got voted down.

Eulalie said her coontie business had fallen off; everybody's had now that so many people were grubbing roots. But the guava jelly was doing real well. "I'm getting letters from people all the way to New Jersey asking for my guava. My boy Jack said that if the railroad brings in lumber, it can carry away guava jelly."

"He's a right smart young fellow."

"He can't read worth a hang. His daddy couldn't read at all. Only difference is Jack has been to school. His daddy hadn't."

"Reading doesn't mean a hill of beans when judging if a fellow's smart. Lots of other ways to measure. How well he sizes up a situation. How fast he moves. Things like that."

A panther screamed from somewhere beyond the ridge. She turned toward him, matched him head to toe, and realized she was taller. "Some things you move as fast as lightning, other ways you're about as slow as a turtle."

"I can't, Eulalie."

"What do you mean, you can't?"

"I mean I can't is all."

"You didn't lead me down the primrose path if that's what you're thinking. I came up here on my own free will."

"I know that, Eulalie, and it makes me pleased as punch. But the business between a man and a woman . . . I'm trying to say this the best way I know how. My parts don't work anymore. I don't know why. It's just so."

Eulalie assumed that all men, even old ones, could. It had to do with the clump their boots made when they walked, or the timber of their voices that always found you, even when you weren't listening.

She put a gentle hand on his shoulder. "I had a man who could," she murmured, "and I didn't love him. Leastways not in all the ways a woman's supposed to care about a man. I had another man who could and he didn't love me. He might have for a while, but when it suited him, he shut off his feelings like he was turning a spigot on a barrel. Maybe it'll be different with a man that can't."

"Which two men are you talking about, Eulalie?"

"One was my husband. The other was another fellow. I loved him so bad it hurt."

"I know what you mean. Had one of them hurtin' romances, pains you worse than a toothache."

"The girl is his."

"The child is pretty. He must have been a handsome fellow."

"He was." She lay on her back, her hands cupping her head. "Galilee said you were in a turpentine camp. Is that true?"

"True enough."

"What were you doing there?"

A chameleon skittered across the floor. Virgil watched it disappear into a crack in the wall. He said he did not ask to go. He left a logging job to find better-paying work in a phosphate mine, then got arrested for vagrancy and sent to box trees in the piney woods. They were

159

chained to their beds at night, manacled by day. When the boss was dissatisfied, he watered them, forced liquid into their stomachs through a tube. Sometimes he hung them up by their thumbs, just inches off the ground. We got even, he said, we fed powdered glass to his dogs.

"How long were you there?"

He turned his head away and curled into himself like a snail seeking the recesses of its shell. Eulalie unbound her hair and spread it about them like a curtain. They spent the night in a passionless embrace, he breaking away from time to time to cough, she ministering to him as if he were a child.

It was a chilly December. The new sheet-iron kerosene stove was lit almost every day. The trees were covered with flocks of migrating birds. Virgil took advantage of the dry season and had begun to frame the dormer windows that would turn the loft into a second story, and Jack returned from Miami to report that seven Jewish shopkeepers had been fined a dollar apiece and court costs for keeping their stores open on Sunday.

Using wicks from cotton cord, Eulalie made Christmas candles in a mold fashioned from a baking powder can. Gray-green and squat, the pine-scented candles managed to lend the house a festive look. Virgil tacked stockings to the windowsill and told Eulalie that she needed

160

a mantelpiece. When he was through with the dormer windows, he was going to build her a chimney, break through the wall, set in a real fireplace with a mantel and a hearth. On Christmas morning Virgil gave Eulalie knitting needles, Eulalie gave Virgil a tin of Dr. Ballou's cough drops and Galilee a real leather truss with padding. Jack gave Eulalie a ledger so that she wouldn't have to figure in her head, and Bristol crept through the palmetto to give Maude a pair of shoes while Eulalie scraped the breakfast dishes into a compost heap.

When Eulalie saw her daughter wearing patent leather hightops that required a button hook, she went straight to Evangelist Street to look for Caroline. She found her on the deep, shaded porch of her narrow house, dressed in white from head to toe as befitting a deaconess, but to Eulalie's taste, arrogantly overstepping her station. "What call do you have to buy my child shoes?" Eulalie demanded. "I know your boy didn't buy them."

"It's a Christmas present."

"We don't need it. And if we did, we certainly don't need it from you."

Caroline pulled her gloves over her fingers. "Maude does."

Isaac McCloud opened the door and came down the steps. "Any problems, Sister Caroline?"

"No, Mr. McCloud," she replied, "you go on ahead." She stopped just inches short of

Eulalie. "I see that child in her brother's ugly old cast-off shoes, I hear about her tied any more to that banyan, I'm going to make more trouble for you that you can shake a stick at. I'm going to see that folks start asking questions again. And you know what questions I'm talking about. I know all about you and him."

"I don't know what you're talking about."

"Yes, you do. Thomas told me everything."

Eulalie's hands curled into fists. She pressed them against her thighs, remembering her father's stories of how impudent slaves were punished, fairly but soundly enough so that they never forgot.

Eulalie spent Christmas night entering her accounts with a shaky, angry hand, determined not to let the sassy nigger or the new rock wall on the other side of her guava shack that blocked her view of the bay make her forget that it was the Lord's birthday. She worked under the murky orange light of the kerosene lamp, annoyed by the sputter of a badly trimmed wick, remembering the diary that she had once kept and the moment she put it aside.

Just before dawn, by the time the black-inked ledger entries turned to brown, her eyes began to sting. She thought it was from working so closely until she smelled smoke too thick to be someone's smudge. When Virgil came home, she would ask him to find out who was burning trash at night.

The next morning the sun was hidden in a

162

charcoal sky. The hummingbirds that had roosted the night before on her coral bean tree were gone and so was Virgil. When he did not return that day or the next, Eulalie sent Jack through the veil of smoke to find him. The boy returned from the newly incorporated city of Miami covered with soot.

"A big fire burned down the whole business district!" he said. "Sparks are still burning on the tree branches, ashes are floating in the air so bad you can't breathe."

"The buildings were too close together," said Eulalie. "Where did it start?"

"In Brady's grocery store. It spread to the Bank of Bay Biscayne, then to Chase's pool hall. Twenty-eight buildings in all burned to the ground. They tried to fight it with a bucket brigade. Some men tried to beat out the flames with branches and gunny sacks soaked in brine, and Mrs. Tuttle even brought her pump, but everything's gone up like kindling wood."

"Is there anything left?"

"A few brick pillars, a couple of tin cans, piles of broken crockery, black timbers falling across each other like kindling sticks. A man got killed."

Eulalie put her hand to her brooch. "Who was he?"

"A Jew merchant. A cylinder of gas in the bottling works next door exploded. Flying metal came right through the wall. They're taking his body to Augusta, Georgia, to bury him

163

because Miami has no Jew cemetery."

"Someone is bound to say," she said, "although I'm not the one saying it, that the Lord saw fit to punish him for keeping his store open on a Sunday."

"You work on Sunday."

"That's different. Chores don't count. The main thing is, I don't sell to anyone on Sunday. Was anyone else hurt?" she asked.

"Some people got burned. A man got hit in the head with an ax. Dr. Jackson fixed them up and sent them home."

"There must be lots of folks still clearing up the mess."

"If you're talking about Virgil, Momma, I looked everywhere I could, I even asked questions, but I didn't find him."

She grabbed his shoulders and fixed him with a stare as if she were pinning a butterfly. "Go back," she said. "We have to find him and help him. He needs me. You understand, boy?"

"I'm trying, Momma." He pulled away from her grip. "You're pinching me bad."

Maude hung in the shadows. Eulalie wheeled in anger. "What are you doing there spying on folks? Get on outside."

"She doesn't want to, Momma. I think she's afraid of the fire."

"Hellfire's a whole lot worse than a fire that's miles away. So is the fire I'm gonna put in her britches if she doesn't get out the door. Look sharp, Jack. You'll find him. I know you will."

Chapter Nine

When the steel battleship USS *Maine* was blown up in Havana harbor, panic spread along the southeast coast of Florida like a riptide. "This means war," residents told one another in hushed voices amid escalating rumors that the Spanish fleet might slip north from Cuba through the Straits of Florida and shell the southeast coast, worse, come ashore to burn and pillage.

In June, over seven thousand perspiring soldiers dressed in heavy dark blue flannel leggings, broad-brimmed campaign hats with bedding rolls slung across their shoulders, arrived by rail. They outnumbered the residents six to one. Clutching travel folders distributed to them on the train, their disillusion was quick.

Instead of a promised tropical paradise, troops from Texas, Alabama, and Louisiana found a raw frontier settlement, a hellish jungle immediately beyond the perimeter of their encampment, with hordes of mosquitoes, unrelentingly terrible heat, and no shade. The elaborate compound of the Royal Palm Hotel suggested in the brochure was a single building for the exclusive use of officers and press. The depicted stretch of beach lined with palm trees was at best a narrow strip, bordered with impenetrable mangroves and palmettoes, and covered with offal and dead fish. Camp life in the city of row after row of tents through which the rain and mosquitoes found easy access was unbearable.

Out of six regiments, four were placed too far west, out of reach of the city's sewer system, a wooden trough that was flushed out daily. Since hard rock prevented the digging of regulation latrines, the resultant improvisation was inadequate and unsanitary. Half barrels were used for buckets, planking for seats, the barrels when full, carried away and dumped, spilling their semi-liquid contents on the ground. Often men simply ran into the bushes, and the complaint arose that one could not walk anywhere without soiling his shoes.

Shortly after the troops' arrival, typhoid fever broke out. Townspeople became accustomed to the measured slow beats of the band playing the death march as mule-drawn wagons bore coffins draped in American flags to the cemetery at 20th Street or to the depot, where escorts stood at attention as coffins were placed on the train.

Because of the heat, troops could drill only in the early morning and in the late afternoon. As a result, the town was overrun with men looking for something to do. Shooting galleries and lemonade stands sprung up overnight.

Troops tossed dice and made chili con carne in washtubs over camp fires with an iron gate to hold the tubs, picked fights with ice picks and shovels, and visited the jook joints just beyond the city's dry boundaries.

Bored, frustrated, tired of inactivity, the soldiers soon brought chaos. Fearful that while their comrades were sent to Cuba to fight, they would die of typhoid or yellow fever in a hellhole, suspendered troops used coconuts for target practice, swam naked in Biscayne Bay, scandalized and sometimes terrorized the residents. A murder occurred nearly every night. Some troops tried to force their way into homes, and one was shot in the attempt. No family let their women or their children out of the house alone. With the only civil law enforcement a city marshal and a few deputies, townspeople started carrying guns.

The Negro population fared the worst. Whenever the soldiers were particularly bored or frustrated through the heat-glazed summer, when they wanted a fight with little opposition, they harassed the colored people who lived near the camp.

The troops were particularly vengeful when they heard that Roosevelt's Rough Riders had left Tampa on a transport. They rioted again with the news of Manila Bay and the victory won by Admiral Dewey, and again when it was rumored that now that the Spanish fleet was destroyed, the Miami encampment was to be sent to Jacksonville. Then came the news of the storming of San Juan Hill near Santiago de Cuba, with descriptions of Rough Riders led by Colonel Theodore Roosevelt holding their rifles across their chests while they slipped and stumbled their way upward in the smooth, high grass.

Caroline had three concerns. The first was the safety of Bristol, whom she made promise not to take his shoeshine box to North Miami, not to sell bottles back to the honky tonks, not to go junking, in fact, not to leave Coconut Grove. Her fears in this regard were particularly heightened after Galilee and his mule were roughed up and his cartful of guava jelly hijacked by members of a New Orleans regiment. Her second concern was that because most trains had been commandeered for the military, she be able to obtain Bristol's rail passage in August. Her goal was to get him north in time to enroll in high school in North Carolina, the only option for young Negroes, for whom secondary education in Miami was not available. Her third concern was the constant, increasing headaches of her employer, Julia Tuttle.

The morning before, Mrs. Tuttle had sent Caroline to buy a headache remedy called Coca-Cola. When the patent medicine didn't work, Caroline placed a wet collard leaf on the widow's forehead, pleading with her to lie still because her remedy wouldn't do any good once she rose. She tried to explain about high blood being too sweet and low blood being too bitter, and the need to balance the blood, but Mrs. Tuttle turned her head and breathed a deep sigh that trailed away like a moonflower vine.

The soldiers were never out of sight. They paraded up and down the streets and on the grounds of the Royal Palm Hotel. One shot himself in the mouth in Mrs. Tuttle's garden. Caroline found the body floating in the lily pond, caught by a suspender on a jagged piece of coral rock. The week before she had witnessed from a bedroom window the electrocution of three men, but had shut out the lightning flash, the crash of thunder, the tree split in half with light, and the steel bayonets that acted as conductors, as she had the lynching of Jesse Jones.

To avoid harassment, Caroline was permitted to leave for Coconut Grove in the early morning, while the troops were still drilling, with instructions to return the next morning before sunup. Despite a late start because she could not find rosemary water to add to Mrs. Tuttle's borax and olive oil shampoo, Caroline rode through warm, humid air that dampened the chalky lane with a shiny film. Huge drops of moisture fell like rain from the canopy of oak and gumbo-limbo that shaded the road. Already the sleeves of her shirtwaist clung to her arms and sweat trickled behind her knees.

Caroline had slid into marriage with Isaac McCloud. It was not his persistence that won her over so much as his presence. He was always there. It was an effortless slide; any resistance she might have felt was gradually eroded by his quiet devotion, as unobtrusive, yet as dependable as an easy chair.

Their life together was limited to whatever married living could be crammed into a Sunday. Once a week they listened to each other's complaints, ate, argued, planned, made love, discussed their investments, decided what needed to be done around the house, and arranged for Bristol's future, a detailed and single-minded plan that included high school in North Carolina, where Bristol would live with Isaac's sister and her family, then Howard University.

She wondered if Bristol remembered to bring her laundry basket back from Lulu Ryder, who had probably spent the night before ironing Caroline's things by the light of a sooty, smoking oil lamp. For sure, none of Caroline's menfolk, including Galilee, had clean shirts for church. It didn't matter that Bristol was as smart as a whip and Isaac strong as a bull, it didn't matter if she was gone all week and had all she could do when she got home just to keep her head above water. When it came to taking care of themselves, all three were as helpless as wet chicks.

Her biggest trial was Galilee, who was getting forgetful. Not wandering-forgetful, where you had to scramble through the undergrowth to fetch back an old one who had gone astray.

170

Just name-poor and sometimes place-poor, when he remembered that he had something but didn't know where he put it. Like the week before when they had looked all over for the copper sheeting that he bought for his still, only to find that he hadn't bought it in the first place, was only fixing to do so. Caroline decided that after church, when she had a moment to herself, she would fix him a cup of sassafras tea. It would help to jar his memory.

Bristol was on the front porch beside his crate of broken glass, old rags, and bits of tin, waiting with his chin in his hands. When he saw her, he smiled and sprang down the steps to tether the mule to the poinciana tree still in a blaze of scarlet flowers. The tree threatened to take over the whole backyard. What it didn't cover was littered with Galilee's still, his manure-covered sacks of corn sprouts and a barrel of mash that she hadn't seen before.

"What's that?" she asked.

"Galilee said you don't have to cook it. It only needs three, maybe four days to sour. He's waiting for the crust, then he's going to break it up and mix it in, and leave it for another two, three days until it sours again."

"It's bad enough he's got those evil-smelling sacks all over the yard, sprinkling them, flip-flopping them like he was roasting chickens. This barrel better be gone before I leave." She reached into the cart for her tote bag. "You see the child?" she asked.

171

Bristol choked down the hurt that was tightening his throat, that might make his words come out squeaky and flush his eyes bright with tears. "How come you always ask about Maude first, Momma?" he asked. "She's not your kin, I am."

Caroline did not tell him of her most recent confrontation the week before with the Coombs woman. "You hurt this child again," she had said, "I'll put a spell on you. Fix you so bad, you'll dry up like a conch. You hear me?"

"I hear you," Eulalie had replied, then went on to talk of her father's shirts, made of the finest lawn, and of his orange groves in Palatka.

"Don't you be talking about this and that, out of your head, thinking to confuse me," Caroline had said, "I know you understand." The little girl had stood still, obediently lifting her hand over her head as Caroline removed her soiled garment. "I'll have this back in no time, honey," she said to the child, "clean and starchy stiff, as if it was brand-new."

Caroline smiled at her son. This was not the time to ask him to return the dress, now folded in a sheet of tissue paper. "See if this don't prove that I'm always thinking about you first." She displayed Harry Tuttle's striped cricket cap and shirts with collars that needed only turning, a pair of high-laced shoes that, if you didn't close the top two grommets, would fit just fine, a heavy tweed suit perfect for North Caro-

172

lina, where she heard it could get cold, and a silk polka-dot bow tie. When he flipped without interest through the cast-off clothing, she pointed out the rolls, cheese, white grapes, deviled crabs on the shell, and the jar filled with jellied consommé.

"I don't like that stuff, Momma," he said.

She put her hands on each side of his head. His hair had changed from the gold of his babyhood to a muted tan. He was taller than she by half a head. She wondered when either had happened. "Just what is it you do like, baby?"

He wanted duckanoo. Caroline put down her reticule, rolled up her sleeves, and mixed cornmeal, coconut milk, brown sugar, and cinnamon, which she folded in a banana leaf and tied like a parcel. Isaac and Galilee came through the back door as she dropped the folded banana leaf into the boiling pot.

"Anybody see my sausage mill?" asked Galilee.

"Must be my hearing's gone bad," Isaac said. "I was up on the roof fixing the leak. I didn't hear you come back, sugar." He looked at her as he always did, with a mixture of pride and surprise, not minding that she was making Bristol's favorite dish first. Bristol was like his own son. Isaac had had a son once, but it was a long time ago, when he was no more than a boy himself and the child so young, he had no recollection other than that of baby arms and legs waving like turtle grass from the back of a wagon. "You tell her about the baby?" he asked.

"Not yet."

Isaac pulled in a chair from the front room. Caroline said she would sit only a minute, there was so much to do, then whispered that she wondered how long Mrs. Tuttle would keep her when she found out. Isaac said not to worry. Pretty soon they would not need Caroline's income at all, what with leasing land, building homes, renting the houses, then, with the rent money, leasing more land, building more houses. He fished out a crumpled piece of paper from his back pocket and straddled the chair beside her. "I got it all figured out," he said. "Inside a year, some of this rent money can come back to us."

"Seems like you have all the plusses and minuses spelled out," she said.

"It's not plus or minus, Momma," said Bristol. "It's more like times. Actually, it's geometry because it's a progression."

Caroline tried to keep the pride out of her face, her voice, when Bristol spoke of things that she had never heard of. She frowned instead. "What's this?" she asked. *"Pants. Bristol."*

"The boy needs long pants," Isaac replied, wiping the back of his neck with his pocket handkerchief. "Not that he don't appreciate the ones you carry home in the tote bag. But, honey, they belonged to some short, rich white boy. He may be older than Bristol, but they not the same size. The pants you brought home don't meet the top of his shoes. Bristol needs his own pants. The kind that keep going as long as they has to."

Caroline studied Isaac's calculations, then raised herself to her feet and looked about her kitchen for repairs that needed imminent attention.

"We got chased from the beach," said Bristol. "None of the colored people are supposed to swim there anymore. It's only for white folks."

"Since when?" Caroline asked, reaching for a box of hominy that someone had forgotten to put the lid on.

"Since the railroad," Galilee replied.

Isaac said to forget about it. They would sail out to Ocean Beach. Have a picnic, fly a kite.

"You need a boat to get there," Caroline said. "How you going to get to Ocean Beach without a boat?"

Isaac smiled. "I got friends in high places," he said. "Bristol set his sights on swimming, the boy going to swim all he want."

Caroline went to make a tour of the rest of the house with Isaac, Galilee, and Bristol behind her. While she checked for new cracks in the plaster and new leaks under which they would have to put a tin can or a bucket, Bristol said he was going to write a letter to the editor of the newspaper. Lots of people did it. What kind of letter you fixing to write? she asked, straightening a picture of Christ before Pilate. I been telling him not to, said Isaac. Caroline fingered front room curtains that hung limp and dank because someone forgot to close the window during a rainstorm. What kind of letter, she asked, somebody better tell me. Bristol said he read in the newspaper about Nassau niggers being shiftless and lazy. He was going to write that it wasn't true.

"We're not from Nassau," she said.

"They don't just mean Nassau, Momma," Bristol replied. "They mean the Bahamas."

"That was a long time ago," she said. "I got papers say we're American, same as everyone else. What difference does it make?"

"It's a lie," said Bristol.

Caroline slipped the curtains off their rods and held one over each arm like a banner. "You fixing to spoil our plan, the one Isaac and me spent a whole year studying on? Every little detail. All the letters we had to write? The money we had to put by? Listen to me good, Bristol. I don't want any newspaper folks to know your name. I don't want them to see your face. Don't you go writing any letter and don't go bothering them at their office. I don't want to have to ask Mrs. Tuttle to get you out of trouble because you were someplace you weren't supposed to be. You hear me?"

"Yes, Momma."

"That doesn't sound like yes, Momma. It

sounds like *make Momma feel better for now.* Which is it?"

"Yes, Momma."

"All right, then. And Galilee, since when does a grub hoe sit in the parlor?"

Then Caroline and Isaac closed the door to their room, and Galilee and Bristol each went off on an unnamed errand. Isaac stood beside the dresser patiently waiting for Caroline to remove her outer garments. Only after she had pulled the hat pin from her leghorn hat and set both on the dresser, when she arranged herself on the bed with a pillow beneath her head and a comforter to her waist, only after she smiled in welcome did he drop beside her. At first he touched only her face, her hair, in soft, gentle, tentative caresses as if he thought she might break.

"Just because a baby's starting," she whispered, "doesn't mean you have to pussyfoot. I'm not glass, Isaac. I'm as strong as you."

When he moved inside her, he stopped from time to time to ask if he was hurting her. Assured, he moved again slowly until emboldened by her soft murmurs and her hands trailing down his back, then seemed apologetic when he rode with his eyes closed, his large, callused hands pressing back her shoulders.

"Whew," he said, "that sneaked up on me."

"You were fine," she said.

"You mean that, Caroline? Sometimes with you I feel like an old man."

"There's only one old man here," she replied, "and he's out there somewhere, messing up the place with his moonshining, probably setting the house on fire."

He smiled. "I'll see to Galilee. You rest yourself." He turned at the door. "I'm about the luckiest man in the world."

They attended afternoon service in a church built of rough planks through which they could see the blaze of day. Before them was an improvised pulpit made from a dry-goods box covered with a piece of carpet. Men sang with voices that broke and with sweat pouring from their faces, while women, many with their eyes closed, clapped their hands and swayed. The low, rhythmic stamp of their feet on the wooden floor sounded like the far-off roll of thunder as members of the congregation called "Amen," "That's so," "Captain Jesus," and the clerical-collared Reverend Sampson with a Bible across his bent shoulders, his head bowed, staggered to and fro.

Two stewards in white passed the collection plate to pay for the funeral of a bonefish guide. The assembly fanned themselves with palmetto leaves and a woman, known as the Queen of Policy, leaned over Caroline's bench to ask what part of North Carolina Bristol was bound for. Crippled with rheumatism that was worse in the fall, she no longer carried her clients' numbers to the wheel in North Miami or spun the wheel herself. Her grandson did that for her.

"He's staying with my husband's people," whispered Caroline, "in Florence."

"What you want to be when you grow up, Bristol?" the woman asked.

"Answer Mrs. Jackson," said Caroline, "but do it quietly, and don't forget your dime."

"A lawyer, ma'am," replied Bristol.

The woman sighed and turned to her neighbor. "Isn't that something!"

At first it sounded like the stamping of feet somewhere outside. Then they heard the shouts of "Help us, help us," "For God's sakes, they're coming," and realized that what they heard was not stamping but running feet and the rumble of wagons. Parishioners in the back row barely got the doors open when colored people from Miami thrust their way in, some of whom they knew, most of whom were strangers, shouting that the Texas and Louisiana volunteers were after them.

Mariah Brown drew herself to her full height as if she could ward off evil just by her girth. "Who they after?"

"All of us," replied a man in gartered shirtsleeves that Isaac recognized as the owner of a boardinghouse. "We all in trouble. They tried to lynch Millard Ross. Said he brushed too close to a white girl. We took them on before they could get hold of Millard, except they had to make roll call. But they came back. We been battling them since they got

179

here. This time they fixing to lynch someone. It don't matter who. We all the same to them. It had to come to this sooner or later. God help us."

The congregation began milling, shouting, scrambling for belongings and loved ones. Some dashed outside into the narrow alleys, and an elderly woman lay on a bench while her son and daughter-in-law fanned her with a hymnal.

Isaac took Caroline's arm. "Call the boy," he said. "We going home." He pulled her from the front door and led them to an open window. "This the best way. I seen doors bolted from the outside, the whole place set on fire. Think you can make it with Bristol on one side, me on the other?"

There were no soldiers in sight. Only an afternoon thunderstorm with dark, forbidding, roiling clouds looming in the west and a home-made sign nailed to the side of the church that read, WHERE WILL YOU SPEND ETERNITY?

Once inside their house, Isaac bolted the door and instructed Bristol to close the curtains quickly. "I can't, Isaac," the boy replied. "Momma's got them drying in the sun."

Then they heard more running footsteps, screams, and the gallop of a horse, and through the curtainless windows saw soldiers in blue shirts and suspenders, all with sticks and bottles in their hands, running from house to house.

"Galilee," said Caroline. "Where's Galilee?"

"Don't you go out," said Isaac. "I'll get him."
He slipped through the back after instructing
Bristol not to open either door for anyone.

Caroline and Bristol stood in the front room,
close enough to the window to see out, far
enough back in the shadows not to be seen.
Two men suddenly darted sideways and cut
to the south side of the house beneath the
fernlike leaves of a wild tamarind which that
morning had been covered with songbirds.

At first they heard nothing, then the thud
of boots on the porch followed by shouting
and banging at the front door. Caroline pulled
Bristol farther back into the shadows as someone
kicked the door, breaking the flimsy bolt and
splintering the wood, and two soldiers, with
holes cut in their hats for ventilation, crashed
through to stand in Caroline's parlor with sweat
pouring down their faces and their mouths
locked in anger.

One man peered around the narrow room
and into the rooms beyond and spat on the
floor. "Nothing here, Dwight," he said. "Just
two coons who don't look like they know what
day it is."

His companion grabbed at Caroline's wrist.
"Is he right? Is it just the two of you, or are
there more hiding out back?" He faced Caroline
and smiled. "Let's see what all of you looks
like, gal. Take off that dress."

"The nigger probably stole it," said the first
man, while Caroline struggled to break free.

"It's a white woman's dress for sure. She's even wearing stays. Lookahere at all this lacy stuff around her throat. You ever see a nigger in anything like this?" He ripped off her fichu. "You steal this dress, nigger?"

"How old do you think she is?"

"You can tell by their tits. Let's get the whole thing off!" The other man grabbed Caroline's collar from the inside and began to rip the shirtwaist from her shoulders when Bristol grabbed Galilee's grub hoe, swung it over his head, and brought it down on the head of the man who was dragging his mother across the floor by a torn sleeve. The soldier looked startled, crumpled to the ground as if he had wilted, and Bristol struck him again. The boy swung to do it a third time, but the first man lunged for Bristol, caught him at the knees, and knocked him to the ground. The soldier straddled Bristol over the chest and began to punch him idly about the head, when Isaac burst in and lifted the man up as if he were pulling off a cur. "Let's see what you do against a grown man," he said.

Galilee followed with a rake in his hands while new shouts were heard outside. "The Commodore's here," he yelled, "with some white men from the Grove, Frow, Pent, Peacock, some others, they're ordering those boys back to camp. The Commodore's got his gun, he's threatening court-martial."

The soldier slipped out of Isaac's grasp and

made for the splintered door, then turned to Bristol. "I'm leaving," he said, "but that's my buddy on the floor. I know how to find you, boy. Don't think you look alike to me. Maybe Yankees say that, but home folks know the difference. I can pick you out from a hundred. And that's the truth."

He left and Isaac covered Caroline with a blanket. Together they knelt beside the soldier on the floor.

"Is he breathing?" she asked.

"Can't tell," replied Isaac. "My hearing's not so good."

"He dead," said Galilee. "You don't believe me, we just has to sit here and watch him stiffen up."

Isaac opened the soldier's shirt and put his ear to his chest. Then he looked up at Caroline. "We got to get the boy out of here."

"We can send him to your sister," she said. "He'll just go a little earlier. He doesn't have to go by train. We'll send him on a boat." Isaac remained silent. "By mule cart if we have to."

"No," he said, clutching her blanket closed around her neck. "Not to North Carolina. They'll find him there for sure. We told too many people where we sending him. We got to get him out of Coconut Grove fast. Out of Miami. To somewhere else."

"To Eleuthera. To Papa Hanna. He's old, but he'll look after him."

"That's the first place they'll look," he replied. "It's in your papers."

"Where, then?" Her hands began to flail.

"I thought of a place. It's the best one I know. It's safe. The Cypress Indians. Deep in the 'Glades. The white folks will never find him."

"How long?"

"Three, five years. Maybe longer."

Caroline sank to her knees and clutched Bristol around his legs. "No!" she screamed. "He's my baby. My firstborn! I didn't want to ask about the girl," she cried. "It's always you, my baby, my Bristol." Caroline began to keen on the ground, thinking that Obeahman had gotten her after all, had stretched out that stiffened hand all the way across the Grand Bahama Bank and grabbed her boy.

"Caroline," whispered Isaac, "you saw what they did to Jesse," and she stood, slowly, held onto a chair, and turned her head.

Despite the heat, Bristol began to shiver as his mother keened.

"I didn't mean it about the white girl," she said. "I just said it."

"I know, Mama."

"I don't care what happens to that child. You my son. You hear? You my baby. Bristol." She sank to the floor. "How we going to get him there? It'll soon be dark. There's alligators out there and snakes. Lord, Jesus."

"Jack knows the 'Glades like the back of his

hand," said Bristol. "He's been there lots of times."

"You ain't telling no white boy nothing," said Isaac.

By the time Galilee slipped outside with Bristol, the melee was over. The soldiers had gone, leaving vegetable gardens trampled and wash pulled from the lines, residents with cuts and bruises, some with broken noses, and a cottage set on fire where both whites and blacks were beating out the flames with palm fronds. Galilee's thump barrel, heater box, drain pipe, and condenser lay strewn about the yard.

"They messed up your still," said Bristol.

Galilee held a lantern. "It don't matter, boy," he said. "I can put that thing together in a minute. You the one we got to take care of now."

Galilee carried Bristol by cart to Brickell's dock, where three Seminoles were camping overnight. The old man told Bristol to wait while he made the arrangements. In a moment Emathla stood and beckoned.

"Go with him," said Galilee.

"Aren't you coming too?"

"I can't go with you, boy. You scared?"

"No, sir," said Bristol, clutching his carpet portmanteau packed hurriedly by Caroline with catnip against colds, clothing, eggs, cheese, bread, a jar of jellied consommé, a blanket, additional mosquito netting, turpentine against mosquitoes, and a mortar and pestle that his friend Jack had once given him to grind peanuts in.

"It's okay if you are. Emathla here, he'll take care of you. Ain't the first time a black man had to hole up for a spell. Won't be the last. Might be you could learn something out there."

"How long will I have to stay?"

"No telling. Till this thing blow over."

"I won't get to North Carolina in time, will I?"

"You young. You got lots of time for school."

They traveled by moonlight through the tips of the thick sawgrass, where torrents of water had raked the land beneath, covering the rush prairies so that only the hardwood hammocks festooned with ferns, orchids, and bromeliads stood above water. Fireflies glowed on the backs of alligators in the sedgy lagoons. There was only the blackness and the sounds of rippling water, an occasional scream of a panther, the rasp of crickets and frogs, the calls of owls and limpkins, and an occasional night heron.

"How you kill white soldier?"

Bristol fought to keep back tears and the image of his mother clutching at his ankles while Isaac pried loose her hands. "I hit him with a hoe. I didn't mean to kill him. I just wanted to keep him away from my momma."

186

The moonlight shone on an opossum swinging from a gumbo-limbo, then on the forest of cypress, standing solitary in water, their branches draped with Spanish moss, here and there cabbage palms and mangroves.

"White man want to drain swamp," said Emathla. "Where put water? Sea in three directions. Not need more water. Need swamp."

"I thought Seminoles owned the 'Glades."

"No own. Never own," said Emathla. "Washington say not give Indian deed to swamp. Only can live here."

They arrived in daylight. Bristol had fallen asleep. He awoke with the warmth of the sun on his face, the whine of mosquitoes trying to slip through his net, and the rude reality that made him seek the shelter of his dreaming. Emathla pulled up his dugout near a curl of a water moccasin drifting in the clear water. A dainty white-tailed deer sprinted away at their approach, and a red-shouldered hawk screeched above the tangled vegetation.

Bristol first heard the soft, low voices of women. Then, through a veil of vines and spiderwebs and zebra butterflies, he saw them near their cook fire, wearing brightly colored calico sacques and skirts that did not meet at the waist, with their hair combed out over a frame that ended at a large rolling pompadour above their black, beadlike eyes. One was grinding corn while another took a pitcher to a well, lifted a plank, and dipped in the pitcher beside a floating corn cob. Flies buzzed around the foodstuffs and cooking utensils. A few scrawny, nuzzling pigs and dogs stumbled over the damp ground while a little flock of chickens scampered through the leaves and the spongy hammock floor.

Bristol clutched his portmanteau to his chest, pulling it away from a rooting pig. There was nothing to learn out here, he thought. Galilee didn't know what he was talking about. The red man was worse off than any colored he had ever seen.

White-haired Billy Sunshine, wearing a tattered, mildewed red velvet doublet with beaded garters, shuffled toward him on dropsied legs. His dark face was nettled with weathered creases. "How many summers, you?" he asked in a voice that was as thready as his garments.

Bristol reckoned the aged Indian to be even older than Galilee. "Twelve," he replied.

"You man. Stop cry. Can farm?"

"No, sir."

"Black man good farmers all. Why you not?"

A woman with a dangling arm, broken six years before and never completely mended, squatted on the end of a log. She offered Bristol coffee in a tin cup and a spoonful of thin gruel made from a meager supply of crushed corn that had been soaked in wood-ash lye. He accepted the coffee and watched a garfish simmer in the ashes of a campfire while someone came

188

with another garfish speared through the head, and threw it, still feebly wiggling, into the fire. The woman shook a sack with her good arm. The sack began to squirm.

"All gophers," said Emathla, pointing to freshly cleaned shells lying around the campfire. "Land turtles. Gopher hard to find."

"Does anybody work?" asked Bristol.

"All work," replied Emathla.

"I mean for money. You know. Jobs."

"Take alligator skins to trade. Take plumes. Not too many now."

"That about it?"

Emathla said that they were paid thirty cents a gallon for huckleberries when they were in season and a dollar apiece for railroad cross ties, but the wood had to be cured and it was not easy to cure hardwood in the swamp. Then he put a hand on Bristol's shoulder. "Time now," he said as he led him to Willie Tiger's chickee.

Since the death of his sister, Willie Tiger lived with the family of his nephew's wife. The old Tustenugge sat hunched on his platform, coughing and weak despite the remedy made from the scent sac of a skunk prepared by Sally Cypress against lung sickness. Feeling his spirit drift from his nostrils, he had no interest in the Negro boy brought to his chickee by Emathla, not even when Emathla said that the boy brought silver. Instead he sent them both to Miami Doctor's chickee with a wave of his hand.

189

"We wait," said Emathla.

The sun was directly overhead, less an object than a blast of light, when Miami Doctor, carrying a curlew and a whooping crane draped over his short, triangular cape, returned from foraging with Charlie Billie and two other men. Emathla conferred with the group, then Miami Doctor broke away to stride to his chickee, where Sally Cypress sat cross-legged at her sewing machine, indifferent to her three children playing in the dirt around her.

She turned the wheel with her right hand, sewing two-inch strips of cloth together. "Where we put him?" she asked, nodding toward the sleeping platform where the family slept. "No room. Not enough room for us."

Bristol unwrapped a handkerchief filled with silver dollars. "Isaac said he and my momma are going to send more."

Miami Doctor took the coins. "Buy rifle for Charlie Billie, canned milk, coffee, sugar for cooking chickee, medicine bottle with picture for Willie Tiger."

"Maybe you could buy land with it," suggested Bristol.

Sally Cypress cut the finished band diagonally into narrow segments, each composed of contrasting blocks of color. "Brown boy same as white," she said. "Know nothing. Can do nothing." Worse than his stupidity, she remembered that his mother, Caroline, had spoken harsh words to her white friend Oolalee. Oolalee's enemy was her enemy and that extended to her enemy's children. She looked at Bristol with contempt. "My son Tommy younger than you. Already put live coal on his wrist. Not cry. Fire go out. New coal put on. Him seven summers." Despite an earlier rancor brought about by Billy Bowlegs' privilege to use the bubbling stick that was forbidden to her, she proudly announced that her son was ready to go with the medicine man into the swamp. "Not eat for eight days. Drink black drink."

"Enough," cautioned Miami Doctor, and she continued her sewing.

"I don't know about any hot coals on my wrists," said Bristol, "but I brought something you can grind corn in and I can fish. Without any bait. Just a little piece of dough."

"Fish don't bite too much," said Miami Doctor. "Water too high."

"Well then, maybe I can teach the kids to read," said Bristol with a sigh. "I can teach anyone who wants to learn. As soon as my momma sends me some books."

"If you teach our children knowledge of white people," said Miami Doctor, "they will cease to be Indian."

"I'm not white, and reading hasn't hurt me none."

"Not speak for you. You have no ways. Your people taken from their ways. Read and write is good for white men but very bad for red man. Long time ago, some of our fathers wrote upon a little piece of paper. When agent called Indians together, he said paper was treaty that brethren made with great father at Washington. They found that their brethren, by knowing how to read and write, had sold lands and graves of their fathers to white race."

"I bet that agent doesn't come around anymore." Bristol slapped at a mosquito, then remembered the bottle of turpentine in his bag.

"Different agent," replied Miami Doctor. "Bring us things from agency, overalls, overcoats, leggings. Agent supposed to be on side of Indian. Give us useless gifts and tell us Washington decide state can have Pahahokee. State only have to ask for it. Agent say they going to reclaim three million acres, then have most valuable farmland in United States."

Sally Cypress finished rearranging and resewing the multi-colored and multi-patterned strips into new bands, then left the chickee to gather palmetto leaves. Her children, a girl of nine, a boy of seven, and a toddling boy of two followed, while Bristol smeared turpentine on the back of his neck.

"Emathla say white man want to hang you," said Miami Doctor.

"A white soldier is lying dead. I killed him. My momma and Isaac are scared they're going to come after me."

"Hanging bad. Spirit trapped in body. Cannot leave mouth. Forget hanging. We take you hunt alligator soon. Start quick. Learn quicker."

That night Bristol slept fitfully between the six-foot-long, box-shaped mosquito bars, standard equipment of all Seminoles, with the under side open over the palmetto leaves that Sally Cypress and her children had spread on the ground. He fell asleep in moonlight, trying to hold back tears and anger. He hoped that Galilee would come for him and tell him it was all right to come home, thinking that he could not stand being in the swamp one more day, much less weeks, or months, or even years.

The worst part of the alligator hunt was the dysentery that Bristol had developed his third day in camp. They went at night, Charlie Billie and a second man in one dugout, Bristol and Miami Doctor, with a bull's-eye lantern attached to his forehead, in another. Miami Doctor propelled his dugout with long, dextrous strokes. Silently, slowly, the dugout cut through the dark waters, stealthily gliding through lilies and floating branches. When they reached a deep bayou, Bristol was handed the lantern and directed to throw the light quickly over the water. Two balls of fire suddenly shone in the darkness. Without a ripple Miami Doctor glided his dugout within ten feet of the alligator and shot it between the eyes with a .38 Winchester, blowing the top of the creature's head into fragments that flew against the bank. Before the reptile could flounder out of reach, the Indian grabbed the carcass and pulled it into the dugout, then severed the spinal cord with an ax.

Other alligators nearby began a vibrating roar, seesawing their heads and tails as Miami Doctor fired another shot, rendering a second alligator so lifeless that he did not cut its neck but hauled it in on top of the first, loading the dugout to the water's edge.

They turned back, gliding once more through lilies. "Used to be more alligators," said Miami Doctor. "So many eyes, used to shine like stars."

At first Bristol paid no attention to the low breathing. His thoughts were on Sally Cypress' remedy for dysentery, an infusion brewed from tiny leaves and red berries that he had left behind in his portmanteau. Then the movement grew more definite, invading his consciousness with its change from random to purposeful. Bristol drew his feet up just before a great mouth opened and began snapping angrily, the alligator's body writhing, twisting, as it lashed its tail from side to side.

Miami Doctor brought down his ax quickly upon its neck, then picked up his pole and glanced down at Bristol. His face in the moonlight was solicitous, kindly. "Brown boy afraid?" he asked.

"Brown boy sick as a dog," replied Bristol.

The next day, after the alligators were skinned, Bristol read a note from his mother while the women cut alligator tails into strips, sprinkled them with lemon juice, and dipped them into batter. Emathla had been the courier. The paper smelled of wild grape leaves. Caroline wrote that their house was being watched, so they all had to be careful. Someone was even watching Mrs. Tuttle's house, although Mrs. Tuttle, whose headaches had seriously worsened, had forbidden the man to step foot on her property. Lawmen were also watching the trading posts for contact between any Negro and any Seminole. Caroline ended by cautioning him to wash out his socks every day and to sprinkle rice around his head at night. Bristol remembered the rice, untouched in his bag. No wonder, he thought as he put down the letter and lifted himself on one elbow.

Two of Sally Cypress' children sat cross-legged in front of him, the girl with the younger boy close at her side, while the older boy stood beside them. Bristol ignored them and absently watched the women from his pallet as they prepared alligator steaks.

Sally Cypress stopped sewing rickrack to the bands of multi-patterned cloth. "No eat alligator," she warned. "Make sicker."

"I wasn't planning to," he replied.

"Better eat sofke," she said. "Baby can eat sofke. Old people can eat sofke. You can eat sofke."

"I can't," he said. "I feel like a tunnel. Food goes right through me. You understand what I mean?"

Later, when everyone was at the cook fire

eating alligator steaks, Sally Cypress returned with a spoonful of sofke. "Eat," she commanded. "You die, husband say my fault."

Bristol's dysentery disappeared before the Green Corn dance. By then he'd learned to like pumpkin bread and hush puppies made of cornmeal and bacon drippings almost the way his mother prepared them. He'd learned to handle a rifle and to track a deer, knowing when to be still by watching the animal's tail waggle, a movement made before the creature lifted its head. He had even observed sex between Miami Doctor and Sally Cypress, an activity he had never seen before, although he had heard it when his mother and Isaac went into their bedroom and closed the door, and earlier, a dim remembrance of his mother with a yellow-haired man. The gropings that he witnessed nightly on the sleeping platform of the chickee looked cumbersome and clumsy. Bristol couldn't understand the reason for all the jokes made back on Charles Street, all the elbows dug into his ribs, the smiles that stretched sideways, the running report of who was doing it with who, and, other than the urgencies that he was able to relieve alone, he couldn't understand what all the fuss was about.

By summer's end, the time of Willie Tiger's death, when Bristol was learning to chop a cypress trunk into a dugout, Emathla brought the news. The troops were gone. Two months

196

after they arrived, the war was over.

"Can I go home now?" asked Bristol.

"Too soon," said Miami Doctor. "White man still look for you. Agent asked about you. We say we not see. He afraid of lung sickness. He soon be by with handkerchief on mouth, carrying more overcoats and leggings."

Bristol realized that Miami Doctor had taken Willie Tiger's place, just as he realized that he would be among the Seminoles for a long time. When Billy Bowlegs painted one of the dead man's cheeks red, the other black, Emathla explained that Osceola, with the death struggle upon him, had risen from bed and painted one half of his face, neck, throat, wrists, hands, and knife handle with vermillion, the marks of a war chief, and although Willie Tiger had never been a war chief, he could have been. Then they placed a bottle of sofke in the log pen in which his body was interred so that he might eat on his long journey. All the women had pulled their hair down over their faces. And Bristol thought that he was like the corpse, confined in a log pen with no place to go, nothing to see, nowhere to move, with one cheek red and the other black, and only a bottle of sofke to nourish him in his confinement.

Part Two

1906–1934

Chapter Ten

Maude wished her mother would die. She wished this in the morning when she rinsed her face over the enamel basin and pulled on the hated black stockings that all girls of fifteen wore. She wished this as she did her daily chores, whisking clean the window screens clotted with flies and mosquitoes, washing the floor with coal oil to kill the fleas, and again at night when, in corset and bloomers, she curled her hair in rags.

Every time she saw her mother coming out of the guava shack with sweat dripping from her weathered face, Maude was surprised that Eulalie was still alive, considering the regularity and vehemency of her prayers. She felt nothing for the woman, certainly not the way her brother, Jack, did. Eulalie could die right in front of her, and Maude knew that she would walk over the body as if it were a fallen log.

She hadn't always felt that way. When she was little and Eulalie kept her tied to the banyan tree with an orange and a pitcher of water in its shaded hollow, when Eulalie came upon her with a sudden, cold-eyed rage, quoting Scripture while she switched her legs, making them burn worse than if they were bitten by fire ants, Maude would wonder what she had done wrong to make Mama so mad.

Their latest quarrel had to do with the subject of Maude's occupation. Now that she had finished eighth grade, and mindful that idle hands were the devil's workshop, Eulalie wanted her daughter gainfully employed despite the fact that most young women, even those grub-poor, which they were not, did not work outside the home. The options were limited. It was doubtful that Maude would ever earn a living as a dressmaker if the clumsy sewing aprons she made in the Pine Needles Girls' Club were an indication of aptitude. This left two remaining choices, a course in stenography, which Maude refused to undertake, and the most realistic aspiration, that of teaching school, dashed during the qualifying examination when Maude failed to name all the war governors of Florida, trace the water routes from Kissimmee to Key West, and name the county seats.

Maude opened the parcel before her. It contained a pair of embroidered stockings and a shirtwaist. She knew it came from the Negro woman Caroline, as did the boxes of shoes, gloves, trinkets, and ribbons that old Galilee slipped to her from time to time. Maude wondered if she stole them from the people she worked for. Mr. Headley said they all did that. When Maude was small enough for Jack to carry on his shoulders, she used to catch

202

glimpses of Caroline standing silently nearby, usually in fragments of vision seen between the leaves and ferns of the hammock, a pair of eyes, a mouth, a pair of hands clasped patiently at a thickened waist. Once, after a switching from Eulalie, the woman came to the house. After that something happened. It was long ago. Jack remembered best. The woman's son had killed a white soldier and ran away to hide. Right after that the presents stopped. Then, when the car trolley tracks were installed, the gifts began again.

Maude had been playing snakes with the oldest Headley boy on the front walk, stuffing a black cotton stocking, coiling it, then jerking it with a string from behind a bougainvillea. Galilee had jumped as they hoped he would, although he did not cry out. Disappointed, they came out from behind their hiding place. Galilee handed Maude a package.

"Someone want you to have this," he said.

The box contained eggs and a jar of olive oil, more disappointing than Galilee's failure to react to the cotton snake.

"What's this for?" she asked.

He lowered his voice to a whisper. "This for you to take against the consumption. Someone I know worry about you. Someone I know think you too thin. This so you don't cough yourself to death."

Maude asked Galilee why the Tuttle maid kept sending her things.

"Miss Caroline, she have a big heart," he replied.

She slipped the stockings into a bottom drawer and left the shirtwaist on top of a chest of drawers. She would never wear the shirtwaist. She kept it only because the sight of another present from the Negro woman would upset Eulalie. It was cheap, shoddy, with none of the trademarks of well-made garments that Granger Headley taught her to look for in the clothes that she would wear someday very soon, hand-stitched satin labels and seams that were doubled, French seams, he called them, where you couldn't see unfinished edges.

It was hard to remember the time before Maude and Granger Headley became special friends. He had singled her out one afternoon, watching her scramble with other children around the ice wagon, scooping up ice splinters while the ice man chipped away at a three-hundred-pound block with an ice pick. "You've grown since last year," he had said. "You just might be the prettiest thing I have ever seen."

Startled, Maude had looked up at the rich man who spent his winters in the eleven-room coral rock house next door and whose wife objected to the guava shack.

"Don't be shy, Maude. You know who I am."

"You scared me, is all," she replied. "I didn't hear you coming. Anyways, I don't have any more ice."

He laughed. "I don't want any of your chips."

"And my mother is never going to get rid of that guava shack."

"I'm not here to talk about your mother. It's hot enough to fry an egg. Why aren't you swimming?"

She told him there were too many conch shells at the water's edge, too much seaweed to tangle up her legs. He asked her if she wanted to sail on his forty foot sharpie to Ocean Beach, a faraway fringe of mangroves across the bay where she could swim and climb the jetties. Once under way, he told her he couldn't get close enough to Ocean Beach because of the current. Instead he dropped anchor in the bay.

"Here's where you'll swim," he said.

"I thought I was going to wade. I can't drop into the water with all these clothes on. I'll drown."

"Swim nude," he said.

Maude shook her head. "I can't do that. I can't let you see me without my clothes."

Granger Headley stroked her cheek. "I'm a father, Maude. Don't you think I have seen children without their clothes before?"

"I suppose so."

"Then don't be such a silly goose."

After she climbed up the ladder, dripping from her swim, he dried her with his sweater, then tied a black velvet band about her neck, gave her ice chips to suck, and followed her about the deck, squeezing the bulb on a big, boxy Kodak camera.

When Granger Headley was through taking pictures, he pulled Maude onto his lap, then stroked her back, the knobs of her spinal column, the velvet band that clasped her small, thin neck.

Maude studied declamation before an oval, floor-mounted mirror with a manual in her hand, her golden hair tied back with a ribbon. Jack promised to take her to amateur night at the Alcazar Theater, and she practiced the repertoire that would make everyone in Miami sit up and take notice, that would win first prize even over Richard Clemons and his mandolin. The artful, stylized poses were not too different from the act she did for Mr. Headley, in which she dressed in her outgrown pinafores and tied a big bow in her hair. He liked it when she lisped. She lisped to make him whimper at her feet like Jack's dog, kiss her toes, and tell her that she was beautiful.

Other people besides Granger said she was beautiful. Maude herself knew this to be so. She had seen pictures of beautiful women in *Liberty* magazine and knew that she was every bit as pretty. She had seen the way men and even women sometimes caught their breath when they looked at her, and how boys opened their mouths to speak and how nothing came out. "That's a one to be watched," people would say, or, if they were the mother of an ugly girl, "Beauty is as beauty does."

Jack watched her from the arm of a green-fringed davenport, a touring cap pulled down over his forehead. "I would end with patriotism. It's a sure winner."

"You mean like this?" Maude took her stance, the right arm extended, hand raised to her eyes, the left arm extended, wrist on a level with her waist, the right foot before the left, and both hands open. "Breathes there a man with soul so dead, who never to himself hath said," Maude raised her left arm and pointed, "This is my own, my native land."

"You're the cat's meow, Maudie."

She faced her brother and practiced a pout. The idea was to look as if a bee had stung her lips. "How did I sound? My words are supposed to be perfect, like new coins from the mint."

"You sound fine."

"How did I look?"

"You're so vain, Maudie. You sound fine. You look fine."

"It's not enough to look fine. I want to look splendid. Don't you want to be admired?"

"I'm happy the way things are," he replied.

"I'm not. I hate this old house. I hate the clothes Mama makes me wear. I hate reading up on stuff just to take the teachers' qualifying examination again." Maude smiled, relishing the secret of a journey north to Newport on a Pullman car. "Anyway, it's a silly waste of time."

"Why do you say that?"

"I may not be here long enough to take it."

"What are you talking about, Maudie?"

Maude opened her manual to *defiance,* thrust out her chin, and changed the subject. "Don't you feel peculiar working for a Jew?"

"Mr. Levy's all right. He's kind of bashful. Keeps a lump of sugar between his teeth and sips tea from a scalding hot glass that he holds in the palm of his hand. Why don't you give him a chance? He's stopping by this afternoon. Meet him first. Then make up your mind."

"I don't know that I want to. I hear they smell funny."

"Actually, he smells of citronella. What did you mean when you said you may not be here that long? Are you planning something foolish?"

"Hush, Mama's coming."

Now that Eulalie had been made a member of the Daughters of the Confederacy and she was speaking in tongues, possibly even in the Hong Kong dialect, she was feeling herself again, sturdy and sure, and she took off her shoes to bang them against the steps.

"They cut through the wrong direction," she said. "They're going to have to lay those water pipes all over again tomorrow, and that means two days' wages instead of one all because you, Jack, were too busy to watch them. You're going to have to stay with them tomorrow and that's all there is to it."

"Mr. Levy is expecting me at the store. In

fact, he's coming by in a little while to fetch me back to town."

"I don't want that man in my house," said Eulalie.

"You don't want anyone in the house, Mama," said Jack.

"That's not true. I like to have visitors from time to time. I haven't forgotten that if it wasn't for that peddler, you'd still be helping me out."

Jack pulled his cap down over his forehead as if to blot his mother out. "I've been hearing you say that all my life. 'If it wasn't for this person or that person doing some such thing, then everything would be fine and dandy.' You have people to help you in the guava shack."

"A lot of good that old nigger does me. Half the time his day-worker friends don't show up, and the other half I have to bring him back home because he forgets where he lives."

"We need to get something straight, Mama. I was earning a living playing the piano at the Lucky Pelican before I met Levy. I'd still be playing if that temperance crowd of yours hadn't shut it down."

"And good riddance," said Eulalie. "The county's going dry. If not this year, next year for sure. The sheriff's running their tails ragged, and there will be no place in Miami for any of those sin palaces."

Galilee called from the yard to say that the roots of the poinciana tree were in the way of the pipes and that they needed either to reroute the pipes or trim the roots. Eulalie sighed and banged open the screen door to tell them to trim the roots.

Maude heard the clip-clop of hooves on the rocky lane before she saw the horse and buggy. The first thing she noticed when Zalman Levy jumped down from the buckboard was that his brown eyes were as dark as the inside of a sunflower. Beneath his jacket he wore a shirt with a celluloid collar that she knew he wiped clean nightly.

He tipped his hat to Eulalie. "You came to my store," he said. She nodded briefly, like someone trying to dislodge something from her eye. "I gave you a donation. Remember? For the portrait of that Jefferson Davis fellow."

"I'm beholden to you," said Eulalie stiffly.

Zalman Levy fingered the brim of his derby. "How do you feel, missus? I hear you have bad spells in the rainy season."

Eulalie frowned at Jack, on his way down the steps. "I'm not as bad off as some folks make me out to be. Excuse me."

"That was my mother," said Jack.

"Nice lady."

"And this is my sister."

Maude remained in the shadows of the porch. Her hands were small and graceful like the hands of a trapeze artiste Zalman had once seen at a circus in New York. That was before he experienced aches in his bones that he thought only old people got and bought a railroad ticket to Miami, filled a drummer's sample trunk with notions, and after two nights sleeping upright on a train, stepped into the heat and humidity of Dade County and wondered how one did business in a steambath.

"From what I can see of her, your sister is a rose. Maybe not yet a rose, better a bud. Where's your papa?"

"He's dead. He died when I was a kid."

"A pity."

"I don't know about that. He was a sorry bastard."

Maude came to lean against the porch railing. From the lift of her nose, Jack knew that her pose was *disdain*.

Zalman tipped his hat. "Me and your brother are going to look for a place to put a moving-picture theater. What do you think of that?"

Maude shrugged and pulled her hair ribbon tight. "I've never seen a moving picture. I have a friend who says they flicker. He says they ruin your eyes."

"Don't listen to him," said Zalman. "Take my word, you're gonna love it and so will your friend. And if you'll pardon me for saying so, eyes like yours can't be ruined so easy."

"My friend knows more than you do. He knows about everything."

"Sounds like a smart fellow. If he rides a bicycle, tell him I could use a messenger."

Maude knew why her mother had disliked

Zalman Levy sight unseen. For a foreigner who couldn't speak English very well, he was too sure of himself, too quick to answer. Right-thinking folks spoke slowly, if at all. "Why do you go where you aren't wanted?"

"Maude," said Jack, "that's a rotten thing to say. Forgive my sister, Mr. Levy. She's always playacting and saying things she doesn't mean."

Maude ran past them down the steps while Zalman put a restraining hand on Jack's arm. "It's a free country, Jack, let her say what she wants. Believe me, it's all right."

"If you don't come back and apologize, Maude, I won't take you to the Alcazar."

"See if I care," she said. "See if I want to go anyplace with a brother who smells of horse-flies and citronella."

Jack and Zalman Levy followed the boulevard past unpainted fish houses and pelicans swooping down on the jumping mullet to the livery barn where they had left the rented horse and wagon, then ran two blocks to hop aboard a yellow trolley. All the cane-covered seats were occupied and they stood, holding onto straps in front of a woman with a parasol.

"What did you think of the location?" asked Zalman.

"The location is okay, but it's a whole lot smaller than your other store."

"That's the beauty of it. All you need is an

upstairs and a downstairs, the top floor for a projectionist booth and an office, the bottom floor for seats, a screen, and a space for a piano. The ticket seller you put out front." Zalman pointed at his new Keds shoes designed with canvas uppers. "Eventually I'd like to build a theater with sides like the tops of these shoes, so that when it's not raining, we can roll back the canvas to let in the breeze."

"You have good ideas, Mr. Levy. I just don't know where the people are going to come from. To buy tickets and all."

"Look, my friend, Flagler thinks this is just a little fishing village. He thinks we're all here to service his hotel and his railroad. He's in for a surprise. A word to the wise. When they finish digging the Panama Canal, Key West is going to be three hundred miles closer to Panama than any other American port. For Miami that spells business and people. Do I have to say more?"

At the Second Avenue corner, the trolley jumped the tracks with a slow, grating screech. The motorman got off and settled on his haunches to study the situation, then called to the conductor, who brought a crowbar and asked all the men passengers to get out and help lift the trolley back onto the track.

Jack and Zalman jumped down with three other men onto a street paved with wooden blocks. It had recently rained, and swollen blocks popped up to turn the roadway into a washboard. The trolley was lifted in minutes. As they climbed once more on board, the woman with the parasol smiled at Jack.

"You're a good-looking fella," whispered Zalman. "I'll bet the women don't leave you alone."

"I can take them or leave them."

"Get yourself a wife," said Zalman. "Look around. You'll find one. The first time I met my wife, Gettel, I almost missed her. She was sitting on a sofa between her parents. It wasn't until her father got up that I saw her with her hands folded in her lap, serene and modest, a pearl, like a jeweler had just pulled her out of a velvet bag. I made up my mind while her father was trying to untangle the doily from his head. We were married by a rabbi who came down on the train from Jacksonville." Zalman leaned forward to whisper in his ear. "When a man is not chasing, he can take care of business."

Granger Headley was dressed as he always was, with his hair oiled and combed straight back, his four-in-hand tie neatly knotted, his trousers showing new cuffs. The skiff was dry-docked for repairs and the boathouse was cramped. They met in the tool closet at the rear. Maude told him that she was spitting mad at her brother. Granger told her that brothers and sisters argued, that one did not say *spitting mad,* that he loved her southern accent, then handed her stockings, garters, a lace undergarment, a hat and a coat.

"Put these on," he said.

"I don't want to put the coat on. It's hot."

"That's the idea. I want you only in the teddy beneath the coat. Please. For me. Haven't you always been my obedient little girl?"

Maude unbuttoned her shirtwaist. "You promised to take me to the Royal Palm for tea. When are we going to do that?"

He cupped her chin in his hand. "We can't do that now. I explained it to you. Only after my mother approves so that a divorce can be arranged."

Maude let her skirt fall to the floor. "She's an old lady. And you're grown up. I don't see why you need her approval."

"You must learn to leave everything to me. Put on the stockings."

"I forgot everything you want me to do."

"It's simple. Look surprised. That's the main thing. Go out, then come in again. Look around. Then notice me. I will move toward you. You will think nothing of it for a moment, until I open my trousers. That's when you look surprised. That's the main thing. Then you must try to run away."

Maude entered the small tool room with the flourish Granger Headley had taught her.

"Are you lost, little girl?" he asked in a throaty voice. "Can't you find your mother? If you stay, I can promise you a big surprise." He opened his pants. "Act surprised, Maude.

215

Nervous. That's not nervous. That's angry. Do it over again until you get it right."

Maude reentered, this time the hat, too large for her head, having fallen over one ear. When she registered surprise, Granger tore off the coat, ripped apart the camisole, and pulled her onto his lap so that they were seated face to face, with one of the hat plumes in his mouth. He inserted himself with a shrug. "Show me shock, horror," he whispered hoarsely.

"This is silly," she replied. "I'm not shocked. I knew what you were going to do. It's what you always do."

He gripped her buttocks, one in each hand, while he rammed himself into her body. "Show me horror," he gasped, "or it isn't going to work. That's it. Yes, yes, that's my good little girl."

When Granger had finished as he always did, with a long, whistling sigh, he nuzzled his head between her small, pink-nippled breasts. "You know you're driving me insane. You know that, don't you?"

"Where's my prize?"

Granger Headley put his hand into his pocket and pulled out five dollars in gold coins. "That disappoints me, Maude. That doesn't sound like you love me."

"That's only half. I want the rest and I want to get off." She flung the hat into a corner and began to dress in the gloom of the tool closet. "Jimmy Ferguson asked me to take a spin in his father's Model T," she said.

Headley pulled his suspenders over his shirt, then slipped on his vest. In a few weeks his wife expected that they would be taking the waters in Saratoga Springs. If, however, all worked out as he planned, in a few weeks he would be free, with Maude under his wing, tamed and captive. Once his mother understood how impossible was his marriage, she would see to it that Emily was well provided for and give him her blessing. A man was entitled to a life. "I'd rather you didn't have anything to do with that boy. Trust me. I know people a whole lot better than you do. I've met the chap. He's not sincere."

"He said he loves me," she replied as she went to the door. "He said he wants to kiss me all over."

"You little bitch," he said. "When did you become a little bitch?" He strode to the door, where he caught her downy soft arm and pulled her against his chest. "I didn't mean it. My own sweet darling." He dropped his voice to a whisper. "I have been looking at train schedules."

Maude's eyes brightened. "Will it be soon?"

"Sooner than you think. I'll arrange everything. You don't even need to pack. In fact, I don't want you to bring your own clothes. They won't do."

"What's it like on a train?"

The thought of the throbbing wheels, of

Maude vibrating beneath him in the narrow berth, made Granger Headley feel once again like a boy of seventeen. He pulled off his vest.

When he whispered hoarsely that there were flowers on the tables in the dining car, Maude rebelled. "I'm not taking everything off again," she said.

"You don't have to," he replied.

A few days later, Granger Headley's wife, Emily, invited Eulalie to tea. They sat in the chintz and wicker parlor, a true parlor as distinguished from the front room that Eulalie called a parlor. This one had double doors and an oriental rug. Dressed in a high-waisted, hobble-skirted tea dress with matching lavender hose, Emily Headley served cookies and ice cream molded and shaded to resemble four-leaf clovers. She poured the tea with two delicate hands, spread like bird's wings, one on top of the other on the silver pot. "We've been neighbors for over ten years," she began.

"And I'm still not about to move my guava shack."

"It's not the guava I wish to talk about, Mrs. Coombs. It's your daughter."

Eulalie placed her napkin on her lap, accepted a cup and saucer, which she balanced on a knee. "What about her?"

"Well, frankly, I'm not sure. I think it's a schoolgirl thing, at any rate. I think she has

218

a crush on my husband."

"That's foolish talk," said Eulalie. "Maude is fifteen. Your husband must be forty if he's a day."

"Actually, Granger is forty-three."

"All the more reason to know how stupid the idea is."

"I want you to stop her."

"From doing what?"

"From throwing herself at my husband."

Eulalie stood, and brushed the crumbs from her lap. "Now I've heard everything. I liked it better," she said, "when you put dust covers on all your furniture and left in March."

Eulalie came home to find Galilee and his crew connecting the water pipes to the kitchen sink while Maude stood watching, holding a bottle of sarsaparilla soda. "I've got no time for such foolishness," she said. "Made me miss two hours of daylight."

"What kind of foolishness?" asked Maude.

"Nothing fit for your ears."

"Tell me. I'd understand."

Eulalie bent to wipe the tracks of mud that the men had trailed over her kitchen floor. For the first time her knee hurt, and she groaned as she stood. "Emily Headley said you had a crush on her husband."

"That's not true."

"That's what I told her."

Maude relished the speaking of the words, delivering them as newly minted coins from the purse of her lips. "He has a crush on me." The expression of the men working at the sink had not altered, as if they either had not heard or had not understood.

"Watch what you say, Maude. Remember Colossians chapter three, verse nine. Do not lie to one another."

Maude faced her mother head-on. "He does too have a crush on me. He says I drive him wild."

"What are you saying?"

"I'm saying we do it. I'm saying we get naked together, except he makes me keep my stockings on."

"Hush your mouth. Hush that evil mouth right now. What's gotten into you?"

Maude laughed. "He has. Mr. Headley has. And he's been doing it since I was twelve."

Eulalie waved a hand before her daughter's face like a fan, then grabbed the hand with her other and brought both to her mouth, unmindful of the men who shook their heads at one another and bent to their task. The sins of the fathers shall be visited on the children, she thought. There was no escaping it. The girl was out-and-out evil because she had been conceived in evil. Eulalie bent her head, but the tears would not come. They had long since curdled. She turned her thoughts inward to her father, Octavius, who had owned one of the largest plantations in Palatka and who had worn shirts of only the finest lawn, grateful that he was not alive to see a granddaughter fallen in debauchery.

Jack returned from the Everglades with a canoeful of baby alligators in exchange for fifty pounds of notions. The torrent of Everglades fresh water that flowed down the newly dredged Miami River to the bay carried him downstream like a feather.

Levy met him at the dock. "Is that what you brought me, a canoeful of lizards?"

"It's all they had," said Jack.

"For fifty pounds of notions? It's a good thing I didn't send you with two canoes."

"It was hard enough to handle one," said Jack. "I can't get around the way I used to. They're draining the 'Glades with the darnedest piece of machinery you ever saw. Dredges blowing black smoke everywhere. Cables and booms two stories high. Big gears on deck that keep up a godawful rumble whenever the dipper comes up from the muck. They're drying out the swamp. It may be good for the white man, but it's bad for the Indians."

"It's progress," said Levy. "That's what happens. It can't be helped. The Indians will find a place. You'd be surprised. A corner here. A corner there. They'll make out."

"I don't think so," said Jack. "They're bad off as it is. They're living on garfish and cabbage palm buds."

"A person can survive on a piece of bread,"

said Zalman. "Believe me, I know. Is there something you're not telling me?"

"No," said Jack, thinking of his encounter the day before with Bristol, the first time he had seen him since he had hidden in the swamp. His childhood friend, who had survived the last eight years on a hammock island in a fly-filled chickee, was taller, his hair now a honeyed brown, garbed in a patchwork medicine dress to his knees and a kerchief at his neck. An Indian girl had stood at the cook fire, heating lard in a skillet from which a light smoke rose. Beside her was a child with curly hair. The meeting was short, awkward, with neither knowing what to say to the other. Bristol remarked that things were bad in all the camps, and that he was still in hiding. Jack decided not to mention the attack on Isaac McCloud, telling his friend instead that maybe he was better off where he was, since there had been three lynchings of Negroes in the last two years.

Zalman squinted, trying to find good in the barter. "Don't look so sad, Jack," he said. "It's not a total loss." The solution came to him the way it had come to him to rent chairs for the nickelodeon from the funeral parlor and to seat only 199 patrons to avoid a yearly $500 license. "First we make little orange crates," he said, "the size of two fingers. One for each alligator. Then we put on a shipping label. We call it a souvenir from Florida. People can send it north like they send postcards. The trick is to keep them alive."

As soon as the sidewalk was swept and the nets of baby alligators doused with water and crammed on storage shelves, Zalman invited Jack for supper to the apartment above the store where Gettel was grinding coffee by hand. Smelling of heliotrope, she invited Jack to sit, then sprinkled the coffee with chicory, stirred in sugar, except for Zalman who preferred the skin of the boiled milk to cover his coffee like a cloak. She served them chopped liver with a radish, a bowl of chicken soup with mondlin as brown as nuts, and boiled beef flanken with horseradish.

Jack's eyes watered from the horseradish. "Did you ever have a good friend, Mr. Levy? Someone like a brother?"

"I had a brother. He was taken by the cossacks to hammer railroad ties for the czar. Why do you ask?"

Jack realized that he had gone too far and put aside the painful image of Bristol exiled to a hammock island in the middle of a swamp. "No reason."

They ate in silence. Gettel excused herself, then went into the bedroom for a hat with two plumes, which she carried on her head like a jug. Zalman explained that his wife was the secretary of the sisterhood of the newly formed B'Nai Zion and a member of the committee that was organizing a seder for the Passover holidays. Even though Miami's tiny Jewish community numbered under sixty, he said, the woman had meetings. Go figure.

Zalman refilled Jack's coffee cup from the steaming pot. "Before you leave, Jack, don't forget to give the lizards another spritz. And next time, boychick, try to make a better deal. It's not enough to know your way around the swamp. You also have to have a head for business."

When Jack returned home with five dollars in his pocket and a pouch of powdered foxglove from Sally Cypress for pains in the heart, Eulalie was in a rage, shouting that Maude had taken none of her clothes, had given no warning, had simply vanished.

"What are you talking about, Mama?"

Eulalie stormed from one part of the house to another. "How could she have left her home without a by-your-leave? How could Granger Headley have left his wife and children for a fifteen-year-old girl?"

Jack followed after his mother, the floor creaking beneath his weight with every step. "How do you know this?"

Eulalie waved a piece of paper. Galilee had found the note in the crotch of the banyan, beside an abandoned raccoon's nest. "I'm going to Rhode Island," she read. "I don't expect to ever see you again." She crumpled the paper and threw it on a hearth of blazing knots. "Did you know any of this?"

Jack said he couldn't explain it, although

Eulalie held him clearly accountable. "I never much liked her," she said, "and that's the shameful truth for a mother to admit, but I never expected her to go to the bad. What are you going to do?"

Jack shook his head, dumbfounded that his younger sister had not confided her intentions. "I'm not sure what to do."

"Don't you want to find them? Avenge your sister's honor?"

"They're a long way from here, Mama. I wouldn't know where to start."

"That's poppycock. Rhode Island is the smallest state in the union."

Jack went to the new wooden telephone mounted on the wall.

"Levy's a smart fellow. I'll ring him up. See what he says."

Eulalie grabbed the receiver out of his hand. "And have everyone laughing at us? You'll do no such thing. I've changed my mind. She's made her bed. Let her lie in it like I had to lie in mine." Eulalie brushed her hands. "Actually, we won't be so bad off. It'll be just you and me, the way we were, Jackie, in the old days before all the trouble. See if I'll take her in when she comes crawling back."

Jack knew that without Maude, the house would be a grim place to live. "I don't know how you can say that. You're always quoting Scripture. What about the prodigal?"

"He was a son. I would always forgive you,

225

Jackie. I would forgive you anything."

While Eulalie told herself and anyone else who would listen that Maude's bolt was good riddance, she fretted over the girl in the quiet of the night, with the only sounds a hooting owl, the rain dripping from the eaves, a pillow smothering her sighs. Then she tossed and turned, thinking of Maude and of Thomas Sands, confusing get with sire, feeling across the years the same keen knife-blade pain of desertion and abandonment.

When in September the telephone jangled in the middle of the night, Eulalie's heart jumped, then hardened. It was too late. She would never take Maude back. Jack called from the front room that it was Central, advising everyone on the line of the telegraph from Cuba that reported that a hurricane had struck, taking five lives, and that the officials were hoisting storm flags. From the distance they heard a locomotive toot its horn.

Eulalie kneeled on the floor to roll up the carpet. "I should have known a storm was coming. That girl's got me so flummoxed I wasn't paying attention."

"I didn't notice any drop in the barometer," said Jack.

"I don't mean that. Plenty of other signs. I should have known. So should you. Sand crabs migrating from the mangrove thickets, a real good mango crop, the Lovells' cat perching on a fence."

Before daylight, great sheets of rain were driven against the shuttered house. They heard the sounds of snapping, of groaning, of tree limbs breaking off. When the eye of the storm brought with it an eerie calm, they went outside in a yellow glare to find that a royal poinciana limb had crashed against a window, that telegraph poles had been blown down like matchsticks, and that many of the docks had been washed away, only their moorings remaining like fingers pointing skyward.

In the sodden rubbish beneath the banyan tree, Jack found the bone shaped like a fishhook, the broken pot with the faded diamondback design, the string of beads, then remembered the mortar and pestle that he had given long ago to Bristol.

"How did these old things get out here?" asked Eulalie.

Jack slipped the objects into his pockets. "Maude must have hidden them in the tree."

Eulalie wheeled. "I don't ever want to hear her name again. And I'm sure I don't know why you want that old trash in your pockets. It's about time someone threw them out."

When the back end of the storm unleashed its fury, Eulalie scurried indoors into the shuttered gloom and lit a hurricane lamp, while Jack put the ancient objects into a tin Borax box and wondered if he would ever see his sister again.

★ ★ ★

Eulalie blamed Maude for the chicken bone that lodged in her throat. She knew it would never have stuck, she would never have had to force it down with chunks of bread if she hadn't been worrying herself to death. The Daughters of the Confederacy, with whom she was having supper, had smiled and clucked their tongues. They told Eulalie that although Emily Headley, who had taken to her bed with ice packs on her forehead, was up and about, the unfortunate woman was still groggy with bromides. Eulalie was going to give them a piece of her mind when the bone got stuck. She didn't think anything more about it until aching pains began in her stomach from which she had suffered for days.

The pains first struck two mornings later when she was in her front yard, enjoying the sweet candy smell of the yellow-flowered acacia. It was a beautiful April day, and except for a pervasive worry that held her in its grip like a corset, she almost felt like a girl again. Gray kingbirds roosted on new shoots springing from the old gumbo-limbo trunk that had been toppled in the hurricane. Monarch and zebra butterflies flitted through her fingers as she weeded periwinkles and pink hibiscus that in the afternoon would turn red. When she reached up to touch the soft yellow skin of a custard apple, someone drove a needle into her belly.

Later, nauseated, pale and sweating, she fi-

228

nally sent for the doctor. The first thing he said when he palpated her rigid abdomen was that Rhode Island was cold and damp this time of year, a feature of the North that just might drive her errant daughter home. "You may have a perforated bowel," he added. "From the chicken bone. We'll have to wait and see."

When her heart began to race like a runaway train that crashed in the Grove on its way to the Keys, the doctor said she had peritonitis. He didn't address himself to Eulalie. It was Jack that he told to wait and see, for there was nothing medically that could be done for her.

In the morning Eulalie's voice grew thready. By evening, when she couldn't get enough breath to both speak and breathe, she took to her bed. Jack sat beside her in a chair with his elbows resting on his knees.

"You ever think about your daddy?" she asked.

"Not if I can help it."

"He did the best he knew how, Jackie. A body can't expect much more than that. If we had called you Quincy Octavius like we were supposed to, you might have felt more of a kinship. Maybe you thought you were short-changed because he passed before his time."

"I never miss him, Mama. All the time chasing me around the yard with a switch when he was feeling bad, thumping me on the head when he was feeling good. Maudie did. She used to ask me about him all the time."

"She's only partly your kin," she said, trying to keep herself awake so that the early morning hours would not take her.

"What do you mean, Mama?" asked Jack beneath the flickering light bulb.

"You and Maude don't have the same father."

A night breeze ruffled the curtain at the window. "It doesn't matter. Maudie's still my only sister. I hope Headley treats her right."

"You think I'm a bad woman?"

Jack put his hands out to take one of hers. "People do funny things, Mama. Who can say whether another person is good or bad? We just are. You don't have to tell me who he was unless you want to."

"You know who he was."

Jack suddenly remembered only the curly blonde hairs on the backs of the man's hands. "Thomas. That's why he stopped coming around."

Eulalie reached up to clutch his shirt, pull him closer to the bed. "That's not why. I'm going to tell you the deepest, darkest secret of my life," she whispered hoarsely. "Your father killed him, stuffed his straw hat and his shirt somewhere in this house to punish me, to remind me all the days of my life, as if I could ever forget."

"Hush, Mama. You're talking out of your head. The fever is making you say things you don't mean."

"Feel my forehead," she whispered. "There's no fever on me. I'm as cool as a pitcher. I tell you he did this. John Quincy Coombs took the life of the only man I ever loved. If you don't believe me, take a good deep breath. Let your nose tell you what your mind will not see. The smell of bay rum is still in the house."

Jack looked out the open window into the night, thinking about his father murdering Maude's father when it should have been the other way around, and about his mother, who had been confined day and night to the torment of her dead lover's scent. "We all have secrets, Mama."

"Not my Jack. You're like an open book."

There was nothing he could say, not to Eulalie, certainly not when she lay so sick. His shame was hidden as deeply as had been hers except that he would have to carry his alone.

Jack's thoughts wandered to the summer before.

There was only the two of them in the Jacksonville armory. The other members of their National Guard unit, the Miami Rifles, were on the parade ground. Richard came behind him, unbuttoned Jack's shirt, then ran his hands over Jack's naked chest, his nipples. To Jack's surprise, his nipples hardened, became erectile nubs. When Richard put his lips on Jack's neck and wrapped his arm around Jack's narrow waist, Jack saw that veins snaked around his

231

lover's arms like vines.

"Am I going to see all of you?" Richard whispered.

Jack had looked anxiously to the barracks door. "Don't worry about it," Richard whispered. "The drill will take an hour." Jack found himself swimming in desire as if underwater. He stripped off his uniform trousers, let them fall to a puddle of olive drab around his ankles, while Richard bent over him and told him that he had been waiting for him for months.

Jack shook himself from his reverie to turn his mother's pillow.

"Can you ever look at me without loathing?" she whispered.

His voice was hoarse. "I love you, Mama," he replied. "Nothing could ever change that."

When Eulalie developed a fever, Jack asked if she wanted him to send for Sally Cypress. He told her that he had seen the Indian woman only the week before when he had brought a dugout full of buttons and rickrack into the Everglades, and he knew where to find her. Eulalie told him to wait awhile.

"I will pass this bone," she said. "I feel it working itself down."

Then Eulalie went into convulsions that caused her narrow body to stiffen and flail. When at last, exhausted, the twitching had stopped, she turned her face to the wall.

Eulalie heard them talking somewhere over

her head. She was too tired to open her eyes, and so she kept them closed, seeing wiggling lines dance inside her lids. She wished Jack and the doctor would go away and leave her in peace. She would like to get some rest. She would like to get some peace. The white-winged Holy Spirit was with her and she was not afraid. So were her father and mother, and Sally Cypress as she had looked when she was young, even her mother's Tallahassee cousin who had been scalped when she was a baby, now with a head of hair even, although she had never met him, Jefferson Davis, whom she recognized from his portrait.

She tried to tell them to go away. She felt her lips move, but nothing came out. She heard the doctor say that an abdominal catastrophe always ends this way. After convulsions comes coma. How long? asked Jack. Two, three days at the most. And then? And then she will have earned her final rest. It's what you want, Jack, after all. She heard Jack cry. She wanted to touch his head, but she couldn't find him. She wanted to tell him not to cry, but now not even her lips would move.

Maude sat in the paneled foyer, her patent leather slippers tapping impatiently on the marble floor. Granger had left her to speak to the owner of the brownstone, a widower with married children whom Granger said he held in high regard, a man of wealth and prominence

233

who would like her very much, who would want to protect her.

"You mean marry me?" she asked minutes before as he handed her down from the hansom cab.

"Not marry, Maude. But Mr. Forrester would care for you as I wanted to do. As I tried to do."

"You didn't try very hard."

Granger led her up the steps. "My hands are tied."

"I don't know that I care to meet some old man. You're about as old as a body can stand."

"Would you rather I put you on a train back to Miami?"

"I never want to see that place or anyone there again. Ever. Except maybe my brother. I miss my brother."

The black and white tiles seemed to dance. Maude had them almost counted when Granger reentered the foyer accompanied by a man even older than he wearing a smoking jacket with velvet lapels.

"This is Mr. Forrester," he said. "John, this is Maude. What do you think of her? Was I wrong?"

The man was kind. He extended his hand. "If anything, Granger, you understated. How do you do, young lady? Granger was correct. He said you would be the most beautiful creature I had ever seen. Won't you stand for me and turn?"

234

"You mean here, now?"

"If you please."

Maude stood and slowly turned, glancing over her shoulder at the old man in the smoking jacket.

"Unpolished," said John Forrester, "because of her tender years and inexperience, yet with enough grace to show me that she can learn. Would you like to live here in New York, Maude? Would you like to have your own car and driver, your own maid to dress your hair, to lay out your apparel?"

"I don't know how to fix anything to eat except hush puppies and collard greens."

John Forrester laughed. "You're not here to cook. I have a kitchen staff. On some occasions you will dine with me. On others, you will dine alone. You will have your own private apartment upstairs. Naturally I would see that you had suitable clothing, tasteful jewelry. I would engage a tutor."

"I don't need any more schooling," said Maude.

The older man smiled. "He would instruct you in etiquette."

"There's nothing wrong with my manners."

"Indeed there is not. But you would learn the forms of propriety, the art of conversation, how to leave a calling card, how to sit, walk, and enter a room, when and how to remove gloves, hat, which fork and knife to use, and the proper pose to take when standing back

235

from a painting, things like that. Perhaps even a smattering of French so that you would be able to read menus. In return, you would be expected to show your appreciation."

"Like how?"

John Forrester turned to Granger Headley. "This is awkward, Granger. Didn't you explain?"

Headley shook his head. "I beg your pardon, John. I thought she understood. Maude, don't you know why you're here?"

She was there because Granger Headley had rushed her north in a Pullman car, then taken her to his family estate in Newport with the idea that if his seventy-year-old mother understood, could explain it to Emily, arrange whatever settlement was necessary, a divorce could be arranged.

Before the meeting with his mother, Granger had cautioned Maude to be sure to fold her napkin, not to speak unless it was about the weather, and that when she smiled, not to show too much teeth. He brought her into a place with potted palms he called the morning room to meet an old woman who smelled of violets. His mother nodded her head in introduction, then, before Maude could sit down, asked her to excuse them, sent her out to the terrace with the butler, the way one might send a pet. Granger emerged from the morning room chastened, looking like a crestfallen boy instead of a forty-three-year-old man.

236

"I'm here because you're a big old mama's boy. You can't keep me so you're giving me away."

"There's no need to be unpleasant. Do you understand what Mr. Forrester wants?"

"He wants what you did until your mama told you you can't. He wants to put it in me."

"Oh dear," said John Forrester. "I had no idea the girl was so rough around the edges."

Granger put on his hat and yellow chamois gloves. "Well, I guess I'll say goodbye," he said. "You're in very good hands, Maude. I hope you have the sense to take advantage of this opportunity." He shook hands with John Forrester, then bent to kiss Maude on the forehead.

She turned her head, pushed out her lower lip. "You're nothing but a great big baby," she said. "A mama's boy."

"Maude, this is not the time to be unpleasant. Don't you want to say goodbye?"

"I hope you swell up like a toad."

When the door closed behind Granger, a white-gloved servant picked up Maude's portmanteau and opened the brass grating of the elevator. Maude hurried to catch up with John Forrester, but he disappeared into a hallway.

"This way, miss," called the footman. "You'll not be accompanying Mr. Forrester. He has an engagement. And there's no need to cry. If you had your wits about you, you'd know that this is the best thing that could happen

237

to a girl like you."

Maude stepped into an elevator for the first time and held her breath during its slow ascent. When the gate opened, she followed the footman down the corridor. "I wasn't crying and I'm not staying very long either. I'm going to be an actress. On the stage."

"Foolish girl. There isn't a lass behind the footlights who wouldn't trade places with you."

They entered a bedroom with a ceiling as high as the lobby of the Royal Palm Hotel. A crystal bowl of dried roses and cinnamon glistened on a bureau. Window drapes matched the bed drapes, everything a sky blue silk with tassels everywhere and an Aubusson carpet underfoot.

The footman set her belongings on a leather rack. "Don't be putting your feet on the bed until Margaret turns the covers down."

"You must think I was raised in a barn. My grandfather Octavius had the biggest groves in Palatka. And my mother is a Daughter of the Confederacy. Her guava factory is making scads of money. Not that we need it. My people are somebody."

The man tugged at his striped cotton vest. "Of course they are, darling. I knew it the minute I laid eyes on you. If you'll be wanting anything from the kitchen, the bell pulley's over there, but then I'm sure you are used to such things."

He closed the door behind him. Alone for the

first time since she had fled Miami, Maude thought about writing to Jack, then decided that a postmark would only tell him where she was and make him try to find her. She didn't want to go home. She didn't want a tutor either, but if schooling meant clothing wrapped in tissue paper, she would read any old stupid books they gave her.

She sat on the bed, then wondered when he would come to see her. Except for being a Yankee, which he couldn't help, she imagined that Mr. Forrester was like her grandfather Octavius must have been. It was puzzling why old men didn't want ladies of their own age. She reasoned that older ladies probably thought that what they liked to do with their private parts was silly. Maude thought it was silly, too, except that it was barter. It got her away from Eulalie and out of Miami, where it was hot, and full of mosquitoes, where everyone was pokey slow, and where to be beautiful, when your mother made guava jelly, was a hazard.

November 17, 1907

Dear Jack,

I don't know why you fell out with me. I feel bad that Mama is dead but not for the reason you think. I would like to tell

239

her how mad I am at her. But I suppose she knew that. She was mad at me too. I never knew why. Maybe you did.

Jack, are you going to stay in that creaky old house by yourself? It has too many dark corners and too many shutters that bang shut and frighten you to death. Why don't you come visit me in New York? Mr. Forrester wouldn't mind. He's got lots of rooms. Most of them will be empty. Can you imagine having rooms that no one uses?

He is not a bad man, although I know you think so. He treats me very nice and buys me beautiful clothes and hats and gloves and shoes and everything a body could want. I hardly ever see him. When his family comes to visit I have to stay upstairs by myself or go riding somewhere. I have my own car and driver. His name is Leopold. We don't go anywhere much except to museums with my tutor. My tutor is trying to walk my feet off. I know that for a fact. We go from gallery to gallery and look for triangles. Sometimes I say that I see them, but I don't. I just say it so he'll move to the next picture. He gives me so many books to read I also believe he is trying to make me blind. He gave me one to read last month called House of Mirth *by Edith somebody. Did you ever read it? He asked me to discuss Lily Bart's predicament. I know what her predicament is. She used to have money and now she doesn't. Any fool can see that. I'm surprised he asked such a simple question.*

I am studying hard so that Mr. Forrester will take me to the ballet. You have to sit perfectly still without moving a muscle. You can't search for your program or open and shut your fan or look everywhichway. I am practicing looking straight ahead. It makes my neck ache, but if I succeed then I get to wear a new pearl necklace with a diamond clasp and my maid will fix my hair on top of my head. Mr. Forrester says that people will look at me and sigh.

I hope you won't stay mad at me. You are the only person in the whole world I care two hangs about. Did you find the old bone fishhook and the beads and the other old Indian things? I hid them before I left because I knew that if she had got a hold of them, she would throw them out. They are my keepsakes. You gave them to me to stop me from crying. You said they were magic. Do you remember? I'll give you a hint where they are. The place I hid them starts with B and rhymes with canyon. My tutor helped me look it up.

With love, from your sister, Maude.

Chapter Eleven

MIAMI DOCTOR

Life in the Pahahokee struggles to keep up with the changing land. The sparkling pools that once broke the rhythms of the sawgrass have become dark puddles spotted with patches of water hyacinths that shoot arrowheads of purple blossoms. Rusty black snakes coil in the sun on pilings of small new bridges while baby turtles cover old logs in the shallow waters of the canal.

Some things have not changed. Seminole women do their laundry in the old way, washing every garment including the clothes on their backs, which they put on wet.

I watch my wife kneel with difficulty beside the drainage ditch, her knees stiffened with age, her long, trailing skirt in which she has woven pieces of her life swirling on the ground behind her. Sally Cypress has still not given away any of her beads, even though our daughter, Mary, was married and is herself a mother, and my wife's neck is encased in shimmering glass.

"Your head is threaded with enough iron,"

she said, laundering with care the pale pink roses, remnants of Oolalee's long-ago gift, now patched into a rainbow band of color. "You should have the wisdom of a medium elder as well."

I do not argue, for she is right. I too wonder when it comes, this clarity of vision that my mother's brother, Willie Tiger, had, that Billy Bowlegs and Billy Sunshine had, that my friend Jimmy Jumper had when he was yet a young man, that I am supposed to have accumulated like rings on a tree.

I know of no answers, only questions and there are many. Why, for example, does the white man try to sell us liquor, often bad, then arrest his brother for doing so? Why does alcohol seem to affect our people more than the white man? Can it be as Sally Cypress says, because we eat no sweets? Why does the agent instruct us to wear shoes so that our elderly and young do not become enfeebled with hookworm, then take away our hunting lands so that we do not have the means to buy them?

It was easier when I was young, when the white man needed our help to survive from one season to the next. Now he brings dredges to shrink the Pahahokee like a drying sponge while he crowds us with his truck farms, like water hyacinths choking a pond.

My daughter, Mary, and my four-year-old granddaughter, Emma, pound clothes beside my wife. Mary's hair resembles the brim of a hat, first drawn to the top of her head and tied like a switch, then secured to a piece of cardboard over her forehead with a net made of black thread. It is an eyeshade against the sun. When Bristol returned to his own people after the council ruled that Mary and Emma must remain with the tribe, my daughter let down her hair like a widow. I am glad to see that she has put it up once more, although not in the traditional manner.

Emma is quiet, as are all our children. Bristol always found fault with his daughter's sober look, her great, dark, unwinking eyes. I tried to tell him that our children are quiet from a heritage of silence when one sound meant death or capture, but he continued to pull up the corners of her tiny mouth, instructing her to smile as if that could change her nature. Now, thinking that it will bring her father back, Emma smiles into the reflection of the water and asks me if he can still hear the alligators honking in the night.

The agent tells us that when I take my camp to the new reservation, there will be a sofke spoon for everyone. If we had wanted this isolation, we would have fashioned spoons for everyone long ago. There is something to be said for food that is passed from hand to hand, or mouth to mouth, that the white man cannot understand. They will teach you to build fences, he says, we who hate fences. They will teach you to be yardmen, to make bows and arrows to sell as souvenirs. A few, like Shirttail Charley, Josie Billie, and Tiger Tiger, have gone. Some have already begun to dress like the white man, discarding the medicine dress for ten-gallon hats decorated with beaded bands, canvas shoes, leather belts with silver, and, like my son Tommy, the white man's trousers, which Sally Cypress refuses to wash.

Because a black box on sticks is taking his image in Miami, Tommy wears his hair cut and greased in the white man's way. Tommy explains that a man cranks this box like a woman making sofke. What comes out? I asked. Nothing comes out, he replies. Something goes in. Why do they want your image? I asked. It is like the stories you tell, Father, he explained, only the story has a life of its own. It will be seen. If it is a story, I said, then tell it to me. It is about a white man and woman and brown-skinned people in grass skirts who dance before a stone, he replies. How do you know how to do these things? I asked. The director tells us, he replies. His name is Griffith. Griffith hands us spears, then shouts to us through a horn. When we are too far away, he signals with colored flags. I have heard of no such white man in Miami, I said. He comes from California, Tommy replies, on the other side of Arkansas.

The agent tells me that if we move to the reservation where the government has already planted citrus trees, we will earn money to use in trade for chewing gum, beef, coffee, and canned fruit. We will no longer have to grind the coontie root, but can discard the mortar and pestle for store flour. The agent will give us seeds to start vegetables. A doctor will set our broken bones, lance and drain the pus from the swollen hand of Charlie Billie, and examine our night soil under a glass to see how many worms we have. Best, the agent promises, an Indian can hunt all year on reservation lands, unlike the white man, who must obtain a license.

The small face of the moon is that if we move to the reservation, my eldest son may never return, even when this moving story will be finished. He has already told me, speaking with the sparks of Jimmy Jumper, that he will never again be under the white man's thumb. He is thinking of the ranch where he and Bristol worked for the man whose untended cattle now hide in the scrub where cabbage palm and pine have returned to thicken his land like cornmeal.

Behind me is the high ground where the deer was killed and burned on the spot to bring about the cure of Bristol and Mary's ailing son. It was an ill-fated day. I remember hearing a fox howl while the sun was still up, and I knew that the child would die. Sally Cypress said that Bristol brought this bad luck upon himself when he dropped a piece of gopher meat and put it in his mouth. We tried to teach him that food fallen to the ground must not be picked up, that to do so is a discourtesy to a ghost, Willie Tiger, for example, or Billy Sunshine, who might be hungry, but he would not listen.

"I'm the one whose gut is rumbling," he said. "Not some haunt that you don't even know for sure is there."

It is hard to know when it began between them. As soon as Mary bled for the first time, her mother put her in her own chickee, where she ate neither salt nor deer meat for four days, then cautioned her to avoid bear tracks and the medicine bundle, now passed into the hands of Charlie Billie. Sally Cypress told her nothing else because Mary and Bristol had become like brother and sister.

At first the tribal council refused to let them marry. But when Mary became round with Bristol's child, the one who later died with swollen cheeks, we did not send the Negro youth away, nor did we think to end the life of the child, as had been done so many years ago with the half-white thing that Sally Cypress bore. We reasoned that Bristol too was forced into the swamp and, while not a red man, shared our heart.

After eighteen years, he was almost one of us. He spoke our language, understood many of our laws, knew how to hunt and fish and how to build a chickee, shared our black drink at the Green Corn festival, could hear a swarm of horseflies in time to fire the grass around

247

his cattle. Like Tiger Tiger, he could even smell a snake and armed with only a stick with a nail, pin his catch to the ground, grab it by its head, and stab it through the backbone.

When Emathla first brought him to our camp, he was like a tadpole flip-flopping in the mud, turning his head from our food, sleeping in the alley between our sleeping platforms so that he was always in the way. When the children played games, he would pit himself against the others, not understanding that the Seminole does not wish to dominate, as rivalry is the white man's sport.

He would awaken yelling in the night like a wounded spirit, then by day, sit waiting at the water's edge for weeks for word from his mother. When it finally came, he would burn the paper, scatter the ashes beneath his feet, and speak to no one.

Everything for him was a trial, even the storytelling time before we fall asleep. One warm, musk-scented night I related a familiar tale of the red, white, and black man, and of the three boxes that floated to earth, of the white man's box that contained pen and ink, and of the red man's box of tomahawks and traps. Before I could finish the legend, Bristol asked what the black man got.

"Hoes and buckets," I replied, and he became angry, demanding that I change the story. I could not. What untruth would I change it to? I then told of Coacoochee, who took up Osceola's fight until the white man took Coacoochee's daughter hostage and forced him on a trek to Arkansas, when Bristol once more broke the thread of recollection.

"He should have known that was going to happen," he said. "When are you Indians going to get smart?" And because he was so heated, I did not finish the part about how Coacoochee fled south with his people to the land called Mexico, which didn't matter since all the others under my chickee had completed the tale for themselves.

Three days before Bristol left our camp, the agent traveled up the widened waterway of the new canal by launch to tell us that he wanted to put our names on his rolls. Bristol warned against this. "Don't give him any," he whispered. "The white man is trying to collect you like beads on string." And since we cannot lie, it was Bristol who supplied the agent with the names of Indians long gone over the curve of the night, Bristol who gave false locations for our small, scattered bands, and Bristol who invented new names as fast as the agent could write them down.

Then the agent asked, "What's your own name, boy?"

Bristol looked him straight in the eye. We thought he was going to give him the name of another dead Indian. Instead he told the truth. "Bristol," he replied.

The new agent did not appear to have heard

of his name. Bristol waited for the man's memory to jar loose. When nothing happened, he became emboldened. "I'm black," he said.

"Yes," said the agent. "We know that many of you have a lick of the tar brush," and Bristol knew that it was safe to go home, that the white man had forgotten. Unlike those who went before him, this agent had no instructions to search among the Seminoles for a Negro fugitive.

In his actual leave-taking, Bristol was split like a cypress felled by lightning. One half wanted to remain with his wife and child, the other to return to his own people.

I knew that it was time for him to return. Sally Cypress did not agree.

"Who will read for us?" she asked, with Mary beside her, choking back her tears.

"The missionaries will do it," Bristol replied sadly, his child in his arms. "I told you it was time your people learned to read."

We consider the missionaries who try to destroy our beliefs as children who spill out the food in cooking pots. My wife snorted. "What about Mary? Emma? Can you desert your wife? Your child?"

Bristol replied as a man with only footprints whose feet have already gone. "I want to take them. You know that."

"Council says no," said Sally Cypress. "Not good for Mary. Worse for Emma. She is both black and Indian, and the white man hates both. She is a bird who must crawl on the ground."

We learn from Jack Tigertail that a white man has bought the land upon which we camp. This white man is not sending us off. Instead he wants us to stay and build a village, bring in more of our number, so that the white tourist can watch us at our work.

Sally Cypress is not for this thing. "We will be like animals in a cage for a white man to poke a stick at any time he likes," she argues. "It is not our way."

"A starving people cannot have ways of any kind," I reply, "just pains in their bellies. Only people who are fed can have their ways."

"If Bristol were here," she says, "he would say no."

"Bristol is not a member of the tribal council. Neither is he a Tustenugge. At this moment he is at home with his own people."

"He is my son," she says.

This tries my patience, worn thin by attempting to measure such paths as taking our camp to the reservation, where we answer to the agent, or to the depths of the drought-stricken Pahahokee, where we would walk where one has never walked before. Or the third path, to become an exhibit for six dollars a week salary, a food allowance, yard goods, and a doctor. My wife's dream-talk jumbles these thoughts.

"You have two sons," I reply, "and he is neither. He is no longer married to our daughter. So how can he be your son?"

Sally Cypress replies as if I have been lost in the brush. "Tommy and Josie are number two and three. Bristol is my first. The baby left in the tree to die."

This makes no sense, yet sense is not always to be sought. "What tells you this?" I ask.

"When he first shared our chickee, he used to weep in the dark. He tried to hide his night cries in his arm, but I heard it through his flesh and bone. Except for its depth, it was the same cry as the baby in the tree. A mother can never forget the lament of her firstborn child."

Chapter Twelve

Caroline stood beneath the entrance arch of Villa Serena, where scarlet bougainvillea vines crossed over her head. Wearing a shawl against the bite in the January air, she viewed the oval patio as if she were one of the three hundred expected guests, trying to judge it as if for the first time, checking to see if anything was amiss. She needed to remind a groundskeeper to pick up a yellowed frond from beneath the row of stately royal palms, but the poinsettias on the second-story windowsills were draped gracefully over the ledge, and the large tubs at the edge of the wood behind her were filled with enough nasturtiums, roses, sweet alyssum, geraniums, foxgloves, and petunias to create what Mrs. Bryan called a profusion.

Caroline at forty-five was once more in service. Thickened through the middle, with iron gray strands threaded through her hair, she walked with quiet dignity, holding her head as high as when she was a girl and carried baskets on her head. As housekeeper, she was allowed to wear her own clothes as long as they were tasteful and covered discreetly with an apron. In the hierarchy of the household she ranked above the groundskeepers, the maids, and the cook, but below the butler, who never tired of telling her that the silver-tongued man for whom she now worked was one of the greatest orators the world had ever known. She learned on the first day of her employment that William Jennings Bryan had been three times nominated for the presidency of the United States, that he had been secretary of state under Woodrow Wilson until just a few months back when he resigned in protest of President Wilson's determination to enter the war. Caroline was not sure what a secretary of state did, just that it was mightily important and guessed that he took dictation as did Mr. Bryan's own secretary, Van Dusen, whose glasses slipped off his nose and whose typewriter, resounding against the glass of the morning room, made an awful clatter.

Mr. Bryan's fame meant little to her in any case. She knew the silver-tongued orator as a stout, kindly old man who dropped frequently to his knees in prayer and expected everyone around him to do the same. He carried himself like a soldier, liked to chop wood, and had recently been diagnosed with sugar in his blood.

Caroline had never trusted the practice of funneling income into new property that would in turn provide additional revenue that would also be refunneled. Now with Galilee addlepated, Isaac too feeble to be of much help, and two younger sons to worry about, Caroline needed sure money, cash in hand.

Unwilling on principle to work for Julia Tuttle's son Harry, who had turned his mother's home into a gambling casino, Caroline had been receptive when word came of a couple named Bryan who were seeking a housekeeper with maturity and experience and who did not object when she refused to live in.

The ever-present din of chirping sparrows was broken by the sounds of buggies and automobiles clattering and sputtering over the rocky hammock lane. Satisfied that the tea service, small cakes, sandwiches made with cucumbers sliced as thin as paper, and fruit punch in a silver bowl that the butler said had once belonged to Thomas Jefferson were laid out on cloths as white as sugar, Caroline smoothed her crinkled graying hair into the bun at the nape of her neck and came to stand behind Mrs. Bryan's wheelchair.

Among the first guests to toss down his hitching weight and line from his buggy was dry-goods merchant Roddey Burdine, wearing a diamond stick pin that glinted in the sunlight. Burdine, who had recently built a five-story establishment that many believed would put Miami on a mercantile map, greeted Mrs. Bryan, remarking on Woodrow Wilson's shortsightedness in accepting Bryan's resignation.

"It is not shortsightedness, Mr. Burdine," replied his hostess with an eye to the guests behind him. "The principal difference between President Wilson and my husband is that the president ranked forty-first in a class of one hundred twenty-two, while in his class Mr. Bryan was first." She extended a cordial hand past Burdine toward Dr. James Jackson and his wife, Mary, indicating to Burdine that it was time to move on.

Dr. Jackson had operated on Isaac ten years before on Caroline's kitchen table, but never seemed to remember either Caroline or the event. Single-purposed, his focus was on the new hospital fund drive and on Mrs. Bryan's feet, which he offered to examine in answer to her question of whether she was suffering from arthritis or rheumatism.

Jack Coombs arrived in Zalman Levy's

Model T with boxes of party favors, which he gave to a waiting butler, lapel pins made of baby alligators, each attached to a little chain.

Caroline thought that Jack looked like his mother, the same straw-colored hair, the same pale blue eyes, only his face was not as pinched with spite as Eulalie's had been. She remembered how Bristol had cried when the teacher sent home a note that he couldn't go to school anymore with Jack or any other white child.

"She's coming home," he said. "My sister, Maude, and her husband."

"I suppose you'll be fixing up the house. Last time I saw it, it looked like it could use some fixing. The front porch is hanging to the side. All your mother's flowers overgrown. Not that it's any of my business."

"They won't be staying with me. They're taking rooms at the Royal Palm Hotel." He smiled. "Maudie's come up in the world."

"Who does your shirts?"

"I guess I do."

"You need to put bluing in the wash water. Or send them out. I know some good women could use the money. For the time being" — she stepped before him and reached up to his collar — "try to tuck your shirt collar under your jacket before you say hello to Mrs. Bryan. It's the first thing she's gonna notice about you." His breath smelled of bourbon and mint. "Maybe not the first. You look pasty. Make sure you get plenty to eat. Cucumber sandwiches

256

and such. It's not what I'd fix, but it'll do."

The tentative sprinkling quickly grew to a sea of visitors in boas and long strands of pearls, in black silk hats and stiff-brimmed straws, spilling over the grounds. The crowd was larger than usual because of the war in Europe, which put not only the French Riviera off limits to guests like William Vanderbilt and Andrew Carnegie, but the British colony of the Bahamas as well.

A handful of celebrities acted as magnets. Zane Grey, who wrote novels about the West, stood in a rumpled suit and string tie complaining to native Miamians that there was no alcohol in the punch. Bushy-whiskered portrait painter John Singer Sargent, who was reported to be designing interiors at James Deering's Viscaya, held court beside a metal lion. A pudgy man in a floppy felt hat named Carl Fisher, said to be transforming the mangrove swamps of Ocean Beach into a posh resort, asked Sargent if the stories of the wild parties at Viscaya were true. His particular interest, which he expressed with a vigorous chewing of his cigar, was in a certain mirrored room on the top floor.

Mr. Bryan, with his huge iron jaw, his bald head with its fringe of hair, galvanized the reception when he walked briskly into the throng. He went about greeting each one of his guests, speaking to this one of his opposition to compulsory military service, to that one of nationalizing the railroads.

To white-bearded Andrew Carnegie he spoke of the dire consequences of breaking diplomatic ties with Germany. Carnegie stood with his hands folded behind his back and declared that if Germany wished to negotiate, it was America's duty on behalf of the allies to demand reparations.

"These are terms that Germany will never accept," said Bryan.

Carnegie lifted a glass of punch from a passing tray. "If that is the case, then we are on a path that will lead us straight to war."

Caroline left Mrs. Bryan's side to find out why the cucumber sandwiches had not been replenished, overhearing as she ducked through the crowd a debate about women's suffrage, and a complaint about a city charter that prohibited one's Negro chauffeur from driving within the city limits.

A plane swooped past, one of the twenty from the naval air station, drumming Caroline's ears as if with machine-gun fire. Planes were daily diving into the bay. She wondered if this plane too would drown its pilot, and its wreckage wind up on a junk heap of wrecked planes behind the barricade on Dinner Key.

She thought of Isaac Jr., who would, at eighteen, be eligible for a draft, and of James, who was not far behind. She noticed that no one in the huge gathering mentioned that the price of bread had risen from five cents to six cents a loaf or that Ocean Beach, which Mr. Fisher and Mr. Collins were calling Miami Beach, had become off limits to her sons. She thought of Bristol, who never got to go there at all.

It was late evening before Caroline left for home. She knew what she would find when she got there. James would be where he wasn't supposed to be, in the front room tinkering with his bicycle, seventy-five-year-old Galilee would be in the moonlit backyard, messing with his still, with Isaac Jr. right behind him, and Isaac would be waiting on the front porch, sitting silently as he had ever since the beating, with his arms draped on the metal frame of the glider.

When Isaac had been bludgeoned in the temple with a hammer twelve years before because he refused to tell two white men where Bristol was hiding, Dr. Jackson had come to the house at the request of Julia Tuttle's son. The doctor ordered a bucket of water, a basin, a cake of soap, and as many clean rags as Caroline could gather, then steeped the rags in a mercury solution, which she squeezed as dry as possible. He operated on the kitchen table, cutting away Isaac's hair, picking out pieces of crushed bone. Tissue like walnuts protruded from the wound. That's his brain, Dr. Jackson had told her as he enlarged the wound with a scalpel, removed the loose splinters, then cut away the projecting brain. Only a tablespoon in all, he said as he inserted a small drain and closed the wound with silk sutures. He won't miss it.

Three days later, Isaac had no fever, felt no pain. With Caroline's help, he could even walk. But he could not speak a word. The silence was terrible. They used to talk by the hour, long into the night, of the boys at home, of Bristol in the swamp, of the lots they were buying, the lots they were building on, the rent they were charging, the deadbeats who weren't paying, the houses needing repair. Now when Caroline turned off the light, there was only silence from the pillow beside her and Isaac's warm, mint-flavored breath on her face.

She had prayed in church, jumping with the others in praise of Jesus while calling for Him to heal her man, to give him back his voice. She prayed in her front room before the framed picture of the Last Supper, burning frankincense that she bought from the conjure man for fifty cents. Still Isaac did not regain his speech. When the conjure man came to the house, placed his fee on Galilee's Bible, then massaged Isaac's tongue, mentioning the names of biblical prophets as he rubbed, Isaac only gagged.

In desperation, Caroline had sought the advice of Aunt Memory, an elderly neighbor who walked with a sprinkling can to wash away witch tracks. Aunt Memory worked in Isaac's behalf with candles and silk. She made him open his shirt at the neck, then told him to face east, then west, then north, and as he made the final turn toward south, she pinched out a white candle and lit a larger black one. When the white candle smoldered, the old woman picked up a small basin filled with yellow liquid, in the center of which were standing a blue, green, and red candle. She lit the candles, took a strip of red silk, dipped it into the liquid, passed the moistened silk over the light of the candles, and anointed Isaac's lips and throat, then the scarred site of the old injury, where she formed the sign of the cross.

Isaac remained mute.

Fish in orange sauce simmered on the stove as Caroline sat on a kitchen chair, letting her weight sink into the wood while Isaac rubbed her neck and shoulders.

"Where's Isaac Jr.?" she asked.

Isaac nodded his head toward the backyard. The month before, the boy had been arrested for vagrancy when he stopped at the edge of Royal Palm Park to listen to a band concert. They marched him down Flagler Street to the Dade County Jail. "They jeered me, Mama," he said. "The whites jeered at me when they took me away." Mr. Bryan had gotten him out.

"College can't come soon enough," she said while James, wearing greasy knickers and sweater, poked his head in the doorway and yanked up his knee socks.

"Galilee and Ike set cornmeal bran on fire to smoke out the stump barrel. Soon as the fire's out, they're going to polish up the copper."

"That old man and his smelly still. One of these days I'm going to tear it down with my own two hands."

"You can't do that, Momma," said James. "It's all Galilee has. Besides the Bible, it's his favorite thing in this world."

"Speaking of favorite things, what's that bicycle doing in the front room? Take it outside where it belongs. Whole place is full of grease. Grease all over everything, including your clothes."

The kitchen door creaked open. Isaac Jr. held it open for Galilee, who hitched in slowly and wiped his feet on the sisal mat. "Seven gallons of pure corn," said Galilee. "Two hundred proof. Have to cut it before we can sell it." He laid a hand on Isaac Jr.'s arm for balance. "Be sure when you add the water, you get a good steady bead in the proof vial. Give it three good thumps in the palm of your hand. If the bead holds, you know you can ship it all the way to Georgia."

"Isaac Jr. is not shipping anything anywhere," said Caroline. "He's got his mind on college."

"Didn't see you, Caroline," said Galilee while Isaac Jr. went to kiss his mother on the cheek. "Rest yourself. We'll take care of things. Tell us about the party. Who all was there? What did they talk about? We going to war?"

"Who cares what they talk about?" said James, helping his father ladle out the fish.

Caroline wanted to forget the long day, the

hundreds of guests, and the punch that someone had spilled on the peach settee. Neither did she want to talk about the war in Europe or the likelihood of a draft. There was time to discuss such things when and if war came. Instead she scolded Isaac Jr. about table manners that would have to improve before he went to college.

"Genteel folks don't use bread to shovel peas on their forks. Use your knife and fork together, like I showed you."

"Some man at the back door, Mama," said James.

"White or black?"

"Can't tell. I've never seen him before. He's strange-looking. Got himself a scarf wrapped around his head."

Caroline's hand went to her throat. When she spoke, her voice was low, almost a whisper. "How old is he?"

"He's grown."

The man with his hand on the screen door was handsome in a scruffy sort of way. His curly hair was the color of the bronze urns on the Bryans' mantel. It was the tilt of his head, the way his eyes met hers and would not let go, that flashed the light of recognition and made her heart lurch in her chest. The boy had crystallized into a man the way syrup hardens into rock crystal. He stepped inside the house tentatively, adjusting to the light, to the people at the kitchen table. Caroline stood and the shawl that had been around her shoulders fell to the floor. She clasped her hands high over her head, began stamping her feet, slapping at him as if to chase him away. When he put his arms around her, she sank her face onto his chest and moaned, "My baby's home."

Chairs scraped away from the table as Isaac moved to clap Bristol around the shoulders and Galilee drew himself upright to shout in a thready, rasping voice, "Praise Jesus."

Caroline turned to James and Isaac Jr., who stood not knowing what to do. "This is your brother, Bristol," she said. Then she straightened Isaac Jr.'s shoulders. "This is Isaac Jr. I was carrying him when Galilee took you away. And this is James. He's the baby."

Isaac Jr. and James stepped forward awkwardly to shake hands. James looked up at the stranger who was supposed to be his brother. "You don't look like a colored man. You look more like an Indian except you have blonde hair. Did you for sure kill a white man?"

"Hush up!" said Caroline. "You make me ashamed! Since when did you become my most foolish child? Your brother is bone tired. He's here in my kitchen safe and sound, all of that is over and done with. You say those kinds of things, you rip open a wound that's trying to close itself up. Who ever did that to you?"

Bristol strode to Galilee, who stood apart, who had been his only contact for almost eighteen years because no one had thought it necessary to watch a dotty old man who often lost his way. The last time he had seen Galilee was five years before, when Miami Doctor found his mother's boarder dehydrated and dazed, poling a canoe through the sawgrass. Galilee said he carried a note from Caroline, but he had lost it somehow in his two days of drifting.

Bristol embraced him. "How you been, Galilee?"

"I been fine."

"You know who I am?"

" 'Course I know you. You the honey man. You the light."

The next weeks were touchy. Bristol settled the problem of where to sleep by bunking with Galilee in the corner of the kitchen. There were improvements that Bristol had heard about but had never seen, electric lights to be switched on, piped-in water to be shut off, a telephone to ring up, a streetcar with a sign that instructed coloreds to ride in the rear, automobiles to stay clear of, a Ku Klux Klan not to rile up. Then there was Isaac, mute because of him, and halfbrothers who were angry because it was to protect Bristol that their father had gotten so badly injured in the first place. Bristol heard them whisper that his real father was not even a black man but some white who wrecked ships on the reef, then stole the cargo. To Isaac Jr. and James, Bristol was less a brother than an oddity, less a hero than a fool.

If they spoke to him at all, it was to ask questions about the Indians. He told them little other than what he wore and what he ate. Only to Caroline did he reveal, while she was dressing for church, that he had a wife and child.

"What are you saying, Bristol?" she asked, slipping on a pair of white cotton gloves. "Are you saying that I have a grandchild?"

"That's how I hear it works. My child is your grandchild."

She turned with eyes bright and shining. "Don't try to put me off with that nasty tone. I want to see her. I want to see my grand-baby. What's her name?"

"Emma. You can't see her, Mama."

"Why not?"

"Because it's gonna tear me up all over again. You know what it would mean to see them and walk away a second time? I can't do it. You understand?"

"No, I don't understand. Why isn't your child with you? Why isn't her momma with you?"

"The tribe wouldn't let them come. They have their way. It's not ours."

"I'm not interested in ways. I want to see my grandbaby. I want to meet my daughter-in-law."

"I been gone almost a month. She may even be remarried."

"Might be she's remarried, but the child's

not. Where are they?"

"I don't know, Mama. They could be anywhere."

When Caroline decided that Bristol had spent enough time staring up at the cracks in the ceiling, helping himself to everything in the pantry, taking daily baths in the big tin tub in the kitchen, enough shaves, enough idle, hands-in-pockets walks that led nowhere, enough listening to his brothers' snipes, she sent him out to find work. There were two possibilities. The first was with Lulu Ryder's son, Percy, filling chuck holes with rock for the city street-repair crew, but that meant checking in with the sheriff. The second seemed more likely. Laborers at Viscaya, a palatial villa being built on one hundred bayfront acres, were earning $1.50 a day, and no one was checking anything other than the breadth of their backs. Bristol went to try to join the work force of one thousand other Miamians, all engaged, under the direction of scores of engineers, stone cutters from Italy, and gardeners from Scotland in creating the baroque mansion's terraces, hidden gardens, grottos, balustrades, canals, courtyards, pavilions, cascading waterfalls, patios, lakes, fountains, pathways, walls, loggias, even its vegetable farm, slat houses, glass houses, and dairy where cows ate from marble troughs and were brushed and combed between milk glass partitions two inches thick.

The household staff numbered thirty-two.

There were two French chefs, four butlers, four housemen whose job it was to set fifty-nine clocks, and six housemaids who wore blue-and-white-striped cotton in the morning and black silk with white aprons trimmed with lace in the afternoon.

Bristol was hoping to be appointed to the six-man crew who worked the annual houses, cutting blossoms to place in the cold room for the scores of daily fresh arrangements. The foreman said that if he showed up regularly, sober, and did his work, there was a chance he could even work the cold room, where it was clean, sweet-smelling, mosquito-free, and cool.

Working the grounds, for the most part, was also solitary work, a way for Bristol to reconcile his present with his past, to try to come to grips with eighteen years lost to this life and gained by the other, to forget sorrowful images of a crying wife and daughter waving from the banks of a canal.

He was cleaning out the lily pond in the center of the forecourt, scraping algae into a bucket, when he thought he recognized the woman strolling past the cascading, water-chain fountains of the piazza. Her hair was blonder than when she had been a child. Now a pale, silvery shade, almost the color of the moon, she wore it coiled in a topknot with soft curls trailing over her ears. She looked like him, a younger, more feminine mirror image, except that his was darker, as if the mercury had been eaten away by mildew, and hers, whitened by powder, like the glass.

She was dressed in a silken gown with a flimsy overdrape that fluttered above her ankles like wisps of blue smoke. Everything about her told him that she was rich — from the collar of pearls at her throat almost as wide as the beads Sally Cypress wore to her pointed slippers held in place by ribbon laces. She glanced once at Bristol the way she might have glanced at a lavabo, a trellis, a marble statue on one of the ancient columns. She gave no sign of recognition, no narrowed brow that showed that she knew him to have once been the boy who brought her hair ribbons and gloves and sometimes sugar cookies from his mother.

The man she was with was older, dapper, with a thin, shadow mustache, a signet ring, a panama hat, and a handkerchief in the breast pocket of his blue flannel blazer. From the way that he looked straight ahead, he was probably her husband. When he caught Bristol staring, he frowned. Bristol bent to his task, his face expressionless, even though Jack Coombs followed close behind.

"It's perfectly all right, Jackie," she said, "I told him about you. And he wants to meet you. He hopes you will play his harpsichord."

Jack checked the creases on his narrow trousers. "I don't know anything about a harpsichord, Maudie. I play the piano. That's all."

"Don't sell yourself short. You're also very handsome. Especially now that I brought you some decent clothes to wear." She smoothed the satin collar of his white dinner jacket. "He likes attractive people. He likes perfection. Fix your bow tie. And slick back your hair. Pompadours are not supposed to wisp on your forehead. Lillian Gish has been invited. We met her in London. She's lovely if she doesn't speak. And try not to act like a dumb cracker. Just remember that if you get into conversation about the house, all this is sixteenth-century Italian Renaissance."

Jack fell back to stop at the lily pond. He came to stand beside Bristol's shovel. "I think I know you. Bristol?"

"Hello, Jack."

"I'm glad to see you back. How are you doing?"

"Can't complain."

"How long have you been back?"

"A while."

"Why didn't you come by?"

"I've been busy."

Maude tapped an impatient foot. "Jack, we're waiting."

Jack waved his sister over. "It's Bristol, Maudie. You remember Bristol."

She walked back in annoyance and took her brother's arm. "Of course I remember Bristol.

270

Hey there, Bristol. Come along, Jack. We're late."

Bristol wiped his forehead with the back of his arm, recalling the time long ago when he had asked Caroline if Maude was his sister. "My mother sends her best regards," he said. "You remember my mother, don't you?"

"I certainly do remember Caroline. You'll just have to tell her that I send my very best regards right back. You'll do that, won't you?"

"Yes, ma'am," Bristol replied, picking up the algae-filled bucket and stepping out of the pond. "I surely will. She'll be glad to know someone is keeping your clothes clean." He watched them leave, swallowing the bitter resentment at the thought that whites had it all, that they would always have it all, even peckerwoods like the Coombs, while the best he could hope for was a job snipping flowers in a cold room.

With her husband and brother on either side, Maude climbed the steps to the entrance loggia, where blue and yellow canvas bunting fluttered in the breeze. "I hear he went to prison for starting a riot."

A butler opened an elaborate wrought iron portal, admitting them into a loggia, the marble floor of which was set in a baroque design of blocks of gray onyx, white carrara, and rust-colored Siena marble from Tuscany that seemed to dance.

"That's not what happened," said Jack. "Bris-

271

tol tried to keep someone from hurting his mother. He never went to prison."

"Well, that's what I heard."

"You were there, Maudie. Don't you remember the soldiers come tearing through the village, all that shouting and shooting at coconuts? Don't you remember Mama bringing us in the house and bolting the door?"

Maude opened her compact and patted her nose with a powder puff beside an ancient Roman tub over which stood a statue of Bacchus, while a maid in black silk took her ostrich-plumed wrap.

"I don't remember anything about it except the smell from Mama's guava shack."

The butler led them through marbled and tapestried foyers embellished with crystal and gold leaf chandeliers, lacquered wall panels, Aubusson rugs, jade trees, marble busts, wooden doors overlaid with bronze cherubim, Venetian sofas, Louis chairs, and moldings, mantels and lintels taken from Italian palazzos, past a center courtyard, to a marbled terrace that overlooked the bay. "Mr. Deering had the whole Ziegfeld Follies here last week," she said. "He gave a stag party. Henry can tell you all about it."

Henry Watson stroked his mustache. "Actually, I didn't go," he said, "but I know some fellows who did. They had a capital time. Every single one of them, if you take my meaning."

"And Deering?"

Maude laughed. "Heavens, no." She dropped

her voice. "He's such a prissy, dyspeptic little man. Actually, he goes to bed early. But he likes to see his guests having a good time. Last month we saw *The Birth of a Nation* in the casino. Have you seen it Jackie? The D. W. Griffith moving picture. It's all about Negro carpetbaggers and the noble knighthood of the Klan, avenging crusaders, actually, sweeping across moonlit roads."

"Avenging hooligans is more like it," said Henry. "Parading down Flagler Street in table-cloths is bad enough. They need to be dissuaded from hanging effigies in front of your court-house. It casts the community in a silly light."

"The Klan isn't silly," said Maude. "As for the moving picture, it's high time someone showed the Confederate side of things."

"It would be more useful, Maude," said her husband, "if your perspective was less paro-chial." He offered his wife the crook of his arm. "Why didn't you wear your diamond ear-rings? When I buy you things, I mean for you to wear them."

"You can't wear diamonds with pearls."

Henry Watson spoke with the assurance of the new American aristocracy, not of the social register, but a well-traveled man of affairs, a polished beau monde at home in London and Paris as well as Des Moines, who, in his case, had made a fortune in tin. "You're my wife, Maude. It's you who dictate fashion. Not the other way around."

273

He led them toward their host, a slight, middle-aged man in white linen whose own family fortune had been made in farm machinery. The man in white linen stood beside a younger, taller man wearing a dove gray suit and vest and a peach tie. The dark eyebrows and mustache of the man in the peach tie was in contrast to his graying hair. To Maude's surprise, he did not look first at her, as most men did, but at Jack.

Maude tapped a cigarette against a silver case, rankling over the encounter in the forecourt. Bristol had looked at her as if she were no more than the dirt he was cleaning up in the lily pond.

"I dropped my compact," she said.

"I'll get it," offered Jack.

"No, don't bother. I remember the exact place. It's hard to explain to someone else."

Before Henry could stop her, she ran back past bronze cherubim and Venetian sofas, through the iron portal into the forecourt. He was nowhere in sight. Maude shielded her eyes against the afternoon sun and walked quickly through the maze of the gardens, her heels catching in the stone as she searched for his wagon. She found it outside a grotto, then stepped into the cool dampness of the niche where a waterfall trickled down limestone ledges. He was cleaning algae from a stone bench.

"What did you mean when you said that

Caroline would be glad to see that my clothes were cleaned?"

"Just that she'd be pleased to know that someone's taking care of you."

"I think you meant something nastier than that."

He turned an expressionless face. "My mama used to worry a lot about you when you were a little kid."

"Why?"

"I don't think she thought your mother was treating you right."

"It's certainly no concern of yours."

"Don't be too sure."

She stepped closer, her eyes glittering in the shadowed grotto. "I don't like your uppity attitude. You better explain yourself."

When he bent to his task, blocking her from his line of sight, she crouched beside him, smelling his sweat, the rich, sweet odor of the dirt that clung to his hands, then brushed her breasts against his arm. "What's the matter, Bristol? Are you afraid of me because I'm white?"

He stood and pulled her up beside him. "It has nothing to do with your color or anything else."

"I don't believe you."

"Look, you better be getting back. They'll be wondering what happened to you. If anyone finds you in here with me, it could cost me my job."

"You should have thought of that before you

said what you did."

He sighed and wiped the back of his neck with a checkered cloth. "All right. What I said has to do with your real father. His name was Thomas Sands. He was my father too. I guess that makes us brother and sister."

Maude stepped out of the grotto into the blinding sunlight. "You vile thing! I'll have you fired!"

"It won't change things."

"If I had a gun I would shoot you."

"That won't change things either. I'll still be your brother. As much a brother to you as Jack."

She narrowed her eyes, balled her hands into fists. "Have you been talking about me? You have, haven't you? Who have you been spreading these evil lies to?"

"No one. I'm not proud to claim you for a sister."

"Liar! You're blackmailing me is what you're doing. You're a liar and a blackmailer!"

Bristol ducked his head beneath the arch of the stoney alcove. "You got it backward. A blackmailer wants something in exchange for his silence. I'd be glad to pay you for keeping quiet."

She flew at him in a rage, flailing at him with her fists. "I will kill you for sure!"

He grabbed her wrists, held them away from his body. "If you insist on getting this close, you're gonna begin to smell like me as well as look like me."

She spoke through clenched teeth, her voice a menacing growl. "Let go, nigger. Let go or I'll begin to holler, and you know what that means."

He dropped her hands, picked up his implements, and placed them in his wagon. "You keep following after me the way you do, I'll get the idea that you're one of these white women who want to make lynching worth my while."

Caroline sat on an upended barrel in the stern of a fishing boat on its way up the Miami River. She carried a package tied in string. Beside her Jack Coombs brushed away a vine that trailed from an overhanging branch, while he kept his other hand on the handles of Mrs. Bryan's wheelchair. It was Jack who had thought up the idea for the excursion and the solution to Caroline's dilemma. Although Negroes by themselves were not allowed admittance into Osceola Gardens, Negro attendants were.

They docked at a place of lush, tropical foliage, with stately royal palms lining a narrow pathway. On either side were cages of monkeys and alligators, a fruit-drink stand, a curio shop filled with bamboo peace pipes, palmetto fiber dolls, miniature cypress canoes, beadwork, and baby alligators, and a silent, sober village of Miccosukee Seminoles. A white man in knee-high boots took their money at the entrance.

While ragged children zigzagged barefoot through apple peels and orange rinds and the offal of a dozen chickens, Seminole boys in long shirts wrestled alligators behind a wooden corral. Most of the Indians remained in their chickees staring silently at the gawking spectators, who talked loudly about the dirty pots and the funny clothes. When a tourist grabbed the sleeve of a Seminole woman who was ladling sofke, then turned to a friend and shouted, "Hey, Bill, want a squaw?" Jack recognized the woman as Sally Cypress.

He led the wheelchair toward Miami Doctor's chickee, where Miami Doctor sat on a platform stuffing an alligator hide with sawdust, ready to run a wire through it to make a lamp. Mrs. Bryan indicated that she preferred to see the cooking chickee, and Jack wheeled her away, leaving Caroline to stand alone.

"I'm Bristol's mother," Caroline said as she reached into the pocket of her apron to bring out an envelope stuffed with money.

Sally Cypress climbed onto the platform beside her husband to stare at Caroline with baleful eyes. "We don't need the money," Miami Doctor said. "We okay now."

"Take it. I owe you my son's life."

Sally Cypress inserted the wire into the lamp. "Buy lamp. Cost twenty dollar."

"I won't feel right until I pay you back for what you've done. It's a whole lot more money than what you'd get for a lamp."

"Buy two lamps," Sally Cypress said.

"Is this all your family?" Caroline asked.

Miami Doctor put up a hand to silence his wife, then told Caroline that his first son, Tommy, was making pictures in Hollywood, that his second son, Josie, was wrestling alligators with Howard Osceola in the pit behind her. Miami Doctor didn't like either situation. "It's against our custom," he said.

Caroline looked over her shoulder as Josie Doctor flipped an alligator on its back and stroked it to sleep while the proprietor in riding boots announced to the audience, "The alligator wrestler doesn't receive any pay from the village for putting on this exhibition. The only money he gets is what you throw into the pool. Now see if you can wake this alligator up."

She turned back as the crowd pitched coins into the pit and asked, as if it were of little consequence, where Mary was. Miami Doctor pointed her out, seated on a platform before a hand-cranked sewing machine in the next chickee, her hair piled in a topknot, a bottle of soda pop at her side, making dolls dressed like her, in skirts of patchwork edged in rickrack.

Caroline ducked beneath the roof of the chickee. A palmetto bug sawed its elegant front legs inches from her face. "You must be my son's wife," she said. Mary looked up but did not speak.

"They not married no more," shouted Sally Cypress.

Caroline ignored Mary's mother and told a lie. "Bristol wanted to come but he couldn't," she said. "He's at work."

Mary picked up the soda pop. "How is he?"

"He's like a fish out of water."

Caroline was about to offer her the envelope of money when the man in riding boots appeared. Mary put down her soda bottle and slid a length of fabric under the needle of the sewing machine while the proprietor told Caroline that she had to move on. The Indians that she was monopolizing, he said, were on exhibit. Other people paid good money to see them, and she was taking up their time. Besides, her mistress was on the other side of the camp, and that was where she belonged. The sewing machine began to whir from the furious spin of Mary's hand as Jack came sprinting through the dusty alleys between the huts. "Is there a problem here?" he asked.

The proprietor hooked his thumbs into his belt. "Your nigger has got to stick by your side. We can't have her wandering about as she pleases."

Jack offered to pay a second admission for Caroline if she could be permitted to stay awhile longer. "We'll be back in no time," he promised. "As soon as Mrs. William Jennings Bryan is finished with her papaya juice."

"Is that who that old lady is?" asked the proprietor.

"Ask her."

"No need. She probably wants her privacy. We get famous people here all the time. The other day we had William K. Vanderbilt himself. Cheap sonofabitch. Didn't spend a nickel except for admission tickets. Liked the monkeys if you know what I mean." He winked, then strode back toward the alligator pit.

Sally Cypress stood before Jack and lifted his pants leg to inspect the old snake bite scar. "You want sewing machine back?"

"No, Sally Cypress," he said. "My mother meant for you to have it."

"Your mother was good woman. Friend." She pointed at a faded silk rose woven into the patchwork of her skirt. "Not like some whose foolish children follow in their foolish footsteps."

A little girl poked her head around a cypress pole. Her hair was not jet black as that of the other children, but a hennaed brown that glinted red in the sun. Her nose was soft and rounded, like Bristol's.

Caroline narrowed her eyes. "Is that the child?" she asked.

"Her name Emma," conceded Sally Cypress.

Caroline knelt on the ground. "Come here to me, sweet thing. I won't hurt you. I'm your grandma."

"She doesn't speak English," said Mary.

"Then tell her what I said."

"She wouldn't understand," said Mary. "She knows only one grandmother."

"Can I hold her?"

"She no want," said Sally Cypress. "She get frighten."

Miami Doctor spoke to Sally Cypress in the Miccosukee dialect, then picked up the child and set her in Caroline's arms.

Emma was silent, spare, without the solid feel of Bristol as a baby, yet there was something familiar, a scent, an aroma that reminded Caroline of her own. "Aren't you the prettiest child?" she crooned. "Isn't my baby the prettiest little girl in the world? Grandma brought you a present." She put the package tied with string in the child's arms.

When Jack returned with Mrs. Bryan, Caroline set the child on the ground. "They're adorable when they're little," said Mrs. Bryan. To Jack she said, "I don't know why you brought us here, Jack. It's all rather depressing. Exploitive, really. Mr. Bryan and I are accustomed to visiting Indian villages in the West, and none of them are part of a tourist attraction owned by whites. I don't like it at all. It's not natural. How much do you suppose they make out of these lamps?"

"I guess they make a fair share," said Jack.

"What do you call a fair share?" asked Mrs. Bryan, while Caroline craned her neck, trying to find her little granddaughter in the tangled cluster of Seminoles and whites, trying to see if someone had helped her open the package and if she was holding the baby doll.

On the boat ride back, Caroline knew that Obeahman had followed her, not only across the sea but in time had stretched his long, bony hand to her grandchild, had seen to it that she witnessed the child's desperate condition, this little girl who was stem to her branch, whose circumstance she was unable to do anything about.

Chapter Thirteen

Miami became a bedlam of swirling dust, drills, hammers, screeching motor horns and winches, and the staccato clamor of a thousand riveters. Quaint bayfront docks and fish shanties were demolished as dredges began pumping land from the bay to widen the boulevard. Demand for downtown property sent prices sky-high while toppling pioneer buildings in favor of modern structures that rose in their places. Merchants who could, updated their stores to the newest rage, the arcade. Every shop seemed to be combined with a real estate office, and in every doorway clusters of paper-waving, handshaking, back-slapping, cigar-offering hucksters proclaimed unsurpassed opportunities to make a fortune. They studied diagrams of desirable subdivisions at street corner cafés and made their deals over sarsaparillas.

The fever extended to the railroad station, where an immense shouting, sweating, coatless crowd wearing cotton knee breeches and purple in the face with the heat and excitement waited for the car loads of gullible northerners, then swarmed around the incoming railroad carriages like a hive of angry bees.

The building boom was accelerated by an equally dizzying pace of land sales, a buying frenzy that left the nation's bankers breathless, with greedy speculators not caring that the lot they bought might be under water since it would be sold by tomorrow anyway. The city issued sixty real estate broker licenses a day. Developers slashed roads through palmetto thickets, put up quickie real estate offices, and lured buyers by auctions, raffles, ukelele music, and strawberry shortcake. Epidemic land speculation, buoyed by the availability of window screens, yellow fever vaccine, a national lust for Florida land, and the automobile, which made it easy to get there, produced an orgy of town building, hucksterism, financiers, construction, and pitchmen, including William Jennings Bryan, who for a hundred thousand dollars a year pitched lots for Coral Gables developer George Merrick from the back of a streetcar.

Salesmen called "Binder boys" worked the streets and storefronts, finding property that they could buy for a minimal down payment, usually ten percent, which they immediately sold for an immense profit. Binders were as good as money. They began by swapping binders among themselves in the crowds that overflowed into Flagler Street. Similar to the margin speculation of Wall Street, it was commonplace for property to change hands two or three times in a day, and many local residents joined in the action, buying and selling paper, sometimes with seven or eight mortgages clinging to it like ticks on a cow, that had value only so long as someone kept buying.

Boom fever was not restricted to the coatless. Everyone was caught up in it, including Henry Watson, one of a handful of financiers who bankrolled the developers. If he could not underwrite a project himself, or interest his friends in doing so, he knew a bank that could. Well positioned, well connected, and well invested, Watson bore the confidence, the look of superior amusement forged at prep school at St. Mark's and Harvard's Porcellian Club, displayed in correct furnishings and cherished equipage and in an art collection that included a painting of a baseball game by Thomas Eakins. If his wife Maude's beginnings were ordinary and tinged with scandal, Watson's fortune and impeccable affiliations, which guaranteed memberships in Boston's Somerset Club, New York's Knickerbocker Club, Philadelphia's Racquet Club, and an exclusive New Brunswick salmon-fishing camp, stamped her with an imprimatur of utmost respectability.

During Miami's season, which began in late November and lingered until April, Henry and Maude attended a round of teas, luncheons, regattas, polo matches, supper dances at private clubs and in the new elegant mansions on Palm and Star islands, performances of visiting artists like Rachmaninoff and Jascha Heifitz, and rode horseback into the surf at Casino St. John. On occasion Henry in plus fours and cap completed foursomes with President Harding before the president died of ptomaine poisoning and the scandals of his administration surfaced, including that of the infamous Teapot Dome.

February marked the height of the season and the Grand Oriental Ball at Casino St. John, where incense, tapestries, scores of imported flamingoes, and turbanned waiters dressed in harem pants provided a tramontane setting for women in fringed and beaded dresses dancing the bunny-hug with men wearing diamond stick pins.

Conversation flitted from the Internal Revenue Service, which had begun slapping Miami's new paper millionaires with huge tax bills, to sweeping runs and angled drives made in the final two chukkers on the polo field. Of lesser interest was the nuisance provided by Klan Number 24's initiation of one hundred fifty candidates on newly built Palm Island, where the public, invited to witness the ceremonies, parked their two thousand five hundred autos along the county causeway and blocked the bridge to the island.

While the women spoke of the impossibility of staffing winter homes with local help, their principal topic was Maude. They gossiped about her hair, bleached to an impossible platinum, about how she had met Henry Watson while she was the mistress of John Forrester, relishing the fact that despite her pretensions and her breathtaking beauty, she had been born cracker poor somewhere in Miami.

Aware that she was being observed, Maude let slip from a shoulder the daring gray georgette chemise designed for the occasion by Lanvin and trimmed in rows of beaded gunmetal fringe that exposed her back all the way to the down-brushed base of her spine.

She wore a strand of pearls that swung to her pelvic bones, and carried a long cigarette holder in one hand and an ostrich fan in the other. Linen bands that flattened her breasts after the birth of a child and a narrow satin girdle confined her figure to a slim, boyish ideal, yet Maude trailed womanly sensuality after her as she did her perfume.

She tweaked her brother's wing collar with the hand that held the cigarette holder. "I'm proud of you, Jack. You're not like the other seedy pioneers that I see around the Grove."

Jack Coombs sipped gin from a silver hip flask. His dark blonde hair was beginning to be threaded with gray above his ears. "I knew the end of Miami's pioneer days had come when I saw men wearing socks on Sunday."

"Fix your tie," she said. "Henry is waving us over. I think he wants you to meet Carl Fisher."

Jack capped the flask, returned it to his hip pocket, then squared his bow tie. They snaked their way through the crowd, executing an abandoned dance across the parquet dance floor where a jazz band called Tommy and the Colonels was playing the Black Bottom.

Maude's husband seemed impatient. "Come along, Jack." He indicated the pudgy man beside him. "I want to introduce you to a true visionary."

"Couldn't have done it without your brother-in-law," said Fisher. "Henry is indirectly responsible for twenty miles of concrete bulkhead and forty-five miles of sidewalk." Fisher chomped on a cigar. "The main thing is, we don't want Miami Beach to ever become a Jewish outfit. It would ruin the hotels and property in general."

Henry suggested that Jack sell real estate for Fisher's development company, then turned to a boutonniered man behind him who had tapped him on the shoulder.

"Sounds good to me," said Fisher. "When can you start?"

"I don't think I can," replied Jack. "It's your right to do what you want, Mr. Fisher, keep Jews out of your hotels and your club. But I can't tell someone that he can't buy land from me because he doesn't go to church on Sunday."

Fisher laughed. If Jack Coombs were not Watson's brother-in-law, he would have dismissed him as a lounge lizard. "You think Collins and Pancoast are any different? Look here, we sell to a restricted clientele. That means we sell to Jews of the right kind. I sold to John Hertz, the founder of the yellow cab company. I even invited Julius Fleischmann to play polo with me. You've heard of Fleischmann's yeast?"

"I heard you didn't let Fleischmann into your clubhouse," said Jack.

Maude took his arm. "Forgive my brother. Sometimes he hangs on like a horsefly."

Fisher appeared to search the room. "Say," he asked, smiling, "where is Deering?"

"I can't answer for Mr. Deering," replied Jack. "I don't know anything about his plans."

"That's funny," said Fisher. "I heard you two were pretty thick."

His jaw clamped shut, Jack turned abruptly and strode out onto the veranda to stare at the moonlit surf rolling softly on the sands beneath a sparkling dome of sky that cupped the earth. A night heron stalked the beach between ghost crabs that scuttled to the water's edge. Maude followed after her brother and caressed the back of his neck with her fingertips. "He never would have said that if Henry were within earshot. You have to get married, Jack.

289

I told you so before."

He sipped from his silver flask. "It's not as easy as that. I don't think I can, Maudie. I don't feel anything that way about women. It would be like telling you that you had to make love to one of your girlfriends."

"If she was pretty, I think I might like it. But she would have to do me first." Maude stroked her arm with the feathers of her fan. "First I would get her to tickle me all over with my ostrich fan. Slowly. Like this."

"Stop making a game of this. Even if I could, it would be a lie."

"What difference does that make? Do you think I really like doing it with Henry?"

"It's different for a man. It's harder to pretend."

"Do what I do. Close your eyes and pretend that whoever you marry is Ramon Navarro." She opened his jacket and touched his shirt over the bulge of his nipple ring. "Why can't you tell me what you do in private?"

He pulled his jacket closed. "Because it's private."

"I wouldn't think it was so awful."

He could not tell her about the rude, thrusting, lubricated fist that filled him to capacity, which violated his inner being as far as the intruding arm could go, until he had given himself completely to the splintering climax and the utter domination by another. Jack hated the rakish, arrogant Chambers, who had said to him with a shift of his pencil-thin mustache, "If you want all this, it is me you have to answer to, not him. I speak for Mr. Deering in all things." Jack hated himself even more for always coming back, for lying naked under a Sulka robe, shivering in anticipation until his lover slipped into the tasseled room and led him by his nipple ring onto the narrow bed.

Jack told his sister that the pine house in which they had spent their childhood was getting too big for one person. It needed too much repair. He was thinking of selling.

She had seen the guest bedroom in which her brother sometimes strayed, the one called Espagnolette, with green silk walls covered with painted arabasques and a secret door cut expertly into the design that led to a shared balcony.

"Where would you live?" she asked. "At Viscaya?"

"I don't think so. I would be one more appointment, like the macaws that swing on their malachite perches in the arcade. Besides, Mr. Deering is ailing. He goes to bed early, so tired he can hardly stand, complaining of pins and needles in his hands, sometimes of pains in his belly. We don't see each other too much. He likes me to talk him to sleep, tell him what Miami was like when I was a boy, make sure he has everything he needs for the night, his little clock, his bedside lamp, a carafe of water, lozenges, his tapestry pull. His valet can do that, Maudie. Mostly I listen to the slap of water against the sea wall. Maybe I'll find an apartment. There are some new ones right on the ocean."

"How would you pay for it? You insist on working for Zalman Levy for pocket change. You won't take money from Deering, you just turned down an opportunity to work for Fisher. Henry might consider setting you up in a business of your own, but he's only willing to match whatever you can raise yourself, and frankly, he doesn't understand why you think you would be successful building boats."

"Shipbuilding in Miami is going to do real well as soon as these northern visitors stop dumping their craft at the end of every season for a fraction of their worth." He capped his flask, put it into his pocket. "Mother loved the house. It's half yours, Maudie. I won't sell it if you don't want to."

Below them luna moths darted in and out of the large white morning glory flowers of a fragrant moonvine. "I couldn't care less about that crumbling old place," she replied. "Sell it if you like." Maude changed the topic to the mansion that she and Henry were building on Palm Island, a white stucco structure with green tile and a separate wing for the child and his nurse.

Jack said that whenever he came to see the baby, the nursemaid was feeding him castor oil.

Maude held out her long cigarette holder for a light. "Nurse says it takes overnight to work its way through. It's the way you toilet-train babies. In the morning she'll put him on the potty. If you wait for a child to decide to do it, it never happens. You and I got doses of castor oil all the time. It never hurt us any. Once Momma made me drink a whole glassful. Then she locked me in the privy. I thought my insides were going down into that evil-smelling hole. I thought I was going to die. But I didn't, as you can plainly see. You were with Galilee, delivering guava. When you came home, you said I looked funny. You picked me up and swung me around and asked if I wanted a peppermint stick."

Jack cupped his hands around the match. "Do you spend any time with him at all? Whenever I come to visit, you're someplace else."

"Bradford's just a baby. He needs a nurse-maid. When he stops fussing over every little thing and can carry on a conversation, there will be plenty of time for us to get on."

"You're his mother. You have to feel something for him."

Her face turned brittle. "Since when does motherhood guarantee feelings? Mother wouldn't look at me. And the truth is, I don't much like Bradford. He's noisy and smelly, and he doesn't like me, I'm sure of it."

"Bradford looks like Mother, you know. You

must have seen it too, Maudie. He's the spit of her."

"That's an awful thing to say. She was a nasty, mean-looking woman."

"She didn't always look that way. The sun did most of it, and time had a hand in it too. She was very pretty when she was young. You saw the pictures."

"I tore up most of them."

"Did you hate her that much?"

"Not always. I used to love her. A lot. I used to dream about her being sweet to me. I used to think I was bad. That I had done something wrong to make her so mean. I used to pray to the Lord to make me speak in tongues like she did until I realized He wasn't listening. Then I found a way to pay her back, and it didn't bother me so bad. Badly." She powdered her face. "Now look what's happened. I think a sad thought and it pops up between my eyebrows." She pressed the line with her thumb, flipped open her fan, and took his arm. "There's something I want you to do for me."

"Name it."

"I want you to get that man Bristol fired."

"Fired? Why?"

"He spoke out of turn to me. Said something terrible."

"What did he say?"

Maude snapped her fan closed. "It's too awful. I don't want to think about it, much less talk about it."

"I can't imagine Bristol volunteering anything, much less saying something out of turn or in turn. He keeps to himself these days."

She tore away from his arm to face him head-on. "That shows how much you know about him. He had the nerve to look me in the face," she dropped her voice to a whisper, "and tell me that he and I had the same father."

Jack leaned over the railing, watching the rollers drench the night beach with foam, thinking that if he didn't meet her eyes he could pull it off. "Maybe you misunderstood him."

"Not hardly."

"It's possible that he believes it, but that doesn't mean it's true."

"Turn around and say that. You can't, can you? You know something, Jack. I know you do."

Jack lit a cigarette, deciding not to tell her of the conversation he had had with Bristol the month before on the grounds of Viscaya. Bristol had been carrying a basketful of gardenias. Jack stopped on impulse to ask if he wanted to go crab fishing that night, the way they had as boys. Bristol said things were different now. Miami was different. The only way they could hunt crabs together was if Bristol carried the lanterns, which he wasn't about to do.

"I can't help being white," Jack said, "and I can't undo the things that happened to you. I wish I could, but I can't."

295

Bristol's reply was curt. "I don't need you to undo or do anything for me except leave me alone."

Jack replied that he remembered the days that they used to talk to each other about everything in the world, that he used to think that they had a lot in common, but he guessed he was mistaken.

"We still have something in common," Bristol had said. "We have a sister."

Jack flicked an ash over the railing. "Just before she died Mama told me that you and I had different fathers. I thought it was the fever talking."

"There. I knew you were holding out on me. But I still don't believe it. She must have started the rumor in the first place just to be spiteful."

"Maybe so."

Maude began to shiver. Jack took off his jacket and put it over her shoulders as Henry stepped out onto the terrace with little clicks of his patent leather pumps. "Here you are, Maude. I've been looking everywhere for you. You look pale, darling. Too many parties. I think it's time I got you home."

Chapter Fourteen

MIAMI DOCTOR

The white man is cutting a new road across the long land from east to west that he calls Tamiami Trail. The work has already divided the water that flows from the north. This causes seasonal drought in the area south of the new road. In addition, the road gives white hunters easier access to our supply of fish and game, so that food becomes even more scarce than before we moved to the tourist camp.

In my mind, I still reckon the Everglades by the old canoe trails rather than the highway. I even find my way by them, although most are now vanished, lost forever like many of our activities before the white man leaked the waters of the Pahahokee to the sea. Like the tales of our ancestors, these trails are only memories carved into my heart.

In the fall I am supposed to journey into the Pahahokee, find families, and bring them back, paying each twenty dollars a month to let the tourists gawk at them as they sit about the chickees. If I have difficulty going about my business with white people staring at me, how can I convince others to do the same? I try to tell them that it is seasonal, only from the white man's new year through the end of his month April, that they will earn enough to get by on for the rest of the year, but some refuse to come.

Some prefer to go to Willie Willie's village at Musa Isle because it is run by an Indian. Many families, such as that of William McKinley Osceola, live in both tourist camps. Willie Willie's village used to be a fruit grove. When the drainage canal caused the water to drop, the grove declined. But Musa Isle had become a great trading post that deals in pelts and hides, those too large to be made into lamps, but sent instead to tanning factories in the north. It is Willie Willie's business, and from it he takes a profit, like the white man Lasher, a buyer of pelts who holds a paper to the river-front property where Willie Willie's village is located.

Because of this, my days have grown unlucky. After Jack Tigertail was shot and killed, Charlie Billie was asked to be head man. Before me. There is nothing I can do about this insult. Charlie Billie can get families to come. I cannot. At first it was I who was Tustenugge, responsible for keeping general order in the camp, for distributing the payroll and handling the grocery money because I could communicate the best in English. Now I am only an old man growing older, sitting on a stool with an opening over a pan of chicken-gizzard linings, waiting for the vapor to ease the soreness of the opening of my bottom.

The proprietor does not want anyone who drinks. This causes trouble for my son Tommy, who has been sent back from the place Hollywood. Tommy has become fat from eating too many of the white man's hot dogs. For this reason the white man no longer wants to capture his image. To forget the place Hollywood, Tommy drinks, sucks at the bottle in the way my old friend Jimmy Jumper used to drown himself into a deep, forgetful sleep. When I see my son seeking so desperately to cloud his pain-filled eyes, I remember things Jimmy Jumper said about the white man and I think maybe he was right. The proprietor has threatened to put my son out of Osceola Gardens if he is drunk one more time, and so I watch Tommy like one watching two gopher holes at once.

"Wrestle alligators," I tell my son. "Like Josie Jumper, Chestnut Billie, and Frank Jimmie. These are the best. They know how to call the alligator, how to keep his jaws tightly closed, how to watch his tail, how to throw him on his back and rub his belly. You can learn from them." No, he does not want to. "Then help us carve totem poles."

"It is not our custom," he replies.

"The tourists don't know that," I say, "carve

them anyway," thinking that working with a knife will keep Tommy from the bottle. I do not tell him that we have to paint the totem poles too.

Josie, my younger son, is another piece of my bad luck. He attends the white man's school because of the agent, Nash. Nash complains that over half of Miccosukee live in tourist attractions. He thinks this is a bad thing. "The cause for the lack of progress among your people is," he tells me, "a lack of a dependable source of subsistence." He says that the problem of securing food and clothing has left us no opportunity for mental development. That is why Josie sits in their school wearing long trousers and a white man's shirt, listening to their teachers instead of to ours. The agent said this circumstance was not easy to arrange. That because the Seminole never signed a peace treaty with Washington, Josie has no legal status. But then Nash speaks to the school headman on Josie's behalf and persuades him to admit my youngest son. I agree because I did not want him to watch his older brother drink and think that this was good.

The Pahahokee is not the only thing that has changed. When I was a boy, I remember when an Indian broke the tribal law by attending the white man's school and the tribe sentenced him to death. He stayed out of sight for a year until the killing fever passed, but he remained a lesson to all of us. Now my son is learning how to read and write and knot the white man's tie, and no one says a word.

Bristol comes to camp from time to time with Oolalee's son, Jack. While the Coombs man waits beneath a royal palm, Bristol stands back and watches my granddaughter with a panther's narrowed eyes. It is not with pride. He does not like what he sees. The child knows this. She would know it even if she were sightless. This is bad, for such thoughts shape the man or woman the way one can shape a tree by first bending the twig.

"Why isn't she wearing shoes?" he asks.

"Your own people go without shoes," I reply.

"No more, they don't," he says. "Travel out of here sometime and see what's happening. Another thing. I give Mary money. Mary spends the money on a truss for Charlie Billie."

I try to explain that it is more important for Charlie Billie to be able to work and earn money than for a child to have shoes, but Bristol does not understand.

"You can get hookworm," he says, "all kinds of disease from going barefoot. There was an article about it in the paper."

"Our women are accustomed to going without shoes."

He struggles with the idea like a fish in a net. "What if I buy them for her?"

"Do you want her to be any more different from the others than she already is?"

This stops him for a while, then he tries a new hole to slip through. "I sure don't like her running after these tourists asking for money."

Some of our children flit like butterflies around the tourists, waiting for tips. When I was headman, I stopped that, but to Bristol I say, "All the children do that. It's their right to earn money just like everyone else."

"It's begging," he says. Again he asks permission to take the child home for a few days. Sally Cypress, who has brought him a spoonful of sofke, which he declines, and a bowl of alligator tails, which he accepts, shakes her head no. I agree. It would only be confusing, she says. What she really fears she does not speak aloud, that the child will come to prefer the place of her father's.

"What about a day, then?" he asks. "Why can't she come for a day? A few hours? We'll have her back before dark. She's my daughter too, Miami Doctor. You're the Tustenugge. Just tell the others that it's your decision."

I do not tell him that I am no longer held in regard as headman. It is too nettlesome even to talk about. "You know that the headman takes his orders from the others," I reply. "I cannot go against the tribe."

"Why not ask her?"

With reluctance I do, but Emma doesn't want to come. She is angry with her father for having abandoned her, for having waited for his return until she was seven, the time she learned to sew rickrack on the sewing machine, when her spinning hand helped her to forget.

Bristol faces me as he did when he was a young boy, legs apart, hands crossed over his chest. "She'll change her mind when I get to my mother's house," he says.

I ask Charlie Billie. If he is headman, perhaps it is for a good reason. His counsel is to let the child go for a day, if only to free her from the tourist stares.

Sally Cypress watches them go through the turnstile, trying to get straight in her own mind why Bristol did not give her proper respect, bring the gifts due a mother. He has been away too long, she says. He has forgotten our ways. "When he return, he bring me something. You will see. He forgot. He sees me now, that helps him remember." But when Bristol returned, it was only to bring his daughter to the safety of the compound, to drop a burlap bundle into our chickee, then quickly turn away, with no words, no sit-down to smoke a cigarette, no string of beads for Sally Cypress.

"Why would he bring you beads?" I ask, trying to soften matters as one hammers an ancient piece of meat. "It is not his way."

"It is his way, stupid old man too blind to see," which is strange, for it is she who is losing sight in one eye.

After Bristol leaves, Sally Cypress says she can smell the others on Emma, traces of the sweat of the dark people who toil for the white. Although her hands are as gnarled as the cypress of her name, my wife fills a bucket from which to bathe her granddaughter.

My daughter, Mary, thinks this is foolish. In the first place, the girl is able to bathe herself. In the second place is only truth. "We toil for the white," she says. "We're no different than the black man."

But Sally Cypress is rooted in her opinion. "We do not toil for the whites," she replies. "When tourists try to talk to me, I open my eyes wide as if I do not understand. And when they stop to watch me work, I not move. I sit like stone. So I do not toil for the whites."

"You do, Grandmother," said Emma. "You toil for the whites, just like my father's mother. You take their money and eat their food. At least she gets to sit down in a chair. You have to stand behind a booth and pour them pineapple juice."

It is soon after that Sally Cypress refuses to eat or drink, and the beginning of my third piece of bad luck. When she sits with her hair down around her face like a widow, the proprietor says that she can no longer work the juice stand because her hair gets in the pineapple juice. I do not know whether her sadness was brought about because Bristol did not give her respect, or because Emma told her she worked for the whites. Mary tries to get her to eat, so do the other women of the village. I try

304

to talk to her, but her eyes gaze past me as if seeing the Great Horned Snake. I tie owl feathers over the entrance to our chickee, but Mary says that it is too late, that the bad medicine has already happened. The agent Nash tells the proprietor to send for Doctor Du Puis, but all the doctor does is look down her throat, listen to her heart, and beat against her body with his fingers as if her back were a drum. Before long she curls into herself like an injured animal, and while I watch, her spirit rides over the curve of the night.

We place her body in a dugout, remove her beads, except for one strand, and divide them between Mary and Emma. I cut away faded blue roses from her patchwork skirt that now rightfully belongs to Oolalie's son. The dugout is placed high in a tree on the bank of the Miami River. Too high for the white man to see. After we return and she is not at my back, scourging me with her tongue, I do not know how I feel. Partly relief, as if some ailing member has finally been severed, its putrefaction no longer able to contaminate the rest. Partly sadness, as with any amputation that brings ghost pains of remembered days, of a wife who did not want to be my wife, who lay in my embrace with eyes that did not flutter, and limbs that did not move, who never failed to serve me first from the sofke spoon or search my head for lice to crack between her nails.

Chapter Fifteen

In September 1926, with Miami still reeling from the bust that followed on the heels of the boom, Jack Coombs came to Zalman's new house with a proposition.

They sat in the living room, which Gettel had furnished with a Kroehler davenport bed, a mahogany armchair for Zalman, an oriental rug, and a mahogany breakfront. It was almost dusk. From outside came the trilling of a mockingbird. Behind them Herschel closed the accordion file in which Zalman's sales slips and bank receipts were kept, tied it with its strings, and returned it to a drawer in the breakfront.

Jack waited while Zalman looked over his shoulder at his elder son. "Did you get all of the slips out of the cash box?"

"Don't worry, Pop. Everything is where it's supposed to be."

"Except you," said Zalman. "Where do you go at night?" He handed a glass of schnapps to Jack. "Once a week he disappears."

"I'm almost eighteen," said Herschel.

"I don't care how old you are. As long as you live under my roof, you answer to me." Zalman turned his attention to Morty, standing in the driveway in knee pants, flicking off sandy grit from the family's yellow, wire-wheeled, custom Victoria Hudson with a feather duster.

"Use plenty of water, Morty," shouted Zalman through the screen door, "and take the nozzle off the hose. If you squirt it with the nozzle, you'll drive the schmutz right into the paint."

Herschel ran out the front door, jumped into an old Ford and backed it out of the gravel driveway while his brother dissolved soft yellow auto soap in a pail of water. "I'm going to spend the night at Benny Rivkind's house," he yelled.

A fan whirred over a dish of ice cubes, cooling the fragrant, moist warm air that sifted through the screens.

Zalman smiled fondly at the man before him, still boyish in his looks, although Zalman guessed that Jack was close to forty. Their relationship had developed into an easy partnership, limited only by the wages that one gave the other.

"So, Jackie," said Zalman, "what's on your mind?"

Jack leaned forward in his chair, his elbows on his knees. "I came to tell you that it's time for me to move on. Between the ship that's run aground in the harbor and boxcars stacked up all the way to Jacksonville, business has come to a standstill. You don't really need me."

"What are you saying? You're my right hand, Jack," said Zalman. "Things will turn around.

307

When they do, I'm going to need someone I can count on like I could always count on you."

"You have your two boys," said Jack.

"Herschel and Morty? They're pishers. What do they know? You and me, we've been through the wringer."

"I'd like to get into something else, Zalman. I was thinking of building boats, small ones, cabin cruisers."

"What do you know about shipbuilding? Where are you going to get the capital? Banks are calling in their loans, not giving out new ones."

"It's time I went out on my own. I had in mind to offer you a deal. My brother-in-law will give me part of the money. I don't need very much. I have some of my own. I was hoping I could count on you for the rest. In exchange for a share of the profits."

Zalman ran his hair over the back of his balding head. "You put me on the spot, boychick. If you would have asked me for a raise, I would have agreed. Without batting an eye. You're my right hand, Jack. I can't do without you. No offense, but I don't see you running a business."

Jack stood, his disappointment revealed only in the set of his jaw. "You treat me the same way you treat your kids. Like none of us knows his ass from a hole in the ground. I've been helping you run your business for years, but

308

I guess that doesn't count. I'm sorry I put the bite on you, Zalman. Thanks for the drink. I'll be getting on my way."

While Gettel folded a damask tablecloth that smelled of starch, Zalman tucked his shirt into his pants and turned on the radio. "Banks are sagging under a load of binders, and he wants money."

"You still could have listened. You didn't let him finish what he wanted to say."

"I got the bottom line."

The radio began to emit an ear-piercing howl. "Something's wrong in the cabinet," said Zalman. He turned off the switch and raised the lid. "Maybe it's the vibrations in the vacuum tubes."

"Don't touch anything, Zalman," said Gettel. "You'll get electrocuted."

Zalman closed the lid and switched on the radio again. He noticed that the howl grew weaker then disappeared altogether when he stood on the other side of the table.

"I fixed it," he said as an Associated Press dispatch, crackling with static, interrupted to report a hurricane north of Haiti, blowing one hundred miles an hour and pointed at Florida.

Zalman ran out the front door past Morty, who was wringing out a chamois. "Take a look at the Hudson, Pop. No streaks or anything."

"We don't have time," said Zalman.

By the time they boarded up the storefronts and the ticket booth, the slashing rains had begun. They made it home in time to park the Hudson in the garage, before the wires went down and the hurricane began shredding Miami with cyclonic winds that rocked the Levys' house as if it were a cradle. By midnight the city was plunged into darkness.

With only yahrtzeit candles to light the gloom, they sat in the hallway and listened in semi-darkness to the sounds of crashing tree limbs, roofs of houses and giant timbers sailing through the air, and telegraph poles snapping off like matchsticks while Gettel prayed for Herschel's safety.

When it was over, the new skyline had been smashed into a medley of cocked roofs, crushed towers, shattered windows, and suspended beams. Downtown streets were full of mud and fish, shards of glass, and boats nestling grotesquely among the bayfront hotels. Houses stood twisted on their foundations or gaped open, exposing household chaos and half-clothed men and women picking through the tattered debris.

Except for a broken upstairs window and water driven in under the front door that soaked the carpet and caused the kitchen linoleum to buckle, Zalman's house, steamy and vaporous in the heat of the sun, was spared.

Zalman took Morty's bicycle to inspect his enterprises, returned to report that the theater marquee had blown down and that the awnings of both storefronts had been torn from their fittings and wrung like the necks of chickens. He raised his eyebrows in question.

Gettel began to cry. "Herschel's not back, Zalman."

"The Rivkind house is as solid as a rock," said Zalman, his hand on her cheek. "He can't get through is all."

Two days later, when martial law was declared and Zalman was convinced that his elder son was dead, Herschel returned. Clearing his throat with every word, Herschel explained that he had gone to Key Largo to meet a sailboat, that when the storm blew up, he and the passengers took shelter in an old stone house. Gettel, her graying braids flopping over her shoulders, flew into a rage and began to smack her son on the head. "What kind of idiot," she shouted, "goes on a joyride in the middle of a hurricane? You could have been killed."

Zalman then noticed the man who held his cap in his hand, and the woman beside him holding a baby in her arms with a little boy at her side. "What's going on?"

"These are the Bergmans," said Herschel. "They need a place to sleep."

The husband began speaking in Yiddish. Zalman slowly got the picture, one he didn't want to see, one that had nothing to do with the ravages of the storm. "Where are they from?"

"Cuba. Before that, Slovakia."

"At the foot of the Carpathian Mountains," said the man.

The woman took Zalman's hand and kissed it. "Did they come in illegally?" he asked.

"Please, Pop. Don't ask questions. Can we put them up or not?"

"I'd like to know where."

"Don't keep them standing in the doorway," said Gettel. "Bring them in."

"You're both crazy," said Zalman. "The first floor is flooded. God knows when the toilets will ever flush again."

Gettel helped the woman off with her coat, a threadbare wool with a fur collar. "They'll sleep in the living room. We'll open the davenport, and we'll put dining room chairs together for the children. Somehow we will manage."

Zalman turned to Herschel. "You could go to jail for this. What about papers?"

"That can be arranged."

Zalman put his hands on Herschel's shoulders. "You've done this before, haven't you?"

Herschel nodded his head.

"For how many people?"

"Thirty, maybe forty."

Zalman pinched his brows together with his thumb and forefinger. "Tell me something, do I treat you like you don't know anything?"

"It's okay, Pop, sometimes I don't."

"Remind me to tell you how I escaped from Siberia. Get Jack on the phone."

"The lines are still down," said Morty.

"Then get on your bicycle. Find him. Tell him I've changed my mind. Tell him a grateful father who doesn't know his *tuchis* from a hole in the ground is going to give him a stake."

After seven years, Bristol was promoted again, from a flower boy, clumping back and forth between the cold room and mansion with hampers of fresh flowers, to a house boy in rubber-soled shoes, whose job it was to wipe down all the draperies and help set fifty-nine clocks. He learned in the first week that the most important skill in his new job was invisibility. Bristol had looked down on Deering and his guests from the second-floor gallery as they took luncheon in the courtyard. A large Coromandel screen had been adjusted so that no draft would blow on the frail Mr. Deering. Bristol inched from behind a column so that he could see the sparkling silver, watch the guests touching embroidered napkins to their lips, sip coffee from tiny cups. They were talking about the movie star Norma Talmadge, who was coming to Viscaya to be filmed, when Deering suddenly looked up and stared until Bristol retreated behind the pillar. Later, when Bristol had been sent down to empty ashtrays, plump up pillows, the housekeeper warned him that he was never again to make himself seen in the house.

Caroline brought a store-bought cake from Holsum bakery to celebrate the occasion. "I'm almost forty years old, Momma," Bristol said. "I've gone from flower boy to house boy. Nothing worth a cake."

"It's a step up no matter how you shake it."

Caroline set out the cake plates, a gift from Mrs. Bryan, real china from England, white with sprigs of green around the border, with only a few chips that no one ever noticed. It was a Sunday, like most on Evangelist Street. Caroline was the first in the neighborhood to have screens like the white people had, and while the flies and mosquitoes were excluded, the sounds of ducks and chickens squawking in the yards came through the open windows, as did the banter of neighbors socializing from house to house, a discussion about Babe Ruth and the New York Yankees, the blare of a band playing in the street, the raucous calls from a crowd of men and boys outside the boxing gym at the corner of Charles and Hibiscus.

The night before, all the neighborhood hogs had been butchered, and the children were making balloons of the small intestines that they call chitlins. The day promised an orgy of pork eating, of fat boiling in large pots rendered into lard, of cracklings, the crisp remnant of this process baked into pones of corn bread.

Two blocks away, gypsies camped on the road near the wall that separated whites from blacks in Coconut Grove. Caroline knew little about them except that they drove big cars, wore lots of jewelry, and told lies. She instructed

314

Isaac to lock up the chickens and ducks in the shed, then gave Isaac Jr.'s four-year-old son, Willie, ten cents to guard the clothes on the wash line after he finished his cake.

"Are those gypsy people white?" the child asked.

Caroline wiped her hands on her apron. "If you mean do the whites think they're white, the answer is no."

"Actually," said Bristol, "the state enacted a law three years ago that spelled it out. If you have an eighth Negro or African blood, you are legally a Negro. Which means that if you register to vote, the KKK is going to slip a red card under your door, and the registrar is going to ask you to name the last six presidents of the United States."

"You should be in law school same as James," said Galilee.

"I've got a lot of 'shoulds' in my life."

Galilee slipped a strip of cardboard into each of his shoes. "I guess you have at that."

"I don't know why you do that, Galilee," said Isaac Jr. "We're making plenty of money."

Galilee replied that old habits die hard, then asked Bristol if it was true that Jack Coombs had gotten married to a well-fixed widow. He heard he was fixing up his house, putting in a staircase, breaking through the living room wall to put in a fireplace, building a stone chimney, putting in indoor plumbing, enclosing the breezeway between the house and the kitchen, covering the kitchen floor with linoleum, and replacing the old tin roof with cedar shingles.

"Who's doing all the work?" asked Caroline.

"You can bet it's none of us," said Bristol.

"That's not true, Bristol," said Galilee. "Isaac Jr. here's been hired along with Lulu Ryder's son to help with the planting."

Caroline served the first satiny slice of cake to Bristol, careful to include in her cut a blue sugar rose. "You're talking about digging in the ground," she said. "I was talking about building. Seems like plenty of our men do carpentry, plumbing, electric work. Building jobs these days seem to be going to the white boys."

"That's because you have to belong to the trades to work in the trades," said Bristol. "What does the house look like? I haven't laid eyes on it since I was a kid."

"From what I've seen, his wife doesn't know much about planting," said Caroline. "Not like his mother. I may have bad-mouthed Eulalie Coombs, but no two ways about it, that woman had a green thumb."

"That's the truth," said Galilee. "I saw Jack's woman fixing to put a Brazilian pepper next to the house, when everyone knows that inside a year it's bound to choke the power line. Isaac Sr. stopped her. At first she got scared, thought he was having a fit, but Lulu Ryder's boy explained that that was the way he talked. And they're selling the piano."

"Find out what they want for it," said Caroline.

Isaac Sr. grunted an objection.

"Don't you want Willie getting every benefit the white child gets? If you get him a piano, he can take lessons."

Willie flipped his slice of cake onto the floor with an inexpert twist of his fork. It was an accident. His mother, Jessie, crisp and starched in a printed dress with a stiff white collar that fanned like wings to her shoulders, bent to wipe it up. "Is Emma coming back?" the child asked. "And is she really my cousin? Frankie Jay says she's nothing but a wild Indian."

Everyone was silent a moment, remembering the awful day Bristol brought Emma back to Evangelist Street. The child had spoken to no one except Galilee and Willie, and once to Caroline, when she asked where the privy was. When Bristol took her out on the porch, the neighborhood children only stared. Some ran away. Emma refused to come back inside or to step down from the porch, and she sat by herself on the glider until it was time to go home.

"That's your doing," Caroline said. "She acts like a stranger because the child feels like a stranger. And it's no wonder."

Bristol was equally angry because his mother had made arrangements with Jack Coombs before asking him. "Why did you have to bring him into it?" he asked.

"I do what I have to do to bring my grandchild home. Since when can a colored man or woman just sashay in and buy themselves a ticket to these places? And why are you so down on him?"

"Because he doesn't have to do a goddamn thing, Mama. Because he's got everything coming. Everything. All he has to do is slick back his hair. I can't slick mine back. And I'll bet Galilee and Isaac Jr.'s bootlegging business that he still can't read worth a damn."

"Bet something of your own," Isaac Jr. said. "Me and Galilee don't plan on giving any of it away. And it's not true about not being able to slick back your hair. A couple of my friends are getting their hair conked. You lean your head over the barber's sink, he pours some stuff on it. It stings like hell, but it melts away the kinks. The nappy look is gone. Your hair is as straight as a cue stick."

"I don't want to see you doing any such thing to your head," Caroline had said.

Jessie stood at the sink and told Galilee that a man with a cabbage truck with Georgia plates was waiting in the backyard.

"Now, how does he expect to haul bootleg liquor in broad daylight?" asked Caroline.

"He has a false bed," replied Isaac Jr. "It's hollow underneath."

"That man also have a license plate for every state in the South," said Galilee.

"I don't care how many plates he has. Don't

318

bring him in my house. Do your business with him outside."

Under Prohibition Galilee and Isaac Jr. had begun to make good money, rubber-band money, when Galilee discovered a way to burn the smoke for his still by bending a pipe to run out of the side of the furnace, under the yard, and up out of a water-filled ditch.

Isaac Jr. helped Galilee to his feet, and they went out the back door to take care of the low-key transaction that marked all their business. When their operation had been small, they had hidden the fruit jars in the sleeves of all the clothes in the closets. Now the jars were submerged, hooked with clips to a pulley line strung across the ditch.

Isaac Jr. could be heard telling the hauler that other moonshiners sometimes used potash to fake a bead. "That's the same material soap is made of," he said.

"A man ought to be put in a chain gang with a ball tied to him if he uses potash to make whiskey," said Galilee. "Nothing but low-down meanness. He ain't making it to drink himself, and he ain't making it fit for anyone else to drink either."

Caroline wiped her grandson's mouth with her napkin. "Don't listen to them, child," she said. "Go outside now and see the gypsies don't take our clothes. And if they come near you, run inside. You never know what's on their minds."

"He's still working on his rose," said Jessie.

The day before Caroline had tried to teach her daughter-in-law how to pad her ironing board so that her employer's monograms would stand out like sculpture, but Jessie said she wasn't interested in learning how to buck and shine. If it weren't for the boy, Caroline would have long since told Isaac Jr. and his wife that it was time they got a place of their own.

Isaac Jr. and Galilee returned discussing heavyweight boxing champion Jack Johnson, who Galilee said was the first black man to become heavyweight champion, holding his title for seven years. Caroline said Jack Johnson wasn't too smart. He had got himself a white wife, and for a black man that meant nothing but trouble. Then she said that William Jennings Bryan was fixing to go to Tennessee to help in the trial against a schoolteacher who had been preaching evolution, or some such thing.

"What's that?" asked Willie. "That 'lushan' thing?"

Everyone turned to Bristol, who was rinsing his plate at the sink. "Evolution. It's how things change," he said. "It's about how nothing stays the same. It's about mutations."

They whistled at his silver-dollar words, knowing that if he had the chance, if luck hadn't gone against him, he could have been somebody. Jessie privately told her husband that she was getting tired of pussyfooting around his sour older brother.

"You seeing the number man's sister?" Isaac Jr. suddenly asked.

"I don't know what you're talking about," said Bristol.

"Are you sure about that? Pablo Garcia came by to pay off Pop's winning bolita ticket." Isaac Jr. clapped Isaac on the back. "Pop dreamed he saw a blind man. So he played number eighty-four. We saw the number posted on the board of Eddie's taproom. When Pablo came to pay off the four bucks, he said to tell you to stay away from his sister."

Caroline frowned. "Are you messing with a white girl?" she asked, a loving hand on his cheek. "Tell me my baby isn't that foolish."

"It's nothing like you think, Mama," said Bristol. "Pablo's old man has a ranch. He needs someone who knows how to work it. James must have told Pablo that I was a hand when I was with the Seminoles. Garcia invited me over to his house."

"Did you go?"

"I went."

"And you never said a word to any of us? What did he say?"

"Lots of things. He said the sugar industry is collapsing and that Cuban banks are failing, that American capital is ready to take over Cuba, and that his wife is burning candles all over the house."

"What's that got to do with you?"

"He's trying to pull some of his irons out

of the fire. He has a cigar factory, but he's afraid they'll go on strike like they're doing in Tampa. So he wants to fix up his ranch."

"What did you tell him?"

"I said I wasn't interested."

Bristol had arrived on a Sunday afternoon. A woman wearing a silver crucifix admitted him into the darkened house where louvered shutters cast shards of light on burnished woods and marble credenzas topped with paper flowers. She pointed him in the direction of the library, then stalked into the kitchen as if he were not there.

Bristol entered a room lined with leatherbound volumes and marble heads of men with hair rippling to vitreous collars. A young woman with almond eyes and clear olive skin tinged with copper on the bone of her cheeks, the color of the underside of a satin leaf, sat reading before an old man in a wing chair. Bristol thought she was the most beautiful girl he had ever seen. He guessed she was reading in Spanish.

When the old man lifted his head, he smiled with ancient, yellowed teeth. "You are as tall and as straight as a *palma real*," he said to Bristol. "A royal palm," he explained, "one of the scattered sentinels that guard the island of Cuba. If I close my eyes, I can smell the delicious aroma of the coffee blossom after rain."

Bristol continued to stand until Garcia waved him to a seat.

"This is my daughter, Marta. It is through her brother Pablo, who sells bolita tickets to the people of color, that I learned of your familiarity with my ranch. How did this come to be?"

"A man named Alfonso needed hands. I was in the neighborhood. I got the job."

"You are wondering what an old man like me is doing with a ranch. I bought it from a Bahamian planter. It belonged to his son. An arrogant, unkempt fellow named Tatum wanted to remain as my overseer, was quite adamant that he owned part of the property. He even sought to intimidate me with a bullwhip with which he popped a bird right out of a tree. Naturally, I fired him on the spot and hired Alfonso to take his place. When the convict-leasing system proved too costly — one has to supply each with four clean sheets and three pillow slips — Alfonso suggested that we employ Indians. At fifty cents a day they were cheaper than either the convicts or the white vaqueros, who wanted three times as much. Then Alfonso was found dead on a wagon load of wildcats that someone was bringing in for bounty."

"Things happen in the palmetto scrub country," said Bristol. "Cowboys pump their Winchesters into passing trains, cattle disappear, then show up with their old brands burned off or scraped off, men disappear all the time. Sometimes they're found lynched or lying dead in some sawgrass bog."

Garcia bit off the tip of his cigar. "How did you come to work with Indians?"

Bristol replied that he rode fence with a Seminole, shifting cattle from one range to another, keeping mineral and salt boxes full for cattle that would stampede at the crack of a stick except in dry weather when the herd lived on sandspurs. He noticed that as he spoke, Garcia's daughter searched his face and looked deeply into his eyes, not as certain women did to make a man think they were on fire for him, but as if she wanted to understand.

He said that Alfonso paid them two dollars for each unbranded calf they found and that the only thing they did not like to do was dip their cattle in arsenic against the Texas fever tick because the creatures' hides cracked from the drying dip.

Garcia smiled. "You sidestepped my question the way the range cow sidesteps a rattlesnake. Did you know that Florida cattle are the offspring of stock brought by my forebears to this continent four hundred years ago? Now they are creatures so scrawny a man could hang his hat on their hips, which is an advantage. A heavier breed, attempting to cover a range so sparse, would walk itself to death. But I suppose you know all that."

"Yes, sir."

"Let's see what else you know. What causes water rot?"

"Cattle wading deep in warm water, feeding on water grass."

"When are they branded?"

"In the fall, when the weather is cooler and screw worm damage is less severe."

Marta's father spoke of how the ranch could be made profitable again. Bristol asked why he was telling this to him and not to his son.

"Pablo is not one for the country," the old man replied. "His inclinations lie in the city." He knocked an ash into a brass receptacle. "Are you interested in working the ranch?"

"No, sir. I like where I'm at. The pay is all right. The work is steady. Mainly I want to live near my family."

Bristol was invited to stay for the midday meal. While they ate red snapper garnished with almonds, he and Garcia's daughter exchanged a glance as fixed as the seal on a letter. It was not Bristol who made the advance. It was Marta, searching out his face until he could do little else save return the look.

Garcia breathed a sigh, understanding passion that has no reason, no sensibility, that can strike like a blow on the head from which one stays dizzy for a lifetime.

When she moved to pour his coffee, Bristol smelled her soap and the violet sachet that drifted from her dress, and found himself wondering what her body looked like under the filmy voile. She was small and soft, that much he could tell. He felt himself stir and told himself that there were plenty of women to mess with, to have a good time with. Garcia's daughter was not one of them; furthermore, she was white. Bristol had avoided her eyes, looking instead at the crease he was pinching in the flannel dress pants he had bought for ten dollars at Sewell's, at the winking, gaslit crystal chandelier that hung from the ceiling, at the old man asleep in the chair with his chin on his chest.

Despite a studied attempt to ignore her, his mind had become runaway, like a wagon that someone lets down a hill, and he could not keep from mentally stripping her, nuzzling her neck, her breasts, her thighs, running his fingertips between her legs. He said he had to leave.

The old man woke up and protested. "But you just got here," he said, his voice hoarse from his awakening.

"No, sir," Bristol replied. "By that clock on your mantel, I've been here two hours."

In the weeks that followed, it was easy to put Marta Garcia out of his mind. By the time he saw her again, he had forgotten her first name. She was waiting in an automobile with pneumatic tires outside the service entrance to Viscaya. It was summer, when only a skeleton staff was in residence.

Bristol noticed first the car. It was an Oakland. He had heard from one of the chauffeurs that it could throttle down to three miles an hour without changing gears and that the driver never had to do anything but set the choke. He was surprised to recognize the driver. "What are you doing here?" he asked.

She wore perforated driving gloves. Her sleeveless frock was made of the same filmy stuff she had on when he first met her. "The gatekeeper told me where to find you."

"You told me how you found me. You haven't told me why."

"Papa would like to see you again."

"What for? I already told him that I'm not interested in any ranch work."

"He knows. He just wants to talk to you. He thinks you may have useful ideas. He remembered what you said about liking to smell the sun on a saddle. This impressed him. He can't get around the way he used to. No one comes to see him. My mother is sharp with him, probably because he forgets from time to time. He has few pleasures. One is to talk, especially about the things in his past. He likes to talk to you."

It was hot, even though the late afternoon sun had already begun to hang over the horizon like an orange. Bristol shrugged his shoulders to lift the shirt that clung to his back. "I don't know what more I can tell him."

"He's old. Couldn't you indulge him, please?"

"Look, Miss Garcia. I only worked on that ranch a couple of years. I was just a hand, same as my Indian friend Tommy Doctor, taking orders from a guy named Alfonso who neither of us liked very much."

"I knew Alfonso. I never liked him either," she said. "My brother did, but I didn't. He acted like he owned us. All of us except Papa. Mother too." Suddenly she turned the key in the ignition. "It was wrong to press you. You work hard. You shouldn't be asked to spend your time listening to an old man who falls asleep in the middle of a thought."

He put his hand on the door handle. "Hold up a minute. I didn't say I wouldn't do it."

"Don't come unless you really want to."

"I want to."

Bristol arrived in the evening dressed in a shirt and tie and smelling of lime. Marta kept her distance, attending only to her father, appearing disinterested in their conversation about fever ticks and screw worms, while her mother and brother, who had removed themselves to the veranda, acted as if Bristol were dirt that someone had forgotten to sweep out the door.

Bristol noticed that Marta had rearranged her hair, had pinned it up so that its glossy black strands wisped about her neck. Once or twice her hand reached up to tuck back an errant tendril, and his eyes were drawn to the movement of her lifting breast.

Garcia was now weak and dispirited, more

tired than before, and it was a struggle to keep him on track.

"I think senescence starts at the feet," he said, "and moves up. My toenails are yellow and thickened. There is no cutting them. The skin below my knees is as cracked as the hide of an alligator. My water has begun to dribble. Age, however, has not yet reached my head. Thanks to the Blessed Mother my hearing remains unimpaired, and if I forget things from time to time, sooner or later the thought pops up like a duck." He looked balefully in the direction of the veranda. "Some things I can never forget."

"Papi," said Marta, "talk about the things that make you happy."

"I feel like the turtles taken aboard ship with their fins tied together. How can I be happy when I too am slowly dying on my back?"

Bristol decided that now was an opportunity to ask the old man about Tommy Doctor. He said that while he had no interest in ranching, he had a friend who did. Who knew the ranch every bit as much as he did. He asked if Garcia would consider hiring Tommy Doctor.

"An Indian by himself," the old man replied. "Never."

"What if I went to get him started?" Bristol suggested. "I've got some time coming. I could go with him and see that he got set."

"No," Garcia replied. "If you went with him

and stayed, but that would be another matter entirely."

"Then it's no?" asked Bristol.

"What is no?" the old man asked.

When Bristol left, Marta walked him to the door. "You were patient with my father," she said. "And I admire what you tried to do for your friend." A pale blue vein pulsed at her temple. Bristol found himself wanting to touch it.

"Will I see you again?" she asked.

"I don't think your father's much interested in talking to me again. He seemed more worn out this time than the first."

"Not my father. Me."

Bristol looked about to see if they had been overheard. "Look, Miss Garcia, this, whatever you're thinking about, it's not going to work."

"Why not?"

"I'm a black man."

"You're not black at all. You're golden."

"Forget the color of my skin. If you don't know what it means for a colored man to be seen with a white woman he doesn't wait on, I'll tell you. It means trouble. Not so much for you. But for me and my family. Serious trouble. The kind that doesn't go away."

"I intend no trouble for your family. I just would like to know you better."

"What for? That's the question. There's nothing to see me about that won't get me into a whole mess of trouble. Miss Garcia, I'm a nowhere man, with no past and no future."

"I'm not asking for anything but the present."

He hooked his jacket over his shoulder. "I was married to a Seminole."

"I know. My brother, Pablo, told me. But Papa also told me that as Criollos, we have Indian blood in our veins. Perhaps even black as well. So I am not as white as you think."

"It doesn't matter what I think. I'm not the one looking to set crosses on fire. Look, I have a fifteen-year-old daughter. She's part Indian, and she lives at Osceola Gardens with her mother and her grandfather. It's a sad business. I don't think that's something you want to get messed up in."

"I know that too. Now I want to tell you something. I hope I don't sound foolish, but that matters less than saying what I must." She folded her hands before her as if in prayer. "I am hungry for everything about you, Bristol Sands. I find myself saying your name aloud, writing it on a piece of paper, anything to bring you nearer. I imagine you in the night. I tell you things in the day. I don't know why this has happened. But it has. And I don't know what to do about it except to tell you."

"Have you told anyone else?" he asked.

"Only my confessor."

"Why did you do that?"

"Because my thoughts about you are impure."

Soon after began the senseless, reckless encounters of which Bristol lost count. Swimming in desire, stupid with passion, they met anywhere they would not be seen, in the unfinished casino until November when the approaching season made it no longer safe, in the winter months on the outskirts of the estate, scurrying through the moonlit, narrow hammock on a path that led past tiny manmade islands, one stocked with monkeys, to a little-used, Moorish-domed dwelling with tiles on the floor and arabesque designs on the lavender walls.

At first he was gentle because she had never been with a man. Sometimes, at her urging, he found himself trying to split her in half, wanting to drive himself up through her body into her throat. Other times their lovemaking was slow, thoughtful, as if each were made of glass. Then followed sober moments of confessions, of trading everything about themselves, using the revelations they shared with each other as barter.

"I killed a man," he whispered one evening as she lay drowsily in his arms.

Frogs and crickets chirped outside the domed enclosure. "I don't see you capable of malice," she replied. "You must have had reason."

"I thought so at the time. It cost me half my life."

"In prison?"

"It might as well have been. I left when I was a boy, hid out in the 'Glades with the

Seminoles. I didn't see my mother again until I was a grown man who someone still calls boy." He moved away to lean on one elbow. "Right now you're looking at me like you don't know what I'm talking about."

"What did I do to make you so angry?"

"Forget it."

She confided that her father had hired Alfonso only after her mother insisted that he find employment for her cousin. Her father suspected that his wife had other motives for bringing Alfonso out of Cuba.

"You must have noticed that my mother is much younger than my father."

"I guess I did," Bristol said.

"She asks him over and over about the circumstances of Alfonso's death. She accuses him of arranging to have cattle from another range branded with our mark so that Alfonso got the blame. She tries to trick him. How is it, she says, when we first learned that he was missing and I was frantic with worry that you were unconcerned? What would Police Chief Quigley say if I told him of my suspicions? Tell him, my father said. I have suspicions of my own."

"Do you think he was responsible?"

"I can't believe such things of my father," she replied. "I just know my mother scolds him all the time. She's taken over the cigar factory as if he were already dead, then she blames him because the *lector*, the man who reads the periodicals, incites dissent and the workers strike with every straw in the wind. If this keeps up, she screamed, I will have to close the factory down. And then where will we be? Pablo has the bolita, my father said. And I still have the ranch. Broken-down shacks, my mother replied, with smoke in the air so bad a person can't open their eyes. My father smiled a terrible smile. 'When were you out there?' he asked."

Marta dressed slowly, her naked body shining in the moonlight. Bristol usually liked to watch her step into her clothes. This time he sat with his arms clasped around his knees, staring out into the night through the open porticos.

"I want to make it up to you, Bristol," she said. "Everything that ever happened to make you feel bad."

"How you fixing to do that?"

Her dress fluttered over her head and settled below her hips. "By filling our moments with enough love for two lifetimes."

"That's romantic talk. Pretty talk. The chit-chat of someone who doesn't know which end is up. How much longer do you think we can go on doing this? Sooner or later someone's going to find us."

"Not if we marry. Not if we have a place of our own."

When Viscaya seemed no longer safe, they met at Jack Coombs' house. Galilee gave Bristol the key, assuring him that Jack was not expected to return to Miami until October, when he and his wife were going to fix up the interior. The yard was littered with rotten mangos, the house shuttered closed, with ficus vines growing up over the walls as if the hammock were in a hurry to reclaim itself.

Bristol opened the creaking door to flaking plaster and spiderwebs that draped the corners and furniture in dusty filaments. A vine that had worked itself into a shutter, poked into the house like a pointing finger. Pervasive in the dank and humid rooms was the faint odor of bay rum.

Marta sprinkled attar of rose everywhere as if it were holy water, anointing with distaste a carcass, which lay among mice droppings, of a robin that had come in under the eaves. When she was through, she studied the pictures on the wall, one of a seated one-armed man in a Confederate uniform with a sad-eyed woman standing at his side, another of a pretty blonde woman with squinting eyes and a little boy in a dress.

"That's Jack," said Bristol, remembering the last time he had set foot in the Coombs house. "And that's his mama."

"You sure he won't mind?" she said.

"He'd like it just fine."

Surrounded by floating dust motes, they lay on a mildewed down comforter and he fell upon her, enveloped by the smells of attar of rose, talcum powder, and laundry starch.

When they lay quietly apart, she reached out a hand to stroke his forehead. "When will you stop being afraid?" she asked.

"It's not a question of being afraid. It's a question of being smart."

"Then when will you stop being smart? When can we be stupid enough to start living a life?"

He sighed. "I guess now."

"Does that mean we can marry?"

"Is that what you want?"

"You know it's what I want," she replied.

Chapter Sixteen

The brush fires of early spring filled the air with acrid smoke that turned the sunsets red, and in the morning they mixed with the blankets of fog that spread over the lowlands of the sandy range. Barrels of bitter vapor rolled between the solitary pines, over clumps of scrub palmettos, sawgrass, and mulberry bushes, blanketing scarlet and yellow tiger lilies and willow sloughs white with fuzzy, fragrant blossoms, revealing an occasional white ibis flying over the sloughs or patches of men on rugged, stunted ponies.

A seasoned, work-hardened man in his prime, Bristol rode with his foreman and his ranch hands among the cattle. Like the men with whom he rode, his shirtsleeves were rolled above his elbows. His forehead beneath the tan felt pumpkin hat was creased from the sun and from daily battle with Tatum, screw worms, ticks, moss pickers, frog hunters, rustlers who stole his unbranded calves and hid them in the swamps, and rifle-toting night riders against whom he and Marta walked on the far side of the lamps so that when either crossed a room, neither's shadow would fall on the window curtains.

Bristol's foreman, Hub Boney, a former rodeo star with smallpox scars and a bad knee, come upon hard times and glad for a job, even with a Negro, rode herd over the cattle and the hands, Tommy Doctor, when he was sober, and a carrot-headed, freckled boy of fifteen named Red.

Road-weary, frightened, and undernourished, Red had drifted in one day like the early morning fog and asked for a job. He had been a vagrant for seventeen months, never allowed to stay anywhere more than twenty-four hours, except for one time when he worked eight weeks making crates for strawberries. Ever since his father had told him to hit the road, see if he could get work elsewhere, the boy had slept out in the open, in tramp jungles near the railroad tracks waiting to hop a freight. Fellows got killed catching trains. You had to be careful not to step on the cutting lever between the cars and get jerked off the train. In the hot weather he had climbed into the reefers, the space where ice was kept. The best way to travel was to hitchhike, riding at night with the truck drivers. They were not supposed to carry passengers, he said, but they got lonely at night, and were glad for the company.

The smoke stung their eyes and burned their throats, adding to the difficulties of screw worm inspection. Each carried a kit in his saddle pocket of benzol, pine-tar oil, and cotton. When they found an infected animal, someone roped and threw it to the ground, another jumped down from his pony to wad cotton into the wound, then saturated the cotton with benzol that he squirted from an oil can. They allowed the cotton to remain for a few minutes before removing it along with the dead parasites. Sometimes the screw worms did not come out easily, and Red had to pull them out with forceps, then swab the wound with pine-tar oil. Their particular concern was cuts from barbed wires and the navels of newborn calves, a frequent site of infestation that if not treated could result in the calf being devoured by screw worms within twenty-four hours.

After they swabbed anyplace where hide was broken, they rode to a drove of cattle at the side of the road that divided Bristol's property from his neighbor's. Tatum's operation was large, five or six times that of Bristol's, with ten riders and a chef, and three men devoted

338

full-time just to screw worm inspection, who covered Tatum's spread with a two-wheeled horse trailer and a pickup truck.

Tatum's vehicles were parked across the road in the shade of a massive live oak. His men were unloading and saddling their ponies as Tommy Doctor, with Red behind him, scrambled down the opposite embankment to hammer in a toppled sign that read OPEN RANGE, BEWARE OF CATTLE.

"You can keep a cow from crossing the road just by pointing a finger at it," Tommy Doctor said. Then he explained to the boy that cows congregated on the highway because the grass on the shoulders of the roads was the best. The problem was the calves, unpredictable and easily alarmed, often dashing out in front of the cars that frightened them.

Red asked why cattle liked to bed down on the pavement at night. While Tommy explained that the asphalt held the heat, that it was warmer than the ground in the chilly early morning before the sun rose, Tatum's riders went off in a cloud of dust raised by the unshod hoofs of their ponies. One of them called out, "Hey, Hub, put a bonnet on that little redhead boy, he'd be right pert."

Bristol's foreman bent to inspect the hide of a steer. "Don't pay them no mind," he said.

"If you tie a belt around his waist tight enough, you might even get a shape on him," shouted another. They roared with laughter.

339

One fired a rifle into the air. "Ask that nigger boss of yours where his banjo is at."

Hub eased himself erect with a groan and wiped his neck with his handkerchief. "They're just men. They can't do nothing but shout. Razorbacks, now that's something you need to watch for. Men scamper up a tree, anything to get away. Even an armed man isn't safe if they're in numbers. Ordinary dogs are no protection. Too bad you missed hog killing. We do it the first snap of cold. Eat all of the pig but the squeal."

"Best time for hog killing is Saturday morning," said Tommy, "when the moon is on the rise."

"Is it true you were in the movies?" asked Red.

Tommy Doctor mounted his pony. "Hogs butchered on Saturday won't dry out. They won't be attacked by blowflies either."

"Hub said you been in Hollywood. But then you got too fat and they couldn't fit you in the picture."

Bristol had been thinking of something else, lost in concerns of tick fever, of the news of Georgia's double barbed-wire tick fences along her Florida border, where armed Georgia cattlemen patrolled the fence against Florida cattle in twenty-mile beats. Tommy's tightened jaw caused Bristol to shake away his thoughts like raindrops. He beckoned Red to his side. "Don't bother a man about where's he been. And don't nag him about where's he going. Try to stay in the middle. If you need to jabber, stick to what he's doing now."

"Yes, sir," the boy replied.

The frame ranch house was shielded by moss-hung oaks and clumps of bamboo and oleander. It stood beside an older dwelling, a log cabin built by the first homesteaders that now was used as a cookhouse and bunk for the hands. When Bristol and Marta first had taken over the property, they had found permutations of pineapple plants growing wild and haphazard, offshoots and slips rising from old roots, producing fruit that had survived frosts and neglect, flopped over on its tall stalks, and rotting on yellow-tipped leaves. After Marta asked Tommy to dig them up and place them in a proper plot, they now stood in rows three feet apart, a space wide enough to burn brush in a frost, to mulch with compost strips of manure and bone.

Marta was at the screen door with the child in her arms. The baby's skin was lighter than Bristol's, darker than Marta's, a hue that neither of them possessed, the color of vanilla. Her hair was black like Marta's and clung to her damp baby forehead in spongy curls, and like those of her father, her eyes were green. Since the business about the Lindbergh kidnapping, the baby was never out of Marta's sight.

Bristol was always surprised that Marta stayed with him fifty miles from nowhere, that she never once said that she wanted to quit the ranch he managed for her father and return to Miami, that she had married him at all, and that she had diminished herself under the law to do so. They were permitted to obtain a license only because Marta told the clerk that she had a Negro great-grandmother on her mother's side, which made her, under Florida law, a Negro herself. Her mother, Rosalia, had denied this, but Marta's aunt Ileana told her that the family knew it for a fact. Marta didn't care that they had to stand while white couples waited on a bench or that when the clerk asked for her name, she called her *girl*. Marta wanted to be at the side of the man she loved. She closed her mind to anything that did not include this eventuality, just as she closed her ears to the clerk telling the superior who stood over her shoulder, "These octaroons can fool you. She sure looked white to me."

Marta shifted Lilia to her other hip and opened the screen door. "Did they catch him yet?"

"You're the one with the radio. They're bound to get him sooner or later. He's pretty stupid being as he asked for only fifty thousand dollars when Lindbergh has a whole lot more than that. Millions is more like it."

"Are you tired?" she asked.

"No more than usual." He tried to make an equally solicitous inquiry as he stepped inside, but something prevented this, like a bit in his mouth. Instead he pulled off his boots and set them near the front door, under a tinted chromo of the Sacred Heart of Jesus.

"I'll make you *piña fria.*" Marta set the baby down to cut a pineapple in chunks. "Your mother called," she said. "It's Isaac. She asked if we could visit."

Bristol thought of his mother, now working for Maude Coombs. When William Jennings Bryan died, Caroline had retired from domestic service, believing she could live with Isaac off their rental income. After the stock market crash, she and Isaac had lost most of their property. Money was scarce. Jobs were few. She took the only one she could get. The fault was Isaac's. If he had moved faster, been where he was supposed to be, none of it would have happened. There wouldn't have been a white soldier lying dead on the floor, or a little black boy shivering his way into the swamps. Isaac wouldn't have been bludgeoned so badly that he could never speak or work again, Caroline wouldn't be washing out the underwear of the biggest bitch who ever lived.

"This is a lousy time. I got one damned thing after another to see to. You can't let cattle shift for themselves like in the old days. You heard me say that we need better pastureland. Wiregrass is alright, but the cattle need better fodder. The boys and I have to roll in carpetgrass seed on the oat field, that's going to take a couple, three days."

"You said summer was the best time to do that." She pounded the pineapple chunks with ice and sugar while the child lay her face against the sandspurs that clung to her father's jeans.

"That's when you sow carpetgrass all by itself," he said. "I'm mixing it with Japanese clover. Then I've got to take a look at a half-bred Brahmin sire I can have pretty cheap. We need to improve the herd. Brahmins are immune to ticks, their get is a whole lot bigger. With any luck, we could see a crop of his calves by Christmas. Brahmin-sired calves outweigh the other calves by seventy-five pounds."

Marta scooped the sweetened pineapple pulp into mugs. "She's waiting for you to pick her up." She set Sevres plates on the rude planked table. The china had been willed to her by her father along with a bust of Rodin. Both were the source of additional rancor between Marta and her mother, especially after his bequest made specific mention of Marta's finer tastes. "You have Hub," she said. "It would only be for a few days. It doesn't sound good, Bristol, about your stepfather. Your mother says he's turned his face to the wall." She set a folded damask napkin beside each plate. "I think you should take your suit. We could see my mother at the same time. Ask her for money."

That night, Bristol sprayed the crevices of the bedroom against mosquitoes with a Black Flag spray can. "I don't see them," he said, "but I can hear them whine."

The only light in the room was the glow of a crackling candle set on a wooden corner niche that held a statue of Our Lady of Charity. Marta stood naked beneath her robe except for a sacred medal, splashing cologne over her body before an electric fan.

"You could have done a whole lot better," he said.

"Maybe. It doesn't matter. You're what I want."

He set down the spray can and sprawled on the bed like a starfish. "Why? Give me one good reason."

"If I had to name one, I would pick your hands. The knuckles, the veins on their backs. They're the hands of safety."

"You're talking safety, we got every redneck within a hundred miles ready to pick me off because maybe I know something about ranching they don't, or maybe because they think you're too light-skinned for my blood. This is pretty wild country. They make their own law." He told her of the body found crumpled over the carcass of a stolen hog and the decision of the coroner's jury that the hog had met death at the hands of parties unknown, and the man died from the wound that he received by falling on the hog's tusks.

"We keep to ourselves." She shrugged in disinterest and sprinkled talcum powder on a powder puff, dusted herself, dropped her robe,

345

then lay down beside him, melding her body to his with the easy accommodation of the customary.

"Aren't you ever lonely?" he asked.

"Why should I be lonely? I have you. I have Lilia. What more do I need?"

From somewhere outside came the shrill of a nighthawk. They moved together with familiar touches, familiar responses, alternately tender and urgent, wordless except for once when she asked him to get off her arm.

They returned to Coconut Grove to the smell of jasmine and salt spray, and to the Depression. More people on Evangelist Street were out of work than working. They milled about on porch steps and sidewalks, in backyards and vacant lots. They spoke of banks that had closed their doors except for the First National, and tax sales on the courthouse steps, of a boss who had hung himself in his garage, of the price of bread rising to thirteen cents a loaf, of white folks picking off all the jobs, except for digging mosquito ditches in the Everglades for thirty cents a day. They laughed at President Hoover's call for an end to hoarding, his demand that people put their money back into circulation. They talked of the good luck of the two men who had got jobs that week digging up bones from an old Indian mound that were being sent on to some museum in Washington.

Caroline presented an equally grim catalogue.

Isaac Jr. had been arrested for bootlegging, James, in Philadelphia, was out of work, Galilee, who scarcely remembered his name, had to be constantly watched, Jessie's youngest had something wrong with her hands, and Isaac lay shriveling like a leaf in a bedroom that smelled of roses. It was also clear that Caroline hated working for Maude Coombs, although she refused to discuss it. The only thing she said on the matter was "You do what you have to do."

After an unsuccessful attempt to get Isaac to turn and look at his visitors, his daughter-in-law, Jessie, explained Caroline's feelings. "It's not the work. Caroline's been trying to skin her fine lady like a banana, peel back Miss Maude to get to the little child she used to feel so bad for. But she's finding out that there's nothing inside. You get bananas like that sometimes. Empty."

Caroline turned the pillow beneath her husband's head. "Don't speak for me, Jessie. I don't need anyone to mouth my words. I don't care about that woman. Only about Saturday afternoons. That's when I get paid."

"What happened, Mama?" asked Bristol. "I remember a time when she was always on your mind."

"It's never too late to see the light. I don't worry about her anymore one way or the other."

Caroline thought of the mysterious ways of the Lord and of Maude's comeuppance through a man called Johnny, who wore diamond stick pins, Sulka shirts, and an ankle holster, one of Capone's men who Maude was always calling on the telephone. Caroline heard them grunting in the bedroom, saw him pull her with a towel into the pool cabana. Once Maude asked her to bring a bucket of ice into the bathroom, where they both lay soaking in the oversize tub.

They quarreled in her presence as if she were as transparent as the ice cubes that floated in their drinks. The week before, Maude had found out that he had been seeing a nineteen-year-old showgirl, one of Earl Carroll's chorines. She accused him of two-timing her. She called him names, told him that Capone would never be paroled. "You're nothing without him," she said.

"And you're nothing without me. You're a roll in the hay, sweetheart. Period. End."

Then he stopped to knot his loosened tie before the lalique-edged hallway mirror while he shouted over his shoulder, "You think any man would want a has-been, over-the-hill dame with a sagging ass if he could get a doll like that? Are you kidding or something? You're lucky you're getting laid. Look at yourself in the mirror sometime without squinting."

He gave Caroline a twenty-dollar bill and left. That night Maude threw out the clothes that she had kept hidden, including a pair of swim trunks that Caroline brought home to

James, even though the boy had no place to wear them except some rock pit that someone had forgotten to fill.

They retreated to the kitchen. Caroline sat at the table and lifted Lilia onto her lap. The child settled back into her arms, recalling her previous encounters with the woman who held her only as an aroma of violets. One of Jessie's children turned on the radio to listen to *Amos and Andy*.

"I don't want to hear that," said Caroline. "White folks talking like they were us. Switch to WQAM so we can listen to Bing Crosby instead."

Jessie said that all three of her children had been born white, but that they had got darker as they got older like water with a teabag. She turned to Marta. "They going to call her high-yaller, white enough to pass, black enough to sashay."

"What's wrong with you?" asked Caroline.

"She might as well get used to it."

Lilia began to squirm. Caroline brushed the curls from the child's forehead and set her down. Bristol asked about Emma. Tommy Doctor had heard she might still be at Osceola Gardens. Had anyone seen her?

"She doesn't want to see you," said Caroline. "That's for sure. She doesn't want to see me. You abandon a child, Bristol, how you expect her to have any feeling for you or your kin?"

He pushed away from the table. "It's my

349

fault," he said, "I was the one decided to tear up colored town. It was my idea to squirrel me away in the swamp. To keep me there so long, by the time I came out I almost forgot how to read. It was me who decided to keep Emma and her mother in that stinking tourist camp."

There was silence except for the sound of Galilee padding through the house. Caroline cleaned her glasses with a flowered handkerchief that had been pinned to her pocket. "I don't recognize my baby," she said. "Don't you think it was every bit as hard on me? My child was gone. My firstborn. Forever as far as I knew. I died every morning I woke up and remembered you weren't sleeping next to Galilee. It's happening to me again, Bristol. My other boy is in jail with an eyelid half-torn off his face. Sometimes I'm so weary, I don't think I can put one foot down in front of the other."

"You too selfish to live, Bristol," said Jessie. "Your brother's going to some work farm, they have sweat boxes in those places, his daddy's dying, I got an eleven-year-old son learning how to ring cash registers, and you still going around asking for pity. There wasn't a night we didn't sit here and try to figure out, do we stay, do we go up north to Philadelphia with James except he's as bad off as we are? Does just one of us go and the rest follow? Or do we go as a family? And where are we gonna get the money? The whites say

350

we so happy. We supposed to be laughing all the time. You hear them saying that, Caroline."

Caroline set the wire rims over her ears. "I don't pay attention to what they say."

Jessie turned to Marta. "Marta knows I'm right. You'all say that, don't you?"

Tears sprang to Marta's eyes. "Why do you make it so difficult for me to be part of your family?"

"You might be married to Bristol, but you'll never be part of this family," said Jessie.

"Jesus God, Jessie. Don't we have enough trouble? Didn't you see me this morning trying to spoon-feed the life back into a man that doesn't want it? You got no call to speak to Bristol's wife the way you do. This is my house. I won't have it." Lilia began to cry and sought the sanctuary of her mother's skirts. "Now see what you did."

Bristol picked up the child. "I wasn't going to come. I could have used the time. We're here because of Marta. She's the one said we needed to see Isaac. Well, we saw him, and we feel bad, especially for you, Mama. It doesn't look like there's much anyone can do except wait, and you don't need four grown people to do that." He put his hand on Marta's shoulder. "You ready?"

Marta stood. Caroline went to walk them to the door as Jessie called out from the kitchen, "Tell your brother, the numbers man, to stop hustling Galilee for plays."

★ ★ ★

Their visit across the river to N.E. 7th Street was even more contentious. They found Marta's mother, Rosalia, to be thicker and somehow shorter than the last time they had seen her, settling and sifting into middle age with Enna Jettick shoes that seemed to root her to the floor. They sat in the parlor, where Bristol was instructed to keep the child from touching things. Marta noticed that the Persian carpet that her father loved had been replaced with a rug with roses on the border.

"How are you feeling?" Marta asked.

"My health is as good as can be expected. One of my legs swells from time to time, but if I keep it raised on a pillow, the swelling goes away. At least my skin is still smooth and does not have the dried-out look of these American women who shrivel in the tropics like prunes."

Bristol came to the point, swallowed his pride and asked for a loan. He needed to lay more grass seed and buy a Brahmin bull to improve the herd. He and Marta were willing to give Rosalia a mortgage on Marta's interest in the property.

Rosalia Garcia refused. "I am in need of money myself, especially with the cigar factory closed. Times are bad. If you wish, you may return to live with me. I will do my duty and take you in. In any case, Pablo and I want to be paid for our shares of the ranch. If you are not willing to do this, we will petition the court to sell it."

"What does my brother say?" asked Marta.

Rosalia Garcia replied that Pablo, who had gone with his wife on the ferry to Cuba, was in agreement. She regarded her daughter with distaste as she had ever since Marta became a *campasina*, living on barren land with mosquitoes and a mulatto opportunist with dirty fingernails and no prospects, who chased cattle as scrawny as chickens.

"I will remind you that your marriage is one which I neither encouraged nor condoned. Before I was even consulted, you ran off like thieves in the night. You were always a stubborn, willful girl, Marta, partial to your father, turning from me at every chance. Well, you have made your bed and now you must lie in it."

Bristol said that Marta's brother owned no interest in the ranch. Rosalia Garcia replied that she had been advised differently, then became critical of Lilia. Her dress was too short, falling well above her knees, which were skinny and not plump and dimpled as a child's should be. And where were her white knee stockings?

Marta said she wanted to see her father.

"Don't expect him to tell you anything different than I have. In fact, don't expect him to tell you anything at all."

Rosalia Garcia swept out the foyer as soon as they left the house, believing that if she waited until after dark, she would sweep out the Virgin Mary, and wondering how it came to be that a dutiful daughter could turn on her mother like a viper.

Chapter Seventeen

EMMA

When my father left the Pahahokee, I waited for his return, gasping like a fish on the riverbank, until night fell and my weeping mother carried me back to our chickee. Now that I am a woman, my mother's brother Josie, who has become a Baptist minister, preaching before a pulpit cut from a cypress pole, says I have another father, a more powerful one. Sent by the white man to the Bible Institute at Lakeland, Josie Doctor does not mean the Great Spirit, or the white father in Washington. He speaks of a father in heaven, a sky-place where a man in a long white beard sits on a cloud and counts my sins.

I do not resent wisdom from Josie Doctor, even if I do not believe it. He is, after all, my mother's brother. More difficult to accept is counsel from whites. This does not mean that I despise the pale ones as does my brother Sam, or my uncle

Tommy, who battles the white man to save the deer. I consider the white man as the swarming flies. There is little one can do to keep them away, just as there is little one can do to keep away smirking tourists who pay twenty-five cents admission to see alligators and Indians who will not speak to them. There is no remedy against strangers with cameras around their necks who advise us, while the Victrola at the entrance plays "Moon Over Miami," to spray citronella against the mosquitoes, to use fly swatters against the flies.

Like the flies, the white man interferes in all corners of our lives. The agent tells us to send our young on a bus to the new Indian school, where they will learn to wash their hands and face every morning, to take baths twice a week. My grandfather laughs at the idea. When the Indian lived in the Pahahokee, he used to bathe every day, he said, wash his hands and face morning and night.

A visiting nurse whose glasses fall to her nose instructs us to use more salt so that we will not crave as much meat. A doctor charges a dollar-fifty a person to check our nightsoil for hookworm on a piece of glass, and tell us that if we don't stop eating sweets, our teeth will fall from our mouths. The nurse returns and says that if we eat more sweets, we will not desire alcohol which cannot be true, since my mother eats candy and soda pop all the time, yet whiskey made her sick and they had to put her in the white man's hospital. When she woke up, her ideas were bad and she saw her thoughts on the wall.

We no longer expect my mother's husband to cure her. Charlie Billie, once able to suck the evil from a sick man's forehead, cannot cure my mother of bad ideas because someone stole his medicine bundle. No one can recall when such a thing has ever happened before. It had to be a white. No Indian would do such a thing. My halfbrother Sam says that the yaboli bundle with its willow, cedar leaf, and snakeroot was sold by the proprietor, Skagg, for a lot of money. Luck, like the parched Pahahokee when the rain has ceased, cracks even further. Last month Charlie Billie gashed his leg against the side of the coral rock alligator pool. His wound became swollen with fever. My mother, Mary, used to know how to cure red streaks and oozing heat. These are things she learned from my grandmother Sally Cypress. But she has forgotten. Now my mother and Charlie Billie are like dugouts without poles. They spin around each other but go nowhere. He cannot cure her. She cannot cure him.

Old white men in buttoned jackets come to Musa Isle. My baby son stands clutching a pickle jar of milk to his belly while I make hush puppies over an open fire, waiting for the lard to raise a light smoke before I drop in the balls of yellow cornmeal mixed with bacon drippings.

The visitors act important, strut like roosters with their hands behind their backs. A man shows my grandfather a newspaper and says he is a reporter. "This is about you, sir. It's called 'Florida's Forgotten Man.'"

My grandfather wears a derby hat that belonged to his friend Jimmy Jumper, and pretends he does not understand. Like most elders, he will not wear shoes. He still prefers to wear red, thinking perhaps that he is in the Pahahokee and should still attract deer. Most of his ideas are good. It is just his step, his voice, and his eyesight that have weakened with age. Skagg does not think he is useful, yet he leaves him alone. Perhaps someone has told him that the elderly have magical powers.

Skagg gathers us together. He points at two men. "They have been sent by Washington. This is Harold Ickes. He is the secretary of the Interior. This is John Collier. He is the commissioner of Indian affairs."

Collier asks me if we have had enough to eat. I am reluctant to speak. I see Skagg waiting for my answer. I nod my head.

"Do you know anyone who is sick?" the interpreter asks.

I watch my grandfather stumble after a pig. "No," I reply.

They speak of infant mortality. No one translates. I understand that they are talking about death and babies, a natural thing, like women eating after men. I do not tell them, nor do they ask, about my first baby, who died from the white man's measles, or my second, weak and feeble, hardly able to walk, from hookworm. My used-to-be husband Chestnut Gopher said it was not the hookworm but the five days it took us to go from camp to camp looking for a medicine man with a yaboli bundle that killed her. It makes no difference. The baby was already too weak to live, like a flower that has lost its petals.

A man in a buttoned coat approaches Charlie Billie. "Are you happy living here?"

"We would rather live here than opposite a filling station," replies my grandfather, referring to the villages that string like beads along the Tamiami Trail.

Another of the party asks, "Wouldn't you rather live at the reservation?"

My grandfather acts as if he does not understand.

"Where they cut the ground for the Indian," the interpreter explains.

"Your children would go to a reservation school," says a woman wearing gloves.

"And learn to wash their hands," I say.

"Yes." The woman smiles. She is pleased with my response, and with me. "That too. And to read and write English, to repair automobiles — your men are natural-born mechanics. To sew, keep house, raise cattle. Everything. What's your name?"

"Emma." I do not tell her my Indian name. "You're very bright, Emma."

"Sometimes too quick for her own good," says the owner's wife.

I try to give the woman a wide berth. The owner's wife is everywhere, thrashing about like the snout of an alligator as it searches for water. She does not like my earrings or the way I wear my hair, long, loose, held back on the sides with two barrettes. She would rather that I dressed it like some of the older women who wear their hair gathered at the side and held in place with a net, the way my mother used to wear her hair when she did not wander distractedly.

The owner's wife also does not like the shortsleeve sweater I prefer to wear over my patchwork skirt. "Wear the proper Indian cape," she says. "The tourists expect to see it."

I do not refuse outright. To do so would be insulting. I just do not put on the cape. It is the softer, Indian way, not like a hurricane, rather like a breeze. A mark is made against me in a book. It costs me fifty cents a week to wear the sweater. I think it is worth it.

The owner, Skagg, sells heron plumes under the cover of darkness, and runs his hands over the women when they aren't expecting it. He is so fast, so deft, like a snapper swimming in and out of the mangroves, that a woman is never sure that it really happened and so can not make a complaint. He does this even when his wife is around. Especially when his wife is around.

He gets us work in the vegetable fields in the winter and the spring, where we ride twenty in a flatbed to squat over pole beans from sunup to sundown and snap them from their stems for seventy-five cents a day. Out of this wage we pay Skagg ten cents a day. He is the contractor. It is only fair.

The trouble began in his office when I came to pay him sixty cents for the week. He sat on the edge of his desk, poured whiskey into a glass, and offered me a drink. "No," I said, "too strong."

He pushes it in my face. "Come on. I know you like it."

When I turn my head, he grabs my waist. White people smell sour. I try not to breathe.

"I also know you don't wear nothing under that skirt."

He moves too quickly. I am ashamed to scream, ashamed to bring humiliation upon my family. He pulls up my skirt and pushes me back on the desk, then strokes my naked body with a heron plume. "How do you like this?" he asks. "Does it feel nice?"

No Indian man asks such a stupid question. They listen to a woman's breathing to know whether she likes a thing or not. I do not answer.

"Must be you do," he says. "You got your eyes closed."

I am someplace different, thinking of white ibis flocking to their roots, red mangroves crouching like an army, so far away that when he enters me I scarcely notice.

Later that night, I swim in the river. My grandfather comes to the landing as I splash about in my clothing. "Charlie Billie said you were in the water. Is there trouble?"

"No, Grandfather," I reply. "No trouble."

He squats on the landing. "Maybe alligators on land worse than those in the water," he says.

When I come out, I ask him to tell me again of the days with his friend Jimmy Jumper, of his uncle Willie Tiger, buried up to his neck in sand by his mother to hide him from the white soldiers.

Skagg tells me that unless I return to his office, he will not give me a job at the truck farm. I tell him that I do not want to pick pole beans anymore, or dig up potatoes. He says if my mother continues to drink, our family cannot stay at Musa Isle. He holds up a heron plume and smiles.

I go to the gas station and trade a rejected tom-tom for the telephone. I dial the old, faded numbers from a crumpled piece of paper that I have kept so long, and am surprised when my father's old woman answers the phone. I thought that maybe she was already dead, or that her spirit, on its way out of her body, had left her weak.

"This is Emma," I said. "I need you to make a call."

"Who to?"

"I don't know. The police, I guess."

"About what? You in trouble?" she asks.

I have to whisper. The man in the gas station is trying to listen. I tell her that someone is selling heron plumes, and it is against the law.

She tells me that I should stay out of business that is not mine, asks me why I have not been in touch for so many years. I say I'll call someone else.

She says she'll do it. She wants to know what is it that I want to happen.

I want the man to go to jail, I reply.

She says she'll find out who to call. She thinks it may be the Audubon Society. To reward her, I tell her I have kept the pillow, the sweet-smelling, silken white man's luxury that she once brought to Osceola Gardens. She asks if I still have the doll she gave me many years ago. I tell her it is someplace in the camp, but I don't remember where.

Two weeks later, federal marshals raid Musa Isle, take Skagg to jail, haul away cartons of plumes that they say are worth $25,000 of the white man's dollars.

The day after Skagg has to pay a thousand-dollar fine, my grandfather dies. There is no warning, no curling inward like a leaf, no cries

362

of pain. We find him one morning still in his derby hat. Uncle Josie demands to bury him at the reservation in the government cemetery. Uncle Tommy, who shows up from nowhere, says no. All adult Indian men are buried deep in the Pahahokee. Miami Doctor will be taken to some hidden place in the swamp, where not even I, his granddaughter, can go, his body surrounded by a fence of logs and fronds of cabbage palm. Because he is famous, we will keep the campfire going to ward off evil spirits. We will say nothing to Josie until it is over.

After the mourning campfire is out, we drive to the reservation in Charlie Billie's car with hempen ropes around its rear wheels to keep it from getting stuck in the muck. I think my mother understands, but I am not sure. She is wearing the beads that belonged to my grandmother Sally Cypress. The car gets stuck in a rut. The back wheels dig in until it is resting on its running board. Starting it up only bogs it down farther until the water laps the running board and minnows swim over it. My mother behaves as if it is she who died. After Charlie Billie gets us out, he takes the engine apart and dries off all the parts. My mother wants to bequeath the beads to me. She says it is time to start giving them away. I don't want them. They would be like a noose around my neck.

"Then who will I give them to?" my mother asks.

Charlie Billie ties a handkerchief over the radiator to keep the car from scooping water into the fan while I look for reservation signs and do not answer.

Chapter Eighteen

The paralyzing Depression that had forced Flagler's Florida East Coast Railway into receivership and caused George Merrick, who poured millions of his own money into Coral Gables, to retire penniless to a fishing camp in the Keys, had not yet affected the Watsons.

As best as she understood, Maude's husband had been quick to react, alert to some pulse, like the chameleons that skittered across their lawn, inducing him to liquidate his securities before the stock market crash and readjust their way of living by doing away with the chauffeur. "Not so much for expenses," he told Maude, "but for appearances."

Neither had the Depression affected the attraction of Miami. It still glinted like a fish lure for tourists arriving on the railroads, the steamships, and the new Pan American flying clippers, in motor buses rolling in from everywhere, as well as tens of thousands of automobiles rumbling over the macadam and concrete highways, over potholes and waffle-iron bridges, past convicts in striped uniforms swinging pickaxes under the eyes of guards with whips and billboard poems about Burma Shave.

The promise of the repeal of Prohibition was not the bait, since Miami had ignored the existence of the law from the start. It was the excitement of charter fishing for tarpon and sailfish, aerial sightseeing in blimps owned by the Goodyear Rubber Company, buzzing from the Biltmore Hotel in Coral Gables to the Roney Plaza on Miami Beach in an autogiro, which lifted itself straight up in the air. It was the racetracks, dog tracks, jai alai, prize fights, nightclubs, and illegal gambling casinos in the back room of a drugstore in Surfside, nestled in posh residential enclaves like the nightclub on Palm Island, or on the top floor of the Floridian Hotel.

It was close to midnight when Maude, her brother, and his wife, Paula, having just seen Eddie Cantor and Jack Benny at the Floridian Hotel's ten o'clock show, rode the elevator to the ninth floor.

Jack Coombs was still lean and handsome in a double-breasted white dinner jacket, his body as taut as a bowline. If anything, he had had difficulty in the past few years maintaining his weight. With a full shock of sun-bleached graying hair, he looked best in deck shoes without socks, in shirts turned back at the cuffs.

It was his offhand panache that had attracted Paula in the first place. They met at the Roney Plaza, where she had taken a suite for the season. She was soft-spoken and confident, her chestnut-brown hair coiffed in a glossy helmet. He learned that she was a widow, that while still youthful in appearance, was clearly older than he. Soon after Paula invited him to escort her to a charity ball, and soon after that, he became the unofficial host at her Bath Club dinner parties.

It was Paula who proposed during lunch at Hialeah Race Track. She was direct. "It must have occurred to you as it has to me that we can offer each other a pleasant life. I think we should marry." She lay down her menu. "I will make no demands on you, Jack, that you do not care to meet."

He slipped his sunglasses into the inside pocket of his jacket. "There are things about me, Paula, that you don't know."

She stopped him with a hand on his lapel. "I never took you for the bore who insists on baring his soul. Everyone is entitled to secrets, darling. All I ask of you is discretion."

The pre-nuptial agreement was signed in a lawyer's office. Of the event, Jack recalled looking out the window at pigeons swooping down from the courthouse roof and wondering why Paula wanted to spend the summer in the south of France when neither of them spoke French.

Jack had told Maude that in the five years

that he had been married, he had been to bed with his wife less than a dozen times, each occasion an unsuccessful coupling made less than distasteful only because their restrained, chaste attempts had been executed in the dark beneath Porthault coverlets where neither could lose face by trading body parts that did not match.

Although Jack felt no passion for Paula, he admired the flawless style with which she teamed her Molyneax silk suits with diamond studs instead of eardrops and the fact that she never left her bedroom without foundation on her face or perfume behind her ears.

Jack considered their marriage a pact, an accommodation. He contributed his part, she hers. The arrangement was simple. Paula provided the money for expenses, holidays abroad, cars and club memberships in Indian Creek, the Bath and the Surf, and the refurbishment of Jack's pine house, which she referred to as their winter cottage. He provided the white tie and tails, the ability to play a decent game of mixed doubles, select a Bordeaux, recognize when she had a headache, not wrinkle the back of her gown when they danced. In short, he was a devoted escort who wouldn't talk about her sagging breasts in the morning.

They exited the elevator, which did not go any higher, then trudged up a flight of stairs and knocked on the door of what appeared to be an ordinary hotel room. After they were waved in, they entered a closet through which they walked into a narrow frisk room, where they were searched for weapons. From there they stepped into a brightly lit gambling casino with brocade drapes, wall-to-wall carpeting, whirling roulette balls, and clicking dice.

The room at the top of the hotel was buzzing with men in dinner jackets and women in furs worn over graceful, softly shaped evening dresses, casino managers in formal dress, pit bosses in black pinstripe suits and white ties, stick men and croupiers with eyeshades and elastic on their sleeves. Patrons milled around two dice tables, four blackjack tables, a roulette wheel, and a table reserved behind a velvet rope for chemin de fer. Here and there an isolated shill sat to stimulate the action. From above, a ladderman scanned the room for dice mechanics rolling bad dice, dealers making bad payoffs, for card sharks palming deuces.

Jack led his wife and sister each by an arm. "You sure you want to see this?" he asked.

Maude was still miffed because Doris Duke, who was staying at the Roney, had not returned her telephone call. Her voice was petulant. She twisted her huge cerise chiffon handkerchief around a finger. "Paula wants to see it. She promised me she would. And don't tell us again that the girls are doing it because they're hard up for money. It spoils it."

They entered a smoke-filled room that was

fitted with a boxing ring surrounded by benches in front and bleachers along the back. Most of the spectators were men. Jack, Maude, and Paula found seats on the side. Someone behind them said that any bookie who took fight action was out of his mind. "A tanker like this," said the man, "he can go for a bundle."

Two young women, one with taffy-colored hair and sunburnt, peeling cheeks, the other, bronzed with black hair, entered the room wearing shorts and sleeveless jerseys. They were greeted with a mixture of jeers and clapping and a sudden flurry of betting.

Maude leaned over to ask a bookmaker the odds.

"If you bet the favorite," he replied, "you have to lay nine to five. If you bet the underdog, you take seven to five."

"The first way I can lose twice as much as I can win," she said.

"Smart lady."

A man in a powder blue serge suit with a diamond stick pin pushed away from the wall. "He's giving you a two-point spread. Two points is his vig. His cut of the action. You're at the track enough, Mrs. Watson, to understand vigorish."

Maude swept him with her eyes, dismissing him as she had tried to dismiss how it felt to rake her nails across his back. "If I want lessons," she said, "I'll hire a tutor."

"Who was that?" asked Paula.

"No one important. He works for Capone."

Paula glanced back at the man with the diamond stick pin. "You really can't mix with them. Roddey Burdine made an ass of himself. Going to Capone with his hat in his hand to ask for a donation to the community chest that everyone made him give back."

Someone struck a bell. The contenders went toward each other, left hand extended, right high and guarding the jaw, their feet shifting impatiently, kicking up puffs of resin. Quick and nimble, able to avoid each other's punches. In the fourth round, the girl with the taffy hair ducked, then whipped up a left that landed on her opponent's mouth. Blood filmed the woman's teeth and fell on her jersey. Infuriated, the dark-haired girl sprang at the other like a wildcat. Some of the patrons looked uncomfortable, including Paula, who took out a mirrored compact and powdered her nose, but the fight went on, with the girls' hair tangled, puffed faces smeared with blood, eyes glaring from under blue and swollen lids.

Suddenly the blonde girl fell forward on her hands and knees, sobbing and straining for breath. The referee began to count. The fallen girl tried to stand, but her opponent struck her again and the taffy-haired girl pitched forward, head cradled on her arms, blood forming a sticky pool under her face, shoulders heaving.

Then there was silence, broken only by the breathing of the spectators, who began to file out, the ruffling snap of bills exchanging hands, the look of triumph on the winner's face. Suddenly the blonde girl opened her eyes and began to cry.

"It's over," said Jack. "Let's go."

They reached the doorway, entering once more the brightly lit casino. Paula smiled. "My wrap," she said to Jack. "It's still on the bench."

Jack returned to pick up the silver fox cape, then crouched beside the ring and slipped a bill into the hand of the crumpled girl.

"You never tip a loser," said Maude when he returned. "What's the sense?"

"She reminded me of you."

"That's an awful comparison to make," said Maude. "And not very flattering. She's not even pretty."

"If she is," said Paula, "she won't be for long."

The man in the powder blue serge suit stood idly at the doorway. A handkerchief protruded from his pocket in three neat points. "Come back again, Mrs. Watson," he said. "You give the place class."

Maude lifted her chin. "Do you hear from your beer and brothel baron or can't he write?"

He smiled. "I had a lot of pen pals. I hear from all of them. Except one."

"Try the dead letter office. You coming, Paula?"

She declined, wanting to play blackjack. Maude stepped into the pink and crystal powder room and took out her compact, scarcely noticing the uniformed attendant who offered her a towel.

She recognized his footstep, saw him slip the attendant a folded bill.

"Thank you, Mr. Johnny," the woman said, closing the door behind her.

"You don't belong in here."

"I belong wherever you are." They stood side by side while he adjusted his handkerchief in the mirror. "I miss you, baby."

Maude snapped the compact closed, dropped it into her beaded purse, then with her pinky finger, smoothed lipstick into the bow of her upper lip.

"I'm a rough kind of guy. Sometimes I get out of line."

"What happened? Did your little friend give you the gate?"

He laughed. "Maybe I blow off too much steam, you know what I mean?"

"Is this some sort of apology?"

"It's the best I got."

"I don't know why I should accept it."

"Let me give you a reason." He put a hand behind her neck and pulled her toward him. "You have sugar lips," he said. "Did anyone ever tell you you have sugar lips?"

Maude smiled, showing the tip of her tongue, her white, pearlescent teeth. "How much did you tip her?"

"Enough to do some damage."

"How much damage?"

"As much as you want."

Maude didn't want to go to Bayfront Park to hear Franklin Delano Roosevelt speak. Even if he had been elected president of the United States, his public appearance did not warrant getting trampled in a crowd of eighteen thousand and arriving an hour early to insure a seat. She went only because Henry insisted, adopting a tone that was less request than demand. To spite him, she took an extra long time tilting her beret.

The night was warm for February. When they reached Bayfront Park, all the seats were filled, including those on the bandstand. Colored lights played over the aisles jammed with standing people and the stately Royal Palms that encircled the amphitheater.

Henry strode to the podium, where a half-dozen police officers in white pith helmets stood with their legs akimbo. They were polite but firm. They would not allow him on the bandstand. Their instructions were to keep everyone out. "Who is in charge of the bandshell?" he asked.

None of the officers knew.

"Let me know when someone in authority arrives."

Maude's heels kept sinking into the grass. She threatened to return to the car, where she could sit down, when Henry suddenly arranged for two seats in the second row.

"We're not on the bandstand," she said, brushing off the bench with her gloved hand. "People will wonder why we're not on the bandstand."

"My hands are tied."

"What's the point? Roosevelt won't know we're here. Neither will anyone else. I see Mabel Gill up there thinking she's something special when all her husband does is run the electric company."

"She probably got here early. We would have been up there too if you had done as I asked."

Henry was pointing out Mayor Cermak of Chicago when they heard the throb of a motorcycle escort. Within seconds a car carrying police and Secret Servicemen arrived in front of the bandshell. The crowd began to roar as a second car followed, an open Cadillac bearing Mayor Gautier and a waving, smiling Franklin Delano Roosevelt.

Spectators crowded in from the aisles, forcing those in the front row to stand.

"They're shooting off firecrackers," said Maude.

Henry turned to see a small man standing on a bench and brandishing a pistol as shouting bystanders tried to knock the gun from the small man's hand. A woman screamed. Maude ran as the man on the bench wrenched the pistol free and began spraying bullets.

One of Maude's shoes had fallen off. She

bent to take off the other when she felt the explosion of a photographer's flashbulb from somewhere behind her.

Where was Henry? She wanted to leave and he had the keys to the Deusenberg. A warm sensation spread across her back as Roosevelt's open Cadillac lurched forward and the gunman was dragged to a nearby car, then thrown onto the luggage rack. Maude watched them drive away, then wondered why Henry was shouting and why the grass was coming up to meet her.

She stayed in Jackson Memorial Hospital for three days. The doctor who treated her said she was fortunate. The bullet had grazed her, leaving her only with a scalp wound, a nick. Her hair would cover it. There were flowers all over the room, roses from Henry, a basket of wild spring flowers from Roosevelt, potted tulips from Paula and Jack, and a spray of orchids with an unsigned card that read TO LADY LUCK. GLAD YOU CAME UP ACES.

Henry came to see her, read the cards, then kissed her on the forehead. "For your sake, I hope your boyfriend can keep you in the style to which you're accustomed."

Maude frowned. "What are you saying? Are you threatening me with divorce? You can't divorce me, Henry. You have no grounds."

He sat on the chair beside her. He seemed old, tired. "You're like a cat, Maude. You go down scratching. It's too late to consider divorce. Try to understand. Everything is gone."

"What are you talking about?"

"I mean everything is lost."

"You got out of the stock market. I know you did."

"There are other ways to lose your assets. I'm overmortgaged and overleveraged. My lenders tell me that I'm also out of time."

"There must be something left. The house, the boat, the cars."

"You need money to maintain such things."

She retied the bow of her bed jacket. "Don't expect me to change from a private suite to a ward."

"No one's asking you to move, my darling."

"What are we going to do?"

He put his head down on his hands. "I don't know, Maude. I honestly don't know."

In May, the week after Bristol learned that twenty-five-year-old Isaac Jr. had died of a heart attack on a work farm in the Redlands, the cattle tick reappeared. Tests determined that the south Florida infestation was caused by a new species, a tropical tick different from the North American variety, that propagated on deer as well as on cattle. The hostility of local ranchers toward Bristol was redirected to the Seminoles, who refused to kill the tick-bearing deer on their reservation lands. It also extended to the state Livestock Sanitation Board, who ordered that all livestock be dipped in a vat of arsenical solution every fourteen days for the next fourteen months, which meant that all south Florida cattle were under quarantine and could not be sold. Some of the sanitation board's vats were dynamited. Glazed carcasses of deer were found skinned on reservation lands, stripped of hides worth twenty-five dollars a pelt that somewhere were being examined for ticks over the headlights of a motor car.

Thirty professional hunters had been called into the area with deer hounds, to shoot as many deer as they could locate, without restriction to age or sex. The government offered to pay the Miccosukee the same wage as the white hunters, but the Indians, who considered the Everglades an ideal deer habitat, were unanimous that under no condition and for no price would they consent to the extermination of deer on reservation land.

Tommy Doctor found Bristol at the corral repairing the split-rail fence. He said that he was going to the reservation. It did not matter that he had never been there before. He would return to the ranch every two weeks to help with the dipping. In the meantime he would join his brothers. Even without the deer-protection people's protests that Texas was doing fine against the cattle tick without touching its deer, he knew that you didn't need to kill all the deer to get rid of the tick. It was just another trick of the white man to mess where he didn't belong.

A broad-winged Everglades kite hovered overhead, searching for apple snails. "I'm probably going to leave this place sooner or later myself," said Bristol.

"Not you," said Tommy. "You're like the razorback. He rustles the marshes for wampee, a root that burns his mouth so badly he squeals, but he continues to eat it."

A week later, Bristol held the ladder, telling Hub, who was thatching the stable roof with palmetto, that it looked like they could forget about wintering their bulls on cottonseed cake and molasses, much less buy a Brahmin. He might even have to sell off part of Marta's interest in the ranch to Tatum just to keep things going. Hub called down that maybe they wouldn't need a Brahmin, that if they fed their next year's crop of calves bonemeal as soon as they were weaned, it might speed their growth. And if his salary was making the difference, Bristol's credit was good.

Hub's hound dog had caught a rat and was tearing it open near the woodpile. "Speaking of growing," said Bristol, "where's that skinny kid? I sent him to the feed store yesterday afternoon. I haven't seen him since."

Hub came down the ladder. "I've been meaning to tell you. I think someone's nailed him."

"What do you mean?"

"Nailed him. Threw him down."

"How do you know? Did he say so?"

"He didn't have to. See for yourself. He's

378

skittish. You can't tell it now, but when he first came back from town, he walked peculiar." Hub pulled his hat down over his forehead. "They tried to get to you, but they couldn't. They won't mess with me. They're afraid that Tommy will bring the whole reservation down on them, as few as they be. They got to the boy instead."

"Damn peckerwoods. Don't they have enough to do getting their cattle to swim through acid?" Bristol found Red behind the stable, laundering saddle blankets in a big washtub. "Someone bother you?"

"No, sir."

"I mean in a way that they're not supposed to. It's no shame on you if they did. You know what I mean?"

"Yes, sir."

Bristol waited. He went to put a hand on Red's shoulder. The boy flinched. "Next time you want to go to town, wait for Hub or Tommy."

"Yes, sir." Red hung a dripping blanket over the split rail fence. "The man in the feed store said to tell you that he doesn't have any Bahia seed. You have to go to Cuba for that."

The assault on Red cast a pall on the ranch that, unlike the early morning fog of February, did not dissipate with the day. Bristol went about his work, as grim-lipped and determined as before, trying to get along with one less hand, trying to figure out how to manage while

379

waiting out a quarantine, how to tell Caroline that there was no way they could leave the ranch to attend Isaac Sr.'s funeral.

The only immediate threat was from a razorback with a low, elongated skull and tapering snout that stopped chasing a rabbit through the pineapples and went after Lilia instead.

It was Red who picked up the screaming child and ran with her to the steps of the porch, yelling and dashing zigzagged into the path of a scrawny-necked, snorting, squealing hog with a center hump, taking the steps two and three at a time until the screen door banged safely behind him, and breathless, he deposited Lilia on the kitchen floor.

"Razorback," he said to Marta with a lopsided, timid smile. "Nothing to it."

Red was a hero. Hub gave him an old pair of spurs from his rodeo days. Marta made the boy a guava pie that he took to his bunk. That evening, Bristol returned with an envelope crosshatched with postmarks and excitement of his own.

The letter was from a solicitor in Nassau informing him of a bequest made to him by a Bahamian who had died some years before. The delay was caused by the time needed for probate, necessary under a presumption and not proof of the death of the man's son, Thomas Sands, and the time to locate Bristol Hanna who had, for reasons of his own, adopted the surname of the de-

380

ceased. Bristol suddenly remembered the white man with the cane who had come to the Peacock Inn when he was just a little kid. Bristol remembered leading him to the Coombs' house and wondering why the man thought that the yellow-haired Thomas would be there when it was in their cabin that he often spent the night. The letter went on to say that the bequest in the amount of five thousand pounds did not constitute an endorsement of Bristol Hanna as a legitimate heir, only that Edward Sands, recognizing the special affection between his deceased son and Caroline Hanna, had designated a small portion of his estate to the issue of that union. With the proper notarized claim they were prepared to send a bank draft in the stipulated amount.

Bristol and Marta worked through the night with pencil and paper to the eerie cry of a limpkin. After they paid off Tatum's loan, they would offer Rosalia partial payment on her interest in the property. With these obligations behind them, Bristol could concentrate on improving the herd, improving the forage, getting another hand, maybe even getting someone to help Marta in the house. It was not too late to mate their cows with Brahmin sires. It was a good investment, considering that twenty-five dollar native cows mated with Brahmin sires produced fifteen-dollar calves. Bristol would buy two Brahmins, one for each range.

Bristol lay down his pencil and stretched his

hands over his head while Marta stood behind him and rubbed his neck. He reached up to take her wrists. "Bet you didn't know you were marrying a rich man."

"A tired rich man."

He thrust a lingering hand up her sleeve. "Tired but not dead. How much time do we have before Lilia wakes up?"

"Two hours. Maybe three. I hope you're not thinking what I think you're thinking. You can't keep your eyes open."

"What I'm planning to do I can do with my eyes closed. I'll do all the work," he said. "All you have to do is shuck those duds and rest yourself."

The floors creaked beneath their feet. She closed the bedroom door and undressed in the moonlight while her underthings fluttered around her bare feet like giant moths. "I'm getting fat," she murmured. "Sometimes when I catch a glimpse of myself in the mirror, I see my mother."

"You don't look anything like that woman. You look like a melon, round, ripe, just the way a woman is supposed to look." He sat on the edge of the bed and cupped her breasts in his hands. "This is how breasts are supposed to feel, spilling over with plenty, with nipples as soft as pansies." He drew her down beside him. "Lilia," he whispered, "you and me, out here, this is just about as good as it gets."

★ ★ ★

Within the month, Bristol bought a rotary chopper and a flatbed truck. While Tatum's men watched from their cow ponies, Bristol, Hub, and Red used the rotary chopper to remove the palmetto scrub. After the cleared field had been disked, cross-disked, and fenced, Red and Hub distributed giant Bermuda and Bahia grass seed sent from Cuba by Nestor from the back of the moving truck.

Later in the summer with new grasses riffling his range, Bristol was ready to plant soybeans, which promised to yield a staggering thirty to forty bushels per acre. He sent Hub to the house to look for Red, who had gotten the idea that it was his job to take off from time to time to watch over Lilia.

It began to rain, huge drops from bulbous white thunderheads that gathered every afternoon. The drops fell in puffs of dust. A panther ran with her cub to shelter.

Hub returned at a gallop, rainwater pouring from the brim of his hat, to say that Marta was crying, that some men had come and gotten Red.

Who?

Some were Tatum's men. She didn't recognize all of them. They said he stole two of Hardee's calves and hid them in the swamps.

Torrents of water began to rake the land. Bristol thrust his left boot in a stirrup, slung his right leg over his horse, then told Hub to follow him to the house and to stay there. He picked up their tracks from the cookhouse through the vast, flat savannah dotted with pines and cattle. A black-capped caracara, scavenging on the meat of a wild turkey, hopped aside as he rode by.

They were easy to track, even in the drenching rain, which only muddied the wagon ruts and the depressions made by their horses' hooves. The trail ended at a hardwood hammock near Hardee's spread. Bristol dismounted and pushed his way through an outer ring of cocoplum. There in a clearing beneath a canopy of leaves and ghost orchids, Red stood in an ox cart with his hands tied behind his head and a noose around his neck, and Tatum's and Hardee's men on horseback, with their rifles and pistols trained on Bristol.

One of them sat easy in his saddle, with one gloved hand resting on his saddle horn. "The best gator bait," he said, "is a nigger, but the best nigger bait is a red-haired kid."

"It's me you want," said Bristol. "Not him. Let him loose. He's only a boy."

Red's hat had come off and his rain-soaked hair fell into his eyes. "I didn't do it, boss, I didn't do what they said."

"We got the proof," said Hardee. "Good enough to stand up in a court of law."

Bristol moved forward, but a rider shoved the barrel of a rifle in his chest. "What do you want? Is it money? I'll give you what you want. Just let him go."

"There's not enough money in the whole United States of America that can buy back a rustler. This is your fault. Every bit of it. Think you know so much. See what happens when a coon tries to shield a vagrant from the law?"

With grim solemnity a cowman cracked a whip and the oxen moved ponderously forward, leaving the boy suspended wide-eyed from a moss-bearded live oak, his spurs jingling as he kicked his feet helplessly in the air.

Bristol choked back the howl of protest that bellowed from his gut. The sound he made was low-pitched and strained, a growl that rattled in the hollow of his body cavity. When white men shoved the barrel of a rifle into his chest, they were once again shoving injustice down his throat and making him swallow it. The old, shapeless rage returned, only this time it was stronger. Despite a grown man's might, Bristol was as helpless in the face of this injustice as he had been while waiting out eighteen years in the Everglades.

Then he remembered something that Miami Doctor had taught him long ago. It was a bad thing for a man to be hanged, for then his soul could not leave his body. For a moment, Bristol thought that his soul was trapped like that of the boy. Then, when the boy's face lost its color, Bristol turned away, clamping off such sensibilities as if he were tightening a bit.

385

Part Three

1939–1959

Chapter Nineteen

Bristol sealed off the five-year episode of the ranch along with other grim events of his life and moved in with Rosalia. The arrangement gave Marta someone to talk to, while it got him off the hook of involvement. It also provided them with decent housing, since Caroline's house was too small and available Negro housing was often confined to ramshackle one-story shanties that leaned upon one another like drunks.

Rosalia took matters of Lilia's schooling into her own hands and enrolled her granddaughter in Gesu Catholic School, where, for four dollars a month tuition, Lilia learned to play cymbals, make the sign of the cross without kissing her thumb, earn the love of the baby Jesus by sitting up straight, print her best for the Blessed Mother, and to discuss her father as little as possible. When Marta explained to Bristol that the idea of a parochial school for white children was her mother's, he said he would have arranged it himself if he could.

Bristol put up with Rosalia's barbs about idlers and with Marta's sympathetic glances for two years. When he no longer cared about

Black Angus and Brahmin sires, about Bahia grass and soybeans that produced forty bushels an acre, about a skinny kid dangling from the end of a rope, he began to look around for a way to support his family, some operation where he could bury himself, an enterprise in which his only investment was time and money. There were plenty of black businesses in Colored Town: tailor shops, funeral parlors run by licensed embalmers, fruit stands, taxi lines, furniture stores, packing houses, drugstores, insurance agencies, grocery stores, dry-goods stores, and barber shops. None of these appealed to him. They were all daytime operations, after which a man came home at night. Bristol needed insulation. The best arena for detachment was a crowd, where you couldn't see because you were hemmed in so tight, where you couldn't hear because of the noise, where you didn't care because of the press.

He sought the action of Second Avenue, a street called The Stem, lined with beer parlors, nightclubs, dance halls, theaters, and restaurants, many with SRO signs, jammed with taxis and jitneys and people dressed to kill, shouting from one sidewalk to another over the screech of an FEC's streamliner's steel wheels, and the calls of peanut vendors. He bought a two-story building beside the Rockland Palace, and equipped a nightclub that he called the Patagonia.

He hauled over the old piano that used to

belong to Coombs from Caroline's house and which Willie never played. He had it tuned, lacquered a bright, lipstick red, put on wheels, then hired a piano player for five dollars a night to play slow-drag jazz from table to table. He put mirrors behind the bar, bought red velour bar stools that swiveled, turned down the lights, turned on his neon, and served southern fried chicken, barbecued ribs, corn bread, pure corn liquor called white lightning for fifteen cents a shot, beer for ten cents a bottle, and wine for ten cents a glass. The word was out that this sober-faced fifty-year-old cat who puffed on an oversized ten-cent cigar and who had married a white woman was no one to mess with, that he had killed at least two men, had served time, would just as soon shoot you as look at you, and didn't cut his liquor.

The Patagonia became the after-hours club, a hangout not only for black and white people out on the town, but for black entertainers playing other gigs, many in white hotels and clubs where they were not welcome to stay once their performances were over. When they returned at night to bed down at the Mary Elizabeth Hotel, or the Carver, they sought the Patagonia as a place to unwind, to listen to a singer whispering slow, lazy lyrics into a microphone.

Patrons stayed until dawn, knowing that if they hung around long enough, they might see

Fats Waller at the next table, Frankie Brown and His Bombardiers, Duke Ellington, Eubie Blake, Pigmeat Markham, Count Basie, Ella Fitzgerald, even Louis Armstrong. Sometimes the performers were not well known, often they weren't even working. They were just good, like a song-and-dance duo called Butter Beans and Susie, who dressed in matching checks, or Snookum Russell, known for his rendition of "Carolina Moon." They competed in jam sessions, each performer putting up five dollars, then picking up a banjo, a saxophone, sitting at the piano or behind the traps, until the applause decided a winner.

Once in a while the police walked in, looked around to see what they could hustle, asking Bristol the standard question, if he was running a little game in the back room. Bristol waited grim-lipped beside his bartender in the light blue, acrid nightclub haze, like a man who knew that even if you paid someone off, you still had to let them woof.

Marta accused Bristol of drying up like the Everglades, which had sparked a muck fire that cast the city in a gloomy, choking pall.

One late afternoon, she lay on her side staring at the banana leaf shadows that patterned the wall of their bedroom. "You tell me that there's no one else," she said. "You say that it's not me. Yet you touch me absently like a blind man stumbling in the dark. I feel like I'm in bed with a stranger."

392

"I wish I could change things, but I can't," he replied.

Marta rolled to a sitting position, pulled up the straps of her nightgown. "Well, I can. I'm suffocating, Bristol. I'm going to take Lilia to Cuba, where I can breathe, visit my father's people. I haven't seen my aunt Ileana, my cousins Nestor and Flavia, since I was a little girl. I don't care if you come or not. In fact, I almost prefer that you don't."

"Suit yourself," he replied.

Marta and Lilia took the ferry from Key West. By nightfall they were steaming past the Malecon, at night a collar of lights for the restless sea and the fortress of La Fuerza, where, Marta told Lilia, the ghost of Hernando de Soto's widow scanned the empty horizon.

They stayed in the Hotel Alcazar on the American plan for seven dollars a day. In the mornings they braved the lottery vendors, who were as thick as flies, and the speeding crowds darting in every direction from the turntable of the city's traffic, the Parque Central, to tour the Cathedral of Columbus, the old Santa Clara convent, now a headquarters for the department of public works, Morro Castle, where a guide told them that the twelve guns were named for the Apostles. Each afternoon they strolled the narrow sidewalks of the Prado on the way to Nestor's house, beneath a long tunnel of awnings that stretched from house to house, past deep, widely grated windows thrown open for ventilation where they had the inspection of all the front parlors in Havana.

"What do you think of Cuba?" Marta asked the child.

"I like the kettle drums," said Lilia. "And the way the streets smell."

"How do they smell?"

"Like pineapple."

The grilles protecting the windows of Nestor's house were three inches thick. His mother, Ileana, came to the door smelling of violets. While Lilia, who wanted to remain in the hotel so she could listen to the band, stood beside her in sulky silence, Marta sipped Catalonia wine with her father's kin on a double row of facing willow rocking chairs.

They exchanged anecdotes and yellowed photographs like favors. Marta thought that she and Flavia, both softly plump, resembled each other. Nestor, on the other hand, was slender, and carried himself with a masculine grace that Marta had never seen in an Anglo-Saxon. He wore it loosely, like the jacket that he draped across his shoulders, yet it clung to his every movement, his every glance, to every word he uttered.

When Nestor's seven-year-old daughter, Gloria Maraquilla, bouncing in ruffles and flounces and spiraling black curls, took Lilia upstairs to play, the talk turned serious. Nestor told Marta that things were a little better under President Laredo Bru than under President Machado. But

Batista was the power behind the scenes, he said. Laredu Bru was only his puppet.

Nestor knew a German Jew who had purchased landing certificates for his parents from a man named Benitez at $150 each. When their ship, the *St. Louis*, arrived in Havana harbor, passengers were not permitted to disembark. No one knew why. Then they learned that President Bru had suspended all documents signed by Benitez.

"It was Batista who forced Bru to cancel all the landing permits," said Nestor. "Some are even saying that Batista received a request from the U.S. secretary of state asking that the Jews not be allowed in Cuba."

Nestor's wife, Hortensia, turned to Marta. "Was this something generally known by Americans?"

"I heard on the radio," said Marta, "only that the ship traveled down the oceanfront of Miami Beach with a Coast Guard cutter following behind, warning over a loudspeaker that it was too close to shore."

"Why didn't they jump overboard and swim?" asked Lilia. "That's what I'd do. As soon as it got dark."

"Lilia," said Marta. "I didn't hear you come downstairs."

"It's amazing what they pick up," said Nestor.

"Little pitchers have big ears," said Ileana. "Especially that one. I would watch her if I were you, Marta. Her thoughts are too bold for a girl."

"Lilia doesn't want to play with dolls," said Gloria Maraquilla with a toss of her curls. "She said she wants to go back to the hotel."

Nestor put out an arm to the green-eyed child who scuffed her Mary Janes defiantly on the tile floor. "Come here, *niña*," he said. "Tell me what it is you can do at the hotel that you can't do here."

"The band leader lets me shake the maracas," said Lilia.

Marta tucked her purse beneath her arm and thought that the other thing they could do at the hotel was pack up and go home.

Caroline considered herself better off than most. No one in her family was on relief. She had not been cut back like some domestics to room and board and ten dollars a month. Although she woke up mornings stiff, she could still get up and go to work. If the knuckles of her hands were swollen and painful, especially when it rained, they were not as gnarled and misshapen as those of some of the other women on Evangelist Street.

She missed James, she missed the ones who had gone on, Isaac, Isaac Jr., killed God knows how, Galilee. In the first few years after Galilee died, Caroline had still thought she heard the old man prowling absently from room to room. To feed his spirit, she left a piece of orange and a crust of bread on a plate bordered with sprigs of green, until Isaac Jr.'s wife complained that the food was attracting bugs.

"You might as well send them roaches invitations," Jessie said. "What would your church board say if they knew you were still doing that old-timey island stuff? You supposed to be a deaconness, dressed up in your white stockings, sanctified and testified, and then you go setting out supper for a ha'nt."

Caroline wasn't sorry when Jessie remarried and took thirteen-year-old Malvina with her to Jacksonville. What made her feel bad was that Jessie didn't want Willie and told the boy so to his face.

Caroline wondered how the woman could wash her hands of her own flesh and blood. Just because he had made a gun out of a piece of tire rubber, a nail, a wire, and a part of a door hinge and almost blew his thumb away was no reason that she could think of. If Willie had got lost in childhood, it was not his fault. A lot of people got lost in hard times, which for many of the people she knew had always been the general state of things.

Now Caroline lived with a reefer-smoking grandson who wanted a zoot suit, said *reet* instead of right, and who was a shill to a man named Shoebrush, who worked with an orange crate, three nutshells, and quick hands.

If the grandchild she grieved for was Emma, a grown woman with a little boy of her own whom Caroline had never seen, Bristol, her firstborn son, the one to whom she owed her life, was the knot in her heart. Since his return to Miami, he had turned in on himself like a snail. Caroline had done everything she knew how to do, had been patient, quiet when he was quiet, talky when he wanted to talk, which was not very often. Whatever it was that was eating him up had sent him spiraling inward in an acid, sour penetralia. I'm the one should be sour, she thought. One child taken away when he was just a boy, a husband who got his head bashed in, one son lost to the North, another to God-knows-what.

I'm the one, she thought, drove with Lulu Ryder's son to the Redlands work farm where iron vans filled with prisoners stood baking in the sun, I'm the one the guards told that Isaac Jr. had suffered a heart attack.

"He wasn't sickly," she had protested. "He never had anything wrong with his heart." She remembered steeling herself so that she would not cry in front of the white men in their sweat-stained uniforms. "He was only twenty-five years old."

They gave her a slip to sign and handed her a paper bag that contained a belt, a fountain pen that had run out of ink, and a note pad scribbled with accounts in Isaac Jr.'s careful, rounded hand. Missing was his signet ring with the real ruby set in gold.

"Where's his ring?" she had asked.

"Now, auntie," one of them had said, "you know that boy never had no ring."

Lately Bristol's visits had become a thing to get through. While he brought his family, he also brought gloom wrapped around him like a blanket. Caroline felt no different this evening, even watched the clock, knowing she would be glad when he left to go to work. They sat where they always did, in the kitchen. Willie put his new alligator wallet, a gift from Marta, in his pocket while Bristol preached an angry tirade against his nephew for getting himself arrested at a swim-in at Baker's Haulover Beach.

"The bail's not the problem," said Bristol. "You are. Why would you do such a fool thing? Swim in a white beach."

"It was hot."

"You want to do some good, don't get yourself arrested. Get a tin can. See if you can collect some money for the Scottsboro boys. They're not thinking of swimming. They just want to get out of jail. You don't see them rushing to put themselves in the water."

Willie looked up through clear, round eyes. "You were the one gave me the trunks. What was I supposed to do with them?"

Conversation stopped while Caroline served yams cooked in ashes, duckanoo the way Bristol liked it, even gave Lilia a plate to take into the front room so she could listen to the radio. When Caroline eased herself into her seat, she noticed that Marta's eyes were deeply shadowed.

"The house is beginning to run down," said Bristol. "You're not taking care of it like you should, Willie. Hammer down the loose boards, man, fix the leaks, at least get rid of the old rusty still in the backyard."

Willie pushed his chair back from the table and buttoned a jacket that came to his knees. A gold watch chain swung even lower. "Can't do it, Uncle Bristol," he said. "Don't have the time."

"Why not?"

"I got me a commitment."

Bristol lit a cigar. "What kind of commitment is that?"

"I been fixing to tell you." Willie reached for a box that he slapped on the table. "See, these here are Christmas seals, for the NAACP."

"Christmas seals in September?" said Marta.

"You heard about the early bird," Willie said. "The way it is, you can buy a book of one hundred for a dollar, or a book of two hundred for two dollars."

"That doesn't sound right," said Bristol.

"It didn't to me either the first time I heard it."

Bristol bought ten dollars worth of books in exchange for a promise that Willie would tack tar paper over the holes in the roof. Willie said for another ten he would hammer down the loose boards, then pinched the pleats of his peg top trousers and asked Caroline for a dollar on account. He had places to go, people to see.

"You shouldn't be giving him money like that," said Bristol after Willie had left. "Buying Christmas seals is one thing. A handout is another. You're encouraging the wrong things."

"Speaking about encouraging the wrong things," said Caroline, "whenever I see Lilia she's finger snapping and singing along to Bessie Smith records. It's wrong for a child that young to be singing *my man this,* and *my man that.*"

"That's not my doing," said Bristol. "Lilia's not allowed anywhere near The Stem. Besides, I'm not sure you're right. If she's all the time doing like you say, how come I never heard her?"

"How do you expect to notice anything she does," asked Marta, "when you're either asleep or at the club? Or anything I do for that matter, either."

Caroline sighed, put her hands on the table, and brought herself to her feet. "As long as we're spelling things out," she said, "I have something I want to say to you, Bristol. Leave off on Willie. Maybe he's got a little hustler in him, but at least he's trying to do something for his people. Which is more than I can say for you. As far as I can see, you're not any good to any of your people, even those you live with."

They drove home in silence. Bristol looked through his rearview mirror at Lilia, who sat

401

curled up in the backseat looking out the window. "I didn't know you liked Bessie Smith," he said. "What is it you like about her?"

"She chews her songs like gum, slides the notes all around her mouth. I like that."

"Would you like to take music lessons? I could arrange for someone to teach you to play the piano."

"I don't want to play no piano."

"Any piano," corrected Marta. "That's how she talks after she's been with Willie."

"Like a nigger, you mean."

"Don't say such things in front of the child."

"Why not? You think them."

They stopped for a red light. Marta's face was shadowed in the street lamp. "Have you gone crazy? What have I ever said, ever done to make you say such a terrible thing to me? You want to spend all your time away from the house, suit yourself. Only don't think you can say whatever mean thing you please the little time you spend with us."

"I can't win," he said.

"The way we're heading, Bristol, there's no winners here. Only losers, you, me, most of all Lilia."

Several weeks later, the KKK rode through Colored Town in seventy-five cars, each with its license covered over. Wearing sheets and nightshirts, they tossed out hundreds of red-lettered warning cards from their car windows reading NIGGERS, STAY AWAY FROM THE POLLS, and set on fire twenty-five crosses at one-block intervals along the FEC tracks. At 14th Street and the railroad tracks, a lifesize dummy was suspended from a pole with a sign around it reading, THIS NIGGER VOTED. Firemen were called out, but returned to their stations with their hoses still coiled.

Bristol witnessed the parade in silence as others beside him who had come from their beauty shops and beer parlors, from their law offices and taxi stands, expressed disgust with the police, who did nothing about the illegal covering of license plates, with the fire department for not extinguishing the blazes.

"Isn't that the damnedest thing?" said a man named Shadrach Ward, another proprietor from The Stem.

Bristol lit a cigar, made no reply as he watched the straw-filled dummy swing from the pole.

"What's the matter with you, man?" asked Ward. "You too stupid to care or you scared shitless? Which is it?"

Bristol returned to the Patagonia and worked through that night, making sure that Hartley Tootes and His Honey Boys got the music stands they asked for, that the waitresses rotated their stations, that the dishwasher showed up, that the show went off on schedule, that the bartender didn't switch bottles. When early morning came, the chairs placed upside down on the tables, the cash counted, the kitchen and the bar closed down, Bristol yanked out memories as if they were splinters. He thought back to the eighteen years he had been forced to hide in the Everglades, to the insults Marta had borne on his behalf, to the white boy swinging from the rope, his eyes glazed over, no longer looking to Bristol for help, to the rage Bristol had been forced to bottle because he had been unable to do a thing about any of it. He slammed his fist against a wall. It went through the thin partition, leaving a hole with a plaster collar.

Bristol drank cold coffee, one cup after another, and waited until dawn. At seven, determined and resolute, he washed his face, thinking that it was time to take the lid off the thing that had been eating at him all his life, time to put an end to all of it, time, like Willie, to do something about it. He locked the door behind him and walked to the polling station, the firehouse at 14th Street and North Miami Avenue that the night before had been so ineffective against the blaze.

Soon others fell in beside him, spilling from every street, a thin trickle that quickly became a stream. Rather than turn people from the polls, the KKK demonstration inspired a record Negro turnout. Some had forgotten about the election. Others had been apathetic. Bristol, like many, had been frozen in rage. Now all of them, a thousand strong, marched to cast their votes at two voting machines that had been set aside for colored voters at the 14th Street entrance to the fire station, while white voters used the North Miami Avenue entrance, and a ring of police officers stationed by Chief Quigley rimmed the perimeter.

After Bristol had cast his ballot, he stepped into the morning sun and rolled up his sleeves. It was going to be a hot day if the shimmering sidewalk was any indication.

Shadrach Ward hurried after him. "That feel as good to you, Bristol, as it did to me?"

"It's like the sun," said Bristol. "You know it's going to get as hot as hell, but it's nice to know no one can stop it from shining on you."

When Bristol came home, Rosalia and Marta were standing beside Marta's Plymouth, making a last-minute inspection of Lilia's pilgrim costume. "Why the glad rags?" he asked. "Isn't she going to school?"

Marta looked dismayed. "You must have forgotten, Bristol. Lilia is in a pageant. You don't want to come, do you?"

"I guess not," he said. "It's been a long night."

Marta opened the passenger door, helped her mother in. "It's almost nine o'clock," she said. "Where have you been?"

"Taking care of business."

"The club's been shut for hours."

"There's all kinds of business. Some deals get opened. Some get closed." Bristol bent to kiss Lilia's forehead. "You don't look like any pilgrim I've ever seen."

"What's wrong with the way she looks?" said Marta.

"All the pictures of pilgrims I've ever seen showed these washed-out, worn-out folks as gray as dishwater. My green-eyed baby girl looks like an electric wire that's shorting out."

"What nonsense to tell a child," said Rosalia through the open window.

Bristol continued to stand by the fender.

"What is it?" Marta asked. "Is there something else you want to tell us?"

"It'll keep. You all go on."

Marta slid behind the steering wheel and put the car in gear, noticing that her husband looked rested, as if someone had ironed out the lines in his face, which was strange since she knew he hadn't slept in twenty-four hours.

Chapter Twenty

EMMA

The haze on the horizon is not another muck fire set by hunters looking for alligator caves. This blaze, which turns the sunsets red, will burn deep beneath the fissured surface before it is extinguished by the rains. I have seen the smoldering fires at night glowing from the crevices of the hardened peat, while I and my small son, Ray Gopher, go with gunny sack and flashlight to catch frogs.

We return to the tar-paper-covered barracks smelling of smoke. Careful to avoid the mules that are kept in the space beneath the floor, we climb a ladder to reach the single room that, for the past six months, we have shared with thirteen Negro women and children.

With no windows in the barracks, the air is muggy, close. A woman sits with a baby in her arms that is taking gravy from a bottle, Even though she has punched large holes in the nipple, the gravy clogs the nipple and she shakes it loose. The woman in the next bed offers me a tomato. Her name is Winona. She reminds me of the black woman who calls herself my grandmother. I think that dark women are harder than the Indian woman, yet at the same time softer, like the carapace of a turtle with the soft underbelly beneath.

We have two weeks to pick the tomato field clean before we move on to another field, another crop. Every morning before dawn, while others ride to the packing house with its corrugated sheet-metal roof, I take my child, climb into a truck with other pickers, men and women carrying buckets, baskets, gunny sacks, or just their aprons, and hope I can get a few baskets filled before sunrise.

Ray Gopher picks silently at my side, kneeling in the black Everglades mud in his patchwork shirt and cotton pants. Around his neck I have tied a bandanna, its ends run through a beadwork ring. When the basket of green tomatoes is full, he lugs it to the end of the row to dump its contents into a rectangular crate. It will be dark again before we return to our quarters.

I talk to my son of how the white man cannot be trusted, how he has stolen the medicine bundle from Charlie Billie, how my grandfather's uncle, Willie Tiger, was buried to his neck to hide him from the white soldier. I tell him of the days when there was so much water in the Pahahokee an Indian could pole his dugout all the way to the sea. I talked to him of the ancient father of Corey Osceola who stuck a knife into the white man's false treaty.

"Who was your father?" he asks in the Miccosukee dialect.

"I have no father," I reply.

"How can that be, Mother?"

"Look around," I say. "Do you see your father?"

"No."

"Then everyone does not have to have a father. We are falling behind the others," I say. "If your tooth comes out tonight, you can throw it toward the rising sun in the morning and make a wish."

The boy turns to me with large, unwinking green eyes. "I will wish to return to the village where white people give you money."

"Don't waste a tooth on that wish."

"Then I will wish for more chewing gum."

"That is a better wish."

I think of my uncle Tommy, who says that next year he will take the boy to the medicine man for black drink, of my uncle Josie's argument that the study of Jesus would do Ray Gopher more good in the white man's world than a week of fasting in the swamp.

The white man's world is a treacherous place. An organizer was here last week, some white man from something called the CIO, to tell us that the government is going to come in and build a model migrant camp with showers and flush toilets. He said that the workers could make it a bad camp or a good camp. It was up to us. He said we should elect a council. I say that I am not going to stay. I am chosen anyway.

While the mules below knock against their tethers, the women make ordinances that no one can object to, even a crew boss. Dogs cannot run loose, a man cannot beat up his wife, part of the rent will go for a nursery school for children under three. Then the man from the CIO disappeared. Two of the women said that some men hustled him into a car. I am not surprised, for the last time I saw him, an owl hooted on the roof of the barracks.

The crew boss, who carries a loaded rifle to chase away rats, tells me that my charges at the company store are running way up. I feel like I am swimming backward, like a fish with red scales who has lost its direction. The way I am going, it will take me a year to pay everything off. But he will do what he can. It would help matters some if the boy went to the packing house. Another year was all he could stay with me anyway, for when he is eight, the boy will have to bunk with the men.

Months later, when it was cold enough to huddle before a kerosene stove, we returned early on a Sunday afternoon. The night before, we hunted for frogs. Now we peel back the legs and fry them in a cast iron skillet. At a nearby bunk a woman wraps her child's spindly legs in brown paper soaked in vinegar.

Ray Gopher asks if we can go to the Green Corn dance in the spring, reminds me that we missed the last one when suddenly we hear the sound of trucks spinning their wheels on gravel, of crew bosses running excitedly about, of a radio's volume turned up high. The women peer through the cracks, but all they can see is a flash of a running jean-covered leg, a beckoning arm, a straw hat lifted from a sweating head.

Then the woman whose job it is to feed the mules climbs up the ladder. "They're saying that Japanese people bombed Pearl Harbor," she says.

We look at one another. Many do not know what or who Japanese people are. No one has ever heard of Pearl Harbor.

When it is dark, I whisper to Ray Gopher to get dressed. "Where are we going?" he asks. "Frog hunting?"

"To the Green Corn dance," I reply, even though the season is wrong.

We wait in the darkness, then untie the rope that binds the mule and lead it quietly down the bank, across the shallow canal, dry now in December, and up the other side. Once in the shelter of the pines, we ride it past the barbed-wired blimp station of Richmond Field and the large wooden hangar that looks like a giant beehive, through the night on a path that parallels U.S. 1 until, before the morning's first light, we tether it to a signpost on Le Jeune Road and walk north.

I find them at a shabby, three-chickee camp on Tamiami Trail, west of 27th Avenue. They ask what the life was like in a migrant camp. I reply that it was tight, like wearing shoes.

Mary is thinner. I can see all of my mother's bones, as if the skin that covers them would soon split and shed, like that of a snake. Charlie Billie hunts but game is scarce. Sometimes he brings in a raccoon, sometimes a string of garfish. Sometimes he finds an herb or a stone or some other thing he needs to complete a new medicine bundle, the stems of wild grape,

411

the root from the east side of a swamp lily, the side with the greatest sun's potency, the scent sac of a skunk. He says that by the time Ray Gopher grows to reach his shoulder, he will have his deerskin bundle purified and rolled.

Sam's earnings at a defense plant near the airport bought their groceries and a 1938 Dodge with a B sticker that entitles Sam to all the gasoline he needs to get to work and back.

I dip the sofke spoon for my son, direct my eyes on the ground, on the far horizon, separating my questions with silence as if they were beads.

I ask if there are Indians at the defense plant, and Sam tells me that Mike Osceola works the day shift. Then I ask if there are guards with shotguns. He says there are guards but no shotguns. I follow my halfbrother to his car. "Do they have a company store?"

Sam checks the spark plugs. "They have a commissary. Where you buy food already cooked. I like the beef stew. If you put lots of pepper on it, it's all right."

When Sam says that half the workers are women, I decide to go with him. Wearing a bandanna to cover my hair and an ID badge pinned to a pair of overalls that I buy at Richard's Department Store for $1.89, I begin working an eight-hour shift, the time after midnight when foremen are too tired to criticize.

I work through the dry season, the fire season, the rain and squall season, earning money to give to Mary for tennis shoes that the clinic people say to wear every day and not just when she comes to the clinic for her B-12 shot, to Charlie Billie for epsom salts, to Ray Gopher for a bicycle, to my uncle Tommy for the dentist, and to my uncle Josie for his mission. I am learning to make a template when the sheriff's deputy comes to make the arrest. He charges me with the theft of a mule and a debt of $223 to the grower from whom I ran away. Then he takes me to the jail at the top of a courthouse, from where I can see all the way to the little ocean in one direction, to the Pahahokee in the other until the steel door of the detention cell slams behind me and I can see nothing except a single light bulb, a toilet that has overflowed, and women sleeping five to a bed.

When my trial comes up the following month, the judge gives me the choice of a year in jail or return to the migrant camp to work off my debt.

Sam advises me to go back to the camp. "Indians die in jail," he says.

"The camp is jail," I reply.

I and Ray Gopher return to days of kneeling in the hot sun, to nights of cheap wine and dark, damp corners, to babies who seldom cry, and other children with insect bites that they scratch until they bleed.

In the early evening, when it is still light, Ray runs in the fields and practices catching Indigo snakes and corn snakes, the releasing of which, Charlie Billie has told him, will give him power.

The woman named Winona tells me that Ray Gopher belongs in school. "Pickers' kids can go, you know."

"No," I reply. "Two people working. Quicker pay back what we owe."

"You don't owe them anything. They just the ones with the books. That's all. You know how to write? Figure?"

"Little bit."

"That's what you got to do. Unless you want to spend your life picking beans and tomatoes."

During the next year, Ray Gopher, like the other older children, learns not to make eye contact with sheriff's deputies or men who wear business suits, with bossmen in flat-brimmed Stetsons with pencils in their pockets. He learns to do only enough to get by. "This boy of yours is turning into a lazy picker," warns the crew boss. "You don't watch him, he'll soon be just another boozing buck."

That night Winona asks me what the crew boss was so angry about. "He wants our blood," I reply. "My son is trying to keep some for himself."

Winona pours bacon gravy over biscuits, offers some to the boy, who sits cross-legged on the floor, and groans as she eases herself upright.

"I'm getting too old to get down on my knees and pick those beans."

She reminds me of Caroline. "You same as woman who calls herself my grandmother."

"How's that?"

"Looks like her."

"You means she's black?"

"Old, too."

In the summer season of torrential downpour that turns the fields into tidal flats, the truck passes rows of old barracks set between the dense thickets of pines near U.S. 1 and North Kendall Drive. White men mill about the barracks in dark blue denim uniforms with the letters PW on their backs.

"Used to be a CCC camp," said Winona. "Now it's German prisoners of war. They got them working as carpenters, mechanics, road workers. Guarantee you they have it better than we do."

"I not care about the war. It between white men. They all the same."

"Ain't that the truth."

On a late afternoon when frost threatens the tomato fields, everyone rushes to cover the plants, to burn smudge pots and strips of old rubber tires between the planting rows. Ray Gopher finds me carrying a bundle of burlap and a handful of wooden stakes. He tells me that he has just knocked a half-sleeping mockingbird out of a tree with a rock, has cut the still beating heart from its body, has eaten it to assure himself skill in learning healing songs from Charlie Billie. Then he whispers that he wants to live with me again.

"We are not warm either," I say.

It is not the cold. He is afraid of the crew boss. "He wants to do a woman thing with me."

"Did you do it?"

"One time. I did not cry. He hurt me but I did not cry. The next time he came for me, I am gone, hidden in a place he is afraid to go."

"Where?"

"Near an alligator hole where I can search for owl feathers for Charlie Billie. But now I cannot hide in the swamp because of the white men with letters on their backs. They also try to conceal themselves, but they make too much noise."

My opportunity comes when Jeeps pull up with soldiers carrying rifles, and crew bosses carrying rifles of their own join them in the search across the canal for white men with letters on their backs. Winona makes the calls when she cleans the office.

A week later, Sam drives up in his Dodge with Josie and another Baptist preacher, a white man with his hat in his hands. They speak to the camp manager in his office while Ray Gopher hides in the reeds and listens.

"The law says she has to work off her debt," the manager says.

The white preacher is polite. "What if it gets paid off?"

"You people got that kind of money? With interest?"

"Yes, sir," says Josie. "We do."

"Then give it here, Tonto. And get that squaw and her papoose out of here before I change my mind."

I give my pillow away to Winona, pick up my cooking pot, then pile into Sam's Dodge with Ray Gopher at my feet. We drive away down the marl-bedded road made of clay, and sand, and the remains of shellfish. The road is dry and the traction good, the sky above filled with streamers of clouds.

"Why didn't she come?" I ask.

"The woman Caroline said she was getting too old to come after you herself," said Josie, "but you were welcome to the money."

When I see a turtle, I tell Sam to stop. Then I jump from the car and wade into the canal that runs beside the road. When I climb up the banks, I am holding a large turtle that paddles wildly in the air. Sam puts it in the trunk of the car, where it continues to thrust itself about as it tries to get out.

"It can't breathe in there," says the preacher.

"No difference," I reply. "We soon kill it."

When we return, Mary and Charlie Billie are eating swamp cabbage. Everything is as if we never left. Sam lifts the turtle out of the trunk. I take a knife and with one swipe cut

417

off the turtle's head. While I detach the carapace, revealing a string of unlaid eggs inside the exposed body, Sam tells me that the war plant isn't hiring women anymore. Discharged servicemen are coming home. They need jobs.

I am no longer interested. "This will make good soup," I say. After supper, I reclaim my beads from my mother's keeping and put them on, one necklace at a time, row upon row of glass strands that belonged to Sally Cypress.

Mary gives me half of her own beads. "Next year I give you more," she says. "Or maybe you will get them all."

Chapter Twenty-One

Jack Coombs preferred to patrol for German U-boats in his sloop, even though the Coast Guard provided the civilian auxiliary with all the gasoline it needed. There was no noise on a sailboat, no fumes, exhaust, no throbbing of the vessel. Under sail he was dependent only on himself, as brisk and as lissome as the currents that blew him, instead of a fifty-six-year-old guy with spider veins on his face who couldn't button his pants over his belly. Paula had been generous. He would say that much for her. He would even admit to missing her from time to time, especially on the sloop. That was when they used to do the most talking, when they didn't have to shout over an engine, or whisper in front of the servants, when there was no one else around for Paula to impress.

The boy with him this night, his sometime companion for the past two months, seldom talked. But then he wasn't expected to. It didn't matter. In a few months he would be drafted. There would be another to take his place. Or maybe none at all. There was something to be said for solitude.

The boy's name was Billy. He lay stretched across the prow, sullen, bored, indifferent to sails, sheets, cleats, winches, and life jackets, complaining that Jack couldn't get it up, that his eyes were yellow where they were supposed to be white, that he liked the cabin cruiser better. When he lit a cigarette, Jack shouted for him to douse the light.

"I don't know why I hang out with an old fag," the boy said, buttoning his windbreaker to his neck. "You want me to do you? Yes or no. I'm getting tired."

That afternoon a blimp had circled overhead, lurching in the turbulent autumn air currents as it looked for U-boats. Just before sunset it released a great yellow ball to mark the spot where a submarine hid in the shallow pale green waters, lying in wait for merchant ships. The ball drifted slowly through the air, tossed skyward again by updrafts, then plunged to the sea, where it bobbed on the current.

It was a shadowed night, both moon and stars partially hidden by low-flying clouds. When the silhouette of the 7,500-ton rear-bridged oil tanker silently glided by, on its way from Galveston, Texas, to Norfolk, Virginia, hugging the Florida shore to avoid the tugging current of the Gulf Stream, Jack almost missed it. Then, in a blinding flash, the tanker was hit and its bridge blown to pieces. Huge sheets of flame leaped high in the air, quickly spreading on the oily water as the tanker became a blazing inferno. The burning ship attempted to beach itself, but a German submarine, streamlined and double-hulled, staggered to the surface, shouldered its way through the burning debris, and with diesels murmuring, fired ten more shells, creating muffled detonations that caused Jack's mast to sway, the deck beneath his feet to tremble.

When the U-boat's steel-plated conning tower sped rapidly away, Jack felt his heart thud against his chest with the rush of adrenaline that honed his senses razor-sharp.

Men glistening with oil dived into the sea as the tanker began to drift northward with smoke belching from her hull that began to cast a pall over the surface of the waves. They floated on pieces of wreckage or swam bobbing in the moonlight, many badly burned, their skin charred and coagulated, and split by seawater.

Searchlights played over the sea as the Coast Guard, communicating to its auxiliary with blinkers, joined the hunt for survivors. Responding to a signal from the Coast Guard to come about, Jack changed tack, told the boy to push the tiller toward the sail and to watch his head, while he hauled tight the sheets to keep the sails filled with wind and driving, until the boat swung around.

Fire from the drifting tanker skewed the horizon with orange spikes, dappling the waves before it in bronze and silver flashings. The boy was the first to see the three men in the metallic water, covered with oil, floating on palm fronds on the starboard side.

"There's guys over there," he cried.

"Throw them lines while I lash the tiller," shouted Jack, pointing the boat into the wind, letting loose both the main and the jib sheet until both sails began to luff. When the sloop bobbed in place like flotsam, Jack threw the rope ladder over the side. Two of the men were able to fight their way over the crests of the waves despite the breaking sea, swim to the ladder, and climb up unassisted. The third was too badly charred. He looked up once in the direction of Jack's shouts but, unable to see over the chop of the waves, floundered in confusion.

It was clear that someone had to go over the side. Jack hesitated for a moment, then jumped into the water, hoping he had the wind to return. With labored strokes he swam to the injured seaman, and with a massive effort that left him gasping, slipped the ring buoy over the seaman's head and hauled him back to the boat. Out of breath, he shouted for the boy to put on a life jacket and help him lift the man on board.

Billy leaned over the hull. "I don't want to touch him. His skin is all black. It's gonna come off in my hands."

One of the rescued seamen climbed back down the rope ladder and helped Jack hoist his sputtering comrade under the arms until the man could be jackknifed over the gunwale.

The burned man lay in a heap. Seawater trickled from the corner of his mouth. While Jack dragged a tarpaulin to cover all three survivors, the man opened his eyes. "Thank you, friend," he whispered. "You saved my life."

Jack placed his folded jacket beneath the man's head. "I saved my own life," he replied.

Then he unlashed the tiller, hauled in the mainsheet, and told Billy to back the jib into the wind. In the deep-water channel of Biscayne Bay, he ran before the wind on a port tack, trimming the sails with each draft that he felt on the back of his neck, thinking that sometimes a man waits his whole life for one special thing to happen. Although he had a navigational chart and a compass to guide him back to the lumeless coast, he didn't need them. Familiar with every inlet, every cove, every shoal and mangrove in the South Bay, he could have done it blind-folded.

It was dawn when, after passing blood-caked, bullet-riddled lifeboats drifting to shore, Jack lowered the centerboard and guided the drifting sloop to its mooring, where ambulances waited to take the survivors to Jackson Memorial Hospital.

Early morning light turned the smoky haze pink while Jack lowered the jib, secured the halyards, and took out the battens.

"If you want me to come with you tomorrow," said Billy, "the answer is no. It's not what I thought it was gonna be."

Jack bagged the sails. "That's okay."

"You owe me money."

Jack reached his hand into his pocket.

"I never liked you," the boy said.

"I never liked me either," said Jack. "Until tonight." His eye was on the spit of land, now part of Dinner Key where Pan American kept its clipper ships, where he and Bristol used to bend pine saplings back and ride them into the water.

With Bradford in the Aleutians and Jack in and out of the hospital, Maude lived alone behind a double set of blackout curtains, but without a service flag in the window since she considered that tacky. The "A" sticker on the windshield of her Plymouth restricted her as a nonessential driver to one and a half gallons of gasoline a week. Unable to afford black market prices, Maude was forced to take the stifling, fume-filled bus. At fifty-two, with her shining blonde pageboy, she could pass for forty if she hid her eyes behind sunglasses. She wore a rhinestone V for Victory pin, and although her patriotism did not extend to painting her fingernails red, white, and blue as Senator Claude Pepper's wife had done, she wrote once weekly to Bradford on V-Mail, obligatory letters scribbled on tissue-thin stationary that folded to become its own envelope.

If anyone remembered her one-time entanglement with a hoodlum, no one mentioned it, either because Pearl Harbor and Bataan, and the nearer threat of wolf packs of German U-boats in the Florida Straits reduced such topics to trivia, or because Maude had thrown herself into the safety of a benevolent respectability that included the Gray Ladies of the Red Cross, and the war bond committee that arranged for Sonja Henie and Sabu the Elephant Boy to parade down Flagler Street.

There were no men in Maude's life, other than a colonel responsible for a jungle-survival course given in the Everglades, who liked to take her to the Pago Pago Club. When no other escort was available, she relied on Jack, although less so since his cirrhosis forced him to stop drinking and to take Vitamin B injections every two weeks. If she felt empty, she put it down to shortages and rationing, to plastic zippers that broke, to the terrible heat and humidity, to having no money.

The old frame house that Maude shared with her brother was falling down around her ears. It was bad enough having to live with memories that she thought she had gotten away from much less disrepair with which there was no catching up. The linoleum was buckling, the floorboards were sagging. In some places they were springy and soft, which meant that someone had to go into the crawl space to reinforce the joists, assuming it was possible to find someone to do it. The wood under the eaves was beginning to rot, and the banyan, whose acquisitive roots had already cracked the clay septic tank, attached itself through its drooping strings to the cedar shingles and was now growing through the roof.

The house, the war, and her job were grinding her down. And Jack was dying. Although he was fast becoming too weak to set his sails, he continued to patrol for the Coast Guard until a month after he witnessed a German submarine shoot down a Navy blimp, when he was admitted to Jackson Memorial Hospital for hepatic failure. The doctor told Maude that they were doing all they could, but she had to realize that her brother was in the end stage of cirrhosis of the liver, that the enlarged veins in his esophagus could rupture at any time.

She found her brother behind a white, gathered screen smelling of ammonia. His face was drawn, angled into sharp planes of light and shadow, his skin jaundiced.

"It's too dark in here," she said. "Why hasn't someone put on the light?"

"I like it better that way, Maudie," he said.

She sat beside the bed, blanching at the fetid odor, the sight of the bag filling with dark brown urine. "You look much, much better."

"You lie through your teeth, Maudie. What do you hear from Brad? He tells me that the Aleutians are jumping."

"All he writes to me about is the fog."

He put out his hand. "You still going to the Biltmore?"

Maude wrinkled her nose at the thought of the hotel that had been converted into an Army Air Force convalescent hospital. "Yes, but I don't know why. A patient has been very rude to me."

"He was probably out of his head. He didn't know what he was saying."

"Yes, he did. He lost a leg. Not his mind. He said I was over the hill."

"You're in your prime, Maudie. His eyesight must be bad."

"And that was after I told him that I had a son in service. He was very nasty. 'You think I'm gonna pity you the same way I would some gold-star mother crying her eyes out?' he said. 'Or maybe a mom like mine, eating herself up with worry over me and my brother? You think that wonderful lady fools with

426

straightening her seams like you do? She wears cotton hose that she mends over a darning egg. She smells like cinnamon and Lysol. You smell like an over-the-hill rich bitch tramp.' "

"What did you say?"

"I told him that I was a volunteer and that he probably got drafted, which is why he couldn't understand someone wanting to do their part. Then he started to holler, 'I'm sitting here next to the window with one leg and I got to watch the early morning golfers walk out to the greens. You want to do your part? Stop them from playing golf. If you can't, take a powder.' "

"And did you?"

"I got real mad. I grabbed his wheelchair and yanked it to the doorway. 'Here,' I said. 'That's about as far away from the window as you can get.' He made me cry. You know I never cry. Never." Maude brought her chair closer to her brother's bed. "How do you feel?"

"A little dizzy."

"Do you want a private-duty nurse?"

"No, not even if you could scare one up. The floor nurses are treating me just fine."

"Jack, do you remember the man who that Negro Bristol said was supposed to be my father?"

He looked out the window. It was rapidly getting dark. Soon a nurse would come to pull down the blackout shade. "What difference does it make? You never knew the man you thought was your daddy. I did, and let me tell you, John Quincy Coombs was a mean bastard. Thomas Sands used to swing me over his head, bring me candy. Take me on his sloop. He's the one taught me to sail. You would have liked him, Maude."

"What did he look like?"

"I can't remember, except that he was . . . sunny. I've been thinking. Maybe John Quincy wasn't always mean. Maybe he got stuck in a pose, like those declamations you used to do." He took a sip of water from a metal cup, then leaned back against his pillow. "Can you still do Repulsion? That used to make me laugh."

"It's been thirty-five years."

"Try, Maudie."

"I might be able to do Remorse." She put the back of her hand to her forehead. "Oh wretched state! Oh bosom black as death." There was silence, broken only by a cart rattling down the hall.

Maude took his hand. "Don't leave me, Jack. You're all I have."

"That's not true. You have Bradford."

"I don't get on with Bradford."

"You don't have to get on with a son. You're just supposed to be his mother."

She rapped her nails on her purse. "I thought that's what I was." Suddenly she brightened, as if a bulb had been switched on. When she spoke, her voice was brittle. "Remember that old guava shack? I never thought I would ever

428

get that awful smell out of my nose."

Jack turned his face to the peeling wall.

She clutched the purse. "Do you want me to tell Paula?"

"No."

"Is there anyone else?"

"Zalman Levy. And Bristol."

"You haven't seen either of them in years."

"I saw Zalman last year when his son Morty got killed at Guadalcanal. He sat on a wooden crate in his socks. He cried and asked me who would say kaddish for him now that his youngest was gone. Call them, Maudie. Soon."

"The time you took me on your shoulders to watch the railroad coming in." Tears streamed down her face. "Do you remember?"

Chapter Twenty-Two

Bradford Watson returned from the University of Florida's law school with a briefcase, a brush cut, a love for red brick Georgian, the recommendation of a law professor for an appointment to the state attorney's office, and a determination to make it big. The commitment to a score was the reason that Bradford did not swap war stories of his three years' service on an aircraft carrier in the Pacific. He was banking on the likelihood that the significant achievements of his life lay before him, not behind.

He pronounced Miami *Mayamuh,* drove a Chrysler, wore tortoise-framed glasses, smoked Pall Mall cigarettes, drank Tanqueray and tonic with a twist of lime, and dressed in white buck shoes, button-down sea isle cotton shirts, and cord suits in which, regardless of the humidity, he never sweated. All in all, he governed himself like a man with a purpose, a man who had discovered in law school that what mattered was not how much money a person had but how he promoted himself.

He also returned from Gainesville with a girl whom he hoped to marry, a Jewish journalism major named Sandra who, unlike his mother, was interested in his every word. He convinced himself that the theological difference between them would not affect a marriage based on mutual respect, a dislike of foreign films with subtitles, and a love of Dizzy Gillespie.

Bradford was not in love with Sandra, although he loved her. More important, he loved how she loved him, how she made him feel. She was pretty in a suntanned, sunstreaked way that spoke of open convertibles and salty shoulders. She was unfailingly considerate, knew how to dress, what to say and when. He did not feel for her the heady excitement he felt for a townie waitress, a seventeen-year-old girl of mixed Greek and Italian parentage with a line of dark fuzz that ran to her navel, who expected nothing from him except a promise that he would call again. Sandra, in contrast, was inhibited in bed, insisting on making love in darkness and under covers, making no demands that could not be easily met. If not concupiscence, she promised a rudder, an antidote to a mother eaten with bitterness, to a father who had shot himself in the head.

Although Sandra's family, denied access to the important clubs, was not as well connected as Bradford would have liked, they were well off. Her father was in the hotel business on Miami Beach, and her grandfather reportedly owned a couple of movie theaters, enterprises that could easily set Bradford up in private practice once he was ready to leave the state attorney's office.

When the couple returned to Miami, they decided to use Maude as a stalking horse and to tell her first of their plans to marry. Bradford took Sandra to the Dade County pine house, where the septic tank was under repair, exposed in a foul-smelling crater in the yard.

Inside, everything was closed, dark, smelling of pine and mildew and a faint sweet suggestion of bay rum. They waited before a portrait over the mantel of Maude seated in a wing chair with her long, elegant legs crossed, one hand idly fingering her pearls.

"That was painted when my father was still alive."

"She was lovely."

"Don't let her hear you put her in the past tense."

The mantel held two photographs, one of Bradford in the yellow helmet and jersey of a carrier deck officer, waving in a swarm of Corsairs. Bradford pointed to a picture beside it. "My uncle Jack. He died a few years ago. Wrote great letters. All the years I was away at military school. He came to visit me a couple of times. His name wasn't really Jack. It was Quincy Octavius."

"What an odd name."

"Not that odd. John Quincy, from my grandfather, Octavius from my great-grandfather on my maternal grandmother's side. Octavius was a veteran of Shiloh. I showed you those sepia pictures that my uncle sent me, the one of my great-grandfather Octavius in a Confederate uniform."

"I remember the sash."

"My grandfather and grandmother Coombs built this house. They were pioneers."

"So was my grandfather Zalman. He said he knew your uncle and your grandmother. Your mother, too."

"You told him about us?"

"Sort of."

"Did you tell him that you just knew me or that we were serious?"

"I told him that you took me to a dinky motel with a plastic sheet on the mattress."

"Quit kidding around. What did he say?"

"He said my father's not going to like it and that my mother is going to be even worse."

Maude descended the rickety staircase, her hand lightly skimming the bannister, disdaining sensible shoes for ankle straps, wearing a dress with a wasp waist and a long, full skirt. While her face was still tightly molded, her skin had begun to take on the fragile look of parchment.

She seemed surprised to see them. "I wish you had told me you were coming, Bradford," she said. "I have to be at work by twelve."

Bradford kissed her on the cheek. The action was dutiful, stiff. "There's someone from the university I want you to meet, Mother. This is Sandra Levy. She's a Miamian too."

Sandra extended a firm hand, her ponytail bouncing as she stepped across the creaking floorboards. "How do you do, Mrs. Watson?"

"I thought I knew all the Miami girls."

"My parents live on Pine Tree Drive."

Maude checked her purse. "That's not really Miami. That's Miami Beach. Coming from Pine Tree Drive, I suppose you think this old house is tacky."

"No. Actually, I think it has a lot of really neat features."

"Like what? I've been looking for one for years. Lock up when you leave, Bradford."

He put his arm around Sandra's shoulder. "We didn't come to see the house. We came to see you. Sandra and I plan to marry."

"Really." Maude found her car keys and

433

snapped closed her bag. "Is there any reason why I'm the last to know?"

"Actually, you're the first," said Sandra. "We haven't told my parents yet."

Maude put a hand on the doorknob. "I can't imagine why not."

"Well, to be honest, they would prefer that I marry someone Jewish."

"Perhaps, dear, you should take their advice."

Bradford's meeting with Sandra's family, while less forbidding, was no less trying. The only reason that the Levys agreed to sit down and discuss the subject at all was that Bradford had a profession. As a lawyer he enjoyed a status somewhere between a doctor and an accountant, an advantage that entitled him to visit the house, but which still did not remove the insurmountable problem of a gentile suitor who refused to convert.

They sat in the Cuban-tiled Florida room overlooking the intercoastal waterway. Sandra warned Bradford that when he was offered a drink, to ask for a ginger ale. Sandra's mother served soft drinks in tall, frosted glasses embossed with pink flamingoes. Mrs. Levy resembled her daughter except that her edges were blurred, like butter that had been left to soften. She said little, busied herself with coasters and napkins, a bowl of fruit, a tray of cheese and crackers, while exchanging anxious looks with her husband when she could get his attention.

Sandra's grandfather Zalman, who spoke in a thick accent in which he brought his consonants down like hammers, remarked that Jack Coombs had died much too young. "We go way back. He worked for me years ago when I opened my first movie theater. Even before that when we peddled notions to the redskins. He used to carry the goods in a canoe. I loaned him money for some cockamamie business that never took off the ground, but I never begrudged him. A good-looking fellow," he said. "When I asked him to do something, he did it. Not like some of these bums we have working for us today."

"My uncle was a great guy," said Bradford. There was a momentary silence. Sandra jabbed him with her elbow. He broke the awkward pause, hoping that he was taking the right tack. "I'm interested in hearing how you made the switch from the movie theater business to the hotel business."

Zalman explained that it began when "talkies" failed to return revenues to what they were before the Depression. He hoped the new technicolor cartoons would do the trick, but the economy continued to keep attendance down. "I did everything, introduced sweepstakes night, gave away toasters, a fifty-dollar jackpot. Then I got slammed with the double feature because the distributor insisted on block booking. If I wanted to take the good one, he said I had to take the dog. I'm not saying that

435

we personally had hard times, but you're talking to someone who knows how tough it is to make a buck. You're talking to someone who earned money for his first inventory by shaving the other passengers in the steerage hold for five cents apiece."

"It was clear to me," Sandra's father, Herschel, interrupted, waving an impatient hand, "that the theaters were only breaking even, while the hotel business was a sure winner. In spite of the shortages, the city expected to double its tourist trade. Even in wartime, people needed a place in the sun."

"I made the deal," said Zalman. "I knew a fellow with heart problems who needed a partner with operating capital. It was before Morty got killed." He sagged in his easy chair. "He wrote to me once that he felt at home in Guadalcanal because it looked like Matheson Hammock."

Sandra took her grandfather's hand and squeezed it while Herschel recounted how they had bought into the pink and green portholed hotel on a lease arrangement for forty-thousand dollars. "It wasn't all easy street," he said. "As soon as we mirrored the lobby with green glass etched in seashells, the Army Air Corps took over the hotel."

"Seashells and palm trees," said Zalman with a sigh, "and I want you to know that during the entire year and a half that the Army had it, I could hear the soldiers in my sleep, slam-

436

ming their duffel bags into the mirrors."

Herschel picked up a stuffed mushroom and popped it into his mouth. "After Mussolini and his mistress were hung upside down, the government returned the hotel in time for the season. I replaced the bunks with twin beds, painted over the *Kilroy was here* signs with a tropical pink."

Zalman said they offered their guests the American plan so they wouldn't have to worry about where to go to eat, hired a rhumba band, printed monogrammed matchbooks and put them in the mail slots, sent a box of oranges to every guest, a crate to big spenders. Then he leaned forward in his seat, groaning with the effort.

"You're a lawyer," he said. "See what you think of this. I have a friend has a hotel like mine. A couple of weeks ago, a city detective came to tell him to get rid of his bookie, that it might be a good idea to lease the pony concession instead to an S. and G. bookie, a guy who belongs to the local syndicate. My friend doesn't want to do it. A promise is a promise. But his son disagrees. His son wants to give the bookie back his money. The question is, what should I tell my friend?"

Bradford swirled the ice cubes in his ginger ale, glanced sideways at Sandra, and winked. "I can't give you a legal opinion on something that's illegal. But off the top of my head, I would say what's the difference which bookie he uses, as long as his guests have a place to lay their bets."

"I like the way the boy thinks," said Herschel, offering Bradford a cigar.

When it was time to leave, Bradford shook hands all around. He stopped before the old man and smiled. "Thanks for your kind words about my uncle."

"I also knew your grandmother," replied Zalman Levy.

"No kidding? My mother never talks about her. What was she like?"

Zalman made a tent of his hands. "That's hard to say."

"My uncle used to tell me that my grandmother Eulalie was genteel and gracious, an old-fashioned southern lady."

"He said this?" Zalman locked his hands behind his back. "Then that's what she was. Who remembers better than her own son?"

"Is that a question?" asked Bradford.

"You'll have to get used to it," said Sandra. "It's rhetorical."

"Listen to my college girl," said Herschel Levy.

When Sandra later confessed to her mother that she had gone all the way with Bradford, that, although she was no judge she thought he was circumcised, and that just possibly she might be three weeks late, the wedding was on.

What Bradford had always known, ever since

438

he was five and had not been allowed to attend a birthday party for Al Capone's son, now was blasted daily in the newspapers, on radio, and on television. Miami had become a haven for gangsters, whose most powerful weapon was official corruption. Since the war, organized crime had entrenched itself in the resort industry, becoming the heaviest contributor to Florida political campaign funds, boldly operating prostitution rings, slot machines, and gambling casinos.

When the Capone gang muscled into a local syndicate operating alledgedly under the full protection of the Miami Beach City Council, when the personal assets of Dade County's sheriff soared, pressure grew for a shutdown. Some of it emanated from the local racetracks, whose pari-mutuel handle had fallen because cabanas were more convenient. In response, a handful of prominent citizens together with the Dade County Bar Association organized the Miami Crime Commission under the heading of former FBI agent Daniel Sullivan. Offering evidence that Miami was the wintertime hub of organized crime, Sullivan convinced Senator Estes Kefauver of Tennessee to bring his Committee to Investigate Organized Crime to Miami.

As an assistant state attorney whose office was under the gun to cooperate to the fullest, part of a multiple-agency investigation, Bradford spent his days and most of his hot summer nights jotting notes, interviewing witnesses, sifting through boxes, and gathering files to place at the disposal of the Kefauver committee.

Being assigned to the investigation was the most important thing that had happened to Bradford since he had been sworn to office, especially since he had spent the past six months trying misdemeanors. Now petty larceny and shoplifting took a backseat to bird-dogging evidence, to running a thing down to where it had no place to hide. It was a chance to build his reputation, an opportunity that could leapfrog his career. When Sandra complained that he was never home, that even her parents said he was working too hard, he said he was doing it for her, for the baby, to keep her eye on the brass ring.

On the July evening that Senator Kefauver and his committee flew into Miami, Bradford worked in his shirtsleeves beside a window air conditioner that rattled and dripped. An associate named Ernest wedged a file into a box. His face was round, pleasant, his expression that of someone who believed that his duty was to present the evidence, push a calendar, and not make waves. When he spoke it was as if he were announcing ball scores. "Broward County's sheriff admits to an interest in a novelty company. It's another way of saying bolita."

"The sheriff isn't the only one on the take," replied Bradford. "One of his deputies made enough money in four years to retire. Kefauver's team already has three ex-deputies ready to testify that they were under orders not to make arrests for bookmaking. It's no secret that our own hands were tied unless a case was worked up by the sheriff, and you know how often that happens."

"By the way, Brad, your wife called."

"Did she say there was a problem?"

"No, she didn't."

"Have Edith call her and tell her I'm tied up." He taped the box shut. "I'm going to run this over to the Columbus. Kemble is waiting."

Bradford lugged the box of cardboard files to a suite of rooms in the Columbus Hotel. Outside the door were dollies of used dishes. In the rooms, beneath a thick blue haze, where countless documents lay scattered in profusion, a dozen men sorted through several packing cases of records. Surrounded by a frenzy of activity, Senator Kefauver chewed on a cigar stub. Everyone seemed to be speaking at once.

Bradford recognized the tall, rangy Tennessean by his plastic-rimmed glasses. Nearby, Senator Hunt, an older, rotund member of the committee, raised his voice from time to time in righteous indignation.

"The Capone group," someone was explaining, "under the direction of bad actors like Greasy Thumb Gusik and Loud Mouth Levin, held the wire service like an ax over the local gamblers to control their operations. They also threatened certain state pressure to gain their ends."

Kefauver scribbled notes on little bits of paper.

An investigator in a brown suit held a list. "Anybody know anything more about our ten key missing witnesses? The marshals haven't been able to find them. They're all missing, including all five members of the S. and G."

Kefauver fished a note out of his bulging pocket. "The committee doesn't care if they show up or not. We can prove our point without them."

Bradford put down his box while someone came in to report that the television newscaster from WTVJ, Ralph Renick, was on the telephone. Kefauver waved to him to wait, then smiled, a quick, ingenuous flash to Bradford. "Do you have any information for us, Mr. Watson?"

The challenge of a quick response after minutes of standing idly by reminded Bradford of carrier duty, when after endless games of bridge in the wardroom lounge, he had been suddenly called out to whip the chocks from the squadron leader's plane.

"Yes, Senator, I do." Bradford opened his notepad. "Abner Zwillman, a close associate of Bugsy Siegel, has checked out of the Martinique. Frank Costello has checked out of the Saxony. We located Johnson in Jacksonville, but when we called we were told by a maid that he was out of town. Sam Cohen has had an operation in some hospital that his brother Ben declines to name. Harry Russel, who fronts the Capone people's interests in the S. and G., is in Palm Springs. Meyer Lansky is in the royal suite of the *Italia*. It's part of the Cunard Line. We've tracked a lot of them to Havana. At this moment we're zeroing in on where. Some of the Capone group have already begun to ship their paraphernalia to Cuba. And we located John Patton in Phoenix."

Kefauver thanked him and turned to Jack Younger, president of Miami's newly formed Crime Commission. "We are not setting ourselves up in competition with any law enforcement officers, the Department of Justice, or the state of Florida. Our hope is that we can work in cooperation with these agencies and present to the public the tremendous importance of the whole crime picture."

The brown-suited investigator made a note in a margin, then looked up at Bradford. "I'm surprised that you have not recused yourself, Mr. Watson."

"Sir?"

Mallory Kemble led Bradford into the foyer. "There wasn't time to tell you. We uncovered a connection between your family and John Patton."

"That's impossible."

"I'm afraid not. Three, possibly four sources. It seems your mother had an intimate relation-

443

ship with Patton awhile back. Lasted a few years."

Bradford shook his head in disbelief over Kemble's startling revelation and how it would impact on him. "This is crazy."

"That's what I thought when I first heard it. You'll have to trust me on this. There's even evidence that Patton paid the tab on your military school tuition. While we're confident that there is no continuing connection of any significance, there are some who might charge that as an ex-officio member of the team, you have a personal interest in the outcome of these hearings. If it were to come out, it could reflect adversely on the commission. In order to avoid the appearance of impropriety, it's incumbent upon you to recuse yourself."

Despite his bitter resentment, Bradford registered little on his face except attention. It was an expression he had learned in military school, the stiff upper lip in the face of momentary defeat. "I'll return to my office, then," he said.

Kemble stepped back into the room, stopped at the doorway. "I hear your wife is expecting."

"Yes, sir. In August."

"The best of luck. Don't forget to send me a cigar."

Bradford found Maude wearing a white coat behind the perfume counter of Saks. "Who is John Patton to you?"

Maude continued to smile brightly as she arranged bottles on a tray. "No one."

He wiped his glasses with his handkerchief. "Don't lie to me, Mother."

"You sure don't know beans about picking a time and place. He was someone I knew a long time ago."

"How well did you know him?"

"I'm working, Bradford. Can't you see that I'm working?"

"Did he pay for military school?"

"I don't think I'll ever get used to standing on my feet. Where did you get such a fool idea?"

"My office has copies of the receipts."

Maude sighed. The corners of her mouth dropped and suddenly she looked old, tired. "Not at first. In the beginning, your father paid for your tuition."

Bradford thought of the man who had dressed daily in a coat and tie, his trousers creased just over the tops of his brown and white wing-tipped shoes, the cane he had carried with the silver knob of a dog's head.

He lowered his voice to a harsh whisper. "He killed himself because of you, didn't he? Because of your infidelity."

"Hogwash. Your father committed suicide because he lost all his money. Because he had nothing left."

"You must have helped him along. I wouldn't be surprised if you loaded the gun. You were a rotten wife. Jesus, does everything you touch turn to shit? You were even a lousy mother."

"You don't know what a bad mother is. Ask me. I had one."

A woman wearing slacks and cork-soled shoes leaned against the counter and asked to see a bottle of Tabu. Maude sprayed the inside of the woman's wrist. "You have to give it time," she said. The woman thanked her and left for another counter.

"They do that, come in for perfume that they have no intention of buying." She raised her eyebrows. "Now what is it?"

"If you couldn't give me anything else, at least I should have been able to count on you for the truth."

"The truth? The truth is, nobody really cares. All this old business you're so worried about. I wish you would stop wanting things from me. You always wanted something from me. You still do. You're too needy, Bradford. I'd like you a whole lot better if you weren't so needy."

"There's no point to this. I'm leaving."

"How is your wife? The last I heard she was living on Saltines."

"That was months ago."

"I suppose you want a boy. All men want boys."

"Actually, we'd like the first one to be a girl so we can name her Eulalie."

Maude caught her lower lip in her teeth and

blinked back tears. "You're too mean-spirited to be believed."

By the early 1950s, people were calling Miami's Colored Town Overtown. The district had become one of the hottest pockets of Negro entertainment in the nation, where black celebrities like Eartha Kitt, Sammy Davis, Jr., Josephine Baker, and the Ink Spots, performing before whites-only audiences on Miami Beach, would drive across the bay to play late at night at the Harlem Square, where Sunday's door prizes might be a grocery cart filled high with neck bones, cans of peas, and cartons of cigarettes, or a chance to sit at the same table with Jersey Joe Wolcott.

The first time Lilia saw Bradford Watson, he was sitting ringside at the Patagonia with a table of other white men with loosened ties. Whites were nothing new. They often crossed Miami Avenue to witness nightlife that they heard was seamier than their own. She noticed him because he seemed uncomfortable, twirling the paper umbrella in his drink, looking at the neon exit sign, at the colored patrons around him, trying to act as if proximity to a Negro who wasn't cooking his breakfast or mowing his lawn didn't bother him. But it did. He couldn't hide it. She saw it in the stiff, unyielding angle of his head, the restless, edgy movement of his hands as they reached to straighten his tie, pat the wallet in his pocket, tie his shoes, clean his horn-rimmed glasses, scribble a note on a little pad.

She had a featured spot that night, won under protest from her father, who had never wanted her anywhere near the Patagonia in the first place. She told him that she was going to sing somewhere, either at his place or at someone else's. The owner of the Rockland Palace had already approached her saying that if her father wasn't interested in a diamond in the rough, he would be glad to polish her and provide her with a setting.

Her father had always tried to discourage her. There were so few spots for Negro performers. Duke Ellington is the greatest composer ever, he said, but white audiences think that Paul Whiteman is the last word in jazz. He told her that if she went into the business, to expect gigs in smokers and conventions, and that if her boss knew some political bigwig, she would have to go out with him. She would be overworked and underpaid. If she worked in a club owned by whites, the toilet would be reserved for white women, she would have to come in through the kitchen, get dressed in the hallway, work until three in the morning. If she went on the road, she couldn't stay in any of the hotels. If she was lucky they would let her sleep on the circus grounds. And if she met up with the wrong people, they would trash her like a mess of pork rinds.

He wanted her to enroll in either Florida A & M, St. Agnes School for Nursing, St. Augustine's College in Raleigh, or Tuskegee Institute if they could persuade the admissions office to overlook the grades of her junior and senior years. It wasn't too late. Lilia said that she didn't want to learn to be a secretary or a nurse, or even a teacher, that Bristol was too old to know what was what. Marta stepped in between them. This idea that Lilia had gotten into her head Marta attributed to the day Lilia was told that Gesu was transferring her records to another school. The humiliating experience was enough to dampen Lilia's interest in schooling, to threaten her self-esteem. Naturally the girl sought approval in other ways. Besides, her voice matched a new pulse that the customers seemed to want, even if it was a shade too sultry, its phrasing too abandoned, for one so young.

Defeated, Bristol agreed to a compromise. Lilia could work the Patagonia but only the eight-thirty show, despite her protests that no one important would be there that early.

Wearing fuschia Chen Yu lipstick, her hair Vaselined and coiled into a bun, Lilia opened the early show singing "Jennie Made Her Mind Up" dressed in a white tulle overskirt over a slim white sheath, and when her father wasn't looking, white satin gloves with rhinestones.

When she stepped off the stage, weaving her way in and out of the tables with the long microphone wire trailing over her gloved hand, one of the other white men at Watson's table reached out to touch her tulle overskirt. The patrons at the next table, galvanized by the recent terrorist bombings at Carver Village and by the appearance at the Mt. Zion Baptist Church of Thurgood Marshall, chief legal counsel for the NAACP, who advised them of their civil rights, turned impassive, angry stares. The white man in the horn-rimmed glasses said something to his friend, who took his hand away.

The next time she saw Bradford Watson, he was alone, sitting in the rear, even though there were empty tables in front. When she got a closer look, particularly at the cleft in his chin, which you could punch your thumb in, she thought he looked familiar, that she had seen him before outside the club. Then she remembered that she had seen him a few years before, in front of her parents' new house, right after they moved in. He had stood beside his car and watched them empty trash. She might have taken him for a dynamiter, except she didn't think that the KKK wore loafers without socks.

They had decided that it was time to move out of Rosalia's house a short time after Lilia was told that she would be happier with her own kind at St. Francis Xavier at 4th Avenue and 16th Street, a parochial school for Negro children.

While there was little available in the proposed Negro projects like the new subdivisions on the outskirts of town, Coconut Grove offered a few ill-defined neighborhoods, small pockets neither black nor white, in which Marta might be more comfortable. In one such gray area there was a house for rent, an old pine cottage with a banyan in front, vacant since Maude Coombs Watson had moved to an apartment. Bristol took it on the spot, even though he suspected that Maude agreed to the deal just to spite her dead mother.

Its fragrances of earth and decay, of pine and blossom, came through the walls, the windows, up through the floor itself. Crotons and hibiscus leaned out toward the sun while at the same time crawled inside the front door. Bristol told his family that he had played in the yard when he was a boy, rode pine boughs with the son of the people who built it.

The banyan tree had taken over the entire yard, its stolons forming a gnarled and massive structure, with apertures and vined apartments and covey turnings in its upper canyons where a child might hide.

The first thing Bristol did was to hire two men to replace the rotten wood under the eaves, pull up the kitchen linoleum and install square blocks of black and white vinyl over the old black tar that had hardened like slate. Shag carpet with fibers long enough for coins and collar stays to get lost in was laid wall to wall,

451

metal venetian blinds were hung, the roof was repaired, the banyan trimmed back, the plumbing diverted from the septic tank to the city sewer pipes, and the porch reinforced with new supports and outfitted with shade screen that filtered in the light but kept out the sun.

An attic fan was installed to suck the hot air through the attic vents. Window air conditioners were placed in all the rooms except the kitchen, and casement windows were replaced with jalousies. When they tore down the wall between the old parlor and the small bedroom behind it to create a larger living room, Bristol found a rotted bundle between the sheathing and the plaster, shreds of mildewed fibers and rags with a faint, sweet aroma, that fluttered to the ground when he tried to pick it up.

Marta said to throw it out. He bent to press it to his face, saying it reminded him of something, but he wasn't sure what.

"What does this smell like to you?" he asked Lilia.

"I don't know. Like a barber shop."

"Bay rum," he said. It bothered him. He had smelled it before, sometime long ago. Then he remembered the night old man Sands had placed a coin in his hand to lead him to the Coombs house, this house, the search by flashlight of the wells and privies for the white man who had slept beside his mother.

"How long are you going to smell those rags?

Let me throw them out, Bristol, for heaven's sake."

A young man in horn-rimmed glasses stood beside his car watching Bristol and Lilia carry boxes of trash to the sidewalk. Bristol thought he looked familiar. He called across the narrow lane to ask him what he wanted. The stranger said that they had moved into his grandparents' home.

Lilia took offense. "I don't see their name on it."

The young man said he had expressed himself poorly. He meant to say that the house once belonged to his grandparents, more recently to his mother until she moved into an apartment.

"Your grandmother told me not to mess up her floors," said Bristol. "I don't remember your grandfather very well. He was away most times."

The young man crossed the narrow, winding lane. "I wonder if there's anything in that trash from my grandparents' time?"

Bristol stuffed the bundle of rags into a can. "If there is," he said, "it's nothing that you would want." He cleaned his hands on the side of his jeans. "My mother used to work for your family when you were just a little kid. Her name is Caroline."

"I think I remember Caroline before I was sent off to military school. I didn't know she had a family."

Back inside, Lilia turned in annoyance to

her father, "How come you had so much to tell him?"

"There's more," said Bristol. "Some of it I don't think he wants to hear."

"Like what?"

"Like nothing you need to know," said Marta with a scrub brush in her hand.

Lilia decided to speak to Bradford Watson during a voodoo incantation act, a wild, flamboyant number with drums and dancing that the whites assumed was the real thing. He seemed like a fish out of water. She passed his table, then turned as if in an afterthought. "You've been here a lot."

"I like the music."

"No, you don't. You can't even beat it right. I watch you slap the table. You do it like all whites. Straight on. You don't know how to slide the beat."

He smiled. She noticed that he had a cleft in his chin and white, even teeth. "I could learn."

"No, you couldn't. You're too far gone. You're also strange. I remember where I saw you the first time. It was when we first moved into our house. A couple of years ago. You stood on the sidewalk watching my father throw out the trash."

"You have a sharp eye."

"This is lame," she suddenly decided as she turned toward the bar.

454

Bradford stood and scraped his chair into the table behind him. "Have a drink with me."

"My daddy wouldn't like it. Neither would our other paying customers, the ones who can't go to your clubs. They wouldn't like it one bit."

He caught up to her at the bar, where a bartender in a bow tie cleaned glass rings with long swipes of his rag. "I'd like to see you again."

"You can see me here all you want, every night at eight-thirty except Monday."

"I mean to talk."

"How you fixing to do that? You gonna honk for me on the sidewalk and I'm supposed to jump into the backseat? That's why we call you honkies. Did you know that?"

"I wasn't intending for you to hide in my backseat."

"Then what? Where you think we can go in this town?"

"You could pass, you know. Easily. Anyone would take you for white."

"What makes you think that's good?" She swiveled slowly on her stool, came to rest, facing him head-on. "You make me jumpy. I wish you'd quit looking at me like someone starving."

"If you mean like someone hungry, I'm guilty as charged."

"Not hungry. Starving. You can fix up someone hungry with a sandwich. Someone starving needs an ambulance. You also look like you're married."

"What makes you say that?"

"You're either married or you're hiding out from the police."

"How can you tell?"

"The way you keep looking over your shoulder."

He laughed, offered her a cigarette, tapped his own against the pack. "How come you're so smart?"

"We're not all dumb."

"I didn't mean that the way it sounded."

The bartender looked Bradford in the eye before he moved to the other end of the bar.

"You really are a knockout," said Bradford. "I'm not kidding."

"You should have quit when you were ahead. When you say you're not kidding, it sounds like whatever else you said is a lie."

"If you were a guy, I'd tell you to go to law school."

"If you'd tell that to a black man, you for sure don't know which end is up." Lilia put out a tentative finger and touched his cleft. "How did you get that thing anyway?"

"I guess I was born with it." He grabbed her pointing finger, held it playfully. "You sing like an angel."

She pulled her hand away. "You are so jive. Who wants to sing like an angel except someone who's dead?"

"All right. I think you sing better than anyone I've ever heard."

"You are really full of it, you know that."

He stubbed out his cigarette. "It's like my cleft. Take it or leave it."

"I guess I'll leave it." Lilia made her way through a haze of blue smoke to a neon-lit exit.

Bradford followed after her. "Wait a minute. Don't you want to hear how much we have in common?"

Lilia turned. "Like what? You're not colored and you're not an entertainer."

"I'm a lawyer. A lot of what I do is on my feet like you, up in front of an audience. Especially in the appelate division when you don't argue about this shooting or that stabbing. You argue points of law, of procedure."

"I'm waiting for the connection."

"A singer argues points of musical style before an audience who understands it."

"You really know how to stretch it, don't you? Are you any good?"

"I could be. If they ever give me the chance. If not, I've got a spot waiting for me in my in-law's hotel."

"That doesn't sound like something you want to do."

"It's okay, I guess. It's just that a front desk is no judge's bench."

Lilia pulled off her gloves, studied his eyes, his mouth, the butch wax that stiffened his crew cut. "I'll meet you in the parking lot. Don't wait outside your car. Get in. It's only a drive. Nothing else, you understand?"

"Wilco."

"You make any kind of move on me, my daddy will mess you up long, wide, and continuous."

"How about if you make a move on me?"

"Don't hold your breath."

"You going to tell me what made you change your mind?"

"It sounds like you got put on ice. I know how that feels."

Caroline's home smelled of duckanoo simmering on the stove, twenty pounds of fried chicken covered with wax paper, and the Orange Blossom perfume that she poured into the rinse water to wash her floors, not kneeling as she used to, but stooped with swollen knees and arthritic hips over a string mop.

She had begged everyone not to make a fuss but was secretly pleased that her family and friends had gathered to celebrate her eightieth birthday, that James and his wife, Ruth, were bringing Willie, whose driver's license had been revoked, Willie's latest girlfriend, Tonetta, his son and daughter from a previous girlfriend (the third child, a boy, had drowned in a rock pit), and that Bristol was willing to leave his club.

She was hoping that Bristol wouldn't arrive

too late and that James wouldn't stir things up too much with his Urban League talk, wouldn't keep everyone on edge by rehashing the experience of Tonetta's mother, bound for New York City to see her sister, denied a place on a Greyhound bus when there were several vacant spots because the driver would not seat her beside a white.

When they returned from church, Caroline removed her gloves and went into the kitchen. The other women shooed her out, told her that it was Her Day. While unfamiliar hands rummaged through her cupboards, she sat and listened to Lilia tell how Katherine Dunham had taken Aly Khan away from Rita Hayworth, to the men talk of Joe Louis' visit to Bunche Park, where for five hundred dollars cash and forty dollars monthly, a colored veteran could buy an all-tile roof, CBS, two-bedroom house, of the youth Kelsey Bethel, who had lost his left eye when he was beaten by a policeman, of how slum clearance kept getting blocked, from the City Commission all the way up to the Florida Supreme Court.

"The city is doing all kinds of tricks," James said. "They had plenty of time to file for an extension to apply for federal funds. They sat on their hands. They let it lapse. You ever see Goodbread Alley? Three hundred block of N.W. 14th Street, no baths, no electricity, toilets that don't work?"

Bristol lit a cigar. "What makes you think

they're going to do anything for Goodbread Alley when Dorsey High School has only four toilets for one thousand kids?"

James said that the public officials who owned property in the slums were behind the effort to block their clearance. Willie said that he was dead wrong. "You blind as a bat, Uncle James. It's the bolita people behind the block to clear the slums. That way bolita has a place to operate."

Tonetta had been featured on the float of the Sunlight Beauty School in the King Coconut Jamboree, Overtown's answer to the whites' Orange Bowl Parade. The recognition gave her a confidence that learning to straighten hair with curling irons did not. "Willie's right," she said.

James patted his mother's hand, then stood to get a plate, piled it high with ham hocks, fried chicken, and cole slaw, and carried it back to the musty, mildewed sofa. He said that things needed to be speeded up.

"Didn't you ask for space in the Orange Bowl?" said Caroline. "And didn't you get it?"

"In the end zone, Grandma," said Willie. "The ofays get the best seats."

"They didn't give us the end zone because we asked politely," said James. "Reverend Culmer from St. Agnes had to remind the commission that we were prepared to bring civil action. We held a hammer over their heads."

"Civil rights is like a lava flow," said Bristol.

460

"It may look like it's creeping, but it's coming down one way or another. And nothing or no one is going to shovel that lava back up that volcano."

When Caroline heard a dish break, she decided that it was time to blow out her candles.

Late afternoon sunset cast the house in pale yellow. There was soft talk, murmurs mostly, while Willie's son, Denver, dropped cake on the carpet and rubbed it out with his shoe, and Caroline told the story again of how she and Bristol had sailed to Florida in a storm. She left out the part about Obeahman, knowing that James would wink at Bristol, that her church friends would think she was a backslider, also knowing, as did anyone with half a brain, that if blacks could survive in a world with whites, there was room for both Jesus and Orisha.

Ruth congratulated Lilia on winning the Miss Bronze Miami title with its all expense-paid trip to the Bahamas and a professional screen test. Lilia thanked her aunt absently while she thought about Bradford Watson. She wondered what they would think, any of them gathering crumpled wrapping paper and ribbons, if they had seen her yesterday on the boat, when she had taken off her strapless two-piece bathing suit and sprawled on her belly on the deck, her head cradled in her hands, deliberately shifting her weight from hip to hip, while Bradford tried to concentrate on working the sheets. Or the week before on the way to Key West, stopping

461

in the motel on Islamorada because she had him so bothered he couldn't concentrate on the road. Driving him crazy was what made it exciting, getting him to trip in his trouser legs in his hurry to get to the bed, to lose his button-down white face as he lay moaning beneath her, clutching her hips, his eyes closed, his lips soft and open, getting him to tangle himself up in the ropes of her life while he forgot his own. Best, she liked to taunt him with her plans to go to New York, then to Paris, where all really good entertainers went. Not to Hollywood, where all the parts a colored girl could get were maids or natives in Tarzan movies, but to France, where she would wear feathers and rhinestones like Josephine Baker, and take the Aly Khan away from Rita Hayworth.

The presents had been opened and laid carefully on Caroline's bed, dishes were being cleared, James and Ruth were making leaving noises when Tonetta noticed the strangers. "There's a couple of Seminoles on the porch."

Caroline turned to Bristol. Her eyes were brimming. She spoke slowly, as if she had just woken up. "Go get your daughter. Bring her in to me."

Emma entered the living room with Ray Gopher behind her. She was wearing a long patchwork skirt, sandals, a T-shirt, her hair cut short, her neck encased in beads. Ray Gopher was taller than she, with green eyes and straight jet black hair. Dressed in jeans and sneakers, he seemed to Caroline distant, aloof, like the panthers she used to see years ago on her way home through the hammock.

Solemn and unsmiling, Emma presented Caroline with a beadwork belt.

Caroline stood slowly. "Child. I'm so glad to see you. How did you know it was my birthday?"

Emma pointed at Marta. "This white woman drove to our camp."

Bristol and Emma faced one another awkwardly, each searching the other with narrowed, puzzled eyes for something to remember. Emma turned to her son. "This man is Mary Doctor's first husband. That old woman is his mother, Caroline."

"How are you, Emma?" asked Bristol.

"We get along fine. Ray Gopher finished the white man's school. Not make difference. He still drive tractor."

Everyone milled about. Denver and his sister, Lucille, stared frankly at the quiet, somber strangers while Lilia stood in the shadows of the dining room.

"Do you need money?" asked Bristol. "I might be able to help."

"We don't need your money," said Emma. "We not here to see you. We here to see your mother."

Ruth offered her hand. "Your grandmother, you mean."

Emma turned angry eyes toward this dark

woman who wore pearls and shimmering hosiery. "My grandmother Sally Cypress. She dead."

Caroline embraced her. "I don't care what you call me, child. I'm just so tickled you're here. And with your boy. This is the best birthday present of all."

Willie put out his hand to Ray Gopher. "Frail my nails, cousin," he said.

Without a word Bristol went out to the back porch, where the poinciana tree that had been there as long as the house was aflame with bright red blossoms. Caroline went after him, found him staring at the remnants of Galilee's liquor still with tears in his eyes. He was still tall and sturdy, still handsome, with hair turned gray, green eyes glinting like his father's, although more dimly than they had when he was a boy, shaded by lids that had drooped and narrowed with age, by corners that had crinkled with distrust.

"Crying is a good sign," she said. "It means the feeling is coming back. About time. You're over sixty. Shake it off your back, son. Shake it like a duck. You're too old to be grieving for what was and what might could be." His shoulders sagged. "You made a good life for yourself. You got plenty of money, got yourself a real nice wife, two daughters. That boy in there is your grandson. Isn't that something?" She bent down to whisper in his ear. Her back creaked like the old wicker rocking chair nearby.

"You're still my favorite. My firstborn child. My honey man."

It was almost dark. Lilia said she had a date. Marta asked her if it was with Brunell Brown. Lilia lied. Emma, Ray Gopher, Willie, Tonetta, and Willie's children, Denver and Lucille, sat on the steps of the front porch beside a tub of burning citronella.

Willie leaned against the railing, his eyes on Ray Gopher. "Your people ever go on the war path sure enough?" he asked.

"Not now," said Ray Gopher. "A long time ago, maybe. Now everyone is learning auto mechanics."

"A man can't fix his own carburetor," said Willie, "he might as well put on an apron. I never talked to no Seminole before."

"We're not Seminole," Ray Gopher replied. "You're talking about Muskogee people. We're Miccosukee. We're a separate tribe."

Willie threw his head back and laughed. "Take a good look at yourself some time in a mirror, man, then tell me you're not a Seminole. You play the numbers?"

"No."

"Don't miss out on the numbers. You have a dream last night?"

Ray Gopher did not tell him, just as he would not have told a white, about the soul that left the body in sleep and wandered far afield with nightly adventures. "I dream every night."

465

"Well, what was it? What did you dream about?"

"Spark plugs. Maybe. I don't remember."

"You got to recollect your dreams. They all mean a different number. If you remember one, come to see me. I'll tell you what number to play and I'll sell you a winning ticket for sure." He lowered his voice. "I hear tell Indians like to sniff gasoline. You ever try reefer?"

Caroline appeared from the side of the house. She stood before the front steps, her hand on the railing. "What you talking about so quiet?"

"Nothing, Grandma," said Willie. "Me and Ray here, we just passing the time."

"Sit down with us, Mrs. McCloud," said Tonetta.

"If I do, I'll never get up again." Caroline glanced at everyone on the porch. "Look at us. Every color in the rainbow."

Lilia slammed the screen door and ran down the steps, then stopped to kiss her grandmother on the cheek.

"Where are you going?" Caroline asked.

"Out with Brunell Brown. Nowhere in particular."

"Tell that to your mama. Not to me. Someone you ashamed to bring around?"

"He's married, Grandma."

"Sounds like there's more to it than that."

"He's white."

"Lots of colored women been with white

466

men," said Caroline. "You're not the first. You won't be the last. Most times it wasn't their own choosing." She took Lilia's arm, walked with her to the cracked and crumbling sidewalk. "Long time ago, I loved a white man. He was your daddy's father, but I guess you figured that out."

"I never thought about it much. How come you never talk about him?"

"I used to wait for that man to warm up my life like someone waiting for the sun to rise. I even remember the way he smelled. If I close my eyes, I can bring it to mind. Bay rum and salt."

"That must have been a popular cologne way back then. I remember when we first moved to the house. There was some old rags we threw out that Daddy said smelled of bay rum."

"What kind of rags?"

"I don't know, Grandma. Old."

Caroline sighed. "That was the evidence."

"What evidence are you talking about?"

"That family was the worst kind of trash. My hip is acting up. It hurts me to stand here."

Lilia watched her grandmother hitch herself slowly back to the front porch, climb the steps, then disappear into the house. She unlocked the convertible top, folded it back into the well. When she climbed back into the front seat and turned on the ignition, Bristol came running down the steps.

"What did you say to her? She's crying in there."

"I didn't say anything."

"You must have said something. And put that top back up. I don't like you driving alone in this town at night with the top down. It's just asking for trouble."

"What's the sense of having a convertible if you can't drive with the top down?"

Bristol slapped the door. "You wouldn't recognize sense if it came out and bit you on the leg."

It was the unbelievable colors of the Bahama bank that Lilia noticed first, its deep channels of azure blue, its dark green patches of sea grass, the pale blue-green scallops of sandy underwater plateaus that failed to breach the surface.

The seaplane dipped its pontoons in the shallows of an out-island fringed with coral, where tides swirled in and out of the cuts and a pile of conch shells rimmed the lonely beach. On the far side of the dock, an open lorry waited on the sand.

The lorry carried Lilia and Bradford over a rutted dirt road, past small houses that straggled up the hillside and lines of scored and salted fish curing in the sun, to a stucco lodge that smelled of sugar apple and thyme.

While Bradford signed the register, Lilia rapped her nails on the front desk and smiled, curving her dimpled cheeks into scimitars. "Anyone ever come here who's not cheating on his wife?" she asked.

The room clerk raised his head. The whites of his eyes were tinged with yellow, his irises even blacker than his skin. As he handed Bradford a key, a vein twitched at his temple.

Bradford hustled Lilia away to the louvered door of their room. It opened with a creak. "He thought you were bad-mouthing his hotel."

"No he didn't. He knows jive when he hears it. Not like some folks I know."

A ceiling fan spun lazily overhead. Bradford went to adjust the shutters that admitted the dappled morning light while Lilia dropped into a wicker chair to unbuckle her ankle strap shoes.

"You gonna let me out to listen to some real goombay?" she asked.

"Anything you like, baby, as long as it's not in Nassau."

She threw a shoe at his head. "You think you're a real mean cat sneaking off with a colored girl, don't you?"

"For Christ sakes, Lilia. That's not it and you know it."

"How do I know it? How am I supposed to know anything when you never let me in? You never talk about your wife, your little girl. Why?"

"They have nothing to do with us."

"They have everything to do with us. *Us*

469

can't be *us* because of them. The least you can do is tell me what they're like."

He sighed. "We're wasting time. What exactly is it you want to know?"

"Start with your wife."

Bradford took off his madras shirt, slipped out of his white duck slacks, and hung them in the narrow closet. "Sandra is sweet and dependable. She's as different from my mother as it's possible to get. Maude, as I may have told you, is selfish and as cold as the ice in that bucket. After twenty years of her poison, I needed an antidote."

"Who are you gonna get to take the sting out of me?"

"Look, this is crazy. Nobody could be better for me than you, Lilia. I'm alive with you. I didn't know it was possible to feel this good. Isn't that enough? What else do you need to know?"

Lilia unclipped her earrings. "I told my grandmother about us."

"That wasn't very smart. Why would you do that?"

"To make it real. Okay?"

"It's real, Lilia. Believe me, it's real. You're never out of my mind." He snapped his glasses closed and lay them on the dresser. "I have a question for you. Sometimes in bed, when I look at your face, I can't tell whether I'm seeing passion or anger. What I'd like to know is, do you have to be pissed at me to get off?"

"Maybe. I don't know. Maybe I'm mad at myself for going along with your program, for getting involved with a button-down square in the first place. Maybe I'm mad at you because I let you treat me the same way you treat them."

"How is that?"

"You've got all of us in an egg carton, each one in a separate little compartment. When you're through you stick us back in the refrigerator. I told you before. I've already been put on ice. I'm not about to let some white man do it to me again."

"Putting you on ice is the exact opposite of what I have in mind."

Bradford knelt before the wicker chair and nuzzled his head between her knees. "What would happen if we called a truce?" He began to kiss the insides of her thighs, pulling aside her nylon panties while she pushed herself forward to the edge of the chair and grabbed his hair in handfuls.

"How I am supposed to yank this out of your head," she said, "when you keep getting crewcuts?"

September 10, 1958
Miss Harris' School

What I Did on My Summer Vacation

In June we took my great-grandfather Zal-

471

man to the Jewish Home for the Aged. I miss seeing my great-grandfather Zalman except on Sundays. His kisses used to suck the air out of my ears. Timmy doesn't miss him. Timmy is afraid of him because his spit runs down his chin. I am not afraid. I wipe it off with my handkerchief.

In August, I went to stay with my grandmother Maude because my mother went to meet my father in Cuba and my grandmother Sylvia took Timmy to the Catskills and she could only watch one grandchild at a time.

My grandmother Maude's apartment is small. You have to be careful where you walk. You can't run around corners. I forgot once. I broke a vase. Grandmother Maude said next summer I would have to go to sleep-away camp where there are no vases. She said I was too old to break them.

Maude's face is kind of young but her hands are old. Sometimes I can see through her skin. It is like looking at an ant farm. I spent the month of August watching her veins carry her blood around.

She lets me go through her closets and try on anything I want. She has furs and beaded gowns and a string of pearls that reaches to my shoes. She has loads of perfume samples. She taught me to put it in the cracks of my knees and my elbows. She said she will show me the other places when I get older. My grandmother Sylvia says Maude is an anti-

Semite. When I asked my grandmother Maude if that was true, she curled her lip. I wish I could do that. She says she has nothing against Jews. She just knows that my father married one to spite her.

I am the only one in the family who likes her. Even my father doesn't like her. He was away the whole summer except for two weeks in the middle. He had to stay in Cuba and work. He is tired of the hotel business in Miami. I heard him tell this to my grandfather Herschel. My mother called him on the telephone a lot. When no one answered, she cried. My grandmother Sylvia said that she needed to get a grip on herself. I wonder where.

When my father comes back from Cuba, I will clean his sailboat. I will polish everything with toothpaste. Toothpaste is the best for getting things to shine. We will go to the bay to watch the manatees feed in the turtle grass, then we will go to the cemetery to put flowers on my great-grandmother's grave. She is buried with the Daughters of the Confederacy. I am named for her.

Eulalie Watson

Chapter Twenty-Three

RAY GOPHER

Old folks have real good memories. Charlie Billie can't walk, but he has a memory that will not quit. He tells me to do this, to burn that, to bury something else. I don't mind. Makers of medicine make demands like this all the time. It is how they work. When his second yaboli was complete, he cured my grandmother Mary. He called the second ghost of the crew boss who used me as a woman to his campfire, threw it into the flames, and burned it. The next day the crew boss had a fever and died. I did not have to see this to know it was so. Then Charlie Billie called the white man's first ghost and threw it too into the fire. The white man never was, and the bad medicine in my body vanished like the smoke from Charlie Billie's fire.

Charlie Billie and me, we're not the same clan. He says he's Bird, although everyone knows he's really Little Bird. He teaches me his medicine because he says I am deserving. He has done this since the Green Corn dance when I was twelve summers and was given a new name, when I brought him a splinter from an oak tree that had been hit by lightning. He said I gave him strong thunder medicine, and he put it in his deerskin bundle. After a wind moon of black drink and herbs, he began to teach me all the proper chants and formulas. Since that time I have learned songs of the corn, alligator, catfish, and screech owl, mourning chants, and curing chants like the chants to dog and buzzard for dog disease. He taught me that the common cause of disease is the loss of the second ghost, which leaves the body in sleep and does not always return. To discover the cause of the sickness, a medicine man must study the sick person's dreams. If the second ghost wanders at night to the north, then returns at dawn, there is no problem. But if the ghost refuses to return at dawn, if it heads west, a dangerous direction since the dead travel over the Milky Way, it is necessary to go deep into the Pahahokee to obtain the proper herbs before one can blow breath through a medicine pipe.

Sometimes medicine is not the only reason to go deep into the Pahahokee, as far from the white man as it is possible to get. The white man muddies thoughts like someone stirring up muck with a stick. I do not know how he does this. We think he cannot think straight because his second ghost is lame. That is why he walks and talks in crooked paths, like an ant zigzagging on an ant hill.

I began to see this in the Season of Lightning,

when I was sixteen summers and reservation Indians like my grandmother's brothers went to Big Cypress and sued Washington for fifty million dollars. They could do that, our council chief, Buffalo Tiger, said, because the white man's council established a claims commission. But the Tamiami Miccosukee did not want money. We wanted only land. Buffalo Tiger hired a lawyer. In Smoke Season, when I was almost twenty summers, we sent a petition written on buckskin and decorated with egret feathers to President Eisenhower to protest the claim filed by the reservation Indians, to say that the Miccosukee did not give consent to such a claim, that we were a separate people, that they should send someone to talk to us. Ten Indian people signed. Buffalo Tiger translated. The lawyer told us that Eisenhower did not reply because he thought we were only a band of renegades.

That was the time my breath came fast for Louise Jumper. I liked her eyes, the way she cooked acorn stew and fried bread. She liked me too, but we couldn't marry because we are kinfolk. My mother told me to marry Betty Tigertail, who is of the Otter clan. I didn't like her. I had nothing against her clan. It was just her voice. When I heard it, it was like getting scratched with garfish teeth behind my eyes.

The next year, reservation Indians went to Tallahassee to the custodians of reservation oil money. They said that they needed oil money for their children and the sick. The white man danced around this idea as he does around all Indian ideas. In that way he does not have to light, as does the fly on deer meat. He is always safely in the air.

After my mother took me to the celebration at the house of the black woman Caroline, Governor Collins sent white men to Jimmy Tiger's camp on the Trail. Fifty, maybe seventy-five Miccosukee came. Miccosukee people ask that area number three of central and southern Florida flood control be assigned to the tribe. White men say Tallahassee wants our children to go to their schools. They will trade this for a hunting and fishing reserve.

We think now they will give us two hundred thousand acres of area three. They dance again, hold a meeting at Miami Shores in the Season to Plant Late Crops, the time when Charlie Billie's medicine could no longer help my grandmother Mary. Eighty-six white hunters and fishermen ask why we refuse hunting and fishing rights for this land. Lawyer says, give my clients land, then we will negotiate your hunting and fishing rights. The white people laugh.

Lawyer tells us that flood-control man says Indian people can have land, but his people can flood it. A Washington lawyer comes. He says that if state gives land, then state admits it owes much money, even though lawyer tells him that Miccosukee don't want money. That we want only land.

Then a knot that only the white man can make. The lawyer is the knot. Washington says that the agreement signed by Miccosukee tribe and the lawyer means that the lawyer will hold a lien on the land and that is not possible. Traditional Miccosukee like Ingraham Billy and Sam Jones break away from the lawyer. They say all he wants is money. Not a good idea, Buffalo Tiger says, to start up with another white man and have to tell him the same thing all over again.

Buffalo Tiger goes to Washington the next year, in the wet Season of Roads Covered with Snakes, for a meeting at the Bureau of Indian Affairs. This was the time that Louise Jumper and I chased the chickens out of my uncle Sam's Chevy and shared our bodies in the back-seat. While we kept our guilty eyes on the ground, Washington promised the Miccosukee people use of flood land, but Tallahassee people changed their minds. Instead they would buy up all the campsites on Tamiami Trail and place them under state control.

When my mother went in anger with her skirts flying before her to talk to Louise Jumper's mother, Governor Collins appointed a committee of white men. They never meet with us but they decide that we do not intend to live on the land, only plan to lease it for profit. This is false. Then suddenly, like the sting of a wasp, the commissioner of Indian

478

Affairs, Emmons, says on television that land claims are not the responsibility of Washington but of Tallahassee.

It is this time that people come from the white man's college with a tape recorder to capture our stories. They want me to tell them because I speak English better than anyone else. Charlie Billie said not to do it. The white man is your enemy, he says. He is rabbit, the trickster. They have taken everything. They break their promises. If we give away our wisdom, they will use it against us. He reminds me of the legend of Stolen Fire, when the fine, handsome rabbit came to the Green Corn dance, crept closer and closer to the blaze, stuck out his hand, and stole the secret of fire.

This is also the time I am in a fever waking and sleeping, thinking as poorly as the white man, when I dream about Louise Jumper and enter her body until the dawn, driving her into the ground with the stake of my own body, when I awake in a sweat and think that it is not a bad idea to marry Betty Tigertail. This is also the time I ask Charlie Billie about medicine that will shake the white man's brains like beans in a rattle to cause them to settle in straight, even rows, about medicine that will help me feel light when I see Betty Tigertail, so that I too might be able to think and act with reason.

Chapter Twenty-Four

Bradford's disenchantment with the family hotel business did not originate with Kefauver's shutdown of gambling in Miami or from the bad publicity from the testimony of an ex-deputy sheriff that New Jersey racketeers made their winter headquarters at the Sand Dollar. By the next season it was business as usual. If anything, reservations were up as were the numbers of sucker clip joints that sprang up in place of the folding nightclubs, where, after a few drinks with some B-girl, a man's wallet was missing or lighter by a few hundred dollars.

Nor did his disinterest have anything to do with any regrets he might have experienced over leaving the state attorney's office. His boredom came from the business itself, from his father-in-law Herschel's constant preoccupation with the books, his mother-in-law Sylvia's meddling with the way he did anything, and Zalman's rambling phone calls from the nursing home, droning in his ear like the surf. It was too predictable, too tame. There was no action.

Bradford was tired of replacing gin rummy cards soaked with sun-tan oil, of announcing on the loudspeaker that one lady was needed for canasta. When he first came into the business, Sandra's grandfather Zalman told him that he didn't need a *Yiddische kopf* to succeed. "The hotel business is easy. Buy a hotel. The guests will tell you how to run it." Zalman was right. Everyone was a partner. Guests sat in overstuffed chairs in the lobby and counted the check-ins and check-outs. They walked around with their hands behind their backs and scrutinized the ceiling for cracks, the upholstery for rips. They accosted Bradford in the lobby and whispered, "I don't care what anyone says, this is my ninth year here and you can't beat it," then proceeded to tell him what was wrong.

His marriage was as dull as the hotel business. Close to forty, with all his hair and a ribbed, washboard stomach rock-hard from playing handball, Bradford was approaching an age when the good things of life, like his footprints, lay behind him. Although sweet and loving, Sandra, who was beginning to look like her mother, never left him alone. She telephoned constantly about things she should have taken care of, who to call for the crack in the pool, what to do about Timmy, who was writing his letters backward, should she get her hair cut in the new Greek-boy style, and couldn't Bradford do something about his mother, who insisted on taking Eulalie to B-rated movies.

Bradford also wanted to get away from his secretary, Linda, a thirty-year-old, long-legged former Orange Bowl Princess who once could never get enough, who used to accost him in the office, give him blow jobs beneath the desk, sometimes even when he was on the telephone, let him do her in the file closet. Then, as soon as he began paying her rent, it was as if someone had thrown a switch. Linda's bird-nest hairdo could not be messed up, neither could her nails. She had headaches, backaches, stomachaches. She began to make other demands that Bradford was not inclined to fill such as getting a divorce. In the office, Linda was a knockout, as shimmering as the hotel's marquee. In her apartment, she was a silent, frigid, Midol-consuming wraith in maribou and backless lucite heels who threatened to tell his wife.

Bradford attributed his good fortune in the remedy of all situations to connections that had never been severed, and which, in fact, had contributed to his fall from grace in the state attorney's office. When he finally decided to get away, if only ninety miles, he resurrected a few, including one made years ago by his mother.

The deal was sweet. Everyone wanted part of the action. Batista put up half the cash on a dollar-for-dollar basis. You could buy in, not the old casinos of the past, but hotel-casino complexes like the ones in Vegas, have something to do with the operation, while Lanksy retained control. It was all right with other partners, who were content to let Lansky handle all the flak. It was certainly all right with Bradford, who bought in on behalf of the Levy family, comparatively speaking, with peanuts.

Batista, who took a cut of everything, which was expected, made it easy. Corporate taxes were waived, import duties on building materials, which usually ran as high as seventy percent were removed, the license fee for a casino was only $25,000, and all pit bosses, stickmen, and dealers were to be considered technicians and eligible for two-year, instead of six-month, visas.

The Riviera cost $14 million to build. Covered in turquoise mosaic, the 440-room, skyscraper hotel-casino was the first to have central air conditioning hissing silently from ceiling vents, in contrast to the Capri, which had individual box units that rattled and dripped from every window. The structure swept back from the Malecon in the shape of a tremendous *Y*, with cantilevered balconies at every end. Nestled beside it like a gilded ostrich egg was the casino, a curved and windowless dome covered in gold mosaic.

The nut was tremendous, even aside from political shakedowns. Since no casino could survive the limited action of the average tourist, who, while spending freely in the nightclubs and shops, usually dropped ten dollars in a slot machine, Bradford's job was to arrange junkets for serious, high-stakes rollers, men who thought nothing of writing a $20,000 check for an evening of gaming. With the help of Pablo

Garcia, a numbers man from Miami anxious to lay off his cash, Bradford orchestrated charter flights to fly high rollers to Havana from New York, Tampa, and Miami at no cost. He arranged for free limos, girls, rooms, cigars, ringside tables, and lines of credit. On the plane rides back to Miami, Bradford had a second responsibility that made up for his lack of contributing capital. He was a bag man.

The millions being made that were not carried by courier to Switzerland had to be dry-cleaned before they could be returned to the United States. To handle the vast amount of cash, a bank on South Beach, where Bradford made early morning deposits in the name of foreign corporations set up under the laws of Cuba and Panama, was created by the syndicate in January 1955.

Bradford came alive in Cuba's brisk winds and whispers of vice, in the sun that shone on the stone and fountains of the colonial section, in the noisy Old World web of alleys and squares near the docks that were tied to the plate glass and Cadillacs of the newer sections by the laurel-shaded Prado. Cuba had the most accommodating girls, the finest cigars, marijuana if you wanted it, the strongest daiquiris. He liked the music of the white-tuxedoed orchestras, evenings spent beside men in black tie and kid-gloved women in mink and serious jewels playing baccarat behind a rope and blackjack dealt from a box, days spent at the race-track, where you could buy two separate daily doubles and three quinielas, or at the Casa Marina near the airport, where you could get a virgin if that was your style or a gorgeous courtesan who knew how to thread a frozen, knotted rope up your ass and pull it out at the moment of orgasm. Best of all, he liked being one of the boys, a businessman with clout.

The excuse to travel between Miami and Havana gave Bradford the challenge he craved. He rationalized his absences from his children with the idea that kids needed their mothers more than their fathers. In any case, Eulalie and Timmy were end-of-the-day annoyances, problems to be dealt with as soon as he walked in the door. There was nothing he could do for Timmy that a tutor could not do better. And Eulalie was an outright disappointment. When she had been a toddler, he imagined that as she grew that she would maintain the same angelic appearance, the same rim of white gold curls, an adorable, precocious child like Shirley Temple that people would stop you on the street for. Instead, Eulalie had become an ungainly, awkward girl, shy, timid, hovering in the background like a shadow. She seemed to want something from him that he was at a loss to give. The bottom line was that her presence was a guilty reminder that neither of them was what the other expected.

After Sputnik was launched, Bradford flew Herschel to Cuba for the opening of the Riviera Hotel. Because rooms were in short supply, he put him up at the Nacional, a hotel on a rocky bluff run by the Cleveland syndicate, with curved loggias that looked down over the Malecon and the plumes of spray thrown up by the sea-pounded ocean wall. He took him to the razzle-dazzle show at the Tropicana, where palm trees lit in red and blue waved over the floor show, to the lavish, open-air San Souci, to the Capri to have his picture taken with its official host, the actor George Raft, to the cockfights, where Herschel said he wanted to get back to the Nacional so he could watch the show girls sunbathe around the pool.

The night before Herschel left for Miami, they sat ringside at the Copa Room to see Ginger Rogers. "She can wiggle her ass," said Herschel, "but she can't sing a note." After the show, Herschel expressed concern that his unknown partners who ran the elegant, brocade-draped, elaborately chandeliered casinos might all be mobsters.

"Who do you expect to find running the games?" said Bradford. "John Foster Dulles? Nobody but an experienced gambler can run a gambling joint. Anyone else would go bankrupt from crooked players, not to mention employees on the take. The gambling here is legit. You can bank on it."

"It's Las Vegas with a rhumba beat," said Herschel.

"It's nothing like Vegas," said Bradford. "Vegas was built from scratch. This whole operation is built on an already thriving metropolis. That's the beauty of it. And the Cubans love it. Thousands of jobs have been created for construction workers, croupiers, musicians, what have you."

Herschel stood before a mirrored pillar and straightened his bow tie. "What's with you and Sandra?"

"Nothing. We're fine."

"She doesn't look fine. I want my girl to be happy. Maybe we were wrong to get involved in all this."

"We can't make a mistake in Cuba, Herschel. Trust me."

"What happens if Batista falls from power?"

"Nothing. A new set of deals will be made with a different set of politicians."

On the way to the airport, Bradford took Herschel to an exclusive shop in the corridor of the new Havana Hilton, where his father-in-law bought a matching red crocodile bag and shoes for Sylvia from a salesman in a pleated white linen shirt with pearl-buttoned pockets.

"Take the belt that goes with it," Bradford advised.

As they were leaving the plushy carpeted shop, a bomb exploded somewhere nearby, deafening them, shattering the glass from the patio

487

enclosure of the Hilton as well as the windows of the shop. Behind them, the salesman stood confused and bloodied, with splinters of glass clinging to his face and shirt like sequins.

Bradford pulled Herschel behind a shoeshine stand while whistles blew around them and passersby scrambled in every direction, criss-crossing blue-uniformed men who Bradford knew were the secret police.

"What the hell was that?" said Herschel.

"Nothing major. Keep your head down," said Bradford. "It may not be over yet."

"I don't mind telling you," said Herschel, his face pressed to the sidewalk, "that this street resistance is scaring the shit out of me."

"It's nothing that organized, Herschel. They're just a tiny band pretending to be guer-rillas. This was probably some pissed-off campesino squatter who thinks he should own the farm."

When they stood and brushed themselves off, Herschel turned to his son-in-law. "This busi-ness can only get worse. It's time to think about cutting our losses."

"I keep telling you there's nothing to be afraid of."

"Tell that to those fellows in the blue uni-forms. They looked plenty worried to me. As my father Zalman would say, it's not enough to know your way around Havana. You also have to have a head for business. That includes when to get in and when to get out."

When Bradford arrived at the hotel for his appointment with Pablo Garcia, he was testy from the moment he entered the hotel room. Meetings with his junket partner were always peppered with a kind of double-talk that made Bradford inch his way through the exchange as if through a mine field. This one was no different.

The plump, middle-aged numbers man pulled a list of junketeers from his inside coat pocket along with a sheaf of rubber-banded markers, slapped both on the bed, then mixed a drink from a nearby brass dolly while Bradford scanned the list, flipped through the markers, then scribbled something on a piece of paper. Pablo glanced at the bottom number, said it was short.

"I'm not paying for Rupert Smith or Franklin Rivkind," said Bradford. "Smith was looking for a free ride. The house is sending him a bill. And Rivkind's play never measured up."

"Someone made a mistake," said Pablo, swirling his drink in his glass. "These guys are high rollers."

"The pit bosses never heard of either one. It's no mystery. They never checked in. Never got themselves clocked. They know the routine. That means they never played. Or if they did, they gave their action to the wrong casino, not the one who paid for the bodies or were ready to pay a commission on their losses."

"What about Smith's marker?"

"Someone else must have signed his name. Don't show it to the house unless you want them to tell you where you can put it. I told you before, get cash up front. That way you guarantee the play."

"You're asking for a lot of paperwork, Bradford. I'm not a pencil pusher. There's other business. The airline is talking about upping the charter fee. Am I supposed to eat that too?"

"Nobody's eating anything. They're just testing the waters."

Pablo tossed down the rest of his drink. "Okay. Don't say later that I never told you. I gotta run. My niece is playing the Nacional. I promised I'd catch her act before I went to the airport."

"What's her name?"

"She goes by Lilia. No second name. Just Lilia. She's big in Europe. You ever hear of her?"

The hallway outside the dressing rooms was noisy and crowded, piled high with beer crates, lit by lonely naked bulbs that dangled overhead. Pablo rapped sharply with his knuckles. "It's me, Lilia, your uncle Pablo. I brought someone who says he knows you."

A uniformed maid opened the door. Inside Lilia Sands sat before a mirror, creaming off her makeup. Only minutes before she had undulated on the stage in a shocking pink strapless feathered gown that rustled at her feet, a gorgeous, exotic performer with magnetic green eyes that swept over her audience and a throbbing, throaty voice that was as intimate as a heartbeat. Now she sat in a flowered silk kimono, pulling off a strip of long, false eyelashes that she set in a box. She looked up once. "Hi, Uncle Pablo. Look what the cat dragged in. Hello, Brad."

Bradford stepped into the room. It smelled of talcum powder and the steam from an iron. "Last I heard, you were in Paris."

Lilia chattered idly about Europe, about Monte Carlo, where she had met Frank Sinatra and Edith Piaf, about sailing on the French lines because the American lines discriminated and the British lines were not much fun. She mentioned that she traveled only first-class with Louis Vuitton trunks and took her meals at the second sitting when civilized people ate.

Pablo looked at his watch. "You were great tonight," he said. "But get the management to make your name bigger on the billboard. And get another picture. The one they have makes you look too dark."

"That's what I am, Uncle, dark."

"Not that dark. I have to get to the airport. I'll call your mother. Tell her I saw you." He waved from the door, told Bradford that they still had accounts to settle, then left.

While the maid handed Lilia her clothes behind a mildewed, faded taffeta screen, Bradford lit a cigarette.

"You doing anything in Cuba besides slumming?" Lilia asked.

"We have a small piece of the action."

"I thought you were a lawyer."

"I went straight. What do you think of all this? All the construction going on?"

"Not much. The Riviera Hotel cost the Cubans six million to build. If it makes money, all the profits will be siphoned off to the U.S. If it loses money, the Cubans are stuck with a six-million-dollar white elephant. What kind of deal is that for Cuba?"

He pulled up a chair, turned it around so that he straddled it backward, his hands resting on the rungs. "Cuba can only win, Lilia. Havana could soon be the hub of a major tourist circuit. They're talking about running a ferry that will bring one hundred-fifty cars from Key West in three hours, another chain of ferries and highways to link Havana with Mexico's Yucatan peninsula, to Haiti, Puerto Rico."

Lilia came out from behind the screen dressed in slacks and a silk man-tailored shirt, her hair tied back with a ribbon. "You haven't changed. The only thing different is that you've given up that butch cut. Don't you know what's going on in the mountains?"

Bradford knew that there were bearded rebels in the jungle-covered, almost impenetrable

Sierra Maestra Mountains. He also knew about the SIM, Batista's secret police. He had even heard that assassination and torture were routine, that bodies had been left hanging from trees and beside roadways, sometimes with testicles stuffed in their mouths. He knew that guests from the hotel could see derelict Cubans camped out on the sidewalk in a street at the rear of the hotel. But these were local politics at which he shrugged his shoulders.

"Who are we to tell them how to run their country? And why did you leave Miami without calling?"

"Maybe I thought a clean break was the best way. You got me sort of crazy there. It didn't start out that way. It started out kind of like a game. What happened was, when I woke up in the morning, all I could think of was you, which wasn't too smart considering you were waking up next to someone else. You almost made me forget my own agenda. Anyway, you look like you survived."

He dropped his cigarette on the floor, stubbed it out with his shoe. "I thought we had something."

"You had something. I didn't."

"You knew I was married. You knew it from the first. I thought you understood."

"I understood plenty."

"I couldn't believe you left without a word. I went crazy trying to find you, trying to get someone to tell me where you were. You were

493

like the air I breathed. Then suddenly you were gone, and I was inside some plastic bag getting blue in the face."

Lilia retied her hair ribbon. "You know what made me finally decide that it was time? When my daddy died and I couldn't even call you on the phone to tell you."

Bradford stepped closer, fingered her lapel pin. "I took one look at you tonight up there on that stage and it was like the first time I ever saw you. I thought my heart was going to hammer itself right through my ribs. Don't tell me you don't feel anything."

"Nothing that a couple of aspirins won't cure."

He grinned. "Let's go somewhere. I want to show you the town."

"I've already seen it, Brad. Besides, I have plans."

A tuxedoed man came to the door, stayed only long enough to hand the maid an envelope thick with bills. Lilia reached inside the envelope to count the money, then tucked it into her purse.

"That's a lot of cash to be carrying around," said Bradford. "What's wrong with a paycheck?"

"How I take my salary is none of your goddamn business."

"Look, I'm the one who got run out on. The least you can do is squeeze me into your program. Be a sport. A couple of hours

494

is all I ask. I promise."

Lilia agreed to let him come along, but said that the *where* and the *what* were her call, not his. They took a cab to Marianao Beach to a dim club called Chori's that resembled a tin-roofed chapel. Inside, the club's unpainted walls were hung with straw hats resting on wooden pegs. The sweet, pungent aroma of marijuana hung in the blue haze above a mulatto clientele who danced to a raucous, shirt-sleeved steel band. The drummer, Chori, wore a giant crucifix and a necklace of voodoo beads that clattered together when his beat became frenzied.

"If you're planning to cha-cha," said Lilia, "this is the wrong place."

Bradford moved closer. Her breath was sweet. He noticed that she had changed her perfume. "That wasn't what I had in mind."

"And don't get any ideas about getting on the dance floor and trying to do what they do. You don't have the moves."

He took her hand, played with her fingers. "You didn't used to say that. You used to like my moves."

Lilia smiled at Chori, who waved a drumstick in her direction. "Not your dancing. You can't dance for shit."

They were on their second bacardi cocktail when a man dressed in loose cotton pants gathered at the waist with a rope hung a checkered scarf on one of the wall pegs, stood until he caught Lilia's eye, then took a seat in a darkened corner. Lilia excused herself and snaked her way to his table, stopping to talk to him only for a moment.

"Who is that?" asked Bradford when she returned.

"He's a guajiro, a mountain peasant. If you want to know what he does, he cuts cane. He cuts cane and waits for the coffee harvest. They pay him five centavos a tin, he gets up at dawn and works until five in the afternoon, and he winds up at the end of the day with one and a half pesos."

"What's a mountain peasant doing in Havana?"

Lilia snapped her fingers. "I feel like moving. Let's dance."

Bradford grabbed her wrist and forced her back in her seat. "He's a rebel, isn't he? What does he want with you? Better yet, what do you want with him?"

"Let go of my hand. It's nothing you would understand."

"Try me."

"All right. But I don't think it will do any good. It's not just about overthrowing Batista. It's about human rights and injustice. You're probably not interested, but in Oriente province there are two hundred thousand peasant families who don't own between them a single acre of land."

He slipped his fingers beneath the cuff of

her shirt and stroked her wrist. "Maybe some things are unfair, but you have to figure the odds. The rebels are only a handful up against the entire Cuban army."

Lilia pulled her hand away. "Batista's soldiers have already begun to cross the lines. Don't you hear anything in those posh places where you strut your stuff, or you go around with casino chips in your ears?"

"Where do you get all this information?" His eyes narrowed as he dropped his voice to a murmur, brought his chair closer so that they were face to face. "I think I just caught on why you want to be paid in cash. This isn't smart, Lilia. If some of the wealthy Cubans give money to the rebels, they're betting on a long shot. What's in it for you? Your gig in Havana is over. Why put yourself in jeopardy for a lost cause?"

"You said you'd leave when I gave the word. I'm giving it."

Bradford loosened the knot of his tie. "How long are you going to keep this up? We need to get somewhere fast to a room with a lock. You want to. I want to. You're as hot for me as I am for you. Why are you putting all this bullshit in the way?"

She pulled off her earrings and dropped them into her purse. "See you around some time."

"I'll come with you."

Lilia stood. "You just don't get it. You can't come with me. I don't want you to come with me. Neither does he." She nodded toward the guajiro, who pulled his checkered scarf from its peg and wound it about his neck. The edge of a machete glinted from the folds of his shirt. Lilia hurried after him, thinking of the ride ahead to the damp, dark wilderness of the Sierra Maestra, with its green mountain folds and ferns higher than a man, where Batista's planes swept low over the jungle, dropping bombs blindly and the small band that never slept more than two nights in the same spot.

Even more impelling were the brief encounters as charged as cocaine highs, of one-sided conversations with the bearded rebel leader, a lawyer in green fatigues who spoke with enthusiasm and passion of unemployment and violated pension funds, of struggle and revolution, a man who smelled of soap and cigars and who shared her cot almost as an afterthought, sometimes without even taking off his boots.

Reservations for New Year's Eve of 1958 had been brisk and busy. On his way to the Copa Room to make sure that his junket sat ringside, Bradford was told by the maître-d' that the hotel had received two hundred cancellations. It was puzzling. Where better to go for a New Year's Eve bash?

Later that evening, in the almost empty Copa Room, a bartender told Bradford that when he left for work that afternoon, he had seen groups of cars loaded with women and children and baggage enter Camp Columbia Military Headquarters near his home. It wasn't until one in the morning, when American consular officers called the front desk for lists of visitors' names in case an evacuation became necessary, that the hotel learned that Batista had fled the country.

Throughout the remainder of the ominously quiet night, Bradford stuffed his pockets, his jacket lining, his false-bottomed suitcase with cash, thinking that it was unbelievable. Castro was in Oriente province, five hundred miles away, Batista had fifty thousand, maybe one hundred thousand men completely armed, in full control, according to big-money Cubans, of practically every single garrison. The only answer was that more than just a few big-money Cubans were slipping the rebels money on the side. Insurance.

Lilia. The last Bradford had heard, she was still in Cuba. He didn't know where. She wouldn't tell him. He had seen her twice in the past few weeks, both times at places and moments of her choosing, once in a glitzy glass and chrome apartment near the Vedado, the second time in his hotel room. She said she was determined to get him out of her system once and for all, that he was a selfish prick, that they had nothing in common.

Both occasions had begun like so many times before when in their urgency they tore off each other's clothes. The difference was that now

499

neither spoke. Instead they spent the moments in between frenzied couplings grazing on each other's parts, licking, sucking, teasing swollen tissues with lips and tongues until each roused the other to another mindless excitement that had more to do with anger than with passion. Yet even then, exhausted, locked together shiny with each other's sweat, Lilia's eyes had wandered and Bradford knew she was thinking of someone else.

He took a cab to Chori's. The guarded jubilation of a handful of patrons came to a halt when Bradford entered the open archway of the club. He found Chori at the bar.

"I'm looking for someone," he said. "She's a singer who goes by the name of Lilia."

Chori smiled, showing two gold teeth. "I don't know of such a person, Señor."

"Can it. I was in here with her a few months back. You waved to her with your drumstick."

"Is she pretty?"

"She's beautiful."

Chori laughed. "I wave to all the pretty women with my drumstick." A woman in platform heels with a rump that projected like a shelf laughed with him. Chori reached over to pinch the woman's cheek.

"Listen," said Bradford, "I know you know her. I've got to get a very important message to her." He peeled off some bills, thrust them across the bar.

"Perhaps it's possible," said Chori. "Relay

the message to me."

Bradford was aware that all eyes in the club were on him. He took the chance. "Tell her that Batista has left the country."

"Maybe she already knows."

"Then tell her it's dangerous for her to stay. I can probably get her out on a charter. But she's got to get back to me by tomorrow morning. I might be able to hold up the flight."

"I'll do what I can."

"Look, Chori, if you have any regard for her at all, then you'll help her out."

"I'm always ready to help my friends."

Bradford decided to play it safe. He'd call the airport before dawn, gather together his junket in the morning, and get them out a few hours earlier. He awoke at daybreak to the sounds of milling, shouting mobs smashing parking meters in the streets below. It took twenty minutes to get through to the airport. When the line finally cleared, he learned that all charter and commercial flights had been suspended. It was only because he hadn't heard from Lilia that he was almost glad to remain at the hotel.

There was a knock on the door. Bradford peered through the slit before he flipped up the chain. It was Lilia, dressed in a scarf and raincoat.

He grabbed her, held her to him. "Where have you been? I've been looking all over for you. You didn't pack anything. It doesn't mat-

501

ter. Whatever you left behind can be replaced."

"I'm not alone, Brad." She turned her head.

Behind her in the dimly lit hallway were two women, a man, and a small child. The women looked like mother and daughter. Bradford judged the middle-aged man to be the husband of the older woman. The younger woman carried a little boy in her arms.

"These are my cousins," said Lilia, "Nestor Escobay, his wife, Hortensia, their daughter, Gloria Maraquilla Alvarez, her little boy, Pupi. Nestor is the managing editor of the newspaper. He has written certain editorials. He thinks he should get out, at least until things settle down. I told them you would help them."

Bradford waved the family into the room. "I don't know. The flight's been suspended," he said, "along with everything else with wings. Your cousins may be better off in a boat."

Nestor Escobay said that it was crazy on the streets. The news had spread like wildfire. There was talk that members of the Batista regime were already in hiding, that some had sought refuge in Latin American embassies, while others escaped on their yachts.

"I appreciate the problem," said Bradford, "but I have a junket to get back to Miami one way or another. I guess you can tag along." He began to call his list of high rollers. Most wanted to stay, wait for the charter that was scheduled in three days. He told the few that were anxious to leave to have their bags packed in an hour. He would get them out on the ferry between Havana and West Palm Beach, the *City of New Orleans*, which usually ran lighter than the one to Key West.

Bradford's party left in two limos, weaving in and out of autos filled with youthful members of the underground speeding here and there with jackrabbit, screeching starts, past Boy Scouts directing traffic and truckloads of bearded rebels rolling into the streets to wild cheers and shouts of *Cuba si, Yanqui no*, through intersections where the militia had set up roadblocks. Nestor Escobay said he was reminded of the morning in 1933 when Machado fell except this time everyone was so young.

At the ferry dock, they waited for an hour, jammed together on the fringes of a pushing, frantic mob, some in autos, most on foot, a few still in their evening clothes. Lilia confided that none of her cousins had visas.

"*Now* you tell me," said Bradford.

When he saw that the ferry was filling fast, that there were at least five hundred already on board and that they might not make the cut, he shoved Nestor Escobay and his wife into a narrow opening created when a child was suddenly snatched up into his father's arms, an advantage Bradford would have taken for himself. The wooden gates swung down before them. The crowd was waved back. Some tried to jump over the stanchions, but it was too

503

late. The overloaded ferry was already churning away from the dock.

"What do we do?" asked Lilia.

"We keep moving," said Bradford, not sure at all why he had done such a stupid thing. He thought of the stray campesinos he had seen that morning, entering the lobby with their pigs, of the hotel workers deserting their jobs to run out and celebrate. "Spend the day at the beach, tourists out for some sun."

By midday, they were sitting on the rocky sand of Varadero Beach listening to the static of loudspeakers and the sound of gunfire from the city of Matazanas across the bay, where Lilia said they were holding executions.

Gloria Maraquilla sat quietly beside her child, offering him a perfumed violet candy from her handbag. She had made a tent for him of Bradford's dinner jacket. Bradford thought she was pretty but placid, and much too soft. He preferred long-legged women with green eyes and hipbones and little asses that you could cup in your hands.

"Ask your cousin," he said to Lilia, "if it's getting too hot."

"Ask her yourself. She speaks English."

"We are fine, Mr. Watson. Thank you," she said.

In bits and pieces of an awkward interchange, she told him that not all her family thought it necessary to leave. Her father's sister, Flavia, and her husband, a rum distributor, were quite prepared to deal with a new regime. Her own husband, Gustavo, a doctor with a new practice, certainly had no interest in deserting his patients. That left her grandmother Ileana, who was much too old, too comfortable with her familiar rocking chair and her photographs to think of leaving her street, much less her country.

She turned away. Her face had taken on an angry look. She snatched a sharp, dried crab claw from the hand of the little boy. "Why did Eisenhower cut the sugar quota?" she demanded suddenly, tears in her eyes. "Why are you forcing Cuba into the arms of Russia? We're not communists. We are more American than the Puerto Ricans."

The sounds of gunfire had escalated. "No one said anyone was a communist," said Bradford. "The driver is waving to us. I think he wants to get back to the hotel."

When the limo pulled into the deserted driveway, Lilia put her arms around Bradford's neck and kissed him. "I'm not coming with you, Brad. Take care of my family. I know they'll be safe with you."

"Where are you going?" he shouted as she broke away. "Lilia, wait!"

She ran across the street, dodging a careening truck filled with rifle-toting *barbudos*, then vanished into a cheering, running mob.

Three days later, the airlines resumed their flights. Since taxis and limos were no longer running, members of the embassy drove Bradford and his stray junketeers, Gloria Maraquilla and her child, and Pablo, who had spent the past few days collecting numbers receipts, to the airport.

They filed into *la pecera*, the fishbowl, a glass-enclosed holding area for those waiting to leave for the United States. People were crying inside and out. Whispers of shameful assaults made everyone afraid that they would be undressed, or even worse, violated. They moved single file past machine-gun-carrying Cuban militia who asked what they were taking out of the country. Then the emigrés were led outside to the runway, where bearded men looked inside their luggage, including Bradford's with its false bottom.

Gloria Maraquilla identified only a small case filled with a child's things including a scrap of a crocheted blanket faded oyster white. When they asked why she hadn't packed for herself, she replied that she didn't need anything for so short a visit.

Bradford stepped forward, put a protective arm around her shoulder, let one hand trail suggestively onto the front of her blouse. "I'll buy my woman anything she needs on Lincoln Road," he said. He kept his arm tightly around her shoulders, despite her recoil. They were led back inside *la pecera*, where people were either crying or silent, staring at the floor, not knowing whether to look or not at their relatives standing on the other side of the glass. A young child stood alone with a Miami address written on a piece of cardboard strung around her neck.

Bradford looked for the usual immigration people. He knew all of them. If any of them were here, there would be no problem. But they were gone, replaced by the revolutionaries. In the rear of the crowd, on the other side of the glass, he thought he saw Lilia, but he turned when a militiaman, scanning a pile of papers before him, challenged Gloria Maraquilla.

"This woman has no tourist visa," he said.

Bradford winked. "My mistake," he said. "We forgot it. Left it on the bed." He winked again, then, as quickly as he was able to palm a set of dice, slipped the man a thousand-dollar bill folded to the width of a cigarette. He took the child from Gloria Maraquilla's arms and kissed him. "Come to Papa," he said.

The militiaman looked at Bradford, then at Gloria Maraquilla, hesitated for a moment. "You can go," he said. "Take your whore and your brat with you."

When Bradford turned to scan the crowd for the woman who he thought resembled Lilia, she was gone. They were about to leave the fishbowl when a bearded man with a scarf around his forehead signaled for Pablo. He was brought forward by another militiaman while they went through his papers a second time. The bearded man nodded. Pablo was led away.

"Where are you taking him?" called Bradford. "He's not a Cuban. Look at his visa. He's an American."

"Mr. Garcia will go to Triscornia, the immigration prison," said the bearded man, "for Americans."

"You can't do that," protested Bradford. "He works with me. We're here every week. Everyone knows us." He fished out another thousand-dollar bill, folded it so that the amount could be seen if anyone was looking. This time the militiaman affected disinterest. The bearded man stepped forward.

"You Yankee gangsters who run the casinos of Havana are symptoms of all that is wrong in Cuba. Your friend is greedy. He involved himself in our lottery, which we also intend to shut down."

"Give him the rest," shouted Pablo. "Give him all of it!"

The bearded man retied the scarf around his forehead. "What rest is he talking about?"

"I honestly don't know," said Bradford. "My friend is afraid and who can blame him? People say strange things when they're afraid."

"*Vamanos,*" said the bearded man, and they were led onto the runway, where the plane's propellers threw up swirls of dust and the little girl with the sign around her neck began to cry.

Part Four

1962–1980

Part Four

1942–1980

Chapter Twenty-Five

Dear Lilia,

I hope it will not upset you to learn that I had to sell the Patagonia to provide right-of-way for the new expressway. Things change. No one knows this better than my Cuban cousins.

When Gloria Maraquilla's husband, Gustavo, arrived on one of the planes that for the time being fly daily from Havana, all his medical instruments were confiscated. I drove him to the new Refugio, stood beside him in the long line in the April sun while he waited for an application for permanent status, sixty dollars, a first-aid kit, chest X rays, and a polio vaccination, and told me he had not seen you in over a year.

Nestor has a job operating an elevator in the du Pont Building. On the weekends, he takes Esteban to Calle Ocho, where they play nine-dot dominos and smoke cigars beneath the black olive tree. Exile is hardest on Flavia. In Cuba she lived in a home that was patterned

511

*after a Florentine chateau, where every af-
ternoon she and her friends played poker with
perfumed hands. Now those same hands cut
string to wrap bakery boxes, and the poker
she plays is penny ante.*

*Pablito, Pablo's seventeen-year-old son,
who was a member of the brigade which tried
to liberate Cuba, has been captured. I never
thought the invasion would succeed. How could
it when everyone knew about it before it
happened? Did they really expect Castro to
give up with so small a force? His mother,
Celia, with a husband already languishing
in a Cuban jail, is in despair. They don't
talk about you, who remained by choice. It
is as if you are already dead, and this breaks
my heart.*

*We discuss none of this in front of my
mother, who is getting old, although her mind
is still razor sharp, as is her tongue. Her
second husband, Ramon, younger than she
by ten years, a wastrel who married my
mother for her money, offers pastillos on a
tray while she prays the rosary for the release
of her son and grandson, and tells me to do
the same. My mother does not ask if I suffer
in my recent widowhood, and I do not tell
her that I still hear your father's footsteps
on the porch, his key in the lock.*

*I look around her house for wisps of my
father, trying to catch phantasms from the
corners of my eye. I think it is an irony*

512

that the time you really need a parent is when you are no longer young. While it is your father's presence that I yearn for, it is my own father's counsel which I want to see scratched in the vapors of his humid bathroom mirror.

I park in the driveway beneath the banyan that has become its own forest, closing off the light in the front yard so that no shrubs, no grass can grow beneath it. The other trees, like the eucalyptus, whose crushed leaves smell like lozenges, grow crooked seeking the light. Some, like the papaya, have become stunted and die. I brush away the poinciana seedpods that cover Flavia's shrine, then think of your father's shoulder and remember what it was like to nestle in its scent.

I pray for your safe return. I also pray that you will find a man who is true and steadfast, so that you are no longer like the houseboats behind Dinner Key, moored here, then there, with no firm anchor anywhere.

> *Your loving mother,*
> *Marta*

In 1965, the second wave of Cubans, exchanged for ten million dollars in medical supplies, arrived in Miami. Among them was Marta's brother, Pablo, released from El Principe, where he had been imprisoned for six years. No one knew he was coming. His arrival was announced by a Haitian cab driver who shouted for payment beneath the banyan tree in Marta's yard.

Pablo looked the same, wearing his jacket over his shoulders, dark and lean, swaggering like a panther. When he learned that his son, Pablito, had been captured in the aborted Bay of Pigs invasion, he pounded a fist on the hood of his sister's car.

Later at his mother's house, with its crimson velvet draperies that smelled of lavender and mildew while his family tried to ease his detention with their touches, their *ropa vieja*, Pablo suddenly wheeled on his cousin Gloria Maraquilla, his voice husky, his eyes a glittering obsidian. "Where is he?" he asked.

"Who?"

"Watson. The one you left Cuba with."

"What do you want with him?" she asked.

"Six years," said Pablo. "And my son. If I had been here to stop him, Pablito would never have gone."

Her husband, Gustavo, a slight, wiry man with skin the color of an olive, knit his brows.

While everyone rubbed the rims of their demitasse cups with lemon peel, Gustavo led his wife into the foyer beside umbrellas that dripped on Rosalia's tile floor. "I'm going to ask you a question. This Bradford Watson, did he mean something to you?"

"No, Gustavo. Not the way you suggest. He was good to me and the boy. Without him,

514

Pupi and I would never have been able to get out of Cuba. We owe him our lives, all of us. My mother and father too."

"I ask this for a reason. From the look in his eyes, I think Pablo is looking to hurt him. Possibly kill him. The question I ask myself is, why would he want to kill him? He cannot possibly hold him accountable for circumstances over which Watson had no control. It has to be something else. You?"

"No, Gustavo. Believe me. Perhaps it is because Bradford had money with him the day we fled. He was transporting it for others. Maybe Pablo thinks he could have saved him with that money."

Gustavo took her gently by her arms. "I would understand," he said, looking into the deep coffee brown of her eyes. "You were grateful. These things happen."

Gloria Maraquilla shook her head. "There was nothing, Gustavo. On my life."

Bradford came to the door wearing jeans, loafers over bare feet, and a thin gold chain beneath his opened shirt. He had been on the phone confirming negotiations for the purchase of a 285-foot-long Greek cargo vessel, a converted World War II troop carrier with a long, sharp bow that he and his father-in-law planned to turn into a cruise ship.

It took Bradford a moment to recognize the rain-soaked man standing at his door. "Gustavo.

What are you doing here? Get in out of the rain."

Gustavo Alvarez wiped down his wet hair with both his hands. "I have come to tell you that my wife's cousin Pablo Garcia has been released from El Principe prison. He is here in Miami."

"That's great news."

"Maybe, maybe not. I have reason to think he may want to harm you."

Bradford lit a cigarette, stared at Gustavo over the flaming match. "I appreciate your concern. The question is why you bothered to come in person. It's pouring out there. You could have told me on the phone."

"Gloria Maraquilla and I are in your debt for what you did for us. As for the telephone, who knows who listens?"

"Thanks for the warning. I'll take my chances. Will you have a drink?"

"No, thank you. I have to get back to the shoe store."

"When will they let you practice medicine?"

"I have to be retested."

There was a pause. Each man looked at the other, then shook tentative hands. When Gustavo left, Eulalie appeared from a darkened corner of the living room. "Who was that man talking about?"

Bradford turned in surprise to his fifteen-year-old daughter. He had never known what to say to her, even when she was little. If anything, it had become more difficult as she got older, perhaps because her childlike adoration had changed into a sullen, adolescent stare, a silent admonition as unnerving as a summons.

"I didn't see you, Eulalie. How long have you been there? You're supposed to let someone know if you're in a room."

"I wasn't in it. I was in the doorway."

"Don't get technical. The point is, you were close enough to listen in on something that you shouldn't have."

"Is someone coming after you?"

"No one's coming after me. I don't want you to mention any of this to your mother or your brother, certainly not to your grandparents, and that includes your grandmother Maude. You'll only make them worry needlessly."

That her father was lying was clear to Eulalie. She had seen him do it before. What was not clear was why. "Who is Gloria?"

"Someone I brought out of Cuba."

Like so many other times before, Bradford had already canceled his daughter with a blink of his eyes. He was reliving the time six years before when Lilia, dressed in scarf and raincoat, had brought her cousins to his hotel room, and his despair the next day when she disappeared into the revolution. He recalled his anguished phone calls to Chori, to the embassy, to every club in town, and finally the postcard, unsigned, which read, "This is where I want to be."

Then nothing until two years ago and the call from the airport. "I have a three-hour stopover," she said. "I'm on my way to Buenos Aires. Even my mother doesn't know."

She was waiting in a room at the airport hotel, dressed in a white linen suit.

At first he had kept his distance. "You think you can pop in and out of my life anytime you feel like it? One lousy postcard. You know how crazy with worry I was? Do you?"

She put her arms around his neck and there was no more talk, only the muffled rumble of jet planes taking off and landing. They said goodbye at the concourse.

"Don't you know," he said, "that if you're not a possibility, I have no life?"

His daughter's voice broke into his thoughts. "Is Gloria the one who calls you on the telephone?" Eulalie bent to retie her saddle shoe.

"A lot of people call me on the telephone. And speaking of telephones, you've been making long-distance calls and I want it to stop. I had a whopper of a bill last month."

"It wasn't me, Daddy. It must have been Sophie."

"Why would our housekeeper call a prep school in New Hampshire? Does that make sense to you? Think about it. Your mother says you go into a closet every time you make a call. Is

518

that the reason? That you're making long-distance calls?"

"No, it's because she's always trying to listen." Tears filled her eyes. "You don't have to sound so mean. You never talk this way to Timmy. Only to me."

"Timmy doesn't hide in the shadows and spy."

"He doesn't have to. He knows what you're thinking because you tell him. You never talk to me that way."

"What are we doing right now?"

"It's not talking. It's lecturing."

"You're being unfair, Eulalie."

"No, I'm not. Mom noticed it too, but she says you can't help it. She says you're the way you are because of Maude."

"My difficulties with your grandmother have nothing to do with you or anyone else." Bradford looked at his watch. "What is it you would like to talk about?"

"It's no good this way," she said. "You're only doing it because I asked you to."

He sighed. "How is school?"

"School is dumb and so is this," she said, walking away with her ponytail bobbing on her head.

Bradford wondered what he could have done to make it go better and why Sandra had to bring Maude into the picture. He decided that there was no winning with Eulalie. She was a difficult child. He was looking forward to when

519

she would go away to college, and his paternal responsibilities would be happily limited to paying the bills.

The next month, Bradford left for the Bahamas to negotiate with the Bahamian port authority for port charges and a suitable berth, to make sure there would be enough taxis to meet the ship. While he arranged for Bahamian registry of the refurbished vessel, a bomb went off in Miami under Pablo's gull-wing Mercedes, killing him on the spot. It was Fidel, Esteban said, who had ordered Pablo's execution all the way from Cuba. Marta, who helped her sister-in-law Celia make the funeral arrangements, decided that there was more death in life than life. And Eulalie, who heard about the deadly explosion on television, wondered why her mother hadn't figured out that her father was probably only pretending to call from the Bahamas, that he had never left Miami in the first place.

When Eulalie was sixteen, she was surprised to find out that she was pregnant. She thought that a boy had to go inside you all the way. She didn't know you could get pregnant just from the tip. He said it would drip out, especially if she got up and jumped around, that a guy had to go in all the way for sperm to reach the cervix.

Eulalie didn't know who to tell. There was only one person she could trust not to betray her to her parents, and that was her grandmother Maude, mainly because Maude didn't like either one, Eulalie's mother because she was Jewish, Eulalie's father because he was her son.

She found Maude at the Arthur Murray studio, where three times weekly her grandmother took dance lessons. Eulalie's father complained that at the rate of fifty dollars an hour for private lessons, and group lessons at ten dollars an hour, his mother had spent over four thousand dollars on dance lessons in the past year, and that if she kept on signing contracts, he would stop her allowance.

Maude was in a private studio room, spinning before a mirrored wall where she practiced an under-arm turn in the rhumba with her instructor, a shiny black-haired fellow with ramrod posture by the name of Sandor. Maude later told Eulalie that Sandor had spent nine years with the Russian ballet and had invited her to dance with him in the pro-amateur competition.

Eulalie thought that Maude looked frail, almost transparent. She could see her grandmother's pink scalp through the fragile pale blonde net of hair that framed her head. The instructor excused himself, said he was going for a cup of coffee.

"I hope you're not going to ask me for money," said Maude. "Your father isn't particularly generous."

"Nothing like that, Grandma."

"Don't call me that here. Call me Maude."

"I think I'm pregnant, Maude."

"How far along are you?"

"I don't know. Maybe a month."

"It's just a thumbnail. I hope you don't want to marry the boy."

"No. He's not even my boyfriend. He goes with Bobo Gibbs. I don't remember for sure how it happened. We were drinking beer. I wasn't drunk. We were just having a heavy conversation. Really relating. We smoked some pot. I wasn't high either. A lot of grown-ups think you get crazy if you smoke a joint. They showed a film in school called *Reefer Madness*. All the kids laughed. Tucker and I were just relaxed, mellow. That's how it happened."

"I know how it happened. What I want to know is, why are you telling me?"

"I thought you would know what to do."

"That's certainly true. I knew what to do five times. Mostly in somebody's bathtub, but that was a long time ago. Once the woman used a coat hanger, another time someone squirted Lysol so deep inside me, I swear I could taste it. I don't think they do that anymore. Come on back with me to my apartment when my session is over. We'll figure something out. But wait in the foyer. You're liable to spoil my concentration."

The following Friday afternoon, Maude spread towels on the front seat of her car and drove Eulalie into Hialeah.

"What are the towels for?" Eulalie asked.

"For when you come out."

They went to an apartment in a two-story stucco building. A woman met them at the door, took money from Maude — Eulalie thought it was five hundred dollars — gave Eulalie pills, and led her to a small bedroom where she was told to take off her clothes and put on a hospital gown. The woman tied the gown at the neck as if Eulalie were going to have her hair cut, then led her down the hall into a blazing white room where another woman with a mask was bending over a tray beside a high table.

"Hop up," said the woman in the mask, "and don't make any noise. Hold on to my hand if you like, but don't yell. You won't feel much, anyway."

Makeshift rope stirrups hung from the ceiling. As the woman slipped Eulalie's feet into the loops, a man in a rubber apron entered the room, took an instrument from the tray, bent before the table, and jammed something into Eulalie's body. She arched her back against the pain, but the woman in the mask pressed her down. "Now, you know that doesn't hurt."

Eulalie began to whimper. The man in the rubber apron mumbled for her to keep still. When it was over, the woman gave her two pills against the infection with instructions to take another pill every half hour and under no circumstances to go to a hospital.

Maude said nothing until they were in the car. "How do you feel?" she asked.

Eulalie's ankles were rubbed raw from the ropes. She bent to touch them, became dizzy, nauseated, sat up. "Before they did anything to me I was scared. Now I just feel dirty. I feel like a bad person, like I did something horrible."

Eulalie spent the weekend on Maude's couch, drinking mint tea with a drop of bourbon, Maude's remedy for anything serious. She got up only to change her blood-soaked sanitary napkins, watching a television screen with horizontal lines.

The next afternoon, Maude left to go to Arthur Murray's to practice. As a bonus for signing her last contract, she explained, she had been given two competition dances with her instructor for free. This was a very good bargain, she said. Normally they would cost twenty dollars each. She wanted to be prepared.

"He doesn't really like you, Grandma, that guy Sandor. He only smiles when he thinks you're looking."

"I know that. I just like the feeling of a man's hand on my back, guiding me across the dance floor. I like being led by someone who knows how." Maude set a plate of peanut butter sandwiches beside the sofa, then tried to adjust the television set. When the picture turned to snow, she shrugged her shoulders and went for her purse.

"Who was the best dancer you ever danced with, Grandma?"

"The best dancer I was ever with didn't know how to dance. He just knew how to lead."

"That doesn't make sense."

"Tell me that in fifteen years. Where are my car keys?"

"I saw you take them into the kitchen. You may not be here in fifteen years."

Maude searched the tiny alcove that served as the kitchen. "You never can tell."

"Was he the gangster? The guy who knew how to lead?"

"Who told you anything about a gangster?"

"Papa Zalman. Before he died."

Keys jingled in Maude's hand. She dropped them into her purse. "You're supposed to be confessing your own sins before you pass on. Not someone else's. Besides, what did that old man ever know? I'm surprised you listened to someone who had to be put in a nursing home. Now, don't get up unless you have to. And don't answer the telephone. Your parents think we're driving to Naples."

"Did Daddy believe you?"

"He wasn't home. I spoke to your mother."

"What did she say?"

"She was miffed. But I expected that. She said she preferred to be told in advance and that she didn't much like for us to be traipsing across Florida on Alligator Alley."

Eulalie raised herself on one elbow. "Grandma, is it true that you don't like my mother because she's Jewish?"

"Absolutely not. If Sandra and I don't see eye to eye, it's because she's a snit. It has nothing to do with her Hebrew background."

"That's my background too."

"Not all of it. You have another half I prefer to concentrate on."

Willie, his son, Denver, and James' wife, Ruth, sat on chenille spreads that covered the shredding sofa and overstuffed chairs and listened to the squeaking rocking chair on the front porch. Ceiling plaster lay spattered everywhere in large, leaden flakes. From time to time someone would peek through the screen door to see if the old woman was all right.

Denver was on a forty-eight-hour pass from the Marine Corps before being shipped to Vietnam. Months before, a black recruiter had come through Liberty City to let the dropouts know that there was a place for them in the military. Denver wasn't a dropout; he had finished high school, in fact, had quarterbacked for Booker T. Washington High School. The recruiter told him that if he waited until he got drafted, he couldn't get the job he wanted, but if he enlisted, he would get valuable training. "The brother over there is raising hell," the recruiter had said. "We're proving ourselves." Anxious to "find Charlie," Denver enlisted for four years, which reassured his father, who worried over his son's less than masculine disinclination to mess up a lot of girls, leave a few babies behind.

Two nights before, the staff NCO cradling a rabbit in his arms had given a roomful of grunts what he called a rabbit lesson, while he lectured on escape, evasion, and survival in the jungle. When one of the men reached out a hand to stroke the rabbit's silky ear, the NCO cracked it in the neck, skinned it, disemboweled it, and threw the guts out into the audience, telling the men that it was their last lesson before they left for Vietnam.

Denver was still trying to figure out the object of the lesson when Ruth declared that they better come to some decision. "Miss Caroline may say she's eighty-nine," she said, "but I know she's at least ninety-two. The other day when I came to see how she was getting on, I found the range burner on, beet tops in a scorched pan, all the water out, and she's sound asleep in her rocker. She's gonna burn the house down. I brought her oxtail soup I made myself, two quarts, with barley and potatoes, cooked the oxtails for two hours until the meat just slid off the bones, and she didn't touch it. She still keeps her money in savings certificates that she gets from the post office. She's got a drawer full of insurance policies. What she need all that insurance for? The policy man is sweet talking her out of her money is what."

Willie at forty-five was dapper. With a pin-stripe suit, a gold watch, a diamond ring, his hair dyed, fried, and laid on the side, and a stable of four girls, if the money didn't actually flow in, at least it was a steady trickle. "So what you talking about?" he asked. "You talking about putting Grandma away?"

"Don't think of it in those terms," said Ruth. "Think of it as the only way out under the circumstances."

"Shit, Aunt Ruth," said Willie. "You'all are talking about my mama, the lady who raised me up. Stuck by me my whole life, even came to Raiford on the bus the time they had me working the cane mill. Never could get into the tag plant. You needed pull to punch those license plates."

"You have a better idea?" asked Ruth.

Willie's daughter, Lucille, pushed open the screen door. She held the hand of her daughter, Djuna, whose hair was done up in ribboned pigtails.

Willie shot his cuffs. "I just might at that. How about we pay Lucille here to take care of her? That way Lucille can stay home, take care of her kids. Take care of Grandma at the same time."

Willie's daughter shifted her bulk into the easy chair. "I wouldn't want to take her in the projects," she said. "People walking on the grass, writing on the walls, throwing garbage. I don't know why they do their own people like that." She reminded everyone that her six-year-old daughter, sitting cross-legged on the floor, was attending first grade in a previously all-white school. "I still have to take Djuna every morning. You never saw so many mean faces. Even now, it gets so bad sometimes, the teacher lets them out the back door. Point is, I got my mind on getting her to school. I can't be worrying about Grandma Caroline. Besides, it's getting worse, getting real crowded. Lots of new people from Overtown moving in since the Cuban people been taking all the rental property south."

"It's not just the Cubans," said Denver, who decided that the rabbit lesson had something to do with attachment. "It's the expressways, I-95, I-395. Those suckers are tearing right through the heart of the community. Thousands of people have to move. I never heard of anyone getting reimbursed for the higher rents they're going to have to shell out."

"I guess it's the price you pay for urban renewal," said Ruth.

"More like Negro removal," said Denver.

"I'm having a hard time understanding," said Ruth, "why the government doesn't treat its own citizens as well as it does foreigners. Cubans can get welfare, business loans, food, money for college, all kinds of assistance, while we have to fight red tape every step of the way."

Lucille wiped the sweat running between her breasts with a handkerchief. "Point is, it's bad. They're stealing light bulbs out of the fixtures so you have to walk through dark hallways. Fightin' with razor blades between their fingers. It's no place to bring someone who doesn't know what time it is."

The screen door opened. Caroline shuffled in, leaning on a cane. Her eyeballs were yellowed, her temples indented with age. "I know what time it is," she rasped. "It's birthing time. I can see the crown," she said.

"See what I mean? Now you tell me what crown is she talking about?" said Ruth.

"What crown you talking about, Grandma," asked Willie. "Tell Willie."

"I know what Grandma Caroline means," said Denver. "She's talking about the rights march in Washington last year."

Caroline looked from one to the other. "None of you my honey man, my Bristol. They broke his heart. Broke mine too. None of you worth a damn." Her eyes rested on Denver. "Except maybe you."

"Now, you know you don't mean that," said Willie.

"Yes, I do. He's the one got his eyes."

"Denver doesn't have my eyes, Momma," said Willie. "My eyes are black. Denver's got eyes like a cat."

"It wasn't you I was thinking of," Caroline said. "It was the sandy one. Bristol had his eyes. My firstborn. Whenever he looked at me, I knew I was seeing right into the beyond. Now this boy has his eyes. And when I look deep into them, it's like looking into a tunnel."

"Why are you arguing with her? She doesn't know what she's saying. Watch her," said Ruth. "She's heading right for the lamp."

Caroline stopped before the little girl. "Who are you?"

Ruth sighed. "You remember Djuna, Grandma Caroline."

Caroline leaned unsteadily over the child. It seemed as if she might pitch over. "You the one going to the white school?"

"Yes, ma'am."

"Learn until your head swells up. Fold your napkin when you leave the table."

"She eats in the cafeteria," said Lucille. "The napkins are made out of paper."

"You know how to protect yourself against Obeahman?"

"Who's that?" asked the child.

"He can put a spell on you, lasts a lifetime. Come 'round in the kitchen. I'll show you."

"Don't scare her, Grandma Caroline. I don't want her head filled with things gonna give her nightmares."

"I don't care about no obeying man," said the little girl. "I just want something to protect me against Monica Dolan. She says next time she sees me on the playground, she's gonna whip my nigger ass." The child smiled.

"Stop showing all your teeth," said Lucille.

Denver tossed his hat onto Djuna's small, curly head. It settled below her ears, concealing

531

everything but her mouth and chin. "You're a front-line soldier, Djuna, same as me. You can't be afraid if you're the point man. Besides, it sounds to me like Monica Dolan is woofing. Someone tells you what they're gonna do would be doing it if they weren't scared."

"Are you scared, Uncle Denver?"

"The only thing that worries me is you're gonna see yourself in a mirror and run off with my hat."

"My boy's afraid of nothing, ain't that the truth, Denver?" said Willie.

"Anyone afraid of nothing is a fool," said Caroline. "Are you a fool?"

"No, ma'am," replied Denver. "Leastways I try not to be."

"Last time a soldier was in this house he got killed. Right where he was standing. A white boy. Bristol killed him, hit him with a hoe and Bristol only eleven, twelve years old. I can see it like it was yesterday."

"What he do that for?" asked Djuna.

"It happened a long, long time ago," said Lucille. "Some things are best forgotten."

"That's where you're wrong," said Caroline. "Some things are stitched as tight as the love knots on those pillow slips I gave you. A whole lot of other things too, part of the story of this family, including Bristol's white half sister, none of you ever knew about that."

"I think it's obvious," said Ruth, "that it's high time we did something here."

"They killed Thomas. They thought they could hide the body, but I knew where they put it."

"Where, Grandma Caroline?" asked Denver.

"Don't encourage her," said Lucille.

"On top of a mess of Indian bones," said Caroline. "Your grandfather Isaac got the job of digging them out. That's how I know. They stuffed his clothes inside their walls."

"Grandma Caroline," said Ruth, "what did you have for breakfast this morning?"

"I don't recall."

"You see? Who knows how much of this is in her head? Denver, stop egging her on. You're only making it worse."

Caroline bent close to his face, whispered in his ear. "My nose can still bring it to mind. You can smell it if you go to visit Marta, press your face against the parlor wall. It's still there, the bay rum, shaking itself in your face like a pointing finger."

Eulalie fell in love with Jason Friend not just because he survived an encounter with a billy club and a can of Mace, but because he exposed her shortcomings, taught her the difference between a radical and a liberal who ran when the action got rough. Jason's hair rippled to his shoulders, and he switched it from side to side as a horse does a mane. He wore army fatigues, beads, and army boots, and helped her make the break from the straight world of Julia Child to the macrobiotic, from dull thinking to hallucinations, from long weekend cruises to Nassau with her grandmother Sylvia to a riot led by Jerry Rubin at Fort Dix, from the Beach Boys to the Doors.

"Politics should shake, rattle, and roll," he told her one night on his pizza-crusted bunk when he slipped pillows under her narrow hips to give them more bounce in sex. "Buying tickets to Pete Seeger doesn't cut it. You got to put your body on the line."

And she did, skipping classes at Pembroke to attend rallies, having sex with him whenever he asked, even making it with him standing in the library stacks in the Useful Arts section, near a flickering exit sign. She typed leaflets and ran off mimeographs, made coffee when he and guys in beads and tie-dyed T-shirts planned strategies through the night. She attended protest rallies, returning first to her dorm to change into her riot clothes. "You have to go to some of these alone," he told her. "Otherwise I won't believe you're committed." Then, dressed in pants and army boots, her long blonde hair tied around her forehead, she went to join whatever sign-ripping, distributor-disconnecting, draft-card-burning demonstration was on tap. The first time Eulalie went alone, she stood in the middle of a mob that was pulling the wires out of a public bus and trashing a jewelry store, and began to cry. The streets smelled of tear gas and her throat felt as if she had swallowed metal filings. She remembered the course she had just taken on Gandhi and nonviolent change, and believed that her suffering would change the world, in addition to proving her commitment to the movement.

In May, Eulalie asked Jason if he would miss her over the summer. He said she would have to get over bourgeois notions of ownership of another person. He intended to see other women. He expected her to see other men. He expected her to tell him all about it.

"It will help you," he said, "to grow."

When Eulalie came down in June, bra-less, dressed in granny glasses, and a long tie-dyed dress to the ankles, resentful that she would not be permitted to join Jason, whom she designated only as her "dorm-mate," at Woodstock, she had begun to count her parents and all three of her grandparents among the enemy.

Acrimonious exchanges began with Eulalie's recent habit of burning incense in her room, playing nothing but Ravi Shankar records, and creating an overload on the air-conditioning system by insisting on leaving her windows open. Soon hostility between Eulalie and everyone else, like the summer heat, became pervasive. Rancor reached a fevered pitch at the fiftieth wedding anniversary party for her grandfather Herschel and grandmother Sylvia. Sandra insisted that Eulalie dress formally as would other members of the family. The transition from fatigues to fittings with a Cuban dressmaker on an ivory taffeta gown with a sweetheart neckline left everyone on edge and Eulalie speaking to her mother only in short, necessary bursts.

The black-tie affair in July for three hundred people on the rooftop of the Doral Hotel began badly. Herschel and Sylvia had a squabble, their first in over twenty years, that threatened to cancel the whole affair. Sylvia wanted her husband to buy patent leather shoes. Herschel insisted on wearing worn black loafers and threatened not to show up if he had to put on anything else. To up the ante, he told his wife of fifty years that he had never wanted to marry her in the first place, that it was his father's idea. The argument concluded with a mild bout of angina for Herschel, a sobering event that nourished Sylvia's guilt enough to end the discussion.

With her eyes defined with black liner that Eulalie said made her look like a possum and her hair shaped in a Sassoon blunt cut, Sandra planned everything under the specter of her parents' labile affections and her father's ill health. She arranged for centerpieces that were low enough for seated guests to see one another, white gauze ceiling drapes fastened with bee lights, the selection of a 1960 Corton Charlemagne (no red wine, as it could stain), and a gown with a jacket to cover Sylvia's plump and dimpled upper arms.

536

The night of the party, Sandra took Eulalie into the ballroom to show her how it sparkled. "What do you think?"

"The truth?"

"Of course the truth."

"It's a bourgeois celebration of fifty years of Grandma's servitude."

"Don't tell that to your grandmother," said Sandra, who turned to greet a guest.

Maude was openly contemptuous of arrangements made anywhere but at the Surf or Bath clubs. She tucked a strand of her pearls neatly inside Eulalie's sweetheart neckline. "I've been meaning for you to have these," she said. "Under other circumstances you would have made your formal debut this year. You would have carried a bouquet of red roses and curtsied light as a feather on the hand of your father. In fact," said Maude, giving the pearls a final pat, "through your patrilinear descent you are privileged to bow at the debutante ball for Daughters of the Confederacy in Montgomery, Alabama."

The shortcomings of Eulalie's matrilinear descent remained unspoken. Eulalie figured them out, unclasped the pearls, slapped them in her grandmother's speckled hand, called her a hypocrite, and left to search out her father. She found him at the top of the steps adjusting his cummerbund. "Did you know that Maude is anti-Semitic?" she asked.

"It occurred to me," he replied.

"I think you also ought to know that every one of you is a disappointment to me."

Deciding not to take the bait, he turned before a mirror to adjust his bow tie, as seemingly detached as a balloon with its string cut. "People are what they are, Eulalie. Learn to live with it like everyone else."

Sandra disengaged herself from a knot of well-wishers and glided across the floor, her attention directed at her daughter's feet. "What are you wearing?" she whispered. "I see something poking beneath your dress, miss, that doesn't look like shoes."

Eulalie lifted the hem of her taffeta gown to display scuffed and worn brogans laced halfway to their tops. "I'm wearing work boots," she replied. "They're a reminder of the people's struggle."

"You think that's cute? I don't believe you're doing this to your grandparents," said Sandra. "Don't you care about them at all?"

"Grampa is wearing loafers that don't have any heels. Besides, what I wear on my feet doesn't demonstrate how I feel about my grandparents."

"You're deliberately trying to provoke me. Why?"

Herschel Levy stepped away from a cluster of men in starched shirt fronts and stood before his granddaughter, resting his freckled hands on her shoulders. "You're not the only revolutionary," he whispered, displaying his loafers.

538

"These are a reminder of my struggle with your grandmother."

The speeches began during the salad course. Herschel Levy spoke first of his father Zalman, who had begun as a peddler.

"Some of you might remember his first movie theater before they tore it down. The admission charge of a dime included the exhibition in the lobby of a live alligator with its teeth extracted. My father kept a ton of ice beneath a perforated floor and large electric fans that blew cool air into the audience until the second show when the ice was melted." Herschel's voice broke. "I would like to drink to the memory of my father, Zalman Levy, a real pioneer." He looked at his wife. "If it were not for him, I would not be married to this lovely lady."

Then a balding, portly man took the microphone and cleared his throat. "Few in this room know that Herschel Levy is a hero. My family emigrated to Cuba from Eastern Europe. My father sold Eskimo Pies from a box that rested on his stomach. They called Cuba, Akhsanie Kuba, Hotel Cuba, because they were expecting to be able to immigrate to the United States. But in 1924 the United States enacted a law that closed the doors and Machado's secret police began arresting Jewish peddlers for blocking traffic.

"I first met Herschel Levy," the balding man continued, "right before the hurricane of 1926.

My family paid sixty dollars per person to flee from Cuba to Key Largo in a sailboat. Herschel Levy, then a young boy not yet twenty, with no regard for the personal risk he was taking, made all of the arrangements, and met my family in Key Largo. He brought us to his parents' home for safety, where we hid until we could find work and a place to live." He raised a glass of wine. "To a brave man, to his lovely wife, Sylvia, and to a marriage of fifty years."

Eulalie listened to the balding man in amazement. It was impossible to believe that her sweet, slightly befuddled grandfather had ever acted so boldly and defiantly, had ever broken the law. She wondered how all that passion got buried and if it could get buried in her so deep no one would ever find it again.

In August, Eulalie distributed handbills with the Student Nonviolent Coordinating Committee for the Vote Power Rally in Liberty City. The field secretary of SNCC, a student from Florida A & M, wearing an Afro and a dashiki, called her "Miss Ann" and said she reminded him of another pretty little white chick who came to see what it was all about.

"Got picked up by a street dealer," he said. "Cat fed her three thousand mikes, then took her to Peacock Park, where he raffled her off for a gang bang."

Eulalie said it wasn't her and grabbed a

handful of flyers that listed four demands including black control of the ghetto and a guaranteed annual income. She stayed for the rally at 62nd Avenue where Wilt Chamberlain was supposed to show up but didn't. Someone said that there was a disturbance at the Republican National Convention over on the Beach, where Nixon was accepting the party nomination for president.

It did not surprise Eulalie when teenagers began throwing bottles and rocks at passing cars, or when they overturned a truck with a bumper sticker that read GEORGE WALLACE FOR PRESIDENT. When they shouted after the running driver, "Get Whitey," she shouted with them. Neither was she afraid when police cars moved in with bullhorns, shouting for people who had pulled cushions and chairs onto their porches to get inside and shut their doors. She knew where to run, how to tuck herself neatly into doorways, how to pack her pockets with stones.

When youths began breaking into white-owned businesses, the SNCC field secretary found Eulalie on the street, pulled her into the backseat of his Ford Mustang, told her to get down on the floor, and drove her to Biscayne Boulevard, where he let her out on the sidewalk.

"Okay, Miss Ann," he said. "You can go home now. Time to quit playing revolutionary."

When she returned to her parents' home, her mother and father were watching the disturbance on the late evening news with no

541

idea of where Eulalie had been. "Do you think it has anything to do with the Republican Convention on the Beach?" Sandra was saying. "Supposedly hundreds of people were hired for the convention and not one came from Liberty City."

"The cops are carrying flame throwers," said Eulalie.

"Police, dear," said Sandra. "Not cops."

"What makes you think they were carrying flame throwers?" asked Bradford. "I hadn't heard that mentioned."

Eulalie decided not to tell them that she had also seen M1 carbines and tear gas, and the rioters taunting, "Shoot us, shoot us," as they threw molotovs and twisted-off steel security bars like spaghetti.

"They do seem to have legitimate grievances," said Sandra.

Bradford tinkled the ice in his martini. "I don't know what more they want. We've integrated the schools. There's even a colored woman on the city commission."

"A black," said Eulalie.

Sandra smiled indulgently. "It can't happen overnight. It's like baking a cake. It's got to take time." Then she changed the subject. A check in the amount of one hundred fifty dollars had been made out to someone named Jason Friend.

"He's a clerk at the bookstore," said Eulalie. "The money was for books for next semester."

542

"Why didn't you make the check out to the store?" asked Sandra.

"They don't take checks," Eulalie replied. "He laid the money out."

"I don't suppose you can tell us the names of the books," said Bradford.

"How am I supposed to trust you," said Eulalie, "when you won't trust me?"

"She has a point," said Sandra, after Eulalie left in an outraged flurry of macrame and ragged cutoffs.

"She's bullshitting," said Bradford. "She's lying through her teeth."

At the end of the summer, Eulalie returned to school, happy to get away from the hassles, from the tedious, hopeless strangers her parents had become, anxious to get back to Jason, for whom her thighs already shivered in anticipation. Her parents, in turn, breathed a sigh of relief when they dropped her off at the airport. Sandra, in particular, still walking on eggs, never quite sure when she would find Bradford again sitting in a darkened room, was glad that Eulalie was out of the house.

Denver returned from Vietnam to a recession and unemployment with what was called a bad-paper discharge. He accepted the less than honorable discharge rather than risk a court-martial, but when he returned to Miami and found out that he was ineligible for any veterans' benefits, including the VA hospital, despite the shell fragments lodged in his elbow, he decided that he had made a bad trade, that he had been duped into fighting a war that was not worth the effort.

When his sister, Lucille, came with their father, Willie, to clean the clutter in Denver's pullmanette apartment, Lucille put on her sternest face and told her brother that he needed a goal.

Wearing a bracelet woven from the shoelaces of a dead comrade, Denver lay on the sofa staring at the ceiling following the crisscrossing searchlight beams from somewhere outside. "I don't have any," he replied. "They burned up and died somewhere. You know how I got this bad-conduct discharge? For being AWOL in my tent. I didn't report for reveille every morning because too many dudes got blown away by Vietcong rockets while standing in formation. They knew I was in my tent, but they kept marking me AWOL. When Martin Luther King was assassinated, the place went wild. The order came down to get rid of the trouble-makers. I guess a black man who won't come out of his tent fits that description to a T. All my commanding officer had to do was sign the paper."

"You home safe," said Willie. "And you home earlier than you supposed to be. That's all that counts."

"The brothers were pimped by the feds," said Denver. "The government got everything out of us it could, gave us the worst assignments, then cut us loose. Saves them time and money. The administrative discharge is a way for the military to get rid of people they don't dig. All that shit about how the doors swing open for vets is just garbage."

Lucille pushed aside a pile of plates and set two green-sprigged Minton dishes, one of sweet potato pone, another with rice and giblet gravy, on the kitchen counter. "Everything in here has a crust on it," she said. "And none of it is bread."

"I don't like to see you strung out all the time," said Willie. "Maybe you can go to the VA hospital. Get straightened out. I hear they got all kinds of programs. They giving Jackson Freemont's son methadone."

"You don't get it, Pop. I'm not eligible for any benefits. I can't get credit. I can't get any city or federal jobs, which includes the post office and the transit system. I can't even get on welfare."

"You need to go to the unemployment office," said Lucille. "Tell them you're a veteran. Tell them you got a medal."

"You think I'm gonna stand in line for chickenshit jobs that I don't really want, filling out all their forms, find out that 'Nam counts against me, that a white skin means more than a Bronze Star? Besides, there aren't enough openings for people experienced in burial detail. I know a guy spent a year designing an entire

545

village pipeline system, he can't get a plumbing job because of union quotas."

"I don't care about him," said Willie. "You my boy. I don't like to see you acting like a criminal. What I mean by that is you don't need to be in hiding like you do. This candy habit, I've seen too many cats strung out on horse. Besides, it's expensive. No way you can keep it up. I don't want to see you boosting cars."

Denver sat up, picked a matchbook cover from the floor, scooped up some white powder from a bag, and put it up to his nose. "You can't get hooked if you don't shoot it."

The sharp reports of rifle fire cracked from somewhere outside. Denver ducked, looked up to see his father and sister holding their breath.

"All hell's breaking loose just a few blocks from here," said Willie. "Police running around with tear gas and sawed-off shotguns."

Denver lay back on the sofa, feeling his mind stretch apart. "I knew guys hid their horse in empty rifle shells, sniff it in Vick's inhalers; buddy of mine liked us to blow it through the barrel of an M16 right into his nose."

"That was then and this is now. Black men out there trying to cool things down," said Willie. "You should be on the streets, Denver. You spoke real good at your commencement. You the one should be the one helping to take charge of things."

The odor of tear gas drifted in through the

open windows. Lucille went to slam them shut, complaining that in the middle of August the apartment was going to feel like an oven, while Denver turned on his side.

His voice was slow, lazy. "Brother name of Wilbur was here a while ago. We played football together. He's at Florida A and M, working his tail off for SNCC. Tells me that whites are complaining that Vietnam vets are responsible for what's going on out there. If I stepped foot outside this building, saying this was something I wanted to do, guess who'd be the first to get picked up?"

"You only guessing that. Meanwhile people getting hurt out there," said Willie.

Denver closed his eyes. "Getting stomped on isn't getting hurt. We went into villages after they dropped napalm, human beings fused together like soldered metal. You go into another village that's had a daisy cutter dropped on it, you don't worry about taking prisoners because there are none. You don't know if you killed Vietcong because you can't put the people together. Pretty soon it gets to you. You realized you're as fucked over as those welded folks you tried to pull apart, those arms and legs you tried to put together. You wake up mad, you're mad when you eat, mad when you sleep, mad when you sit, just mad all the time."

"You've been back for weeks and you're still mad," said Lucille. "I know it must have been bad over there, Denver, but you're supposed to be setting an example for my kids. What about Djuna? Little Jomo, so scared of you he's hiding in the corner? How am I supposed to bring them around when you never take a bath, just lay on that couch like you're glued to it, smelling funky, wearing the same old rag around your head?"

"Don't bring them."

"I can't believe you said that. Your own sister's children. What's wrong with you?"

Willie ran a handkerchief over his shoes, snapping it back and forth until his wingtips shone. "Ain't nothing wrong with your brother," he said. "I'm beginning to get his point. You go and get a nice car and see what happens. Police stopping you every corner, where's your driver's license? You ever seen them crackers stop and frisk a white man? It's open season on the Negro all year 'round."

"I don't care about any of this," said Lucille. "If Denver won't stop feeling sorry for himself, at least he's gonna eat my food. I cooked it, wrapped it, brought it all the way down here, made sweet potato pone with cinnamon and ginger the way he likes it. You don't have to get off the couch, Denver. I'll bring it over to you, but I'm gonna sit here and watch you eat every bit of it."

Jomo came out of the corner, where he had been trying to fit a penny into an empty beer bottle, and stood beside the man that his mother

548

said was his uncle. "You sick?" he asked.

"No," said Denver. "Just tired."

"Momma fix you Jell-O if you're sick. Slides down real easy. Tastes good too. 'Specially the red."

Chapter Twenty-Six

Just after Neil Armstrong walked on the moon, Eulalie learned that she was pregnant again despite the pill, and Jason drew number eighty-seven in the draft lottery, which placed him in the unlucky first third. Eulalie tried lifting mattresses to bring on her period. Jason lived on Kools and Thunderbird wine for a week to elevate his blood pressure. When he went to the induction center for his physical and was told, after a suspicious eyebrow was raised, to return in three days, he decided that the only way out was to split, to drop out of school, slip away quietly to where no one would find them. They lived for weeks on her credit cards and checkbook. When both ran out and her car broke down, they panhandled on the streets of whatever town they had hitchhiked to. At first Eulalie sent postcards home and called collect. When it was too late for an abortion, even the coat-hanger variety, and Jason heard of a commune in Meadville, Pennsylvania, where they would grow their own wheat and consider Huey Newton and the religion of love versus the religion of fear, Eulalie followed him eagerly.

The three-story ramshackle farmhouse sat on a dirt road a mile from the state highway with no windows, electricity, or running water. Eulalie's task was to help prepare breakfast for the twenty-member communal family. She crawled out of the sleeping bag she shared with Jason, slipped into her Mother Hubbard, and walked softly past a dozen men and women still asleep on mattresses strewn about the floor, careful to avoid an old corn cob that had fallen out from between the beams. After a visit to the bathroom, a tin pail set inside a closet, she went downstairs past a pile of dirty clothes and out the back door to join a woman named Kathy at the open fire. A man wearing jeans had started the blaze from scrap wood gathered from a nearby sawmill. Now he sat Buddha-like, strumming his guitar and looking out over the rolling hills of western Pennsylvania. Eulalie took a wooden spoon and began stirring the pot of oatmeal, while Kathy milked the goat.

One by one, members of the commune appeared, two nude and glistening from a bath in the nearby creek. Rebecca, a divorcee in her late twenties, patted the outlines of Eulalie's belly.

"You're not worried, are you?"

"No."

"Don't be." Rebecca called to her little three-year-old son, who ran naked with a pack of dogs. Eulalie mentioned that she had felt the baby kick again. "For sure you can't do anything about it now," said Rebecca. "You know that, don't you?"

Eulalie nodded while Kathy wiped her hands on her dress.

Jason sat at the feet of a heavily bearded man in his early thirties named George, who rocked in his chair and said that the commune was an extension of a new religion. In a few years there would be communes from coast to coast, just like Howard Johnsons. The disaffection of young people like Jason and Eulalie, he explained, grew from religious discontent. A new religious synthesis would emerge, he promised, blending the best of Christian ethics, nonviolence, and love with the mind-expanding disciplines of Eastern faiths. He compared the similarities of Zen and Christianity, in which both attempted to exchange self-consciousness with a cosmic consciousness, then turned to Eulalie and told her that he wanted her on his mattress that night.

"Your old man will be glad to share you," he said.

Eulalie glanced at Jason, who gave no sign of protest. She had hoped he would. She had told him the last time that she didn't like the way George smelled. Jason said she had to work on her middle-class hang-ups.

The income of the commune was limited to allowances, like the thirty dollars a month Marko got from his father, who, Marko said with disdain, spent his life on the freeway breathing sulfur dioxide, or the one hundred dollars Eulalie got from time to time from her grandmother Sylvia, or handouts from tourists, birthday gifts, occasional work by the men for neighboring farmers, paid in kind, a share of the farmer's crops, selling dandelion wine, earning three dollars an hour for tunneling gardens with an ancient Rototiller that kept breaking down.

Sunday afternoons, townspeople packed up their families and came to gape, their kids' faces pasted to the windows as they crept past the farm. A procession had already begun churning up a continual dust cloud while Kathy gave Eulalie a recipe for dandelion wine, telling her that she had to soak the dandelions for at least nine days, strain out the flowers, add yeast cakes, wait until the concoction didn't fizz anymore. The dandelions reminded Eulalie of the yellow tickseed that grew wild on Sunset Island.

"Check the bottles in a week," said Kathy, her eyes shielded against the dust. "Burp them so that if they're still fermenting, they won't explode. We lost a lot that way."

Eulalie was thinking of the call she had made home the week before from a gas station on the highway. She had spoken to her brother, Timmy. Their parents had been out.

"Where can they call you back?" Timmy asked.

"They can't," she replied.

"Well, what shall I tell them?"

"Tell them I'm okay."

He told her that Grandmother Sylvia might be very ill.

"With what?" she asked.

"A woman thing."

"How serious is it?"

"Serious," he replied.

"Cancer?"

"Nobody's saying. But she had an operation to take something out or off, and now they're shooting her with cobalt. Sounds like it to me."

"Bummer."

"Mom says that's why she wouldn't buy a new dress for her fiftieth-anniversary party. Grandma Sylvia must have known that she was sick and she didn't want to spend the money on something she would only wear once. Lalie, come home," he said.

"I can't."

"The Dolphins are on a winning streak. We might get to the Super Bowl. And Dad's feeling real good because he thinks he and a bunch of other guys persuaded Governor Kirk to stop the jetport in the Everglades."

"Since when does he care about the environment?"

"He's not so bad now, Lalie. He talks to you and everything except he's pissed at Grandmother Maude because she keeps buying her Arthur Murray teacher presents on Dad's credit card. I don't know if she's getting it on or not, but she dances backward better than anyone I ever saw." A truck roared from the highway. "I'm set for Harvard."

"You always knew you would be. If you want my hash pipe, the one with the mesh filter, you can have it. It's hidden under my Barbie doll clothes."

"Lalie, what about if I come to see you? Just me. I won't tell where you are."

"Bye, Timmy," she said and hung up.

"I don't feel like you're paying attention," said Kathy.

Eulalie sighed and bent to wipe her face on the hem of her dress. "I have to wait for the fizz to stop. I have to check the bottles in a week."

"You don't have to snap my head off. I'm only trying to help. I think you should know that some of the others think you don't fit in. You're on probation. George is going to decide, and if he says you have to go, the baby won't make any difference."

Chapter Twenty-Seven

RAY GOPHER

I do not agree with the traditional people who say that there are no good white things. What about electric fans, irons, and mattresses, electricity, hot and cold water, and toilets? On the narrow strip of trust land set aside for us at forty-mile bend, some Miccosukee are replacing open-sided, thatch-roofed chickees with concrete and frame houses, even with house trailers complete with furniture and appliances that are financed by the company selling them. Some of our women like my wife, Betty Tigertail, take their wash to the coin laundry. A few even have electric washing machines. Sometimes there are strange combinations, chickees with television antennae, concrete houses with thatched roofs.

It was not easy for everyone to learn the white man's ways. At first some people piled their clothes on the floors of the closets until they learned how to use clothes hangers. They had to remember to turn the stove burners off and close the refrigerator door. Many of our people were innocent about money. If a new television set didn't work, they threw it in the canal, not understanding that it costs less to fix than to replace. The elderly find change most difficult to accept. My mother, Emma, refused to move into a house. She said she was too old to learn to housekeep.

Even the way we honor our dead has changed. When an Indian died, he was taken out into the forest. Now we bury our dead in cemeteries like my grandmother's husband, Charlie Billie, who we buried with a dish of food and a knife beside him in the casket.

When I was a boy and followed my mother from the white man's vegetable fields to the tourist camps, we scurried from place to place seeking warmth like snakes in the winter. Now that we Miccosukee are recognized by Washington as a separate tribe, with almost three hundred on trust land, another few hundred in scattered camps along the Tamiami Trail, we live in one place on income from land that we lease to the white man, like the people from Shell Oil, who want to negotiate a lease for seventy thousand acres.

All this came about when Buffalo Tiger went to Fidel Castro to sign a treaty of friendship. Soon after, the Bureau of Indian Affairs began to listen to our demands. Last year Buffalo Tiger was named by Governor Askew to head the Indian Affairs Council, which he sits on with Joe Dan Osceola of the Seminole tribe. Now for the first time Indians have a

4–3 majority on the council. We also have a claim against the government after a ruling by the federal court that said that we and our Oklahoma brothers were the legal owners of thirty million acres of Florida. We were awarded twelve million for this land by another court, and some of our people flew to Washington to prevent our Oklahoma brothers from taking more than they should. But we are not counting on it too much. We have to wait and see how much it will really be, how it will be divided, when it will be paid.

Our traditional Miccosukee brothers who live west, scattered along the trail, who refuse to name their people or to accept government aid, are not with us on this thing. They believe that when the white man assigns land to us, it is like assigning air. They do not want restrictions from the federal government just as they do not want its help. They warn that the lease that is held in our name can be terminated, that even now there is talk that the state wants to renegotiate its terms. They say that if the land is not protected by making it a permanent reservation for the Indian people, then the white man will use up all of it for jetports and hunting camps. Last, they say that Buffalo Tiger has made a foolish bargain, for what is the sense of free license plates when the Miccosukee still do not have their own homeland?

They point to the younger ones who have been away to school and want to live like their white neighbors, to the girls who have started wearing jeans and shorts, to the elders who have lost their authority, to the fading of old virtues, to our young men who sit idly and drink alcohol while they wait for government checks.

My mother says that if our young people drink *wyomee* to excess, it is because they find it difficult to straddle two worlds. At every tribal council meeting the subject comes up. Some say the reason is that young tribe members drop out of school because they cannot keep up. Without schooling they cannot find jobs. Others say the problem is that young men are no longer permitted to hunt or fish as they wish, except to gig frogs for the restaurants. They suffer because they can't succeed in the white man's world, and the white man won't let them succeed in their own. The elders complain that our young learn bad things at the white man's school, and bring these bad things back to the tribe to others who don't understand them. They believe that going to the white man's school is a violation of the law of the Breathmaker, which is never to change, to remain what you are until the end of the days.

My son, Bo Charlie, now in the sixth grade, threatens daily to quit. "I want to be nothing," he tells me. Like the elders, Bo Charlie does not share the white man's notion that education is the key to success. Since attendance is not compulsory, he goes when he feels like it. When he was small, he went to Head Start, where he learned English, numbers, colors, and shapes. Now he wears a Dallas Cowboy football jersey, jeans, and sneakers, studies Everglades animals, the perils of alcoholism, and fractions. He tells me he is restless, that his feet move as if by themselves, to the door.

I won't make him go if he doesn't want to. Learning has to come from within. It can't be forced. That would be like pulling open a flower's petals to make it bloom. Perhaps the traditional people are right, that those who try to straddle two worlds fall between the cracks.

The white man brings his clinic twice a week. This does not trouble me, for there is room for two kinds of medicine, although they do not think so. The clinic people are not so worried about coughing sickness as they were when I was a boy. Now they talk about hookworm. They say it is our greatest disease. They have begun a Weight Watchers' club at the Brighton reservation, but our women do not want this, or the prizes that they give to lose one's weight, like the silver pickle fork they gave to Minnie Johns for losing forty pounds.

While I tell my mother's brother Sam that deer brains must never be eaten by a man because they will kill his peter, the nurse tells Edna Jim to stand on her feet to prevent her legs from getting stiff. "We'll have you walking without crutches soon," she says, but when she leaves, Edna Jim comes to me. The nurse checks on a baby's immunization schedule, but tied to the blanket is a small cloth herb bag to ward off evil spirits. The nurse comes to the water's edge to ask me what I put in the bag. I reply that it is medicine and continue to fix my air boat, taking the engine apart, carefully removing the screws, adjusting a lever, opening the throttle until I have a steady roar, and she keeps shouting with her hands cupped over her ears.

The Indian baby may be born in a hospital, but I still prepare the ancient formulas, still hold newborns over coals of fire, with bay leaves placed in the coals and the baby immersed in the smoke, so that when it leaves the camp the first time, it will not get lost.

They ask me to explain my medicine and I do, not so much that they steal it, just enough so that they will leave my medicine bundle alone. While they take notes and smile over my head, I tell them that before you can treat someone, it is necessary first to know what has caused the disease. Loss of soul, for example, or diseases caused by birds, fish, dogs, shells, mosquitoes, chameleons, rainbows, monkeys, smells that get inside the body. Disrespect for the doctor who has cured you will bring a recurrence of the disease. They laugh outright at that. I tell them that if a baby cries and scratches himself, he has monkey's disease.

Stomachache and vomiting are symptoms of dog disease. The bird sickness, which is easily treated with pinweed and bay boiled in water, is caused by the egret and the ibis. Babies are particularly susceptible. You can see it in their thin, greenish stools, hear it in their noises, which resemble bird calls.

Most herbs, I say, are gathered fresh at the time of illness, except for ginseng, which we get from Oklahoma, button snakeroot, red bay, southern red cedar, sassafras, southern willow, lizard's tail, downy milk pea, serpent fern, all of which used to be kept in medicine pouches that now I store in tins and cardboard boxes.

I do not tell them that herbs treat only the symptoms while the curing song gets at the cause of the disease, that during the preparation of herbs I must abstain from eating meat and fish, then rinse my mouth with water before singing the curing song, that if I make any mistake in the recitation, I must stop and begin again, that the curing song is sung facing east, over dry herbs or an infusion blown through the medicine pipe.

They ask to see the bundle given to me when Charlie Billie died, his thunder-in-the-sky, snake-in-the-water war medicine that by rights belongs to someone more worthy than me. I act as if I did not hear them, but that night, after they leave, I unwrap the buckskin bundles to check each item: Thunder Crystal, to make one's enemy agitated as in a thunderstorm, Living Medicine, the white powder to capture the souls of the sleeping enemy, the Small Stone, used to ward off bullets, Shot Medicine, a silver powder that can revive anyone killed with a bullet, Buzzard feather quill that stops bleeding, left-hand horn of the Snake King to attract deer, the Little Tube, a small whistle made of bone that is used to signal the sweat bath ritual, and last, a mortar and pestle belonging to the ancient ones, the ones who were here first, the ones who knew the color of the wind, the music of the stars, whose bones the white man has buried beneath his condominiums.

Some of the medicines in the bundle are so powerful they cannot be touched without implements to handle them. The powders in particular cannot be scooped up if they are spilled, and women are not allowed to come near the medicine bundle, for they would surely be knocked down by it. That's how I knew that the white nurse tampered with the bundle, for what else could have caused her to trip?

They do not understand, nor would I tell them that to be successful in my cures, I must have the living medicine in my body. Charlie Billie gave this to me in a beard fern that he sang over, blew into, which I swallowed. It is this power that became alive in me that I breathe through the medicine pipe into the pot of medicine. To keep it, I must avoid contact with menstruating women. I must not treat a woman during mourning, or bed my wife less than four months after she has borne a child. And if a patient I treat dies, like Caroline, the old woman of my mother's father with skin the color of eggplant, whose time had come to its natural end, and for whom there was nothing to do except make sure her spirit, when it left her mouth, did not get lost, I must purify myself by taking the black drink and waiting two weeks before I try to heal anyone else.

Other than my medicine, there are only a few things that I am certain of. The earth spins in a circle of life which begins in the east and ends in the south, and you always look at an eagle straight on, for if you see him over your shoulder, your neck will turn stiff for good. When you see rain coming down like oil, it means the world is coming to an end.

Chapter Twenty-Eight

Miami's economic slump of the mid-1970s brought construction projects to a halt and left skeletons of incomplete buildings to grid the skyline. With four thousand members of the black laborers' union out of work, the streets in Lucille McCloud's neighborhood were more dismal than dangerous, more hopeless than hostile, the areas that the newspapers reported with the highest crime rate in Dade County almost empty except for occasional bars, pool rooms, and small groceries scattered among boarded-up storefronts. Men hung around on the street corners, looking hopefully in both directions, waiting for The Man in a pickup truck or van to offer them a day job. By midday, when it was clear that no one was catching any breaks, they played cards beneath the trees, smoked reefer, drank wine. Some of the older men collected scrap metal and cans to stretch a Social Security check.

Lucille sat in the shade of an almond and poinciana tree and fanned herself with the scalloped-edged cardboard fan she had got at her great-uncle James' funeral, while her social worker told her that the next time she found a job, to make sure her employer signed her up for unemployment benefits.

They talked outdoors on folding chairs because Lucille, fearful that possession of fine things lowered your benefits, did not want HRS to know about the Minton china or even the lace tablecloth darned in two places willed to her by her great-grandmother Caroline.

The social worker opened her accordion folder, sorting through the papers until she found the one she was looking for. "One of your neighbors said you were pregnant."

Lucille sighed and fanned herself again. "I didn't mean for it to happen but it did."

"Have you considered abortion?" asked the worker. "It's legal now. There are clinics we can send you to."

"I don't want to do that," said Lucille. "To my way of thinking, scraping out your own flesh and blood is worse than getting caught in the first place."

Lucille continued to fan, looking at her worker out of the corner of her eye with the same distrust she regarded all white institutions, like the insurance company that found a reason not to pay her great-grandmother Caroline's policy. Mrs. McCloud had been sick when she took out the policy, the policy man said, so her beneficiaries couldn't collect, despite the fact that during the time she was sick, they continued to collect her payments.

"Someone said you had a man living with you."

"They're lying."

"Our informant said the man wears a large Afro and an old field jacket with its sleeves cut off."

"Whoever told you that is a fool. That's my brother, Denver. If you're worried about him living off my welfare, you can forget it. Denver's got a job, getting paid by this outreach program for finding black Vietnam veterans. Goes everywhere, even to the city jails. From where I sit it seems like he's doing your job for you, so I hope you don't mind if he helps himself to a glass of water."

Lucille stood to fold her chair when her father turned the corner wearing a white captain's cap too big for his head. He was no longer able to totter on six-inch platforms, although he still executed a reputable stork walk, despite arthritis in one of his hips and the loss of his stable girls to a younger pimp.

Willie managed by zigzagging through his welfare income, paying some bills, letting others slide, catching catfish in the Tamiami canal, picking turnips and collard greens from a backyard garden, and making side deals in The Life, as he called it, which he was not ready to give up.

He complained to his daughter's social worker about his landlord, who evicted people without notice. "Most folks afraid to say something because they know the landlord knows there's always someone waiting to take their place. Then he sends a rent man at dawn to bang and shout at the door. He won't make repairs. You try to wash a wall, the paint comes off with the plaster."

"You have to tell your own worker, Mr. McCloud," the woman said. "You know that." Her clothing was beginning to stick, and she plucked it away from her skin.

Willie set his cap back from his forehead. "I do. I also know you're a pile of shit."

The woman shook her head, snapped shut her folder, and left while Lucille poured her father lemonade. "Why did you have to do her like that?"

"I felt like it." He gave her a string of catfish rolled in a newspaper. "Where's Djuna?"

"She stayed after school to work on the newspaper."

"Tell her I found her a bicycle."

"How'd you manage that?"

"Thing fell right off a truck. I made an arrangement with the driver. If she don't like it, might be I can get it painted another color."

"Why don't you give it to Jomo? Djuna's always got a pencil in her hand."

"I want to give it to Djuna. If it isn't Djuna, it's nobody."

"Have you seen Denver?" she asked. It looked like rain. Lucille tucked a folding chair under each arm, then climbed the stairs, puffing with every step.

"No," said Willie, following after her. "And I don't want to see Denver either. Denver makes my pressure go up. I can feel it hit the top of my head as soon as he starts to talk. Gets himself in one damn thing after another, and nothing makes him any money as far as I can make out. First it's the firemen; he's mad as a hornet because the city's slow in hiring blacks, they only has two, he says.

"I'm settling down to watch the game, he says the city's record of how they treat black sanitation workers is one of the worst in the South. Said that the situation is as bad as Memphis when King got shot. Tells me, like I don't know, about the men who report for work every day at the sanitation yard, with no guarantees. Like I never heard that if the city can't use them, they lose a day's pay. It's not enough he's agitating to get them civil service status. The most foolish thing he's doing is running these groups over at the vet center. Ain't no money in that. Had himself a good job. Lost a steady hundred-twenty-dollar a week gig installing sprinklers with all this shit. I've gotta go see about taking care of business for my son. Too much hustling in The Life. Denver's not cut out for making deals. I'm gonna see if I can get him back into sprinklers."

After months of lying on his sofa in a mindless, heroin-induced oblivion, Denver finally bottomed out when he found himself lying in an alley with his head wedged between two packing crates, his lips cracked and dry, his wallet and his stomach empty, two teeth knocked out of his mouth, a dull pain in his head where someone had kicked him, and his nephew Jomo standing over him, calling his name. His habit shriveled up with his money, and Denver began the slow, rocky crawl back to being clean.

The way was not easy, beset by moments like one of his neighbors asking if Denver could kill women and children like the guy being court-martialed. He stiffened. "I can't judge him," he replied, "it could have happened to any of us." Or at his great-grandmother Caroline's funeral when his uncle James advised him that it was time to get a job. Denver lost his cool, despite the somber occasion when bits and pieces of who and what Caroline was had been assigned to the mourners like her pots and pans. He told his uncle about months of job hunting, cataloguing for him a string of skeptical employers worried about Vietnam vets going berserk, forming guerrilla armies, or operating forklifts in their warehouses while stoned out of their gourds.

"One of them asked me flat out if I learned to use dope in 'Nam. I told him I was strung out on heroin the first fifteen months I was there. I told him no one really cared as long as you went out to get shot at."

"That's why you're not working," said James, who had fought in World War II. "You have to get this chip off your shoulder. You have to get into the mainstream of America's fiscal life if you hope to get into the mainstream of its political life."

"What makes you think brothers coming up want to move into the mainstream?" Denver asked. "You think we want to be a part of this system?" By the time someone handed him a piece of coral rock and told him to throw it down on top of the casket, Denver felt himself stringing out, needing the spray of pepper on his brain that would make him straight.

It took a year for Denver to solder the pieces

of his life, to get it together. He was running a rap session at the vet center, sitting in a circle with men dressed in olive drab fatigues and jeans, when someone came in to hand him a note. One of the group members, a plump, placid-faced man in a green and black crocheted skull cap was saying that when he first had returned to Miami, someone spat at him at the airport. Denver read the note. It was from Lucille telling him to come home, that something had happened to their father.

"They treated us like we did something wrong," said a second man sitting propped against a wall with his feet on the rung of his chair. "We didn't come home. We sneaked home."

Denver stood. "Something happened to my old man," he announced. "Keep it going."

"We're cool, baby," said the plump man with the long sideburns. "Do what you have to do. We know the drill, same as you. We're gonna get it together just like you were here. And, Denver, when you get around to it, see if you can get us a new coffeemaker."

Denver ran the four blocks to the projects, up three flights to Lucille's apartment and banged on the door. The last time he had been in his sister's apartment was to caution his nephew Jomo that if he wanted to run numbers, he couldn't do drugs the way Denver used to do because folks wouldn't put up with some spaced-out kid fucking with their money. He hoped Jomo got the message.

Lucille was crying into a dish towel. "I haven't been over to his place yet. Djuna has. She can tell you everything."

Djuna told her story from the bed that she shared with her baby brother, Akibo, who lay sleeping in the corner. She had gone to get her bicycle. When she got to her grandfather's apartment house, there was yellow tape around his car and across his apartment doorway. She ducked under the tape. A policeman told her that her grandfather had been shot and killed. Djuna looked around for Willie, but he was nowhere to be seen, only his captain's hat, which she took, and a lot of blood in the hallway. No one could tell her anything else except not to put her hands anywhere, and that her grandfather had been bleeding for a couple of hours. Denver figured out why Willie hadn't gone to the emergency room of Jackson Memorial. The ambulance cost twenty-five dollars. "That's too much," he said, "when you're trying to live on a hundred-fifteen a month welfare."

The bicycle, like Willie, was nowhere to be found. Only a tire pump and a pink handlebar basket in the backseat of Willie's car.

Two weeks later, while Denver lay in bed with some white girl whose freckled, sunburnt skin peeled off in his hands, some man called from the office of Small Business Loans. He sounded like Denver's great-uncle James. Did Denver want to continue his application?

"What application?" asked Denver.

"The one that we have on file," the man said. "Your father filled it out for you. Said you asked him to do it. We need to finish up the paperwork. You may be the kind of guy we're looking for, someone with drive and ambition, someone put off by the white man's business world. Often in the arena of finance, our people are bewildered by a banker's questions, the red tape. The white man is faced with this too, but he brings along his lawyer and his accountant."

Denver leaned on his elbow and pushed the girl aside. "You say my father filled it out?"

"That's right."

"What did he list as my qualifications?"

"That you were a smart, mouthy vet."

"Mouthy?"

"That's what it says. I'm reading right from your file."

"This isn't going anywhere," said Denver. "I'm not in a business. I don't have anything to sell."

"That's not always important. We try to size up the loan applicant, what he's done, what he's looking for. There's no pat system."

"What I've done is nothing," said Denver. "I'm just looking for the pain in my head to stop. My father, now, he was an operator. If he had you to stake him twenty, thirty years ago, he's a man would've made something of himself. One more question: Is there a space on that form for the business that I'm supposed to be interested in?"

"Yes. It says you're involved in sprinkler systems."

For the first time since he had learned that his father died, Denver laughed, and then, later, after the girl pulled on her bell bottoms and went home, he cried.

When Jason left the commune without warning, leaving no note, only a message relayed through Morgan that it was time for him to split, Eulalie had already become one of George's women.

Gone also for Eulalie were the mystical feelings of oneness that she had sometimes felt, in the creek on a moonlit night, while minnows nibbled at her feet. Once she could reach out and touch another body and feel there was no difference between what she felt and what she did, between her and the minnow, between her and the water. All that was left was a fierce but impotent protectiveness toward her four-year-old daughter, Starlight, and a determination not to make George angry. Despite his talks of love and peace, he was capable of unexplained rages. These resulted in beatings, in deprivations. Recently he had punished Eulalie by chastising Starlight on the porch, spanking the startled child while everyone looked on. Eulalie prayed that it would stop and soon be over, while Starlight, with her pale blonde hair like a dandelion puff, cried and looked in her direction for help.

She kept her feelings to herself, just as she had learned not to protest at night when George had poked a toe at Jason to move away, or when George's hands traveled over her body, and others in the room could hear him admonish her to show some response. Eulalie stayed because she believed she could no longer live with straights, least of all her family. She had no plan, no way to get out, only some notion that the only way to leave was to somehow get on the highway, take Starlight with her, go somewhere far away where George couldn't find her and where there would be no recriminations.

The day that Jason left, George came back from town to tell Eulalie that he knew why Jason split. Ford had just granted amnesty to draft evaders and military deserters. George also had bad news. He said that the townspeople were making moves to get rid of them. He came to sit beside Eulalie on the step, slipped his hand beneath the hem of her long dress, ran it up her thigh, and caressed her absently while he told them that he was going back into town to attend the protest meeting at the Fire Hall to learn what he could. Meanwhile he wanted the men to continue digging the foundation for the coffeehouse where straight and communal cultures might meet.

"You don't learn," said Rebecca, when George

rumbled off in the VW bus. "Be extra sweet when he returns, Eulalie, and when he touches you, try to act turned on."

When George returned to the farm, he said that he had had to listen to a lot of yelling. A state senator had pledged that he would do all in his power to move the hippies out of the county, hinting that he might even introduce a special law into the state legislature if he had to.

George told the commune that the only answer was to play the straight game. They had to have an attorney, and attorneys cost money. "We have our own Patty Hearst," he said. "Eulalie's family has bread. Not major bread like old man Hearst but big enough. I want you to get to a phone booth, Eulalie, call home, tell them you need money for an operation. Say anything you have to, but get it."

Eulalie continued to pummel bread dough. "They won't give me any more. I've asked them."

"You haven't tried very hard. That's your problem in all things, Eulalie."

She wiped her hands on her dress, hoping they could not tell how fast her heart was beating, and reached for Starlight's hand.

"Where are you taking her?" he asked. "She's not going. You are."

"I'll watch her," said Kathy. When George put Starlight on his lap, then told Eulalie not to expect the keys to the bus or to return

575

without the money, she ran for the highway.

Eulalie was surprised to reach her father on a Sunday afternoon. It could only mean that small-craft warnings, typical of early September, had kept him from his sailboat. It had been a year since they last spoke. He dispensed with the small talk, asked her if she was ready to come home, and told her that he hoped this wasn't about money like her last two calls.

"I don't know if I'm ready to come home. I just want to get away from the farm."

"What's stopping you? If you're at a phone booth, seems to me you're already away."

"I can't, Daddy." She began to cry.

"Why can't you?"

"They're keeping my little girl. They said I can't have her unless I get the money."

Bradford was silent. Eulalie watched the cars go by while she listened to her father breathe. "You never said you had a child. Don't you think that's something we'd want to know?"

"I thought you'd try to get us back."

"You're right on that score. If what you say is true, Eulalie, you're talking about kidnapping, and extortion, and a whole lot of other ugly things. I'm not giving you money to give to them. And as trustee of the money that your grandparents left you, I can tie that up until you're thirty. I won't support that life. But I will support you. I'll help you get your baby back. I can do that much for you. With luck I might be able to get there tonight, tomorrow

576

for sure. Why don't you wait for me in a motel?"

"I don't think they'll let me register," she replied. "I don't have any money. Except the quarter I used for the phone call."

"All right, I'll do it from here. Give me the name of someplace local, Eulalie. By the time you get there, arrangements will have been made. Just go to your room, stay there. Order in if you're hungry and charge it. Don't let anyone know I'm coming. Do you understand?"

"Yes," she replied.

When Bradford saw Eulalie for the first time in five years, he was struck with pity at the sight of the bedraggled, disheveled woman that was his daughter. He bent to kiss her cheek. She pulled away.

They were served in the restaurant only because of the stern, no-nonsense expression on Bradford's face. Conversation was testy.

"How old is she?" he asked.

"Four."

"You put her in shoes or do you have her going barefoot to make a political statement?"

"I knew you were going to be like this."

"It won't surprise you," he said, "if I tell you that I don't want to see you or your child spend the rest of your lives contemplating your navels. We're living in an exciting time, Eulalie. Look at the space shot."

Eulalie poured syrup over her waffle. "I don't care about sending men around the moon," she said. "Learning new ways to relate to other people is where it's at. New ways of being a woman."

"Sounds good. I wish you meant it. What do you do on the farm?"

"I cook."

"You cook. Do any of the men cook?"

"No. They work outside."

"Do you ever swing a hammer?"

"No."

"Why not?"

"The men do that."

"Seems to me you've created a microcosm of what you wanted to escape. With one exception. Your mother doesn't cook. It's easier to understand what you don't want, Eulalie, than what you do want."

"Stop talking. You're mixing me up."

"No, I'm not. I'm trying to get you to see things clearly. It's the way I've been trained to think."

"It didn't do you much good."

"How do you mean that?"

"The whole time I was living at home, I never saw you laugh. Not once."

There was silence. Bradford wiped his mouth, then folded his napkin and lay it on the table. "I want you to know that I don't care what experiences you've had as long as they didn't destroy your desire to do something productive."

"What's productive? As long as I'm perceiving

the world in all its beauty, I don't have to paint pictures."

"I'd settle for brushing your teeth. Your gums are bleeding, Eulalie. How long has it been since you've seen a dentist?"

"I didn't call you to listen to this. I want to get Starlight back. I don't think they're going to let me."

"They will, Eulalie. Trust me."

"I can't."

"That's the problem, isn't it?" He signaled for the check.

"You never asked me anything about her. How come?"

"Maybe I'm protecting myself."

"You do that pretty good."

"Let's go, Eulalie. They need the table."

The rental car had no pick-up. Complaining that it handled like mush, Bradford held tightly to the wheel. "Your mother wanted to come. I wouldn't let her. You can't drop in and out of people's lives like this, Eulalie. You put us through hell." He adjusted the rearview mirror. "After you dropped out of Pembroke, we traced you on a map."

"I didn't make that many phone calls."

"Phone calls don't tell the story. I get a credit card statement. It shows what city something is charged in. We followed you from Providence to New Haven, then to Newburgh, New York, from there to Scranton, then Altoona. It was clear that you were heading west.

I thought you realized that you were leaving a trail. Your mother said it was because you wanted us to find you. That it was like dropping bread crumbs."

"I never thought about it."

"It seems to me you never thought about a lot of things."

She sighed and looked out the window. "How is Timmy?"

"Timmy's at Harvard. He's into streaking."

"You made me go to a school where I had to wear a uniform."

"Is that what this is all about? For God's sake, Eulalie, a lot of other youngsters go to school in a uniform and come out fine. I attended a military academy for a while. My mother used to put labels in all my clothing with my name written in indelible ink. She gave it to the maid to do. All my labels read *Mr. Brad*. I took a razzing on that the whole time I was there."

"That story is racist."

"How is it racist?"

"You're putting down a black."

"No, I'm not. As a matter of fact, sometimes I think I had more affection for our housekeeper than I did for your grandmother. I really loved that woman. And I have never told that to a living soul."

When they reached the farmhouse, everyone was gone, along with the goat, dogs, guitars, only a knapsack slung over a broken rocker and an injunction nailed to the front of the farmhouse forbidding the use of the premises for fornication, assignation, and lewdness.

Twigs cracked behind them. They turned to see Kathy, who had been camping in the bushes. She told them that the day after Eulalie left, the commune had been raided by the state police. Everyone was packed off in a bus and driven into Meadville. They were arraigned in the offices of some alderman, charged with maintaining a disorderly house. They were also charged with corrupting the morals of one of the sixteen-year-old runaways. In exchange for the district attorney dropping the charges, the group consented to abandoning the farm and leaving Crawford County. Rebecca's child had been taken into custody. Kathy thought the same thing had happened to Starlight. She wasn't sure. There was a lot of screaming and crying going on.

Eulalie hugged her middle and groaned while Bradford led her back to the car. "We're going back to the hotel so you can clean yourself up," he said. "I'm going to take you to a store so you can buy yourself a decent dress, some underwear, a pair of shoes, not sandals, a hairbrush, a pair of scissors. Do what I tell you, Eulalie, if you want to see that little girl of yours again."

Bradford made a few telephone calls, then went to talk to the district attorney. They learned that Starlight had been placed in a foster home. Although Eulalie was not present at the time of the arraignment, she had been charged with abandonment, exposing the child to male nudity and foul language, leaving her to wander about without supervision, and allowing her to live in filthy housing conditions. He did not think the child would be permitted to return at this time to her mother's care, but he would arrange for a hearing in juvenile court.

In a wood-paneled courtroom that smelled of lemon, Bradford took over. The custody battle had nothing to do with Eulalie. It had to do with him. It was as if he had conceded Eulalie's ineligibility. "I am the maternal grandfather, Your Honor," he said. "I am an attorney, licensed to practice law in the state of Florida. My wife of twenty-six years and I are in excellent health. We seek temporary custody of the child Starlight, and request that she be remanded to our care. My daughter has been a victim in this affair, as has the child. I mean to see that both have an opportunity for rehabilitative care."

The adjudication was swift. They were to appear the next day to receive the child.

"Why can't we just go and get her now?" asked Eulalie.

"That's not how it's done," said Bradford.

"You mean not how it's done your way."

"My way doesn't get my children taken from me."

"Didn't it?"

★ ★ ★

Sandra had no idea that Bradford was bringing Eulalie back with him, much less a child, only that he had flown north to get their daughter out of some scrape. She had accommodated to Eulalie's long absence, had learned to dull the ache, as she did the death of her parents, with a roster of activities that began at dawn and a fabrication that Eulalie was pursuing graduate studies abroad.

Bradford walked in first. Sandra kissed him, said she hoped that whatever he had to do for Eulalie hadn't taken too much out of him, told him that Joan Sutherland had agreed to sing in *Lucia di Lammermoor,* and that she had to be at the printer before noon.

"We have house guests," he said.

Sandra put her hand to her throat. "Eulalie?"

"Eulalie and someone else."

"Not that boy, Brad. I don't want him in my house."

"Not the boy."

Eulalie's voice was heard at the front door. "Now, don't touch anything," she said. "They're real fussy."

Sandra flew to the foyer, heels clicking on the marble floor. She came to a stop at the sight of her daughter holding a child by the hand.

"I didn't want to come home," said Eulalie.

"You didn't have to tell your mother that," said Bradford.

583

"It's all right, Brad," said Sandra. "It's the truth." She moved to wrap Eulalie in a guarded, tentative embrace, smelling the familiar sandalwood fragrance of her daughter's skin, surprised that she was not crying, that she was holding it all together.

"What happened to your hair?" asked Eulalie. "When did it get so gray?"

"It's not gray. It's frosting. Actually, I have very little gray."

The little girl came out from behind her mother's legs and looked up at the strange woman standing in the hallway whose fingernails were painted the color of berries. "What's your name?" the child asked.

Sandra gave a little cry, bent down to touch her cheek. "Sandra. Grandmother. I'm your grandmother." She stood, faced Eulalie, her lower lip trembling. "Why didn't you tell us? That was a cruel thing to do, Eulalie. We don't deserve it. No matter what you think we did, we had a right to know."

After supper, Eulalie had little to say. She rummaged through her old room, picking up a Snow Crop juice can that she used to roll her hair with, a book called *Counting Calories with Twiggy*, a Herman's Hermits record, while Bradford and Sandra put Starlight's mattress on the floor so that the child could go to sleep the only way she knew how.

Later Bradford asked Sandra if she knew where she had put the kids' old Dr. Seuss books, then said the first thing in the morning he would see about fencing the seawall. "That's what they mean about grandchildren," he said. "Isn't it? A second chance to get it right."

"You got it right the first time."

"You know as well as I do that's just not so. Somehow I'm the one to blame for the whole mess, although I'm still not sure how or why. Who does she remind you of?"

"Don't say it," said Sandra. "Maude."

"Maude with more fettle. Hardier, less fragile."

"Maude never seemed fragile to me."

"You haven't been paying attention."

He brought out the old sepia picture of his grandmother. They sat on the couch listening to her namesake slam doors while they studied the photograph. "What do you think?" he asked.

"I can't tell, Brad. The woman's squinting so. Maybe around the eyes."

"That's it," he said. "The eyes. That little girl up there is only four, but she looks like she knows everything there is to know."

"Don't put that much on her, Brad, she's only a baby."

"First life drops you down a well so deep you never think you're going to get up. Then it hands you a sunbeam. Where's my old camera? Never mind. I'm going to get a new one. A Nikon. And we're going to enroll her in Miss Cushman's school next year."

"It may be a second chance, Brad, but she's

still Eulalie's child."

"Technically she's in our custody."

"That's only temporary, as I understand it. You know what I mean?"

"I know what you mean, Sandra."

"I just don't want you to get your hopes up. If you allow yourself to get too involved, if you let yourself feel too much, what happens when Eulalie decides to leave, takes the child with her, and we never hear from her again? You have to protect yourself." Sandra flipped off her shoes, swung her legs around to stretch them across her husband's lap. "It's awful to think that that child's going to go through life with a name from a hallucination."

"I like Starlight. I think it suits her."

"I wasn't the one that dropped you, Brad, was I? Down the well?"

"No," he replied, rubbing her stockinged toes. "It was never you."

Lilia Sands returned to a city whose opalescent skyline oscillated in the brilliant sunshine. Impounded drug boats lined the Miami River, an elevated rapid-transit system lay under construction in toppled concrete forms, Spanish was spoken everywhere, and bank depositers shod in alligator shoes bench-made in Bogotá carried oversized wicker suitcases stuffed with cash.

An attendant at a Shell station, noticing Lilia's out-of-state plates, warned her to be careful not to walk around Overtown. His remark didn't surprise her. Lilia was used to a lifetime of people assessing her racial origins by the parts of her that were white (skin and nose), or black (lips and voice). "What is your background?" white people would ask. "Are you Italian?" "Are you Greek?" while black people resented her ambiguity.

The truth was, Lilia didn't feel either black or white, which is why she was sometimes called a honky bitch to her face, and sometimes nigger behind her back.

Lilia pulled out of the Shell station. "He thinks we're white," she told her son.

"No shit," the boy replied.

They drove through a drenching downpour in which sheets of water cascading down the windshield caused the wipers to stop working. By the time they got to Brickell Avenue, the rain had stopped, and the wide-bladed St. Augustine grass glistened in the yellow sulfur haze of the sun. They passed a condominium building with a fifty-foot cube cut from its center in which a lipstick-red staircase spiraled in space.

"Looks like Miami people have holes in everything," he said.

"You'll get used to it."

"I wanted to live with him."

"They didn't want you. I'm the only game in town, baby. Looks like you'll have to play me for a while."

The expressed reason that Lilia and her son, Hunter, were returning to Miami was the letter from her cousin Gloria Maraquilla, which said that Marta's fractured hip was slow in mending and that, while Marta would never complain, it was difficult for her to manage alone. The more compelling reason was that Lilia's career was over and, with child support soon to come to an end, her sources of income were limited. Although Lilia was still attractive, her exotic beauty had ripened into cheeks that were too plump and a pinch of fat beneath her chin that resisted all efforts to slap it away. As if to show that none of it mattered, she cropped her hair short and adopted rimless glasses. It wasn't only her slide into maturity that had made bookings few and far between and a listing on the Metronome Critics' poll only a memory. At forty-eight, the quality of her voice tone had lost its resonance.

During the past twenty years Lilia stayed as far away from Miami as it was possible to get. In the early days with Fidel, it had been exciting to spend weeks in the mountains before wood fires cut that day from machetes from their shoulder packs, while behind them rising thousands of feet in the air were the stony black faces of the Sierra Maestra.

Then there was only his band of *barbudos* who slept around the camp fire in huddled piles of blankets while someone strummed a guitar.

A powerful six-footer, olive-skinned Fidel disdained fashionable clothes, wore a grimy khaki shirt and wrinkled pants. The boots on his feet were dulled with dust, and his dark eyes gleamed wetly with the softly off-focus stare of zeal, his intense face pushed close to hers, while he caressed her breasts and lectured her with a monotonous, whispering urgency.

He carried a rifle with a telescopic sight. "We can pick them off at a thousand yards with these guns," he told her, and she thought that nothing could make her leave such a man.

After the revolution, when she followed him to Havana, she realized that he never stopped talking. She couldn't switch the topic, or reason with him, and she had to listen to what he was saying even if it was in the middle of the night, even if it was instead of making love. Sometimes his voice rose in crescendo, and he became animated, plucking at his straggly beard, pounding the table or the mattress with the palm of his hand. Other times he would step back and jut out his bearded chin, puff up his chest and slap it with his hands, and she knew that he was only rehearsing.

When it was clear that there was nothing for her in Cuba, that the revolution which was romantic in the mountains became prosaic in a Havana with shortages, that moody, unpredictable Fidel, given to lengthy tirades and long absences, treated her as an afterthought, Lilia left for Europe.

She had been in Glasgow with a package tour called Jazz USA when she saw news photos of Birmingham firemen turning their hoses on civil rights marchers, and was glad she was elsewhere. For Lilia, rights activism was an abstract issue, something to believe in, something over which to put her own life on the line only up to a point, which did not include either rationing or police dogs.

When she returned to the States, she married a white man because she was tired of being footloose, because it was easier to get a white man than a black man, and once having gotten him, there was less time spent in easing his hurts. Paul took her to Dayton to meet his family. His parents wore their hair in the same gray brush cut except that his mother's was a little longer. They were polite but distant, shaking her hand in a stiff-armed way that prevented her from coming any closer, even if she wanted to. Lilia and Paul acquired a son, a cappuccino machine, an au pair girl, and hanging ferns. While she pursued her career, Paul was active in the civil rights movement, returning from the March on Washington to tell her that he had walked behind Mahalia Jackson. Paul left her for another black woman the year that Martin Luther King was killed. Lilia remembered watching *Bewitched* with Hunter, wondering when Paul would send his child-support payment and why her agent didn't call, when an anchorman interrupted the program to announce that Dr. King had been shot in Memphis.

Lilia knew about Miami's Liberty City riot in 1968. She had been home the year after, on her way to Mexico City, and knew about the near riots that followed in the early seventies. She thought some of the discontent had been solved after her mother wrote to tell her that the Miami City Commission had chosen a black man over a white for city attorney and that a black man had been appointed superintendent of Dade County's schools. So she was surprised when teenagers threw stones at her car as she drove through the black section of Coconut Grove.

"I hope they didn't mess up my paint. Now, why did they have to go and do that?"

"Same reason the Shell man told you to be careful where you drive. You still don't get it. They're getting ready to tear this thing up and they're on a short fuse, same as everyone else."

"You trying to include yourself in the *everyone else*?" She turned into a heavily wooded lane overgrown and tangled with trees and shrubs, then stopped before an enormous banyan that was suffocating a quilted-leafed wild coffee tree. "We're here," she said.

"All I see is a motherfucker tree turning everything around it into mummies. It's even attaching itself to the roof."

"Don't use those words around your grandmother."

"Okay. I won't say roof."

Lilia flashed her brights, illuminating the old pine house with its gabled roof and dormer windows, its stone chimney that ran up the side like a squirrel, the clapboard siding weathered to a silvered green.

"You were six the last time you saw her. Do you remember her?"

"No. She better not be like my dad's mom. That's one cold bitch."

Someone switched on a porch light, which became quickly matted with scores of fluttering moths. A woman came to the door leaning on a crutch.

"Lilia, is that you?"

Lilia found her mother changed for the worse like the house around her. The front porch sagged as did several of the shutters. An abundant and untrammeled bougainvillea grew wildly over the back steps. Alamander and hibiscus needed pruning. Crotons that Marta had planted long ago had grown leggy and thin in the sandy ground. Pots of poinsettias, with roots poking through their drainage holes, lay on their sides, knocked over by some dog or by the wind. Everything inside had deteriorated, beginning with rotting eaves and soffits, sagging floorboards that creaked, doors that wouldn't close, a stair rail that wobbled, and two of the three window air conditioners hanging idle in their mountings, oozing a rusty precipitate.

"Without your father," said Marta, "it's hard to keep up."

"Mama, he's been gone almost twenty years."

"Has it been that long? I guess I let it get away from me. He wasted away, you know. That's what cancer does. A big, strong man like your father. It ate him up from the inside until there was nothing left."

Hunter complained to his mother that it freaked him out to find the old lady up and waiting for him in the kitchen. "I have to be on all the time, you know what I mean?"

"That's show biz," she replied.

"I don't feel like smiling back all the time, especially when I get up."

"Bite the bullet and smile. It won't hurt you."

Chapter Twenty-Nine

In early 1980, a series of unrelated events leapfrogged in a volatile escalation. In February, the Dade County grand jury indicted Johnny Jones, the black superintendent of schools, for attempted theft of school property. Two months later, Fidel Castro announced that anyone who wanted to leave Cuba could do so through the port of Mariel. President Jimmy Carter flashed a green light. Miami's Cuban community responded immediately with a freedom flotilla made up of thousands of small boats. Anything that would float struck out across the Florida Straits for Cuba's Mariel beach.

Anxious to arrange boat charters at the going rate of fifteen hundred dollars per person, to be there when loved ones arrived, to be a part of what was happening, Miami's exile community occupied every available hotel room in Key West, slept in cars and vans parked everywhere, even in the shadow of the magnolia trees on the grounds of Hemingway's house. Over five thousand Mariels sought refuge during the first week. By May 17, the day the McDuffie case, in which four suspended police officers were charged with manslaughter and tampering with evidence, went to the jury in Tampa, there were already fifty-seven thousand Mariels camped under the bleachers of the Orange Bowl and in makeshift tent cities under I-95.

Alarmed by the size of the flotilla, the United States government sought to stem the flow, but the momentum of reunion was too strong. Miami's Cuban community continued to travel south in cars, trucks, vans, buses, some in chartered planes. Every hour on the hour, radio station WQBA gave an arrivals report while Burger King sent thousands of hamburgers and the Cincinnati Reds sent scouts to search the bedraggled newcomers for Cuban ball players.

Gustavo, like other doctors, went to Key West to offer medical help. He also had an interest in expediting the anticipated arrival of Pablo and Celia's son, Pablito, of whom Gustavo had a photograph, taken when Pablito was a round-faced boy of seventeen. Gustavo traveled in a rented camper in which he set up a makeshift clinic to treat those suffering from exposure, to identify the more seriously ill, to corroborate a few unexplained deaths as the result of carbon monoxide poisoning from diesel engines.

He was treating a bad case of sunburn when Pablito appeared at the Winnebago wearing a ragged shirt, torn pants, and a beard. It had taken a week for his papers to be approved, for the authorities to figure out if he was really who he said he was, a former political prisoner, a survivor of Brigade 2506, neither criminally insane nor one of Castro's agents but an American citizen who needed no sponsor.

Pablito looked older than his thirty-six years. Gustavo quickly determined that Marta's nephew was suffering from malnutrition, anemia, and loss of muscle fiber. He assured him that in six months he would be back to normal, then took down the photograph, closed up his Winnebago, and drove north to Miami.

They rode back in silence, punctuated only by a stop at Alabama Jack's for beer and Gustavo's attempt to kindle a conversation. When Celia saw her son emerge from Gustavo's camper, she ran screaming to the street. Neighbors, even strangers, ran beside her, caught up in the drama of homecoming, while she grasped her son and moaned, "I never gave up hope, never."

Everyone came to hear the story of the hero who volunteered for Brigade 2506 when he was only seventeen, except for Hunter, who had gone to join a protest march at the courthouse with a sign that read, JUSTICE FOR MCDUFFIE. Pablito spoke slowly, haltingly, as if he wanted to be sure that the words were correct, while everyone drank paper thimbles of sweet Cuban coffee.

They had been taken to the military installation at Mosquito Beach, to a cove, with high bluffs on all sides. After two weeks of waiting on the beach, Pablito was told to get into a tugboat. Five or six of the people who went with him were absolutely crazy. One man killed his wife. How do you know? he was asked. He told me, he replied.

Before, they asked. Tell us what happened at the Bay of Pigs.

Pablito sighed, as if unbuttoning a part of his brain with fingers that were stiff. He told them that seven battalions had left Nicaragua at dawn, including the medics and the priests who gave their benediction. They were told to hold on for seventy-two hours, that Fidel had no air power and little artillery. It was almost twenty years ago. But it was like yesterday. It should never have happened.

Because of his youth, he was given ten years, sent to Escambray for rehabilitation, where he picked coffee beans. He was always hungry.

"So what is it like there?" asked Nestor, whose skin had taken on a pale ochre patina, like candle wax. "Terrible, no?"

"The socialist movement is responsible for a lot of good," Pablito said.

They looked at one another helplessly. Gloria Maraquilla ran sniffling from the room.

"If there is so much good," said Nestor, "why have almost one hundred thousand come over in the boat lift? Why did you come back?"

"I wanted to see my mother." They stared at the man, trying to find the plump, familiar boy in the lean, hardened, rehabilitated face, except for Lilia, who regarded her first cousin in the sideways manner one sizes up a stranger. When he was younger he had been soft and arrogant. Their grandmother Rosalia had favored him openly. Now that Pablito looked like a wolf, Lilia liked him better.

"Give it a rest," said Lilia. "He's tired of answering questions." She took his hand, pulled him from the couch. "We're going to take a walk."

"Pablito," said his mother, "these ideas, keep them to yourself. Others would not understand."

Lilia walked beside Pablito on the sidewalk, knowing by other Cubans' disdainful looks that they guessed at once he was a Marielito by his bony shanks, his missing teeth. She bought lemon ices from a vendor. They sat on a bench at a bus stop to lick them.

"I don't think they're glad to see me," he said.

"Sure they are. They just need to cross some T's."

He squinted in the light. "The sun is stronger in Miami. Why should that be?"

Lilia gave him her sunglasses. "These shades might be too small on you," she said.

"No," he said, pulling them over his ears. "I like them. I can see out but no one can see in."

Pablito's remark reminded Lilia of the first time she had seen Denver McCloud.

He had been wearing sunglasses even though it was indoors. It happened when Hunter brought her to a meeting of a civil rights group who handed out flyers on street corners and called themselves PULSE. Denver McCloud had been one of the speakers.

She watched from the second row as a young man raised his hand. "I got a problem, Denver," he said. "My boss doesn't like me."

Denver McCloud had been quick to reply: "You're there to work. You're not there to be liked. Don't think of it as a problem. It's a problem only if you get back on drugs. Think of it as a situation that you can turn around. When I was in 'Nam, we played a kind of Russian roulette. Someone would pull out the pin of a grenade, everyone would toss it back and forth until, just before it exploded, the last man threw it away. The way I see it, you're the last man. The toss is up to you.

What you're tossing is a losing attitude."

For some reason she caught his attention. He took off his sunglasses, stuck them in his shirt pocket, then narrowed his eyes to see her more clearly until someone called to him from the rear.

After the meeting, Hunter brought her to the podium. "This is my mom," he said, then left to hand out flyers.

"I know we're related some kind of way," said Lilia.

"That's what they say," said Denver, who offered to walk her to her car. "They also tell me that you made it big. Don't you sing or something?"

"I used to."

"What are you doing these days?"

"Trying to keep my head above water."

"You seem like you're making out all right. Floating on your back without a worry in the world."

"What's that supposed to mean?"

"I get the idea that you're not interested in serious swimming, that you're one of these folks satisfied just to coast on top of the current."

They passed a man who sat shirtless on the sidewalk, punching pin holes in a cola can. "That's crack in there," said Denver. "He's gonna stick some ashes in those holes he's making, then he's gonna light that rock and smoke it. You don't have to stick a spike in your arm to feel no pain is what I'm saying."

She became angry. "You're the one swimming upside down. You want to say something, say it out flat."

"All right. I don't think you have a clue who you are."

She put her key in the lock. "You don't know anything about me. You might be surprised to learn that I was with the rebels in Cuba when Castro took over."

"You're not there now. You're safe and sound right here in Miami. Floated yourself home." He put his hands in his pockets. "What makes it easy for you is your looks. You're a mean-looking chick."

"Not anymore. Maybe when I was younger," she replied. "Then I was really something."

"You're something now."

"I don't know about that."

"I do. When I saw you out in that audience, your eyes burned through me like searchlights. Come home with me. I'm not asking some candy-ass bleached-out chick who used to be. I'm asking the woman who's here now, a black woman as ripe as a peach, who's been there and back and who's improving with time, like concrete and wine."

She wasn't sure why she went. It was late. She was tired. His apartment was small. He brought her a can of soda from the refrigerator.

"All I have is a Dr Pepper," he said.

She took the soda can and touched his wrist.

"What's this band you wear?"

"It's made out of shoelaces. They belonged to a friend."

"You mean like some kind of friendship ring — he gives you his, you give him yours?"

"He wouldn't know it if I did. His brains got blown out of his head."

"I'm sorry." A siren wailed in the night. "How old are you?" she asked.

"Old enough."

Lilia stood by an open window with a soda can in her hand. "I don't go around doing this. What I mean is, younger men are not my style."

"Times change. Styles change."

"There's no advantage in this for you."

"Probably not."

She put the can on the windowsill. "I've reached the age," she told him, "when I'm not going to strip down in front of you. Put out the light."

"How about if I dim it, like this?" He threw his shirt over the lamp shade. His stomach was lean and muscled. He opened her blouse.

"I'll do it," she said. "There's nothing sexy about a woman taking off her slacks." She turned her back, undressed, then lay on his bed and slipped beneath the sheet. "You're going to think you're in bed with a pile of mush," she said.

He dropped beside her. "I'm in bed with a pair of eyes like searchlights is all I know."

He drew her close, kissing her eyes, the corners of her mouth. "Lilia. I get the feeling you're going to give me a bad time, Lilia. How long you want me to fumble under these sheets like a blind man?"

"You always do this much talking?" she asked.

"Only when there's not much action." He pulled her on top so that she sat astride him while his hands gripped her buttocks. "I'm gonna keep you busy till morning," he whispered.

"Is that a promise or a threat?"

"Which one you want?"

"Don't stop is what I want," she whispered. "Never stop."

Lilia smiled at the recollection as she and Pablito watched a bus pull away. She realized that they were sitting in a cloud of exhaust. The ices were gone. Each held an empty paper cup. Pablito had crumpled his into a ball. "I worked at the Habana Libre," he said. "It used to be the Hilton. I was a busboy. My job was to put water and bread on the tables, carry away trays of dirty dishes. You know the hotel?"

"I stayed there," she said, remembering the days after the revolution when she had followed Fidel from the house in Cojima to the luxurious apartment that occupied an entire floor of the Hilton. She recalled sending out to a restaurant in the Vedado for Chinese soup, her closet with Russian-made shoes that never fit, a French desk with an old typewriter that he told her to learn to use so she could type his notes. What she could not recall was what it had been like to make love with him.

Shortly after Pablito's arrival, an all-white jury convicted school superintendent Johnny Jones, who was sentenced to three years in prison. Three weeks later, at the same time Mariels were still arriving in Miami, an all-white Tampa jury, in less than three hours of deliberation, acquitted four white policemen of the December beating death of insurance agent Arthur McDuffie.

Miami radio stations interrupted programming to report the verdicts. Several minutes later, WEDR, a dico-music station popular among young blacks, began to receive calls from listeners saying that they didn't want to wait until Monday morning to do something about the injustice of the white policemen who had beaten a black insurance man to death for a traffic violation. They wouldn't take it anymore, they wanted to do something now.

An angry crowd, many with large boom boxes balanced on their shoulders, some of the younger ones on skateboards, congregated near African Square Park, site of the largest housing project in the city, where Police Chief Kenneth Harms had just left after addressing a community rally on the rise in street crime.

At first the milling was undirected, random, a shuffle of small clusters that merged, then split apart. Standing with a group from the projects was Denver McCloud, one of the rally organizers, and his two nephews, Lucille's sons, fifteen-year-old Jomo, and seven-year-old Akibo wearing a Miami Dolphins T-shirt two sizes too big.

Like everyone else, they talked about the verdicts. "We watched the trial every night," said a man wearing sunglasses. "All those pictures and witnesses telling how they beat that man to death and then they find them not guilty? Of nothing? That's like saying he didn't die."

Jomo was trying to enter the conversation. "Uncle Denver, how about when they had him unconscious, bleeding, handcuffed, and one of them's talking about how you could break his legs if you wanted to? That's like saying he ain't worth shit."

"This kid got the point," said the man in sunglasses. "Why couldn't the jury do the same thing, being they older?"

"Older doesn't mean smarter," said Denver. "Sometimes it just means you can't run as fast as you used to."

"Ain't that the truth."

In the late afternoon, the first rocks and bottles were hurled at cars being driven by whites along 62nd Street. Bystanders shouted, "Get the crackers!" and some older people, elderly men in baseball caps, middle-aged women, their arms pendulous and thick, took out aluminum

604

lawn chairs to watch. A rumor spread that a white man had shot a black child, drawing hundreds more to the street. The crowd grew so large, the rocks and bottles so thick, that the Miami Police Department pulled out its squad cars and set up roadblocks to keep out white drivers.

When Denver realized that the squad cars were leaving and that the police intended to let the violence run its course, he said he had business to attend to and instructed Jomo to get his little brother home. "That means now, Jomo," he said. "Take Akibo now, take any shortcut you know, but get inside and stay there."

Jomo waited until his uncle was out of sight. "Go home," he said.

"Uncle Denver said you supposed to get me home."

"You don't need me to hold your hand, Akibo. I'm telling you to go home. Now do it before I break your ass."

"You can't make me, Jomo."

Jomo made a threatening lunge in his younger brother's direction, and Akibo took off on his skateboard, weaving skillfully in and out of the people in the street.

Jomo stood in the rear of a mob that was throwing rocks and bottles at a cream-colored 1969 Dart. A chunk of concrete hurled by some big guy that Jomo had seen once or twice came through the windshield, striking the driver in the head. The Dart swerved along the center divider strip, across oncoming traffic, and up onto the sidewalk, where it struck an old man and a ten-year-old girl, driving her up against a stucco wall, severing her right leg and smearing the wall with a swath of blood. Cries of horror and anger went up from the crowd. Women grabbed sheets off a clothesline and wrapped up the bleeding girl, while Jomo pushed his way to the front.

"There's one, that's a white one," screamed a member of the crowd.

The mob dragged two men from the car and began to beat them savagely. They were punched, karate-kicked, and struck with rocks, bricks, bottles, and pieces of concrete, shot by a revolver, and run over by a green Cadillac, whose driver then came over and stabbed them with a screwdriver. A woman came and placed towels over the heads of the injured men who lay in the streets, and a shirtless man, his body streaming with sweat, said to Jomo, "I know them crackers got to be dead."

The anger was collective and contagious, and what Jomo felt before as a grievance, an annoyance like a horsefly that wouldn't quit, now became rage. He ran with others to push garbage dumpsters into the middle of the street so that cars would have to slow down, becoming easier targets, while the angry mob that surged around him stoned ambulances and beat back squad cars trying to get to the scene. A woman in a Chevrolet Malibu was set on fire along with her car, and another car turned over, its driver pinned in the wreckage jabbed with sticks, until that car too was doused with gasoline and set on fire, and Jomo forgot about trying to keep out of the face of his uncle Denver.

By the late evening, when a call was placed to Tallahassee asking that the National Guard be sent in, the rioting had spread from Liberty City to Overtown, the black Grove, and around the entire Metro-Justice complex. Doctors and nurses answering emergency calls to Jackson Memorial Hospital were stoned and beaten, the Metro-Justice building itself torched, and a mob shouting, "Justice, Justice," ripped antennae off police cars, inserted rags in their opened gas tanks, then tossed lighted matches at the gasoline-soaked rags.

On Saturday night, all six of Jackson Memorial's operating rooms were going at once, and the hospital ordered 278 units of blood, nearly 35 gallons, from the city's blood bank. The police moved in with face shields and riot batons. At the sight of police in riot gear marching toward him ten-deep, Jomo ran home through the smoke and splintered glass, recognizing Denver's voice coming from a loudspeaker mounted on a van saying, *"Don't let them hurt you, man. They gonna hurt you, baby, they got more troops coming in. Watch yourselves. Go home and protect your families. Get off the streets."* When he got home, Akibo wasn't

607

there. His mother began to scream.

Pupi Alvarez had been assigned to cover the Sunday afternoon meeting of the Community Relations Board, which had been opened up to include police and government officials, black community activists, and media reporters.

Alvarez, who had interned the summer before at the *Miami Herald*, wanted to be a newspaperman like his grandfather Nestor. He wanted to be the first to uncover something, and he loved the excitement of the three-to-midnight police beat that no one else wanted, where you got to ride in a company car with a police band scanner and a C.B. radio.

Now he sat in the rear of the room, stuck with what was shaping up to be hours of squabbling when the real action was on the streets, his reporter's pad flipped open to an empty page while officials announced that the governor had declared a state of emergency, that liquor stores and gun shops were closed, that no gasoline in cans or inflammable liquid was being sold, that bus service had been suspended, a curfew imposed, and that there was to be no trash collection within the curfew area.

The suggestions and counter-suggestions flew almost as fast as the bottles outside — enforce the curfew, lift the curfew, fire State Attorney Reno, keep her, talk to the people, quit talking so much. Mayor Ferre told the gathering that the eyes of the world were on Miami. He said that he had already asked two nationally prominent blacks, Jesse Jackson of Chicago, and former United Nations ambassador Andrew Young, to come to the city the following day to try to help calm things down.

Ferre's announcement was followed by stony silence, then anger of several blacks who resented the mayor bringing in outsiders without consulting them, for implying that the riot was a failure of local black leadership.

A man with a woven wristband who was identified as Denver McCloud said that it was as if Ferre was asking the big niggers to come in and get all the little niggers into line. Alvarez took McCloud's comments down. They had the makings of a memorable quote.

One by one, blacks got up to say what they thought should be done. Charles Cherry, head of the state NAACP, said that black leaders should draw up a list of demands. If the whites agreed, they would take the list into the streets as an inducement against rioting. Otis Pitts, head of a social agency in Liberty City, accused a county commissioner of not pushing hard enough for programs that benefited blacks. She shot up from her seat, said he had no right to criticize her, then made disparaging references to people who made money from being street leaders.

The state attorney, Janet Reno, said that she was bitterly disappointed over the verdict. The meeting ended when Denver McCloud stood,

609

his knuckles on his hips. "It's getting dark," he said, "and we're still here yapping. Get on your armbands and get out in the streets. If you don't, a lot of our young people are going to get killed."

Alvarez chased after Denver McCloud, caught him at the door. "Mr. McCloud, my name is Pupi Alvarez. I'm with the *Herald*. Did you know that the president of the Urban League refused to attend this meeting?" Pupi read from his notes, "His reason is, 'How can you say to people to be rational when they have been treated in an irrational manner?' Do you think he is being irresponsible?"

Denver looked down at the young reporter. He was short, with a thick, developed neck that showed that he worked out. "That depends," said Denver, "on what you think black leaders are supposed to do. Protect white folks or lead black folks."

"Don't you think it's the responsibility of leaders to tell people what to do?"

"No one from the black community can go out there and tell them to hold it down. And I'll tell you something else. The riot damage won't be anywhere near as serious as the damage done to those kids on the streets."

Alvarez followed him to the parking lot. "Eugenio Montoya warned that the situation has gotten worse between blacks and Latins with the recent arrivals of the Marielitos. You care to comment?"

"What's happening out here is not aimed at Cubans or white Anglos. This is a matter of blacks against the system, and it's been going on for a long, long time."

Alvarez stood beside Denver's car. "You going back in there?"

"As soon as you set me free, I will."

"Can I hang out with you?"

"You want me to run interference for you, is that it?"

"No," said Alvarez. "I can take care of myself."

"You're not only short. You're also blind. Come on, then. But don't expect me to do anything for you."

Denver fixed a black sock to the antenna of his car.

"Is that to get us through?"

"It's in memory of Arthur McDuffie. Pupi. What the hell kind of name is that?"

"My real name is Guillermo. You know, a lot of Hispanics feel a solidarity with blacks. We understand the indignation."

"You dig the indignation?"

"Yes, sir, we do. We just don't think that acts of violence are the way to solve anything."

"Pupi, or Gupi, or whatever your name is, you want to hang out with me, don't go mouthing off your opinions to anyone else. I don't want to have to scrape you off the sidewalk. You understand?"

"Yes, sir. I do."

Denver and his passenger were stopped for identification at a checkpoint by National Guardsmen carrying M16 rifles. As they left the perimeter of the curfew area behind them, the din of hundreds of jangling burglar alarms, the sledge hammers of people breaking into businesses, and the hammers of others boarding up their businesses, nailing up signs that read BLACK OWNED AND OPERATED, drowned out the wailing sirens. Charcoal pillars of smoke pointed at the sky, while puffs of low-lying smoke drifted in a wispy pall. A crowd of looters waited for a man to back his car through the door of a furniture store while others hauled booty on bicycles, in supermarket carts, in pickup trucks and vans, some with their trunks tied open.

A mob tried to set fire to a service station that Denver knew was owned by a black man. When it wouldn't ignite, they jump-started the owner's tow truck, drove it onto 22nd Avenue, and set it on fire despite Denver's pleas from his car window that the owner was a brother.

"We shouldn't tear up a black neighborhood like this," he shouted to the small knot of excited, shirtless, and sweating young men.

"You must be an Uncle Tom," cried a youth whose face was gilded by the flames.

"Don't be stupid, man. I just know that if you tear down these businesses, a lot of people are going to be out of jobs." Behind him an unescorted fire engine careened down the street, its firemen pelted with rocks and bottles, while the vehicle, with firemen clinging to the truck, swung south, wheels screeching, and disappeared in a hail of rocks.

Lucille McCloud decided that her family was safer indoors. She closed her windows and her doors, brought everyone inside, including nineteen-year-old Djuna, five-year-old Shira Marie, Akibo, safe after being treated at an area hospital for a fractured wrist, and Jomo, itching to get outside where it was all happening, whom she threatened to sit on if she had to.

When Denver walked in the door, Lucille was on the phone with a friend. "We're doing the best we can," she said. At the sight of her brother, she hung up the phone. "You running off seeing to everyone else, when your own sister's child is missing!" she shouted.

"Seems like you found him."

Lucille stood with her fists on her ample hips. "I had to call the police. No one knew anything. Someone finally told me to call Jackson Memorial. He wasn't there. Then I found out that if you weren't hurt too bad, they sent you to one of the other hospitals. It took me two hours to find out that someone took Akibo to Cedars. I sent Jomo to bring him back this morning."

Akibo flashed a toothless seven-year-old's smile. "Hi, Uncle Denver. I got a cast. Jomo didn't take me home like you told him. I was in the emergency room. Blood was all over the floor."

Denver grabbed his oldest nephew by his arm. "Why didn't you do like I told you? Either one of you could have been killed. Now your brother's got a broken wrist. That's on you, man. It wouldn't have happened if you had done what I told you."

Jomo pulled away. "I told him to go home. He didn't listen."

"He's not the only one who didn't listen. I told you to take him home. Not send him home. I should be able to count on you, Jomo."

Lucille stepped between them, said they were safe now, said she hoped that Denver didn't have to work the streets again. "It may be cooling down out there, but they're not satisfied and settled yet. We hear shots, but we don't know which way they're coming from." She said that several blocks away, Norton Tire Company had burned down. A few blocks in another direction, U-Totem had been looted. Her electric power had been flickering on and off, then was cut early that morning. If it wasn't on by nightfall, she had candles ready to see by, but nothing in the refrigerator would be any good. She seemed to notice Alvarez for the first time.

"It's not safe for white people to be here," she said.

Alvarez explained that he was a reporter.

"It doesn't matter what you are," she said. "They don't want any whites in here yet, I know that. No kind of way." Lucille turned to her brother. "The smoke has gotten so bad, we can hardly breathe."

"Maybe you should get out of here," said Alvarez.

Djuna fixed him with a level look. "Where are we supposed to go?" She turned to Denver and told him that a boy she took classes with had been killed by a security guard at the Jet Food Market on 27th Avenue and 54th Street.

Shira Marie said she was hungry, that her mouth tasted like burned toast.

Lucille sighed. "The child's got to eat when she's hungry," she said.

"How about me?" said Akibo. "I'm hungry too."

Lucille sent Jomo to cut through the alley to Washington's grocery two blocks away, on the edge of a small pocket of safety as yet untouched by violence. He was to buy Goody's Headache Powder, milk, cereal, two cans of tuna fish, and Kit Kats for Shira Marie to take the bitter taste of smoke out of her mouth.

"Be careful," she said. "I'm sending you because you run the fastest. Don't hang around watching anything. Just buy the food, hurry back."

"I'm sorry, Uncle Denver," said Jomo on his way out.

"Sorry doesn't cut it," said Denver.

615

While Denver fixed the lock on the front door, Lucille offered Alvarez lukewarm coffee in a Minton cup. "This used to belong to my great-grandmother Caroline," she said. "It was given to her by William Jennings Bryan. You ever heard of him?"

Alvarez said the name sounded familiar, but he couldn't exactly place it. The sharp report of gunfire came through the open window. Lucille went to close it. "I been listening to that for three days. I told you that you can't tell where it's coming from."

"Those sounded close," said Alvarez.

Running footsteps and a knock on her door brought Lucille puffing to her feet. It was a neighbor with bad news. Jomo had been shot. A blue pickup truck driven by a white had begun shooting in every direction. Jomo had been hit in the head by a bullet. It looked like they weren't shooting at him in particular. Jomo just got in the way. Unlucky, you might say.

With Alvarez and Denver at her side, Lucille waddled down the glass-littered street that reeked of smoke and tear gas, past overturned cars with their tires slashed and fires burning out of control. "Oh, Jesus, is he dead? Is he dead?" she cried. When they came upon the bleeding boy lying on the sidewalk, she screamed. "Someone just drove down the street and shot him in the head. Blew my baby's brains out. Oh, no. Why my baby?"

When Denver stooped to pick up his nephew's body, he was sliced with a painful flashback as sharp as a shard of glass, of slipping a dead comrade into a body bag. Only this wasn't a guy in a combat helmet, this was a kid in high tops, his sister's kid, a kid who hadn't even been born then. Denver choked back his tears. It would take too long for an ambulance crew to find a police escort. He would drive Jomo to the hospital himself, while Alvarez, dimly aware of snipers firing at the helicopter that was photographing the blazes, tried to figure out his lead sentence.

Denver carried Jomo in his arms to his van, hoping that no one had messed with his tires. "Sorry is okay," he whispered to the unconscious boy. "Sorry is just fine."

The weeks that passed with Jomo on life support felt to Denver like one long day. The family's fragile hopes for the boy's survival snapped with each downward turn like filaments in a web. When Lucille signed the paper allowing the hospital to disconnect Jomo's respirator, Denver's own body seemed to deflate like that of the boy.

Several days after the funeral, Denver opened the door to his sister's apartment, never noticing Lilia standing in a corner talking to Djuna.

Lucille came from the kitchen to greet him, drying her hands on a checkered kitchen towel. Her movements were labored, her breathing heavy. She kissed him on the cheek. "Lilia's here to see you," she said.

Lilia stepped out of the darkened corner, her thumb hooked around the leather strap of her shoulder bag. "I read about your nephew in the paper, Denver. It's an awful thing. It never should have happened."

His face was grim, his eyes without luster. "That's for damn sure."

"Your phone's been off the hook for weeks. I even tacked a note to your apartment door. Where have you been?"

"Blending," he replied.

"I don't do too well with doubletalk," said Lilia. "What does that mean?"

"It means he's trying to fade into the woodwork," said Lucille. "I keep trying to tell him that that only works for termites. Help yourself to coffee, Denver. The neighbors have stopped bringing cake, but I put out a bowl of peaches on the counter."

Lilia followed Denver into the kitchen, where he poured coffee into a Minton cup with a sprigged green border. "I even went to the rehab unit," she said, "but they said you haven't been there either."

Denver looked through the window. "What happened to the damn screen? Got a five-year-old child in the house. I told the landlord to put one in six months ago." He turned to Lilia. "I don't much see the point in trying to do for someone else when I can't keep my

618

own sister's kids safe." He downed the coffee, then returned to the small living room. "I'm leaving, Lu. How are you fixed for blades?"

"I have money, Denver, if that's what you mean. Take care of yourself. I worry when you don't get enough to eat. You coming by tomorrow?"

"Maybe. Newspaper people still bothering you?"

"They stopped coming around last week," she said.

"Let me know if they come back."

Lilia followed him down the cement stairs of the open hallway. "Slow down," she said. "I can't take these steps two at a time like you can." The smell of jasmine drifted from the vacant lot across the street. She caught up to him on the sidewalk. "I want to stay with you tonight."

"I wouldn't be much good for you," he said.

"I don't need you to be good for me, Denver. I need you to let me be good for you."

"Whatever," he said.

When they got to his apartment, the first thing Lilia did was to open the window wide. "Whew! Got to get some air in this place. If I didn't know better I'd say you were trying to bury yourself with the boy."

The bulb in the floor lamp had burned out and they stood under the pale fluorescent light of the small kitchenette.

Denver turned away, his hands balled into

fists. "Jomo tried to tell me he was sorry. I told him that sorry didn't cut it."

"We all say things we don't mean," she said.

"What you're talking about, saying things we don't mean, that's a different ball game. It's not even in the same ball park. Somehow or other we get a chance to make it right, to fix it. I want to fix it. I want to fix it so bad I can taste it, but I can't."

He sat on the edge of his bed and cried. Lilia bent over him, saw that the edge of his undershirt was frayed, and thought absently while she held him in her arms, that she would buy him a package of new ones in the morning.

"There's nothing as beautiful as a black man," she murmured. "I guess I saved the best for my old age. Close your eyes, baby. Try to get some sleep."

It was not until early morning that she fell asleep beside him to the sounds of plumbing pipes groaning through the walls and a baby crying in the apartment next door.

Part Five

1982–1992

Chapter Thirty

The Sand Dollar was now a rundown, shabby, portholed hotel for elderly Jewish retirees who cooked on hot plates and Mariels in undershirts asleep in the lobby. It stood in the middle of a dying slum of other ornamented, pastel Social Security hotels. Herschel wanted to tear down the fifty-year-old structure, build something else in its place, a disco or maybe a health spa. Bradford was for a clean break. He wanted to sell.

With Herschel gone to Pritikin to unclog his coronary arteries, the decision was left to Bradford. He parked his bottle green Jaguar on Ocean Drive, paid a kid five dollars to watch it, and walked up the steps, thinking that any hotel built with the narrow end facing the ocean deserved to be demolished.

The terrace was lined with elderly people sitting on plastic-ribboned beach chairs, where they would perch until dark. Despite air conditioning, the lobby smelled of mildew, urine, stale cigarette smoke, and the grease and onion odors of cooking in confined spaces.

"We don't have anything on the first or second floors," the room clerk said. He was a skinny little man with a face like granite. Herschel

623

had said he used to be a jockey.

"I'm Bradford Watson. I'm part owner of this place."

"Sorry, Mr. Watson. But most older people like to be where they can get out in case of fire."

Bradford took a handful of room keys. To demonstrate his vigor, he avoided the elevator and ran up the stairs. Most of the keys did not make it on the first pass and had to be jiggled in their locks. Bradford had forgotten how small the rooms were. He remembered a joke that a comic once had told, about hotel rooms so meager guests had to go in the hall to change their minds.

On his way down to the lobby, someone started yelling from one of the upper floors.

"That's Betancourt in 501," said the desk clerk. "I don't know why he uses bad shit with that wad he carries around."

A little woman, bent at the neck like a question mark, hit the bell. "He's doing it again," she said. "Screaming his head off."

Bradford flicked his nail at a crystal sconce that had been painted over in white, wondering what idiot had decided to do that. He looked up to see a young man strut into the lobby, a cocky little guy with a notepad in his hands who introduced himself as Pupi Alvarez. He said his mother was Gloria Maraquilla Alvarez. Bradford tried to place the name.

Pupi flipped a page. "Did you know that

the Art Deco district is now on the National Register of Historic Places?"

Bradford gave the crystal sconce another flick with his nail. "I do now."

"Maybe you're not aware that the Design Preservation League has little support from Miami Beach officials?"

"I guess they don't see it as a problem, and neither do I. If I want to preserve something," said Bradford, "I'll prickle it in brine."

"They don't just want these old hotels preserved, they want them revitalized. Like the Cardozo." Pupi Alvariz put down his notepad. "My mother says you got us out of Cuba."

Bradford looked at the kid in baggy pants, striped shirt, and flowered tie that somehow looked great together, an outlandish combination that only the young could pull off. He looked like he should be playing with PacMan. "I got you both out. Your grandparents too."

"My grandmother says you saved her life, that you pushed them ahead, gave them your place on the ferry."

"I guess that's what happened. I don't remember. It was a long time ago. What do you do for a living, Pupi?"

"I'm a reporter."

"You can't make any kind of money chasing after news." Bradford bent to check the floor beneath the linoleum.

"That's not the point."

"What is?"

"The truth, as I see it. A lot of people are watching to see what you're going to do with the Sand Dollar." Pupi knelt beside him to offer him a penknife.

Bradford fingered the dusty drapes, which looked as if they hadn't been opened in years, then pulled on the cord. It came off in his hands.

"What do you think I should do, Pupi?"

"Build it back up. It's easy to tear something down. It's harder to put it back together."

"You know what you're asking me to do? The electric has to be brought up to code, God knows how much that will take, it has sagging joists, the rooms are too small. If you enlarge them, you have to line up the plumbing, forget that the pipes are covered with asbestos and have to be replaced. In case of fire, we have a tank of water on the roof leading to a hose. That doesn't cut it with the fire marshal. We would need a whole new fire-protection system, sprinklers, fire pumps, alarms, the whole nine yards. It was a piece of shit then. It's still a piece of shit. Only worse."

Pupi took the pull rope out of Bradford's hands, stood on a chair, and tied it to the ragged end that hung from the valance. "If you decide to renovate, I'd like to do a piece on the renovation. Step by step."

"I'll let you know. Tell your family that I send my best. Tell them they've got a nice kid who likes to spend other people's money."

"My mother says you're a friend of my Aunt Lilia. Is that true?"

"We knew each other, yes."

As the young man ran down the steps, Bradford thought of the fragile scab that used to peel afresh with every mention of her name, that Lilia had left Cuba for Europe, that she had returned to the United States, that she had married and was living in Ohio, that she had come back to settle in Miami. It had taken all this time to be able to pick at it without pain, to hear her name and not feel the empty knot that made him want to reach for the phone so he could hear the soft, sultry cadence of her voice.

Bradford Watson had reached the stage when he understood that life was as good as it was going to get, just as his mild coupling with Sandra was as exciting as bed would ever get — in fact, was all his cardiologist would allow.

Bradford attributed his acceptance of a life without Lilia less to his chest pains than to his granddaughter. With Starlight's picture in his wallet next to his driver's license, Bradford sublimated his disappointments with a crowded calendar that included membership in the most influential, behind-the-scenes force in Dade County, the Non-Group, a select fraternity of a few dozen predominantly white Anglo males, Miami's most powerful businessmen and civic leaders, representing the Establishment in Miami.

And if his daughter, Eulalie, criticized the

Non-Group for its snobbish sense of noblesse oblige, Bradford pointed to the salvaging of the metro-rail project and the creation of the Federal Drug Task Force, complete with frogmen and EC-2's flying overhead, as a direct result of Non-Group intervention.

For her part, thirty-four-year-old Eulalie was less interested in causes than she was in living her own life without interference. Eschewing her granny dresses and sandals for Armani jackets and Guess jeans, she had allowed her long honey-blonde hair to be precision-cut, so that when she pulled it up with the gold barrette from Tiffany's that her grandmother Maude had bought for her sixteenth birthday, it fell smoothly to her shoulders. And while she used cocaine, she preferred amyl nitrate, which gave the same great sex, but which was less damaging to the lining of her nose.

Eulalie showed a predilection for bronzed Latin males, as glossy as the black patent-leather Mary Janes she once wore to cotillion. They were men with questionable occupations, who wore heavy gold chains, silk shirts open at the neck, unstructured jackets, pleated linen trousers, and Papucci shoes bought at the Four Ambassadors Hotel, who disdained sailboats and cabin cruisers for sleek Cigarette-38's that skipped across Biscayne Bay to Bimini at 75 m.p.h., who appreciated the fact that even if she was not eighteen, she was an American girl with pink nipples and pale pubic hair, who knew how to cut a line of coke razor-sharp. She liked the way they strutted like peacocks when they danced, the heady scent of their Paco Robanne cologne, their stash houses in some garden apartment complex in Kendall, the .357 Magnums and the 9mm Browning automatics that they left in their cars. She especially liked the way their eyes narrowed when they wanted sex.

As for her daughter, Eulalie encouraged Starlight to live once more with her grandparents. At five, Starlight had been adorable, and at seven, on at least two occasions, she was bait, but at fourteen, awkward, ungainly, timid to a fault, as tall as her mother, she was not only a hassle, she made Eulalie look old. There had been no argument. All Eulalie had to say was that the apartment was getting too small, especially the closets, that if Starlight moved to her grandparents' home, she wouldn't have to clean her room because her grandmother had a live-in maid, and that Bradford would do anything she wanted, including, when she was sixteen, buy her a car.

Bradford and Sandra came to help pack their granddaughter's belongings on a day that Eulalie was off to the Bahamas.

"This is going to be for the best," said Sandra, grown as sleek and as plump as a seal. "Just you wait and see."

"I don't want to live with her anyway," said Starlight. "She never picks up after herself.

She sleeps till two in the afternoon. Sometimes she comes home stoned."

"How often is that?" asked Bradford.

"I don't remember. A few times, I guess. That's not as bad as when she spills coffee on my schoolbooks and borrows my clean underwear. I kind of like it when she goes away for the weekend."

Sandra exchanged a glance with her husband. "I didn't know your mother left you alone," she said. "I wish I had known that before."

Starlight threw her mineral collection into a duffel bag. "I love my mother, but she doesn't have her head on straight. I'm tired of taking messages and running out to Easy Quik Chek for coffee. Living with you guys is going to turn my life around."

1983 was also a turnaround year for the city. In January the three-point favorite Miami Dolphins played in the Super Bowl for the fourth time, seeking their third world title against the Washington Redskins. A few weeks later, in a swirl of banners and the aroma of shish kabobs and burning rubber, Ralph Sanchez ran the first Grand Prix of Miami on a twisting, rain-sodden, skyscraper-lined course laid out through an eight-block section of Biscayne Boulevard, the FEC railway lot, and the Miamarina parking lot.

At almost the same time, a Bulgarian artist named Cristo Javacheff came to Miami to create a work of al fresco art in Biscayne Bay. His interest was a chain of swampy mangrove islands littered with syringes and used condoms, which he proposed to swath with 6.5 million square feet of flamingo pink polypropylene.

Volunteering for Christo's work force was not Bradford's idea. It was Starlight who told him that some kids from Ransome needed a boat with a shallow draft to skim over the waters of the flats, and someone over twenty-one to sign for them.

Bradford found himself wading beside Starlight at sunup through the mud to clear an island of garbage, sink anchors in the bay bottom to which they tethered immense hexagonal booms and tugged electric pink fabric toward shore, while an island captain walked shirtless among the booms to secure the lines. Starlight's schoolmates worked beside them, giggling at nothing, diving beneath the porous sheeting to grab a scuttling crayfish, dropping handfuls of turtle grass down each other's necks, and Bradford found himself wishing that deadly serious Starlight would do the same.

By late Friday, when Bradford thought he would never again stand up straight, most of the islands were skirted. Starlight looked back from Bradford's outboard at the pine-covered islands surrounded by immense and delicate Schiaparelli pink lily pads, blooming where before there had been nothing but garbage and mud, and told her grandfather that the sight gave her goose bumps.

Uncomfortable with expressing such feelings, Bradford said it looked like a Pepto-Bismol spill.

Starlight hugged him around his neck. "My friends are going to sell their T-shirts for fifty dollars apiece," she whispered, "but I'm going to keep mine forever. It's beautiful, Grandfather. Admit it."

They returned home, mud-caked, smelling of the flats. Sandra said she didn't know what all the fuss was about since the project was temporary. Starlight glanced at Bradford while Sandra complained that draping spoil islands in pink plastic seemed frivolous. "What's the point? Someone explain it to me."

Bradford shook out his rain gear and smiled conspiratorially at his tall, tanned, green-eyed granddaughter, so leggy, so fresh, she reminded him of a colt. "The point is that Pepto-Bismol keeps you in the pink."

"That's funny, Grandfather."

"Thank you, Starlight. I thought it was pretty clever myself."

"Have you taken your pills?" asked Sandra.

"Yes," he replied.

"I worry when you don't take your pills."

Starlight told her grandmother that if she wanted to see the Surrounded Islands, the best bargain was the seaplane because that only cost thirty-three dollars, but that actually, the best view of islands 2 and 3 were from Morningside Park, where she could see them for free.

Sandra said she would think about it. "Did you remember to buy your mother a Mother's Day present and a card?"

"I forgot, but I promise to buy a gift this afternoon if someone will drive me to the Omni. I don't want to be a flight attendant anymore. I want to be a marine biologist. Do you have to go to college for that?"

Events took a downturn when Maude fell and broke her hip while taking a dance lesson at the Arthur Murray studio. Bradford took Starlight to the hospital to see her, angry that his selfish, willful mother had brought this on herself. "What the hell is a ninety-two-year-old woman doing taking dancing lessons?" he said as he and Starlight searched the corridor for her room.

They found Maude in a hospital bed with protective railings. One pale blue eye was clouded with a milky cataract. An oxygen fork was stuck in her nostrils, and intravenous lines ran into her bruised and fragile arms. When Bradford noticed that his mother's skin had taken on the paraffin yellow of the gravely ill, an old despair returned to surprise him.

"I've brought Starlight to visit you, Mother. Eulalie's child."

Maude said something inaudible through parched and cracked lips.

"What did you say, Mother?" asked Bradford.

"I couldn't understand you."

Maude crooked a transparent hand, motioning the girl before her to come closer. Starlight bent her head over her great-grandmother's scrawny chest, trying not to breathe in the stale odor of her hospital gown while Maude whispered in her ear. "She says she did a triple spin with a guy who didn't know how to lead. And she's calling me Eulalie."

Maude died of pneumonia two days later. She was buried near her mother in a section of the cemetery reserved for Daughters of the Confederacy while everyone told Bradford it was for the best. If Maude had lived, they said, he would have had to put her in a nursing home, which for Maude would have been a worse death.

Bradford astonished everyone when he said he wanted his mother's portrait, the one of her fingering a strand of pearls. No one knew what had become of it until Eulalie disclosed that her grandmother had given it to her dance instructor. There was no point in asking him to return it because he refused to give it up, which Eulalie found out when she asked for it herself.

While the family, including Bradford, was still heavy-footed with Maude's loss, Eulalie called to break a date to take Starlight to the movies to see *Terms of Endearment*. She explained that she had been invited to a party at Regine's, the glitzy nightclub on top of the Grand Bay Hotel.

"This is the third time you've canceled," said Starlight. "I thought you liked Shirley MacLaine."

"I'll make it up to you, I promise."

"That's what you always say."

"Don't give me a hard time. There are things over which I have no control. This is one of them. It's not just a party. I'm going to meet stars like Julio Iglesias. I'll even get his autograph for you."

"Don't bother," said Starlight, slamming the receiver into its cradle.

Bradford found his granddaughter sitting on the seawall, blinking back tears. "Forget your mother and her party," he said. "I'll show you real stars."

He took her to the Orange Bowl to see the universities of Miami and Nebraska vie for the national championship. "Keep your eye on freshman tailback Alonzo Highsmith."

They sat in a glass-enclosed box and watched the Hurricanes jolt the surprised, heavily favored Cornhuskers with a furious burst of offense, to make the Hurricanes, with a win of 31–30, the number one college team in the country.

"It's not over till it's over," said Bradford. "What did you think of Bernie Kosar?"

"You told me to keep my eye on Alonzo Highsmith," she said.

Coconut Grove was out of the way, but Bradford was feeling impulsive. He drove Starlight to see the house that his grandparents had built. It was dark and it was late. Lilia would most likely be asleep.

An eleven-story condominium building blocked the view of the bay. Bradford's headlights picked out a Crime Watch sign posted on a telephone pole. Two new houses, half-hidden by the foliage, stood on either side surrounded by high stucco walls.

Starlight opened the car window to get a better look at the old pine house with its shuttered dormer windows and hanging front porch that dropped like a jaw. "It's really old. And smaller than I imagined. I wish we could take a look inside," she said.

"I can describe it to you. The ceilings are high and the floors buckle and dip so badly, you feel you're at sea. For the most part, the rooms are very small. It smells of pine. My mother said that when she was a little girl, freshwater springs bubbled up all around here. And Seminoles camped out in the yard. My uncle Jack told me my mother used to hide in the banyan tree."

"From who?"

"I don't think she was hiding from anyone in particular, Starlight. She was just playing."

"I never did that."

"No, you never did."

A woman appeared at the door with a doberman at her side, then came down the steps.

She wore rimless glasses that glinted silver in the moonlight. She bent to look inside the car. "You still haunting folks?" she asked.

"My granddaughter wanted to see the house."

"You're going to get yourselves shot at," she said, "poking around where you don't belong."

"It's a lifelong habit," he said. "Hard to break."

"I'd tell you to bring the child inside, but the hot-water heater broke and the kitchen is flooded. If you're just going to park, keep your doors locked. All kinds of fools wander around here at night."

When she went back into her house and closed the door behind her, Bradford drove away.

"How come you didn't introduce her to me?"

"I don't know her," Bradford replied.

"Yes, you do. Why did you lie?"

"It's complicated."

"Did you have something going with her?"

"Where do you get your ideas?"

"From you. You said to watch the way someone plays their hand. Yours was too close to the vest. Well, did you? It's no big deal."

"Good God. I'd better get you home. It's after midnight. Your grandmother will have my head."

"You did, didn't you? Was she prettier then?"

They passed the curve of I-95 where the highway hugs the new glass and steel buildings.

On one hung a huge sign reading, MIAMI'S
NO. 1.

"She was exquisite."

"Were you sad to say goodbye?"

"At first. Then I might have been relieved.
I don't remember."

"Why did you bother in the first place?"

"It was a long time ago. I was intoxicated."

"I never saw you drunk."

"Not with booze. Just out of my mind. Someday you'll understand."

"No, I won't. I would never understand acting
dumb because you liked another person. And
you don't have to tell me not to say anything
to Gran. I'm not stupid."

"I never said you were."

She turned to smile at him in the dark. "I
guess this is what you meant when you said
it's not over till it's over."

"Your mother and you, Starlight, that's not
over either. She can change. I did."

"I don't care if she does or not. I like things
the way they are."

Chapter Thirty-One

The last time Starlight saw her mother alive was at the Biltmore Hotel, where Eulalie was an extra on a shoot of *Miami Vice*.

She did not need the seventy dollars or the extra ten for bringing her own wardrobe. She did it as a lark, the result of an acquaintance with a location scout. The woman told her that everyone in Miami wanted to be on the set, that a lot of the politicians were doing it, like the county manager and the mayor of Miami Beach, as well as big-time models who wanted the exposure. She said that if Don Johnson liked her, his bodyguard would give her an appointment at Johnson's trailer. The experience was disappointing, even boring. There were long waits between scenes until they were summoned in anonymous clumps by the first assistant director, who pointed and said, "You, you, and you." Other than a visit to the makeup trailer or to the honey wagon for a sandwich, Eulalie's only diversions were to guess from which angle they would shoot the next scene and to watch the costar tying cherry stems into a knot with his tongue.

It was late afternoon when Sandra showed

up unexpectedly with Starlight. When Eulalie saw them standing behind the wooden barricade, she groaned. "Oh God," she said to no one in particular, then left the extras' enclosure to stamp through the St. Augustine grass in spike-heeled Maude Frizon shoes.

Sandra said she hoped Eulalie didn't mind, explained that she picked up Starlight after school so that she could watch her mother involved in making a film.

Eulalie looked around to see if anyone was watching them. "As long as you're here," she said, "you might as well sit and wait for me. But they don't really like outsiders on the set."

"If you explain that it's your mother and daughter," said Sandra, "I'm sure they won't mind."

Eulalie gave Sandra her canvas chair, stood beside her with her arms folded across her chest while Starlight sat cross-legged on the grass.

"What's all that white for under your eyes?" asked Starlight.

"Your mother is covering her circles," said Sandra.

"I'm not covering up anything," said Eulalie. "Someone else made me up."

"You should wipe it off," said Starlight. "It looks awful."

A man in jeans had been watching them from the trailers. Eulalie knew him as the production manager. He made his way to Eulalie.

His hair was bound at the neck in a rubber band. "'Who's the kid?" he asked.

Sandra realized that he was speaking about Starlight. "She's only fourteen," she said.

"Fifteen in January," said Starlight.

Before Eulalie could reply, the first assistant director called her to the shot, told her to occupy a seat at an umbrellaed patio table, to sip a drink through a straw, not to look up or do anything to call attention to herself.

Eulalie slipped on a pair of sunglasses to mask her eyes. "This could take a few hours," she said. "I wouldn't hang around."

"She never even said she was my mother," said Starlight.

The man with his hair in a rubber band handed Starlight a card. "If she didn't, it's because you're gonna be better looking than she is. You got great bones on you, chica. A friend of mine is setting up a casting agency on South Beach. Give her a call. Get yourself a composite made, body shot, head shot, fashion shot, action shot. Make sure that one of them looks the way you do now, big eyes swimming with tears, lower lip sticking out like a shelf, cheekbones like knife blades."

"My granddaughter is very young. She still has braces on her teeth," said Sandra, "or didn't you notice?"

"You got a kid with this kind of possibility," he said, "you need to groom her early. The business gives her a narrow window. It's over

641

by the time she's twenty-three, twenty-four, twenty-seven if she can hang around long enough to interest the soaps. There's big money in it. Some of these kids are pulling in eight, ten grand a day."

Weeks later, when Sandra was trying to decide if appearing before a camera or on a runway might possibly be of benefit to her solemn granddaughter, a homicide detective wearing an ankle holster came to see Bradford at his office. He told him that his daughter, Eulalie, and two drug dealers, known for running a string of mules from Colombia, body packers who swallowed cocaine-loaded condoms, had been shot to death on a Cigarette in Norman's Cay. The Bahamian police said that one of the men had been tied to a line and thrown overboard. His body was badly decomposed, half eaten by sharks. Bradford should consider himself lucky that that hadn't happened to his daughter. The nine-thousand-pound, one-hundred-thousand-dollar craft, with its red and white racing stripes and Twin Hawk V-8 engines, had been impounded by the INS.

Bradford asked if he had any leads, the detective replied that some cowboy setting himself up in business had probably made the hit. Bradford said he thought the DEA had been making inroads.

"Are you kidding?" said the detective. "The money is coming in so fast these guys don't have time to count it. They just weigh it. They got artillery you wouldn't believe. M16's, M14's are just for openers. We picked up a war wagon in Dadeland, a Ford on an Econoline chassis. It had a sawed-off .30-caliber carbine on the passenger seat, a MAC-10 between the seats, side panels of the truck reinforced with quarter-inch stainless-steel plates, in the rear cargo doors two holes big enough to accommodate the muzzle of a gun, a pump shotgun, a .380 silenced Beretta. If they need someplace safe to hole up for a while, they got *caletas* all over the place. I know this guy on the force, he used to carry a .38-caliber Smith and Wesson. After the Dadeland business, he bought a fourteen-shot 9mm Browning automatic. Look, I'm sorry. You asked."

When the body was returned and preparations made at the funeral home, Bradford was inconsolable. He blamed himself. "I wish to God I could live it all over again," he said.

"What?" asked Sandra. "Live what over?"

"The way it was with Maude," he said.

"You don't mean Maude, dear, you mean Eulalie."

"Did I say Maude? Why did I say Maude? A million dollars in hundred-dollar bills weighs twenty pounds. Can you imagine that?"

"Rest, won't you? Tomorrow will be a difficult day."

Starlight dressed carefully, filed her nails straight across, put on panty hose without being asked and a dress she hated, navy blue with a white linen collar and cuffs. She overheard her grandmother say that the worst thing in the world was for someone's child to predecease them. Sandra looked suddenly old. So did Bradford. Starlight had to decide which one needed her most, reasoned that since her grandmother could still speak, could still tell the maid which trays to put out, that it was her grandfather whose side she would not leave.

"I feel such rage," he whispered late at night after everyone had left. "I'd like to kill the people who did this."

"I'm not mad at them," said Starlight. "I'm mad at her. She did this all the time, put herself in danger. It was like she didn't care about anything, even me."

Bradford was too grief-stricken to console Starlight in turn. Instead he thought of the little girl who had written to him in Cuba, begging him to come home, telling him how she was going to clean the brightwork on his sailboat with toothpaste.

Chapter Thirty-Two

RAY GOPHER

The white man does not have to kill us off. We are doing it to ourselves, splintering off in factions, one against the other, until there will be nothing left. In 1976, the Indian Claims commission announced a final award of sixteen million dollars to the Seminole Indians. Although the Miccosukee decided to reject the money because land is sacred and cannot be sold, the Seminole tribes of Florida and Oklahoma squabble over the settlement while their white lawyers chew away at it like termites.

Even if we do not contest our Seminole brothers, we are at war in the Everglades. Tourists driving on the Tamiami Trail don't see it or hear it. It is a quiet fight, waged with insults, a bitter feud, setting kin against kin, modern Indians like Buffalo Tiger against traditionalists like Homer Osceola, who refuse to let go of the past, and me in the middle, a fifty-seven-year-old Ayikomi with my hearing going bad, trying to keep together the fraying ends of a cord.

When our land-claim dispute was settled

for $975,000, the squabble spilled out. Some of the traditional people denied the settlement made between the United States government and Buffalo Tiger. They called us a fake tribe. They even wrote a letter to President Reagan to protest what they said was a fraud against their nation for paying for Everglades land rights to a group without authority.

Buffalo Tiger says they are not a tribe anyway, just one family, all of them his first cousins, and not to pay attention if they don't recognize us because Florida and the federal government do.

I steam my ears open so that I can hear, then go to try to make peace, to explain that the contract and the money means jobs, which they surely know, since one of their own kin, a sister, holds an office job in our Social Services department.

The traditional people dismiss this. Someone complains about Buffalo Tiger, "He's not doing things the Indian way at all. Buffalo Tiger likes to have a necktie all the time, and have a sports coat on him. Florida is not part of the U.S. anyway, because we've never been conquered. The land was already here. How can the white man give it to us when we already own it?"

I remind him that Buffalo Tiger did a lot for the Miccosukee. He got us recognition as a tribe. He brought us from scattered hammocks, from tourist camps owned by the white man, to a modern village. Because of him our people have electricity, a school system, windows with screens, and law enforcement.

"I remember when Buffalo Tiger first started out," he replies. "He said we were going to put some life into these people out here. Instead these young people are killing themselves. Some of them can't speak their own language. He's not even here all the time. He lives in Hialeah."

I return to Buffalo Tiger. I do not tell him that the traditional people believe that one day the government will cancel its two-million-a-year contract with our tribesmen, leaving us nothing but regrets.

My son, Bo Charlie, wears Porsche sunglasses in the alligator pit. You cannot see that he is angry most of the time, but you can smell it on his skin, a bitter scent, like nettles. As soon as I move into the tribal office, he has advice. "If you're going to be a medicine man," he says, "you shouldn't be involved in politics. It doesn't mix." Then he tells me that the Miccosukee do not have the cash flow that the Seminoles in Broward County have. Neither do we have the bingo and tax-free cigarette stands. Bo Charlie took business courses at Miami Dade. That is why the language of profit and revenue rolls more easily off his tongue.

"Money alone is not the answer," I reply, hoping he will listen intently, as a young man should. "We need more work. We need jobs. I think maybe the government will help us build a hotel at the I-75 interchange, maybe the first in a tribe-owned chain, with camping grounds and riding paths, and a jogging path, maybe fill a lake for boating. That will make jobs."

Bo Charlie interrupts me, a white man's habit that I think little of. He would like to see us less dependent on the white man, even turn back his welfare in his face as did the Canadian Inuits.

Willa Cypress knocks on the screen door. Her roof leaks. She wants to know if it can be taken down and replaced with palmetto thatch. Bo Charlie says he will take a look. She tells him that if he does not take off his sunglasses, he will see the roof as it is at night when it does not rain.

In the month of frost, we crate an alligator to send to Spain. This was not my idea, but you have to let the others have their way once in a while. When Lee Tiger found out that they don't have alligators over there, some of our people thought that the alligator would make a foreign emissary to remind Spanish tourists of Florida's attractions.

The alligator's seven-foot body is packed in a wooden box, and his stubby legs paw at the pine boards while we lock the box, hammer it shut, then secure it with wire for its six-hour flight in the belly of an Iberian Airlines plane. Bo Charlie has roped the creatures mouth shut, yet it is able to make a low ferocious hiss. I write DANGER wherever there is room and suddenly think that what we are doing to the alligator, the white man is trying to do to us. Not send us to Spain, but keep us in a box. Lee Tiger says that the alligator's arrival will coincide with a convention of travel agents in Madrid, then it'll go to a zoo. As if it understands, the frightened creature pushes loose one of the boards and pokes out his green, toothy snout. We cautiously wire the box together again while I try to understand the sign.

Bo Charlie is contemptuous. "If you're going to do business the white man's way," he says to me, "then don't keep your eyes on the ground like the gopher. Set your sight high. Do it better than the white man. Beat him at his own game. Like the Seminoles in Broward. Bingo and cigarettes. That's where the money is. Your hotel and your alligator ideas, they mean pig shit for all the jobs they'll bring."

I am ashamed for my son, for myself. The others walk away with their heads down as they carry the crate to Nelson Tiger's pickup truck.

When the white man's pope comes to Tamiami Park in a glassed-in vehicle that makes him seem as if he is riding in a jar, something from down there beneath my feet begins talking to me. You can hear it if you listen. To most of the young people, like my son, the earth is a dead thing. They do not know how to listen. Like a knife blade that has gotten rusty from disuse, my hearing has gone bad because I forgot to listen.

It tells me that it is impossible to live in balance with the natural world and with the white man at the same time. The skirmishes within the tribe are proof enough, but the war with my own son, who should be listening to me, matching his heart rhythms to mine, to the ground beneath him, who instead scoffs at what I believe, all this tells me that it is time to return to the Old Way.

I will go west, deeper into the Pahahokee than even the traditional people who are still in harmony with the earth. Long before I leave, I try to teach somebody my medicine, but everybody is too busy, except a drug company that asks me for the formula for a potion used to calm nerves, which I would not break tribal law by revealing.

I also want to get the alligator back. I dream about him in the zoo in Madrid, his long green snout contemplating Spanish people who watch him through a fence, longing as I long to see an anhinga spear a fish with its razor-sharp bill, then spread its wings in the sun to dry. I know now that he gave me a sign that day when he broke through the crate. But then, he was not an alligator.

My wife will not go with me. She likes the laundromat, the hot and cold running water.

She is angry with me for leaving. "Who will take care of your mother?" she asks. "She is old, and needs help."

My mother, Emma, says she needs no one to care for her. She surprises everyone when she says she is coming with me, deep, deep into the grassy water to places that she remembers only by the color of their tree snails.

"You will make medicine for our people?" my wife asks.

I tell her that our people know where to find me if they need me, and those who can't would be better off with the white man's medicine. Bo Charlie asks if I will return for the Green Corn dance, if I have decided where it should be held. Now I am surprised, for the younger Indians, like my son, do not regard the dances as we do; still he seems to understand that if there is no Green Corn dance, the medicine will die, and then there will be no more Indians. I am not so sure that he understands that the dance grounds must be hidden from the white man, who makes entertainment of our traditions. I tell him only that I will return in the spring.

We leave in the evening, before the sun has set, when the white ibis flock to their roosts and yellow crowned night herons begin to search for crayfish. Among my mother's pots and spoons, next to an old rusty sewing machine that you work with your foot, is a white man's doll that I have never seen, stained with mold like the north side of a tree.

"Why did you bring that?" I ask. "It is a child's plaything."

She tells me that the doll was a gift from her father's old woman, the one whose spirit I led safely to the north, over the curving shelf of the night. "It will make medicine," she replies. I look at the thing with its hank of yellow hair, glass blue eyes rolling around in its cracked pink face while I try to understand what medicine my mother can be thinking of.

We pass a hunter's camp, one of many just like it, an ugly wooden shack set upon oil drums. A fire smolders in a pit, but no one is there. I pole my dugout to the water's edge, and in a pop of thought, like a bubble that rises to the surface of the clear swamp water, I rip off the doll's hair, stuff it in my belt, and leave the bald, ugly thing on a cypress nub.

My mother's knee pains her. She rubs it with tallow mixed with willow bark that she keeps in a Gerber's sweet potato jar. "I have been saving that doll for a long time," she says. "I am glad you found it useful."

Chapter Thirty-Three

Lilia stood beneath the banyan tree and checked to see that everything outside was tagged. Inside the house, Denver, her son Hunter, Denver's nephew Akibo and his niece Shira Marie continued to haul objects from the attic, the garage, and the closets: a black silk fan, tins of Redman chewing tobacco and Dr. Ballou's cough drops, a Bowie knife, a marble bust, a carton of Sevres china, patent leather high-top shoes, a box of embroidered stockings, a declamation manual, a Galli-Curci record as thick as a slab of butter, a Spanish edition of Amado Nervo's poems, a silver flask, a white enameled kitchen table, electric fans, none of which worked, a hood ornament from a 1927 Hudson, a tinted chromo of the Sacred Heart of Jesus, ration books from WW II, a bill of sale for two Brahmin bulls, a giant poster of Cab Calloway, white satin gloves studded in rhinestones, and a ragged straw hat that smelled faintly of bay rum.

By mid-morning, the mango-littered driveway was filled with cars. Some tag-sale shoppers came on foot with their dogs on a leash, their babies in strollers, others in running shoes, on bicycles, on roller blades, out for a Saturday in Coconut Grove, now traipsing over her lawn and through her house to pick through her life and the lives of those who had lived in the house before her.

"Taxes or crime?" asked a tanned woman wearing shorts, a diamond tennis bracelet, and a purse slung across her chest like a rifle.

Lilia squinted at the hood ornament and scrawled a price on its tag. "What are you talking about?"

"Taxes are driving a lot of people out of the Grove. Either that or home invasion. My neighbor got mugged in her own driveway." The woman picked up the marble bust. "What is this thing? It looks like the head of someone famous."

"That's Balzac," said Lilia. "He was a French writer."

"How much you want for him?"

"It's priced on the tag. Hundred dollars."

The woman spun her tennis bracelet. "I never heard of him. I'll give you fifty."

They settled on seventy-five. As Lilia made change, she noticed her Cuban relatives ease their way past two men carrying the davenport with broken springs. Since Marta's death, they had visited with greater frequency, believing it their duty to keep a watchful eye on their cousin's only child. This time they came to find out if there was anything belonging to Lilia's grandfather, Roderigo Garcia, that they might want.

Flavia, his sister, took Lilia aside.

"As your mother's oldest living relative, the granddaughter to Roderigo Garcia's sister Maraquilla, I have the right to say what I am going to say. We heard that now that you have sold this house, you are planning to live with Denver. What can you be thinking of? Forget that there is no talk of marriage. He is your cousin, no matter how many times removed, and he is much younger, at least fifteen years."

"Twelve," snapped Lilia.

Flavia whispered the last objection. "He is so . . . dark."

"So was my daddy."

"This man is even darker."

"That's the point," said Lilia. "He makes me feel less diluted."

"For you it is going backward. Move only forward, *niña*. Always forward."

"Talk about moving forward, watch that man walk sometime," said Lilia. "No white man or Cuban or what-have-you walks like a black man. You ever see satin shimmer? That's how they move."

Flavia shook her head, held Lilia's face with both her dimpled hands. "Love comes hardest when you get older. That's what happened to your grandfather Roderigo."

Lilia pulled her face free from Flavia's grasp. "These tag shoppers are robbing me blind. I have to take care of business."

"Nestor wants to ask," said Flavia, "but he

is too embarrassed. My brother would like to have the bust of Balzac."

"The bust is sold," said Lilia, "but if he really wants it, maybe I can get it back."

Lilia found the woman in the tennis bracelet examining the walnut headboard. When Lilia asked for the return of the bust of Balzac, the woman refused. A deal was a deal.

Akibo had been sent out for change. He returned, dressed in a rapper's neon yellow running shorts, Nike high tops, and a turquoise Miami Dolphins baseball cap. Like his idol, Flavor Flav, he wore a clock around his neck. He found Lilia frowning before a card table heaped with jars of buttons and a stack of *Saturday Evening Post* magazines. "What's happening? Something wrong?"

"Nestor wanted a little statue of Balzac, but I sold it. The woman won't sell it back."

"Where's she at? I'll talk to her."

Denver carried the white enameled table to a waiting van. "Don't do anything stupid," he said.

The lawn and the house began to empty. Someone's car horn became stuck in annoying blasts, then stopped. Lilia continued to make change while she listened to Gloria Maraquilla complain of how her son Pupi was wasting his time writing about the Miccosukee.

"They want a bingo parlor," she said. "He could say that in two sentences. He should write about Carlos Arboleya, Louis Pantin, people like that. It wouldn't hurt to get noticed by such men."

Akibo appeared with the bust. "This what you're looking for?"

Nestor smiled. His teeth were as yellow as his skin. "Lilia, I hope you didn't go to any trouble."

"No trouble," said Akibo. "It was easy. Just some smooth talking. Explaining the situation, you might say."

"He sounds like someone I knew," said Denver.

"Who?" asked Lilia.

"If I didn't see that clock hanging around his neck I would say that was my old man Willie talking."

Tears spilled down the old man's cheeks as he cradled the bust in his arms, then turned to follow his daughter to her car.

Shira Marie watched them drive away. "He said he would treasure it always. His *always* is just a little teeny piece of mine. He should have said something like *for now*, or *for a while*."

"What are you talking about, girl?" asked Lilia.

"Shira Marie thinks he picked the wrong word because he's not going to live forever," said Denver.

"Who is?" asked Lilia.

"I am," said Shira Marie. "I'm going to live forever and be famous."

Lilia pulled the child to her. "What are you

going to do to make you famous, baby, besides being the seventh-grade spelling champion of Dade County?"

"She doesn't have to do anything," said Denver. "All she's got to do is not die. The word will get around."

By late afternoon, other than a homeless person picking through a carton of trash, the shoppers had gone. The only things unsold were the straw hat and the declamation manual.

"What am I supposed to do with this shit?" asked Lilia. She put the straw hat on her head and tossed the declamation manual into the carton of trash, then locked her hands behind her head and stretched. "Let's pack up what's left, sweep the place, and go. It's time to move on."

Hunter took Akibo and Shira Marie into the Grove for ice cream while Denver and Lilia went into the house. Lilia began to sweep the buckling wooden floors, reach overhead for cobwebs that clung to the beams, while Denver picked up a framed studio photograph made of Lilia holding a feathered fan under her chin. "You were some fine-looking chick." He tossed it into a suitcase. "You're still a foxy lady. I know you're gonna tell me it's none of my business, but this Castro dude, he mean a lot to you?"

"That was a long time ago," she said. "It was over before it started, mainly because he had other fish to fry." She eased her back, turned to look at him. "In a way he was a lot like you, passionate about the things he believed in. Like you are right now, going after the county commissioners about those pockets of unincorporated county in Liberty City that were targeted for street improvement back in Lyndon Johnson's time, trying to get them to dole out federal money for storm drains so when it rains people don't have to walk alongside streams of raw sewage. I know you. You won't let up until you're heard. I guess that's a turn-on for me. With you it's not just your passion that attracts me, but the issues behind it. They spell my name same as they spell yours."

"Anyone else important to you, besides your husband?"

"A white man. You might know him. Brad Watson. He lives right here in Miami. Grandma Caroline used to work for his family. There was something about my father and Watson's mother having the same white man for a father, but no one's been able to pin that one down. Anyway, I was a different person then. So we might as well be talking about someone else." Lilia rested on her broom. "Everyone is telling me this isn't going to work," she said. "You and me."

"Come over here and tell me that." He reached out a hand and pulled her toward him, knocking the straw hat to the floor. She was astonished at the heat he created in her. "In three years I'm going to be sixty," she said.

He slipped his hands beneath her shirt and cupped her breasts. "Is that your way of telling me we're not going to have any kids?"

By the time Akibo, Hunter, and Shira Marie returned, Lilia's bags were packed. Shira Marie said that they had seen Gloria Esteban shopping at Coco's. They watched her through the window buying an Ozbek outfit with glitter and spaghetti straps. When she came out, Akibo tried to rap his new song, but there were too many people on the sidewalk trying to get her autograph.

"Rap to me," said Lilia.

"You're not gonna like it. It's not your style. It's got no past and it's got no future. I'm pissed off and there's no nice way to say it."

"As long as you're not attacking Koreans. Too many people telling me what is and what isn't my style. Let me decide."

Akibo loosened his shoulders, moved to the left, to the right, then spun around as he began to speak/sing his lyrics.

"The dope man gives you the crack pipe
says don't believe the hype, look at me,
I'm still alive, the people who tell you
*   drugs will kill,*
lie to you, they always will, just like the
*   government,*
and white folks on this continent,

but the dope man, he don't use the stuff,
  he hopes you
haven't had enough, hopes to keep you
in no condition to join Jesse Jackson's
  coalition,

the same for passing through the gang
  territories,
they tell you lots of stories, but you got to
  keep your hat
on straight, let your feet cooperate and walk
  on by,
these guys been gangbanging for years and
  they got nowhere
yet, it's time to stand up and be counted
  for, 'cause
nobody's counting no gangbanger unless he's
  dead."

"That's cool music in a cool medium," said
Lilia. "You've got a lot to say. I'm going to
teach you how to say it on stage."

"You were in show business in the olden
times," said Akibo. "Besides, your music was
pretty lame. That's not where it's at."

Lilia checked the pine frame house for the
last time, making sure that the windows were
shut, the water turned off. "Facing an audience hasn't changed. You still need to learn
to phrase a song, to hold an audience with
your attitude, to manage a mike."

Akibo smiled. "See, that's what I'm talking

about. You don't have to worry about that no more. Mikes are cordless. You can put your lips right up to them, kiss 'em if you want to, even suck 'em, the sound engineer will take care of feedback, stuff like that. As far as holding an audience, they don't need to like me. They just need to listen to my message."

They piled into Denver's van while Hunter followed in the small acid green BMW he called his baby beemer. While they rode, Denver advised Lilia that it wasn't enough to talk to people in the health department about the establishment of a clinic in Overtown where residents could go for prenatal care. "You need to speak to the folks at Jackson Memorial Hospital, get them to commit their staff."

When she replied that she was after someone with real clout like a state senator who could get it funded, Akibo began to compose a rap song. "People crying 'bout a bald Zack, and that's a fact, while- I got to worry 'bout a drive-by, a bullet on the fly, an accident, man keeps me in suspense . . ."

"Suspense doesn't rhyme with accident," said Shira Marie. "*Compliment* is better."

"I can't use *compliment*. There's nothing about *compliment* I want to say."

"Then what about *resident?*" said Shira Marie. "What about, 'a bullet on the fly, an accident, no way to treat a resident of the United States.' "

"Girls can't rap," he said. "It's a natural

fact. Spelling isn't the same as rapping, Shira Marie. Keep out of my face." He turned to the front seat. "How much you make today, Aunt Lilia?"

"That depends. Enough to buy a silver fox jacket or a sequined gown that ripples in a key light . . ."

"Or a used Harley," said Denver.

"A year's tuition at Miami-Dade," said Lilia, "or six months' rent for a clinic. You've got to make choices in this life."

"That's what I'm trying to explain to Akibo," said Shira Marie. "He's making the wrong choice. Tell him to take *argument* if he doesn't like *resident*. It's a really good word. And it's better than *suspense*."

In the four years that she had been a fashion model, Starlight's earnings had risen from sixty dollars an hour for gigs after school to five thousand dollars a day for video commercials, runway shows, or print work for magazine ads and catalogues.

Starlight had been doubtful during the initial interview when she was told that the agency wanted to represent her, wary during the courtesy testing by photographers beholden to the agency, who took endless rolls of film from which Starlight might put together a portfolio. Despite Bradford's objections, the black-and-white glossies confirmed it. On camera and off, tall, full-lipped Starlight, with her great cheek-

663

bones, wide-spaced feline eyes, and defined shoulders, represented a new aesthetic. Most important, she had attitude, demonstrated in her matter-of-fact expression and indifferent stance, in her grandfather's Acqua di Silva men's cologne that she splashed on her body.

In March, the busiest season, Starlight accepted a two-day assignment posing for Calvin Klein's fall ad campaign that began at five-thirty that morning and would last until sunset. Dressed in shorts and halter, white socks and black suede Chanel ballet flats, Starlight nibbled on a bagel in an air-conditioned trailer outside a corral in South Miami. The backpack that she carried everywhere, crammed with Hershey bars, lingerie, safety pins, shoulder pads, panty hose, and a photograph of her mother, lay at her feet as she settled into the tall stool before the makeup table, where the makeup artist, wearing an undershirt and bill cap, began by shaping Starlight's eyebrows.

As she worked, the makeup artist cooed in her ear about a model they both knew who had had her boobs done, about another model at the Milan show who had shaved her head and had her skull tattooed. Starlight tuned her out, thinking instead of an injured baby manatee she had helped roll into a sling the day before.

After a lunch of rice and broccoli from a takeout container, the photographer took Starlight outside for Polaroid shots, then told the makeup artist to begin again.

"Too high," he said. "The look is upscale country. I need browns, siennas, transparent terra cottas. Her lips should look as if they were stained with berries."

The makeup artist turned her bill cap backward and wiped off Starlight's makeup, then reapplied foundation with a sponge. "You need to think about what happens when your tear sheets start thinning out. You should be taking acting lessons instead of spending your spare time in a wet suit feeding fish," she said.

Her eyelids once again shadowed, her lashes curled and separated, Starlight jumped off the stool and went into the back bedroom of the trailer, where clothes hung on a rack. There beside a table piled with bags, shoes, and jewelry, she stripped down to a lacy bra and white bikini panties while the clothing stylist handed her a shimmering silk bias-cut dress, a pair of shoes, and a numbered baggie containing clip-on earrings and a rope of pearls.

As Starlight dressed, a hairdresser clucked his tongue over her shorn, curly blonde locks, cropped close to her head ever since she had decided that big hair was fashion oppression and hacked it off with her grandmother's manicure scissors. He ran his fingers over her scalp, used a pick to pull out wisps, slicked random curls with gel. "It's unique, I'll say that much. We're going to do what we can," he said, "and hope it works."

For some reason the gold chain around his

neck reminded her of Eulalie. Or maybe it was Eulalie's boyfriends.

They waited outside the trailer while the crew scurried about adjusting reflectors, positioning black flags on movable stands, rigging white silks over scaffolding to filter the light.

"I feel like I'm in drag," said Starlight.

The makeup artist flicked a powder-loaded brush across Starlight's forehead. "You're frowning, darling. Get rid of the thought. It's killing the look."

"Actually, I like it," said the hairdresser. "It borders on macho. Not butch, just a sweet babe who knows how to kick-start a Harley. You do own one, don't you, Starlight?"

"I drive a Jeep," said Starlight, "a CJ-7."

The makeup artist leaned close. "What's eating you?" she whispered. "Come on. You can tell me. I knew you when the braces came off."

Starlight lowered her voice. "I keep thinking that if I hadn't left my mom, she would still be okay."

"And from what you've told me, I keep thinking that the mom and the kid got mixed up. She was supposed to be responsible for you. Not the other way around. All that was five years ago. It's time to put it to rest."

"I don't know how to do that."

"Sure you do. Same way she put you to rest when she told you to go live with your grandparents. Bye bye, Mom."

The creative director, responsible for setting a mood and satisfying the client, checked something off on a clipboard. "Lock up the set," he shouted. Then he called for fabric, and a grip trained a fan on a length of chiffon.

One of the lighting gaffers yelled from the stable that a senior citizen was there to see Starlight.

"What does he look like?" Starlight called.

"Jimmy Stewart with a suntan."

"That's my grandfather."

Bradford shouldered his way past the waiting crew, found Starlight outside the trailer. His voice was low, angry. "Your grandmother told me where to find you. I've been trying for days to get you on the phone, but you haven't answered my calls. I got a notice from the university that you've dropped all your courses. I think you owe me an explanation."

"Not now, Grandfather. They're going to call me to the set any second."

"I'm not going anywhere."

The creative director put on a tape with an upbeat tempo, Paul Simon's *Rhythm of the Saints*, while chiffon billowed and light bounced back from gold reflector pans that had been set in the paddock.

The photographer called for action. As Starlight stepped forward, he danced in front of her, crouching, standing, shouting, "I love that move! Again, Starlight! Yes! Beautiful! You look incredible," while she whirled and pivoted, flirted and scowled, leaned over the railing, peeked inside the stalls, reached out a hand to touch a horse's nose, until finally, after three rolls of film, he shouted, "I think we nailed this one, Starlight. You can change."

While the photographer's assistants checked light meters and reloaded cameras, and the grips stood on ladders to change the rigging of the filtering silks against the climbing sun, Starlight changed into a cashmere pantsuit and matching hooded coat.

She found Bradford drinking coffee in the tiny kitchen, took a deep breath, and smiled.

He was not to be put off. "I don't want you to wind up like your mother," he whispered hoarsely. "I insist that you get an education. That was our understanding. It was the only reason I agreed to this."

"Taking classes is not where I'm at."

"I thought you wanted to be a marine biologist."

"I don't want to look at the sea through a microscope. Besides, I like what I'm doing. I can tune out anytime I want and it doesn't matter."

He looked pained. "I guess you have to do that, don't you?"

"Sometimes."

"Okay, I understand. But all this is time limited, Starlight. You have another six, seven years at best. Then what?"

"Maybe I can get a job at the Seaquarium."

"Without a degree? You'll be a keeper. Someone who cleans the tanks. That's not what I call thinking ahead."

"I'll deal with it when it happens."

He frowned, slicked his hair back with the palm of his hand.

"You're beginning to sound like Eulalie."

"What are you afraid of, Grandfather?"

"I don't want to lose you too," he replied, setting down his coffee cup, turning toward the narrow exit of the cramped R.V.

The creative director stuck his head in the door. "We need you, Starlight. Okay, Gramps, it's time for you to go home."

"I was leaving," said Bradford. "Don't push it."

"He means it," said Starlight. "I wouldn't crowd him."

The creative director watched the departing figure disappear behind a billowing curtain of chiffon. "I'm sure he's a nice old dude, but come on, what am I supposed to be afraid of?"

"He once had someone's car blown up."

"You're full of it, Starlight."

"It's true. My mother told me. She was trying to convince me that he was really a shit. When I asked my grandfather if it was true about the car, he said he didn't understand the question. That's when I knew for sure. I'll tell you something else. He can get a head waiter faster than any man I ever saw."

669

Chapter Thirty-Four

Pupi was a second-generation Cuban-American, an amalgam of Cuban roots and American education, of Latin temperament and Yankee ingenuity, both cocky and mellow, a chameleon able to shift ethnic gears and move through Miami's neighborhoods with bicultural ease, a hybrid like the burgers with guava barbeque sauce he now enjoyed at the Wet Paint Cafe in South Beach.

Pupi was also short. He had tried to make himself taller, drank quarts of milk, took handfuls of vitamins, when he was eleven, hung upside down from a railing by his knees. He used to include a plea for height in his nightly prayers, along with a request to his guardian angel to finish his rosary so that he could go to sleep. He did this until the age of sixteen when he entered eleventh grade and was no taller than the majority of girls and decided that El Señor, Papa Dios of his babyhood, was deaf.

Once Pupi made up his mind that five-foot seven was as tall as he was going to get, he compensated for his lack of height by increasing his strength. If he could not develop lengthwise, he would do it by building his body sideways at a Little Havana gym called Ulysses. Pupi also learned that if you kissed sitting down, any differential in height was quickly overcome, as was the girl if you knew what you were doing. In fact, according to what he had found out in the past few years, shorter men had an easier time in bed since they could see the girl's face without having to hang their feet over the bed.

Known for his flamboyant ties and his dedication to the Lambada, Pupi's goal was to have a Porsche by the time he was thirty. He told this to the news director of Channel 4, advised him to order the black bean pasta with the red pepper leek sauce, then asked if he knew that the six billion dollars a year in cocaine money that was coming into Miami's banks translated into $11,000 a minute.

When Rick Farren first had asked him to lunch, Pupi guessed that Farren wanted a feature story on the weather twins, sister meteorologists who had recently succeeded a weatherman in a brush cut whose tanned face was as lined as the isobars he plotted. The news director took his time in getting to the point. He said he had seen Pupi's series on the Art Deco district of South Beach, on the Miccosukee, his earlier cub pieces on the McDuffie riot. More controversial was his contribution to the series explaining how the CEO of Centrust had borrowed from Centrust to take over Centrust.

"Where are you guys going with the series?" asked Farren.

"Centrust is going to topple. We're just there to record it."

"Predict it, you mean."

"It's already happening. The regulators want him to reduce the huge junk-bond portfolio he got from Milken. The IRS is hot on the scent. It's only a matter of time before the FDIC comes into the picture."

"The man has done a lot for Miami," said Farren. "He's very philanthropic, serves on some pretty prominent boards. When he took over Dade Savings and Loan, it was going down the tubes. Now it's more than tripled its assets. You don't think he did the depositors a great big favor?"

"The checks he's dropping are Centrust checks. He's living like there's no tomorrow. Better than that shiek with all the cats. He's got a seven-million-dollar yacht with a six-hundred-thousand-dollar state-of-the-art electronic system. Centrust has issued him three million dollars worth of mortgages. If you never saw that sprawling compound he lives in, you ought to go sometime. Did you make the bash he threw for the New World Symphony? A thirty-five-foot raw bar with eighteen hundred stone crab claws and fifteen hundred lobster tails."

"The downtown folks don't see it your way. There's a rumor that he'll be invited to join

672

the Non-Group." Farren changed the subject. He had caught Pupi being interviewed on Channel 10 during a measles epidemic at the Miccosukee reservation. Pupi looked good on camera, was witty, succinct, yet compassionate, said what had to be said with a certain brash style that worked.

When Farren put down his knife and fork, Pupi waited for the hustle. They were a conservative station, Farren began, looking to broaden their image. They needed someone young, someone articulate, someone who understood the news, someone Cuban.

"What are you earning now," Farren asked, "forty, forty-five thousand?"

"Something like that." Girls from the modeling agency in the portholed, mint green hotel next door ran down the steps carrying their impossibly oversized totes. One of the models wore her short, curly taffy-colored hair cut to the shape of her skull and carried a backpack. Her tanned cheekbones were broad, her eyes an unbelievable Caribe green.

"Pupi, are you listening? We'll start you at sixty thousand dollars. If things work out as I expect, that can be renegotiated in six months."

The girl ran to a waiting jeep parked between a photographer's van and a Winnebago belonging to a television commercial crew, threw her backpack into the rear seat, jumped up on the running board, and swung herself into the front seat. "I'll have to think about it."

"She's too tall for you. Think this instead. The *Herald* has a circulation of four hundred fifty thousand, more or less. We have a potential viewing audience of three million. There's an immediacy about reporting the news on television; it's live, it's now, it's the ultimate show and tell. It's not what *happened*, it's what's *happening*. When you write for a newspaper, you're one reporter in a stable; maybe the readers will see your piece, maybe they won't. But on TV if they're watching us, they're watching you. It's that simple. You'll be a star, Pupi, with face recognition. Everyone will know you on the street. Cops won't give you tickets. It may even be a stepping-stone."

"To what?"

"The networks."

"I'll let you know, Rick."

"You have a week to make up your mind. I ought to warn you. You'll have to fight the women off with a stick."

"Who told you?" Pupi put down his napkin. "Thanks for lunch. I've got to check out something next door."

"They won't give you her name, if that's what you're thinking."

"For how much?"

Pupi returned to the pink stucco house on Segovia to find his grandmother and his great-aunt Flavia, as usual, watching the Latin soaps.

On the coffee table beside a Lalique bowl stood an aerosol can labeled *Siete Potencias,* a santerismo potion with which Flavia sprayed her swollen legs. Flavia went to mass on Sunday, to the santero when she had a problem. If she kept a figure on an altar lit with candles, what did it matter if its name was Babalu Aye as long as the figure she was honoring happened to be the image of a Catholic saint?

They were discussing, in the breathless, gravel voice of age, how easily a villainess called Bernarda was pulling the wool over the eyes of a strikingly handsome Argentine actor named Jorge Martinez, who played the part of Fernando.

Hortensia tilted her cheek for her grandson's kiss. "Columba Bush also loves the evening telenovelas," she said. "So don't turn up your nose. The president's daughter-in-law revealed this to your mother. At a luncheon."

Pupi's elderly female relatives regarded him with the same puzzlement as they did a Fahrenheit thermometer that could go as high as 103, a reading that would be fatal on a centigrade, or when they discovered that Pupi, as other American school children, was learning to do his math backward, to write his answers above the number, not below and to the right as it was done in Cuba. They discovered such things in the days when, if Gloria Maraquilla could not come to school during lunch period, Hortensia or Flavia went instead to make sure that

Pupi was eating all his food. "None of the American mothers show up in the lunchroom," the boy complained, but someone appeared faithfully every day, standing silent and watchful, like the visions at Fatima.

At dinner, Flavia announced in her rapid-fire, machine-gun Cuban Spanish that when Gloria Maraquilla took them shopping to Calle Ocho, they listened to a lecture from a man on the street corner who said that Jimmy Carter really had been born in the Havana suburb of Santa Suarez.

Pupi waited until after dinner when they sat with tiny cups of dark, rich coffee that was as thick and as sweet as syrup. Nestor suggested that Pupi do a story on the argument waged on the newsstands among the various free newspapers like *La Verdad*, *La Nacion*, *El Expreso*, *Espectaculo*, *El Mantecero*, in which each hurled daily, well-aimed provocations at the other.

Pupi agreed that it would be a good idea for an editorial, but not for a feature story, then said that he wanted to get his own apartment. When he added that there was one on Brickell that he could rent, his grandparents, his elderly aunt, and his parents, particularly his mother, looked at him as if he had spit on the floor.

"Who will do your laundry?" asked his grandmother.

"I will."

Flavia laughed. "Ay, niño. First you have

to learn to pick up your clothes. Who will cook for you?"

Gustavo asked if Pupi's salary could support an apartment on Brickell. Hortensia pointed out that Pupi would be lonely.

Gloria Maraquilla was not speaking. She was hurt. How could he leave? Why would he want to leave? The Anglos, yes, they did such things, but that was to be expected. They didn't have the same feelings, the same sensibilities toward family. Was he getting married? Was there not enough room and then some for everyone? Did she not do everything in her power to make him comfortable? Where had she gone wrong?

Pupi changed his tack, announced that he had been offered a spot on television. Nestor said that he hoped he refused, that television was no place for a journalist. Gloria Maraquilla lifted her eyes from her folded, French-manicured hands. "You will have to have pale blue shirts made. You can't wear white on television. But then, why do I bother? You no longer need a mother's advice."

Hortensia smiled fondly at Pupi and said that he was handsomer than Jorge Martinez. Maybe not as tall, but better-looking by far.

"They don't want me for my looks," said Pupi.

"Of course they want you for your looks," said Flavia. "Why else do you think you were asked?"

The next time that Pupi, dressed in a tux and white Reeboks, saw the leggy model was on a Saturday night at the new Miami Arena for the Miami Heat's premier NBA game against the L.A. Clippers. The stadium in Overtown was jam-packed with a sell-out crowd of over fifteen thousand dressed in both black tie and in shorts, their excited faces chiaroscuroed with the broken light of blazing lasers and smoke from fog machines, and blasting fireworks that detonated in the ceiling baffles.

It was after Ben Vereen took center stage to sing "America the Beautiful" in the smoky semidarkness. Pupi noticed her sitting motionless in the middle of a rolling wave chanting, "Let's go, Heat! Let's go, Heat!" until the smoke from a fog machine hid her from view.

He caught up to her at halftime in the vestibule. She was wearing a gunmetal beaded tank top and olive drab silk pajamas as flimsy as the smoke that still trailed in the arena, the fabric lightly defining her spare, lean body. Large gold hoops swung from her ears.

"I'm Pupi Alvarez," he said, flashing his credentials. "I used to write for the *Herald*. Now I'm with Channel Four. Maybe you saw my series on dangerous docs. Not important. I'm taking a survey. What is your opinion of what is going on here tonight?"

Her eyes were wide and steady. "About what?"

"After the first four minutes, the sizzle seemed to go out of the Heat. What do you think? Opening night jitters?"

She thought for a moment. When she responded, it was in deadly earnest. "I don't know much about basketball except that until tonight the Clippers were the worst team in the NBA."

"That's good enough. What's your name?"

"Starlight."

"That sounds like a stage name. You pick it yourself?"

"It was my mom's idea." She turned on her heel.

Pupi wondered if she would be closer to his own height if she wore flats. He pushed his way after her in the crowd. She was at least two, maybe three inches taller. Pupi found himself inhaling deeply, as if to inflate himself, make himself lighter than air so that he might float upward and match her face to face.

"I saw you before," he said. "At the Wet Paint Cafe."

"I never eat there," she replied, looking down upon him as if he were an insect.

"*I* was at the cafe. *You* were coming down the steps of the hotel next door."

"So?"

"So, I thought you were very attractive. Don't tell me you mind that because I won't believe you. Why else are you in modeling if it isn't for admiration? Look, Starlight, when I saw you, I knew you were someone I wanted to talk to."

"What about?"

"Anything on your mind."

She ran her fingers through her crop of hair. Her neck seemed small, vulnerable. "Are you finished with your survey?"

A tuxedoed man with a shock of white hair appeared at her side with two soft drinks. "Is there some problem, Starlight?"

Pupi recognized the man as Bradford Watson and was surprised. Watson wasn't known for squiring young girls.

"No problem," she replied. "He's a reporter. He asked me some questions. I don't have anything more to say to him."

"Then let's get back to our seats," said Watson.

Pupi chased after them. "Wait," he said. "Don't you remember me? I'm Pupi Alvarez, Mr. Watson. I came to see you a few years back at the Sand Dollar. About the renovations."

Bradford smiled. "I didn't recognize you." He turned to Starlight. "I brought this young man and his family out of Cuba thirty years ago. How are they?"

"Fine, sir. Everyone's fine. I need to have a telephone number in case there's some question that needs clarification."

"Don't bother," said Starlight. "I don't have anything more to say."

Bradford shrugged his shoulders. "I'm afraid

680

my granddaughter is trying to tell you something, Mr. Alvarez. The interview is over." He took Starlight's elbow and led her away.

Pupi smiled. He liked the way she walked. She didn't undulate like most women did when they knew you were watching. Her stride was straightforward and smooth, a glide really, that pulled her shapely little butt right into her hamstrings. Pupi clenched his fist. "Yes!" he said, thinking that with or without that receptionist bitch at the agency, with or without Bradford Watson's cooperation, Bradford Watson's granddaughter, Starlight, would not be hard to find.

Starlight didn't know why she said yes. For one thing, he was too short. Even though he was good-looking, it was like being with a twelve-year-old. He came up to her ear, which meant she had to look down to talk. For another, he was cocky, arrogant, too sure of himself and too hyper, as pumped up as his eighteen-inch biceps. The third thing was that he was Cuban. Starlight didn't much like Hispanic men. They were macho, impossibly possessive, which became even worse once you went to bed with them. They either ran drugs or alluded to mysterious training in the Everglades that they couldn't discuss. She also held them responsible for the death of her mother. This last was not a conscious objection, just a negative sentiment lodged in the shadows of her mind.

She didn't agree to a serious date, just a quick meeting at the Cuban coffee counter on the second floor of Bayside, where the waitress wore a white carnation between her hair and her ear. It was a half-hour commitment at the most, something like the preliminary go-sees she went on where prospective clients had the opportunity to see her in person. She wasn't even going to drink the coffee.

He was waiting when she got there. He asked if she had seen him on television.

"I caught a few minutes. Your face was too shiny. You need to buy Max Factor Tan Number Two pancake makeup, put it on with a sponge, then dust it with translucent powder. I have some with me if you want to see it."

"I never use the stuff," he said.

She rolled the sleeves on her T-shirt. "Why not?"

"It wasn't in my job description."

"I don't know why anyone would want to go on camera with oily skin unless it was for a Clearasil commercial."

He turned his stool so that their knees touched. "Why don't you show me how?"

"Okay," she said. "I'll do what I can, but don't expect miracles in ten minutes."

He carried a paper cup filled with water to a bench on the bay, where she held his chin with one hand and made him up with the other. Their faces were inches apart. He held his breath. She held hers.

"Don't make it too obvious," he said. "I can't look like a fag."

"Are you?"

"If you were paying attention, you wouldn't ask that question."

She brushed off the excess powder, noticed that his lashes were dark and thick. "Some guys use eyeliner, but you don't need any. Didn't they tell you anything at the station?"

"Not to wear checks, especially houndstooth. It gives a wavy effect."

"You also need concealer to put under your eyes, but I don't have any." She glanced at her Patek Philippe watch, a gift from her grandfather. "I've got a trunk show at Saks. A favor for the designer." She tossed the makeup into her backpack, then slid her sunglasses over her temples and looked out over the opal bay, where a funnel of seabirds twirled in the air.

"What is it?" he asked. "What do you see?"

"A dolphin. There he goes again."

"Where?"

"He just jumped clear of the water, did a barrel roll in the air. If you didn't see that, you need glasses."

"How do you know it's a he?"

"The males are larger than the females. Nothing personal. And they have a more prominent dorsal fin." She began a hasty trot toward the parking garage.

He rushed to catch up. "Wait. When can I see you again?"

"Why should I see you again? Except for the fact that my grandfather helped your family get out of Cuba, I don't know anything about you."

"Sure you do. For openers, you know I can't be a dolphin even though I've been told that my dorsal fin is pretty special."

"Why do I get the feeling that you and your stupid jokes are not going to go away?"

"I get the same feeling."

"I don't like anyone to box me in."

"I'll give you all the space you need."

She agreed to go out with him a second time because he waited two weeks to call and he didn't ask her to wear flats as short men usually did. She dressed carefully for the event in black leather jeans, a white Hanes undershirt, and a motorcycle jacket she had brought back the summer before from St. Tropez. The look was macho, a declaration of the ability to go *mano a mano*. He took her to the toast-and-lilac-painted Marlin Hotel with its outside tables topped by lavender umbrellas. There, in the checkered cafe called Shabeen, they drank fresh pineapple juice squeezed with fresh ginger served by a waitress who looked like Nefertiti.

He wore Bermudas and Raybans, knew everyone, called them by their first names, including Robin Gibbs, whom Pupi said he considered a personal friend. Starlight was not impressed, just as she was not impressed that Pupi was seen nightly on television. Later when he came around the side of his Corvette, opened the door, told her he had a great time, and never tried to kiss her, she wondered if she was a cover or a trophy.

Pupi went out with other women with inevitable odious comparisons, too chatty, too coy, too flashy, too dark, too easy, too short, too eager, too loud. The only time he didn't think about Starlight was the night of Martin Luther King's birthday, during the melee that erupted in Overtown after a black motorcyclist was shot and killed by a Hispanic policeman.

When Pupi reached the scene with his cameraman, the victim lay in the gutter, covered with a white sheet. On either side of the street were empty lots and low-rise apartment houses where packs of cats roamed aimlessly and clotheslines flapped at odd angles, half concealing grafitti on the walls that read, DEATH TO DOPE PUSHERS and SMASH APARTHEID. A few blocks to the east, the Omni and the Plaza Venetia towers sparkled in the night.

The driver of the Buick into which the cyclist had crashed said that he had seen the cycle coming, saw the officer step into the street, take a combat stance and fire. "There was no chance to avoid a collision," he said into Pupi's stick mike. "The guy went flying through the windshield. His brains are splattered all over my dash. Glass was flying everywhere."

Mayor Suarez suddenly walked into the

bottle-throwing crowd with his jacket flung over his shoulder. "Roll on him," said Pupi, he and his cameraman following close behind until, pelted with a barrage of rocks and bottles, they were forced to retreat.

Things escalated quickly. Pupi's cameraman climbed onto a wrecked Buick to get a clear shot of police carrying riot shields, the mayor was escorted to his car by a cordon of young black men shouting, "You can't fuck with the mayor!" and Pupi got whacked on the eyebrow by a bottle.

"Party's over," he shouted as he and his cameraman sprinted for the van while the mob shattered the windshield of a car belonging to an Associated Press photographer. By the time they got into their vehicle and locked the doors, the mob had taken the A.P. photographer's camera equipment and was dousing his car with gasoline.

Pupi fumbled with the keys on his ring while the car across the street burst into flames and a man in a shower cap yanked on the door of the van.

The cameraman climbed over Pupi and grabbed the keys out of his hand. "You got too much property, baby."

He selected a key and gunned the ignition, while Pupi opened a window and thrust his stick mike at the man holding the door handle. "Say a few words," he shouted. The man was taken aback until the van jerked away, jumped a median strip, and turned squealing in the opposite direction.

"I'm gonna find out where you live!" the man in the shower cap shouted.

By the time Pupi returned to his apartment on Wednesday night, there were six messages blinking on his machine, three from his mother, one from the mayor's office, an anonymous threat from someone who said he knew where Pupi lived, and a message from Starlight, who said, "Your face is still too shiny, but that's probably because you were scared. Hope you're keeping out of trouble."

The purple bruise over his eyebrow that had turned the color of a ripe plum meant nothing. For all her offhand attitude, her bitchy, get-lost look, Starlight cared.

By March they still had not gone to bed even though he submitted himself to a blood test and an AIDS interrogation in which he revealed as much of his sex life as he could remember for the past ten years including a statement of preference.

Things came to a head at the Calle Ocho festival. He took her to the block party of one million people, a Latino Woodstock where they danced in a conga line with 119,000 people to the Miami Sound Machine's "Conga," whacked at a three-story-high piñata in the form of a sombrero, listened to an all-women group called Chicas Del Can and a Puerto Rican crooner named Lalo Rodriguez. They ate conch fritters, Nicaraguan beef on a stick, and paella from a two-hundred-pound vat. Pupi bought T-shirts with Fidel Castro's picture and the words, WANTED — DEAD OR ALIVE, which Starlight said that she would rather be dead than caught wearing. Pupi said he wished he had known. He might have given one to his mother instead except that now both shirts were too big.

"Give it to your father," she said.

Everywhere people were moving their arms and hips to salsa and the Brazilian Lambada, which seemed to come from every stage along the twenty-three block route. And everywhere Pupi went, he was recognized by smiling revelers who pranced about until they realized that there was no camera, like the group who danced on top of a yellow frozen lemonade truck as its roof slowly buckled.

Starlight wanted to stop at the booth of a palm reader named Madame Elena who promised to predict *el pasado, presente, y futuro.* Pupi translated. The woman's mustache was moist with perspiration. She said that Starlight was not a stranger to sorrow. That she would fall in love with a small dark man. A man who was *muy famoso.* Pupi didn't translate the part about Latino and gringa mixing like oil and water, but Starlight got the gist.

Later that night, they sat on the patio of the Clevelander Hotel on South Beach and listened to the band. Pupi was wearing shorts, and the plastic of the chairs stuck to the back of his legs.

"The psychic was right, wasn't she, when she said you're not a stranger to sorrow."

"I don't know what you mean."

"Starlight, the *Herald* has a file on your family. I know about your mother. I never wanted to bring it up. I was hoping you would. It was an awful thing to happen. I'm really sorry."

"I don't want to talk about it."

"Let's drop it, then. I'm sorry I mentioned it." He pulled his legs free of the seat. "This chair is driving me nuts," he said. "And so are you." He took her hand. Her nails were squared and polished with a clear shell pink polish. "I can't go on like this, Starlight. It's not normal."

"Then don't."

"Give me a break, baby. I'm so crazy about you I can't see straight."

"I knew this was going to happen," she said.

"You make it sound like something negative. What's wrong with what happened? What happened is great!" He put his hand down. "Don't tell me you're not into guys."

"What difference does it make? You'll never find out."

"Is that it? Do I turn you off?"

A girl with a Russian wolfhound on a leash stepped up to the bar. The outlines of her nipples against her tank top were as big as

689

silver dollars. Pupi never noticed her. His eyes were on Starlight.

She snapped her purse closed and slung it over her shoulder. "Pay the check."

"Now?"

"Now."

His apartment was immaculate. Freshly washed fruit, still dappled with beads of water, filled a Rose Medallion bowl.

"Who lives with you?" she asked.

"No one. What makes you say that?"

"It looks like someone's been cleaning here all day."

He laughed. "That's my mother's maid, Carmelita."

She pivoted as she might have on a runway. "Take off your clothes," she said.

He started peeling off his shirt, his socks, flinging them about the corners of the living room while she stood silently and watched.

"Starlight?"

"You first. Keep going."

"Jesus." He pulled off boxer shorts that were wildly printed with two boxers in a ring of vines, then stood naked while she sat on the sofa. "Do I pass?"

"You're not bad. But you're going to turn to fat by the time you're forty if you don't watch it."

"That's it," he said, collecting his clothes. "I don't need this bullshit. I don't like your games, Starlight." When he was almost dressed, she opened the long ties of her sarong-wrapped skirt and let it drop to the floor.

"I don't belong to you," she said, stepping out of a one-piece teddy. "This doesn't mean a thing."

"That's right," he said, stripping down a second time. "It means nothing, nada, zip."

He kissed her temples, her throat, the hollow of her belly, while his fingers circled her nipples. He noticed that they were the color of the periwinkles at his parents' front door as they might have looked in the moonlight. "Let's go into my bedroom," he whispered.

"I like it here."

"The bed is more comfortable, Starlight. This is a sectional."

"Stop trying to take control."

"Okay. Here."

She drew her long legs up, he pushed them apart, saw that her petaled vulva was moist, lowered himself slowly, poised to thrust, then entered. She looked away and moaned, her eyes half closed as he pinioned her arms over her head.

They shifted positions, trying to get at each other every way they could, once spilling onto the floor. After several hours they fell asleep curled like spoons in a drawer, except for her legs, which trailed over the edge of the sofa.

He awoke to find her dressing. "Where are you going?"

"Home," she said.

"Stay till morning. I'll make you American coffee."

"I want to wake up in my own place."

"Didn't tonight mean anything to you?"

"It was really good sex, Pupi."

"That's it?"

"Really, really good sex. Okay? But I need to get sleep. If I stay, I won't."

"Why? Because of this?" He stood behind her and ran his hands inside her thighs, then hooked his thumbs under the straps of her teddy and slipped it over her shoulders.

"Oh, God," she said, bending over the dining table where fruit still glistened in a Rose Medallion bowl.

The sky was pink with morning. Starlight's eyes were heavy-lidded, swollen with sleep. She awoke in Pupi's bed to find him staring.

"Starlight, you're so beautiful," he said. "Your skin gleams like sheet metal. All of you just shines."

"This doesn't give you an exclusive," she murmured, pulling him to her by the gold chain of his St. Francis medal.

He wrapped her in his arms. "Understood."

"You say it, but you don't mean it. The minute you ask who else I'm seeing, it's over."

"Fine." He nuzzled her neck, her ear. "Is he as good as me?"

"That's it, Pupi. I'm out of here." She jumped out of bed.

"I didn't ask who he was. I asked how he was."

She turned her head. "I smell coffee. Do you have it on one of those timers?"

"Oh-oh," he said. "Better get dressed."

When they came out of the bedroom, Nestor was seated at the dining table over a cup of coffee. Hortensia was in the kitchen setting out a plate of guava and cream cheese.

"These are my grandparents. Abuela, Abuelo, this is my friend Starlight."

"From the looks of things," said Hortensia, "I would say she was a very good friend. I threw out the pizza, niño. The cheese was like leather. I brought you some picadillo." She turned to Starlight. "All you have to do, niña, is heat it up."

Starlight turned to Pupi, who shrugged with a smile. "My family is very close," he said.

A few weeks later, Pupi brought Starlight to the stucco house on Segovia to meet his family. The meeting was as stiff as Nestor's collars. The maid served carbonated pineapple Jupina, a coconut soda called Cocorico, and a beverage called Materva, which Pupi described as a cream soda with zing. Starlight sat on the sofa and crossed her long, elegant legs. Gustavo and Nestor tried not to notice the golden skin of her thighs. They were exceedingly polite, his mother all gentle smiles and soft whispery words of welcome. Pupi returned the next day armed for a postmortem.

"What kind of name is Starlight?" asked Gustavo. "It seems very fanciful."

"Stagey and artificial," said Nestor. "As garish as a neon sign."

"I think her name is suited to her," said Pupi, determined not to lose the battle in the first skirmish.

"We owe a lot to her grandfather, but it is the girl we worry about," said Gloria Maraquilla. "How did her parents die?"

"Her mother died in the Bahamas. In a boating accident."

They made the sighs, the sympathetic exclamations, the ai-ai's of commiseration, then returned to the issue. "And the father?"

"I forgot to ask," said Pupi.

"A girl without family," said Gloria Maraquilla, trailing the sentence as she might a fishing line.

"Not without family," said Pupi. "You know her grandparents. They are very well respected in the community."

"Yes, but they are Anglos," said Gloria Maraquilla.

"You have only to look at her to know that," said Flavia.

"A man should look down on a woman," said Nestor. "She is taller than you."

Pupi smiled. It was time to turn on the

charm. "My biceps are bigger."

"She doesn't understand Cubanismo," said Gloria Maraquilla. "She will give you TV dinners at six and think that you will be satisfied."

"She'll learn. You should see her maneuver her way through Calle Ocho."

"She's not Catholic. You would be marrying a Protestant."

"Not exactly," said Pupi. "As I understand it, her grandmother is Jewish and her grandfather is Protestant. That makes her mother half-Jewish. I don't know about her father."

"It doesn't make any difference what the father was," said Gloria Maraquilla. "The thing is complicated enough." She did not articulate what was really on her mind, the secret that she had confided to Gustavo, that Bradford Watson had had a long-time affair with her cousin Lilia, and her concern that lack of moral commitment ran in the family.

"What about this career of hers, this modeling? Will she want to continue?" asked Gustavo.

"We haven't gotten that far yet," said Pupi. He felt like the man who walked around Calle Ocho with a photograph of Batista hung around his neck. He was committed and he wanted the whole world to know. "I can't tell you anything else except that I love her. I want to marry her."

"This is what comes from taking his own

apartment," said Hortensia.

"I thought you'd be happy that I want to marry Watson's granddaughter," said Pupi. "You always say how much you owe him."

"I owe him something, yes," said Gloria Maraquilla, "but not my son."

"Have you asked her yet?" asked Flavia.

Pupi shook his head.

Flavia stroked Gloria Maraquilla's arm. "There's hope," she said.

Pupi left, thinking that the argument was like the one with the news director, who wanted him to tone down his ties, get some shirts that buttoned down at the collar. That's not my style, he told him. If you want Brooks Brothers, hire Brooks Brothers. Everyone wanted him to be something other than he was. Nobody seemed to get it, that he was both Cuban and American, gifted with American know-how, seasoned with Latin *sabor*.

They turned off *David Letterman* and dressed for a late-night fashion show at Club Nu, where Starlight had a free membership. She put on a pitch-black Lycra minidress and told Pupi that the *Miami Vice* look was out, that he could no longer wear a T-shirt under his jacket, much less an open shirt exposing chest and chains. She dressed him herself in a Hugo Boss shirt buttoned to the neck.

Club Nu was gaudy, giddy with excess, and packed with Miami's glamour fashion industry, international editors, photographers, stylists, makeup artists, and boutique owners, each making a statement. Revolving on the turning stage were models with hair-covered styrofoam balls on their heads, surrounded by smoke from a fog machine and body builders dressed in Mylar space pants. A screen behind them projected the planets.

"What's the point of models watching models?" Pupi asked.

"We all feed off our energy and that's how a scene happens. Part of the scene is the owners of the boutiques, the models, the hairdressers who create the styles to go with the new clothes. It overlaps."

"Why are we here at one in the morning? Why aren't we overlapping in bed?"

"I'm trying to explain it to you, Pupi. If you'd listen, you'd get it. We're all individuals with something to offer, and we all want to share it. Fashion is one way we do it. It's instant. It has impact. It's as close to you as your skin."

"I'm close to you, Starlight. I want to get even closer." He found a table on an upper tier. Starlight ordered a Perrier with a twist. "You can't take this too seriously," he said.

"What do you mean?"

"Basically this is empty, surface. All hype and glitz. It may be duded up and polished to a shine, but it's plastic. It's not the real world."

"You think you know the real world but I don't?"

"I think you've been sheltered."

"I was born in a commune," she said.

"What are you talking about?"

New Age sounds rocked the room. "You said you wanted to get closer. I mean my mom and I lived with a bunch of people in some farmhouse. Or shack. Someone was always playing the guitar. I don't know which one my father was. I was four or five when my grandfather came to get us. I thought you ought to know."

"Did you think it would make a difference?"

"It might."

"You sure pick your time."

"Are you all right? You look funny."

"I'm okay. It's just a shocker. You came at me from left field. It just takes getting used to." The waitress set down their drinks. "What was it like?"

"I was afraid a lot, mostly of some man. I don't remember what he looked like. Just that he had hair on his chest that reached his neck. He used to come at night to our mattress. My mother carried me across the room to sleep near someone else. He used to punish me on the front steps. My mother watched. I remember trying to turn my head. I thought that if she saw me crying, she would make him stop. But she didn't."

"Jesus."

"I try to remember more, but I can't. A friend told me to write down my free associations in a journal. I did it for a while. But it looked like such a crazy jumble, I got scared and I stopped."

"Starlight, whatever happened, happened. You'll never know the truth because there's no one to check it out with. We can't do anything about yesterday. Ask my father about that sometime. It's today that counts. It's you and me. What made you decide to tell me now?"

"My grandfather said I should."

Pupi sweated through his entire meeting with Bradford and Sandra, even though the Watsons were gracious hosts who acted as if they couldn't care less that he was screwing their grand-daughter blind.

Nothing had been easy, starting with the sentry at the gate who took down Pupi's license tag. Bradford, beginning to get the slat-assed look of an aging WASP, was polite but distant. When he enumerated the leadership positions occupied by Cuban Americans — the United Way, the County Bankers Association, the Dade County School Board — Pupi began to suspect that he was being patronized.

Not even Starlight, who chatted with her grandfather in the private shorthand they used between them, helped. It was Sandra who finally came to Pupi's aid, strolling with him after dinner beside the seawall, where boats on winches hung suspended over the water.

"They're very close," she said.

"I know. That's the way it is in my family."

"I understand Starlight has told you of her early years, which is why I am sure you will understand my husband's concern for her future. He wants her to have a beautiful life. The life to which we both think she is entitled. He would like for her to see a little of the world, finish her education before she takes on the responsibility of marriage."

"I plan to give her a beautiful life."

"Starlight is still very young. She is not quite twenty-one. It would be easier if you would agree to wait a few years."

"We're either going to live together or get married. Those are the choices."

"I see. Starlight might have told you that she has a modest trust. You should know that other than her income from modeling, she can't touch the principal until she reaches thirty."

"Starlight never told me she had serious bucks. That puts a new face on it."

"In what way, Mr. Alvarez?"

"It'll make my family come around a whole lot faster."

If the Watsons were lukewarm about the match, Pupi's family was frankly opposed; still, they felt it their responsibility to host an engagement party. Invitations were extended to distant cousins whom Pupi remembered only as a pair of shoes, a belly, a chin wart, a smell.

The question arose whether to invite Emma, Gloria Maraquilla's cousin, Lilia's half-sister, and Emma's son, Ray Gopher. Starlight thought it would be an awesome inclusion. Hortensia and Nestor disagreed. The party would take on the aspects of a sideshow. Lilia's consanguinity extended only through Marta, and the guest list was already beginning to be staggering. Flavia, chastened after a humiliating arrest at a Santeria ritual, declined an opinion. "It was my knee," she explained to anyone who would listen. "If it was not so swollen, I never would have gone. And I have never known them to use animals before. Personally, I am shocked."

A compromise solution was agreed upon, which was to send an invitation to the reservation, the only address they had, but not follow it up with a phone call.

The Alvarezes decided against holding the reception at the Big Five Club in West Dade, opting instead to have it catered at home. Gloria Maraquilla, for whom Raoul Arango was designing a cocktail suit trimmed in bugle beads for fifteen hundred dollars, said it was impossible to plan such an event. November was a treacherous month, often rainy, sometimes windy, always unpredictable. Tents were known to blow away, chafing dishes to blow out, high heels to sink into the ground like golf tees. Besides, it would be like giving two parties. Cubans came late. Anglos came early. Cubans liked to party long and hard. Anglos left early so they could go jogging in the morning. Cubans preferred Chivas Regal scotch and oysters Rockefeller, Anglos, champagne and pâté.

They settled on a menu that included crab claws, asparagus salad, avocado and pineapple salad, plantains in a chafing dish of brown sugar, loin of pork stuffed with prunes, dates, and guava, paella and prime ribs, very well done, followed with a Viennese dessert table that would include flan and bread pudding with rum custard sauce. The party for three hundred would cost, excluding the photographer, two sets of hand-addressed invitations in Spanish and in English, flowers, valet parking, security, a lighting technician, a Plexiglas cover for the pool with lights beneath, and a tent with its poles wound with satin and twinkling lights, twenty thousand dollars.

Gloria Maraquilla told Pupi to request that his fiancée wear flats.

"She won't do it," he said.

"Of course she'll do it. Tell her she must."

"You can't make Starlight do what she doesn't want to do. Besides, what difference does it make?"

"Think of the photographer if you think of no one else."

There were other vagaries. Starlight refused to wear an engagement ring. Instead the couple bought a pair of diamond studs that each placed in an ear. Gloria Maraquilla saw custom and protocol slipping away, the wedding turning into everything that was wrong with the United States. "Next, she will not want to wear white, and it will be my son who throws the bouquet."

Gustavo told his wife to concentrate on the party. "If you think about anything else," he said, "you will drive yourself crazy."

After a few false starts, the tent went up, the Plexiglas dance floor was laid over the pool, ice swans breathed vapor into the late November afternoon, and the salsa band unpacked its guido, casada, maracas, timbales, and bongo. The first guests stood in isolation, as rooted as the shrubbery. Then, pressing their glasses to their lips for support, they danced around one another, do-si-do-ing in a rigid, bicultural pas de deux.

Starlight tottered across the grass, clinging to Pupi's arm for support, wearing an old, ratty mink jacket that belonged to her great-grandmother Maude. Shaved across the back in large letters were the words ANIMALS ARE NOT FOR KILLING.

She introduced herself to Lilia, said she remembered driving past her house after the Nebraska game. Denver McCloud appeared with two drinks in his hand. "You're looking at the former Miss Bronze Miami," he said.

"When was that?" asked Starlight.

"You don't want to know, sugar," said Lilia. "I won a screen test and an all-expenses-paid trip to the Bahamas. My daddy wouldn't let me do either one. You know how they are."

"Actually, I don't. I never had one."

Lilia remembered something about Bradford having to fetch his daughter back from someplace or another. Had she had a child then? Lilia didn't recall. "Everybody has one. Even a bullfrog. You just never got to know yours. Don't feel bad, though. They're not all they're cracked up to be. They can get in the way. Especially when you got yourself some plans."

Pupi led Starlight away. "I don't think you should go around saying that. That you never had a father."

"Why not? It's true."

"This just isn't the time or the place. It puts people off. Makes them uncomfortable."

"Did I make you uncomfortable that night at Club Nu?"

"Yes."

"Then you lied to me. You said it was okay."

"It was, is okay. But blurting it out is not the way to tell people."

"How did you tell your parents?"

"I didn't. I'm working up to it."

"What's the problem?"

"There is no problem."

Starlight's eyes flashed over his face like strobes. "You're a coward. You're afraid of what they'll say."

"That's not true."

704

"Then prove it. Tell them."

"I will."

"When?"

"Tomorrow."

"Today. Tell them today."

"Give me a break, Starlight."

Sandra walked toward them, on the arm of ballet impresario Edward Vilella, who brushed a stray lock back from his forehead, then held out both his hands in greeting.

Starlight turned on her heel. "I don't know which I hate more," she said to Pupi, "you or ballet."

A heated discussion broke out over Nelson Mandela's refusal to repudiate Fidel Castro. At issue was a hotel and convention boycott by local African-American activists, triggered by the official silence of Miami, the only community in Mandela's eight-city tour of the United States that did not extend to him a hero's welcome.

"By this time next year," said Denver, to the small cluster that had gathered about him, "it's going to cost Dade County between five million and twenty-five million dollars."

Bradford said it was time for the boycott leaders to declare partial victory and come to the negotiating table. After all, Mayors Daoud of Miami Beach, Clark of Metro, and Suarez of Miami had all expressed regrets.

"Regrets but no apologies," said Denver.

Nestor was unforgiving. "How can you apologize to a man who has shaken the hand of Fidel Castro?"

Pupi ran to instruct the band to turn up its amps. What the liquor started, as per Gustavo's instructions to his bartenders to hit his guests hard and hit them fast, the music would finish off. Pupi's idea of loosening up a party came from his conviction that it was humanly impossible to ignore salsa, that it was programmed into everyone's biorhythms, even Anglos, once they pulled the ramrods from their asses. He and his father were both right. Within an hour the paseo had turned into a pas des bourree.

When Lilia and Bradford found themselves spun face to face, it was Lilia who spoke first. "Hello, Brad," she said.

"Lilia."

"How are you? I heard you had a bypass."

"As good as new. You?"

"Getting by. I guess neither of us can say the other looks the same."

"I guess not."

"I hate that bullshit."

He smiled. "I know you do. How's your memory?"

She dropped her voice to a purr. "If you mean do I remember that you can't beat time for shit, that you used to use butch wax to make your hair stand up like a brush, and that you had this thing about closing the blinds, the answer is fine." She smiled. "How's yours?"

"Short-term's getting frayed. Long-term is

great. Anything locked in there is as safe as in a bank vault. As shiny and as wonderful as when it was new only not quite as sharp."

She straightened his tie. "It was a long time ago."

"It was yesterday. I hear you're living with McCloud. You happy?"

"Can't complain."

"That's when it's good, I suppose."

"You and I, Brad, we had a different kind of good. But it was like going around all the time with your finger in a socket. I don't know about you, but I've gotten too old for that stuff."

She touched his arm. He was surprised and almost relieved that he felt nothing other than the warm pressure of her hand. Then suddenly she was swept up in the crowd, and he found himself being introduced to Gloria Maraquilla's bridge partner.

When the Viennese dessert table was rolled out, Ray Gopher arrived alone, wearing a string tie and his steel gray hair slicked straight back. He was shy, silent, moving on the periphery of the thinning crowd. He had come on the bus. He told Lilia that his mother, Emma, had died, that he spent part of his time in the Everglades, part on the reservation. He came, he said, because their old ones were woven together and he would not break the strand.

Pupi asked him how the lawsuit over the tribe's right to hunt panthers was going.

Starlight interrupted. "I don't think an Indian or anyone else has the right to harm endangered species," she said.

Ray Gopher answered her slowly, gently. "Federal treaties written over a hundred years ago give us the right to hunt on our reservations. We don't hunt like the white man. We use the panther for food and medicine."

Pupi rushed in before Starlight could make another pitch for the environment. "I hear that the Seminole tribe over at Big Cypress is bringing in antelope. I understand they expect to charge as much as two thousand dollars a kill. Will the Miccosukee do the same?"

"You will have to ask Bo Charlie," said Ray Gopher. "My son knows all such things." Ray Gopher didn't want to talk, nor did he tell them what his grandfather had told him, that all this land had once been part of the Pahahokee. He wanted to feel the old rhythms, smell the old smells, listen to the old sounds that often lingered the way ripples spread in the water, but the young man and his woman kept talking, holding off the ancient heartbeat with their peevish chatter.

"What a nice idea," Sandra said to Bradford on their way out. "Someone thought to invite a Seminole. Will he dance, do you suppose?"

"He's the son of Lilia's half-sister."

"Who is Lilia? I know you told me, but I forgot."

"Lilia is Pupi's mother's first cousin."

"This isn't what I had in mind for Starlight," Sandra said as she handed the valet their car check.

"It's not the wedding yet," said Bradford. "People change their minds, especially twenty-one-year-old girls."

"Speaking of the wedding," she said, "you can't imagine where Starlight wants to hold the wedding supper. A place called Big Fish, on the Miami River, with a tin roof, she tells me, and with barrel seats and tables made out of spools of cable wire. She told me it was a compromise, the only way she would agree to an engagement party. Who is Lilia Sands? I've heard of her before."

"She used to be a performer."

"In Miami?"

"Mostly in Europe. Lilia is black."

"So I gathered, although she could pass if she wanted to. I could never understand why they call themselves black when they're as white as we are."

A valet squealed their Mercedes to a stop and jumped out, leaving their radio tuned to an anti-Castro Cuban talk show.

"Will you drive, Sandra?" said Bradford. "I'm tired."

Chapter Thirty-Five

The rain was driven in silver sheets over the sliding balcony doors of Pupi's Brickell Avenue apartment. Even the choppy bay below flashed with silver. Pupi turned to his mother, who sat at his butcher block kitchen table composing a list. "Starlight has something to tell you."

"Ay, por Dios," said Gloria Maraquilla, her eyes on the girl's flat, concave belly.

"I don't have a father," said Starlight.

Relieved, Gloria Maraquilla reached out to take Starlight's hand. "We know that, dear."

"I will try to take his place," said Gustavo.

"That's not what I mean," said Starlight, securing the back of her diamond stud. "I mean I have one, but he doesn't acknowledge me. I tried to call him. My grandfather told me not to, but I did anyway. He said he didn't remember anyone named Eulalie, told me that Xerox repairmen didn't make much money and not to call him again."

"It means nothing to me," said Pupi. "I love Starlight. I want to marry her."

"Did you know about this?" asked Gloria Maraquilla. Pupi nodded his head. "And you never thought it important enough to tell us?"

"I don't see this as a problem," said Gustavo. "Don't make it one."

"What will everyone say?" asked Gloria Maraquilla. "Others are not so forgiving."

"Others are more forgiving than you suspect," said Gustavo, his eyes intent on hers. "Besides, there really is no need for anyone else to know."

"Yes, there is," said Starlight.

"There's the problem," said Pupi. "Starlight doesn't believe in keeping anything hidden."

"You have only to look at the length of her skirt to see that," said Gloria Maraquilla to her husband in the privacy of the elevator.

Bradford and Sandra invited Pupi's family to sit in their box at the Lipton Tennis Tournament on Key Biscayne. It did not go well for reasons other than the unfortunate history that Starlight had revealed to Pupi's parents. Gloria Maraquilla did not like facing into the sun, Gustavo's beeper kept going off, and Sandra sat behind dark glasses and smiled at no one. When Bradford suggested that because of the differences in religious observances, only a judge officiate at the wedding, the tension strung up everyone as tight as the net.

Between games, Starlight chatted about a reception at Viscaya for Queen Elizabeth and Prince Philip in which Governor Chiles presented the royal couple with a conch shell and a jar of orange blossom honey, and elderly author Marjorie Stoneman Douglas arrived wearing a bright red straw hat and a white lace dress.

"She dresses like Madonna and she's 101," said Starlight. "That proves you don't have to look tacky like Elizabeth just because you're old."

Gloria Maraquilla turned in her seat. "How would you dress the Queen of England?" she asked.

"I'd change the way she carries her purse, for one thing. Someone ought to get her a bag with a shoulder strap."

"What I would like to know is how does one curtsy so deeply without falling? I could never sink my knee that low, even when I was young," asked Pupi's grandmother Hortensia.

"I didn't curtsy," said Starlight. "I was afraid a curtsy would split my skirt, so I bowed."

"Bowed how?" asked Nestor.

"Low, like Pupi."

After the matches, they had supper in a hospitality tent with plastic sides. Fits and starts of conversation sputtered like fat in a frying pan. The families discussed where the young couple would live. Bradford was opposed to renting, in favor of building equity instead. As a trustee of Starlight's endowment, he was prepared to approve the purchase of a house, depending on the property. Gloria Maraquilla suggested Coral Gables. There was a house for sale right behind them. Sandra recommended Cocoplum, where many young couples with means were buying homes. Pupi preferred his apartment at Brickell, where he had just installed a Yamaha remote-control AM/FM CD disc system with Dolby Surround-sound. Starlight wanted to live on a houseboat.

Bradford said he knew of a house. It had not yet been given historic designation by the Miami City Commission because the present owner had not consented. But he had been keeping an eye on it. The owner, who had gotten a little help from the zoning board, intended to use the property for something more profitable than a single-family residence. He was planning to demolish the house — in fact, a permit of demolition had been issued — but he had just been indicted for income tax evasion, and everything was on hold.

"Oh, no," said Sandra. "I hope you're not thinking of what I think you are."

"What is that, Grandfather?"

Bradford pushed back from the table, a general about to place his pins on the war map. "The house my grandparents built."

"Bradford," said Sandra. "You can't be serious. It's a shack. A cabin."

"It's a frame vernacular," he said, "a common form of wood construction made in the early years of settlement in south Florida. There's not too many nineteenth-century post-and-beam frame houses left in Miami. Tall ceilings, exposed rafter ends, protective overhangs, porches, history."

"I remember the house," said Starlight. "You took me there that night after the U of M played Nebraska."

Gloria Maraquilla knit her finely plucked brows and turned to Sandra. "Is something wrong?"

"My husband has a romantic notion about the old house his grandparents built. If it isn't rotted to the ground, they'll have to spend a fortune to get it to look right, smell right. Not to mention the fact that Coconut Grove has become a dangerous place to live."

"The point is," said Bradford, "it's not rotten at all. It's made of Dade County pine. There isn't any around anymore. The wood is impervious to termites, rot, even fire."

"With all due respect," said Gustavo. "There are so many beautiful houses. Why saddle the young people with the headaches of restoration?"

"How old is old?" asked Pupi.

"One hundred years, more or less," said Bradford. "And if you ask for historic designation, there are certain tax advantages in the restoration."

"Your cousin Lilia lived there," said Starlight.

"How do you know that?" asked Pupi.

"I saw her after the Nebraska game," said Starlight. A quick glance at her grandfather making her regret that she had said anything at all.

"Starlight, dear," said Sandra, "no one can make a positive identification in the dark. As for remembering someone's face years later, it's more likely that Lilia Sands only resembled the woman who lived there."

"Starlight remembers correctly," said Bradford.

Sandra turned to her granddaughter with a quizzical smile. "How did you have occasion to meet Lilia Sands?" she asked.

"She came out to the car," replied Starlight.

"How odd. I would think that in Miami no one would approach a strange automobile at night."

Sandra stirred coffee in a styrofoam cup. "Can you remember what she said?"

Starlight invented the lie on the spot. "She told us not to block the driveway."

Bradford looked up from the paper napkin that he had creased into pleats. "All I ask," he said to Pupi, "is that you look at the house with an open mind."

The next day, Starlight and Pupi clumped over the curb in their roller blades. Each wore knee pads, elbow pads, and a helmet. "I don't care how high the ceilings are," said Pupi, pushing aside an overgrown oleander bush. "The place is a dog. We'd be buying nothing but trouble."

"I don't want it either," said Starlight, "but

I promised my grandfather I would take a look."

A salvage truck was parked in the driveway, where two men in undershirts were carting away a pair of wooden shutters. Inside the house were another two men, one, wearing a bill cap, standing in the middle of the empty floor with his hands on his hips, the other with a crowbar, knocking free a decorative wooden door jamb from the plaster that held it in place.

"What's going on?" asked Pupi.

"You the owners of the property?"

"No," said Pupi, careful to avoid the glass-fronted kitchen cabinets stacked against the wall.

"Then get out. I don't need sightseers on roller skates. You stick around, you're gonna get hurt."

Pupi pulled out his press card. "I'm with Channel Four."

The man held out his hands, palms up. "I have a permit to do this," he said. "They're gonna bulldoze this thing next week. I've got seven days to get whatever I can before they bash down the walls."

The two men in undershirts appeared in the kitchen doorway carrying a cast-iron porcelain sink. They stopped to stare at Starlight.

"Wait," she said, spinning around on the narrow blades. "Where are you going with all that stuff?"

"They're putting it in the truck," said the man in the bill cap. "Salvage is a business. I bid a job. For a flat price I get a week to remove the contents for resale. Tomorrow we'll steam off this wall covering section by section. It's hand painted. You can see for yourself. The day after that I'm taking down the banister."

Starlight glanced about the house. The ceilings were high, yet the rooms were small and the floors dipped just as her grandfather said they did. Everywhere was the faint odor of pine. "Where is the mantel?" asked Starlight. "There must have been a fireplace mantel."

"Right you are, sweetheart. Hand-carved and in perfect condition. It's in the truck. I have a buyer for it sight unseen. A penthouse on Brickell."

"Hold it," said Starlight. "Just cool your buns. Pupi, stop them."

"This man has legitimate business, Starlight. There's nothing we can do."

"Maybe you can't do anything, but my grandfather can." She skated across the floor. Pupi skated behind her as the salvager told someone named Ramirez to get on a ladder and take down the copper gutters and downspouts.

Pupi caught up to her in front of a house made of coral rock. "Stop zipping around like a pinball. I'm not the one with a crowbar."

"I want the house."

"You're crazy, Starlight. Think about what you're saying."

"I am."

"What about the houseboat? I thought you wanted to live on a houseboat."

"I changed my mind."

"Well, I didn't. The house is an old piece of shit that's better off torn down. It's no place for us to live."

"Maybe it isn't for you, but it is for me."

He took off his helmet and wiped the sweat from his forehead with his forearm. "This is some kind of crazy thing that has to do with your grandfather." He caressed her cheek. "I admire your loyalty, but you don't need to live in an old shack to prove that you love him."

"It's not him. It's me. I belong here. My great-great-grandparents built this house. You know how far back that goes? It goes back forever, practically to the Civil War. I'm a bead that someone dropped from a string. But not with this house. With this house, it's like I'm threaded. And it's not a shack."

"You really mean this."

"I do."

Pupi dropped his hand. "You know who I'm mad at? I'm mad at your mother. I can't help it, Starlight. All of this bullshit that's in your head comes from her tear-assing around the country so she could screw you up for the rest of your life. Don't get me wrong. I don't care about her not being married to your father like my mother does. I just care about what she did to you."

"You're an asshole, Pupi. And you're short. You're a short asshole that I never want to see again. And it has nothing to do with the fact that your family talks with their hands or that they're never on time."

By the time Bradford obtained a restraining order blocking demolition of the pine house on the grounds of historic preservation, the hand-painted wall covering and the banister were off, as was the wedding.

Later in August on a Saturday morning, a distant swirl of wind designated as tropical storm Andrew, one of several spawned yearly off the West African coast, was described as a developing storm that needed watching. Rapidly growing stronger, with a steady wind speed of seventy-five miles per hour nearest the center and a change of direction from northwest to westward, Andrew was given hurricane status as civil defense coordinators, gathered in thick-walled bunkers, reviewed preliminary evacuation plans.

Starlight spent the morning collecting remnants of Pupi, shave cream, tube socks, tapes of Willi Chirino's salsa, Honey-Nut Cheerios that she tossed into the trash bag. The television set was on. When she heard Pupi's low, resonant voice, and looked up to see him report from the Hurricane Center, where Kate Hale, who headed Metro Dade's emergency agency, was confirming shelter availability, tears stung the back of her throat. Starlight turned off the set, then packed her workout bag and went to the Paradise gym to add definition to her deltoids. Pumping iron helped her take her mind off the breakup, which Sandra told her over and over again was all to the good. When the locker room attendant handed her a towel and told her that there was nothing left in the stores, Starlight nodded absently, concentrating instead on her refusal to think of Pupi.

By Saturday night, the hurricane grew in strength and speed, chewing its way across the warm waters of the Atlantic toward south Florida's long, vulnerable coast. A hurricane watch had been posted from Titusville south to the Dry Tortugas for the storm that had been elevated to a category three with a pre-dicted storm surge of seven to nine feet. Brad-ford called to say that he was taking the Hatteras up the Miami River early in the morning before they closed all the bridges for evacuation, and that he needed her to help him with the lines.

The day was sunny, calm, with an absence of air currents. Starlight drove beneath the ar-cade of banyans on Old Cutler Road to her grandparents' waterfront home on the finger of land known as Gables Estates, where a handy-man was wedging wood in the tracks of the sliding-glass doors and a yard man tossed lawn furniture into the pool. Dressed in shorts and T-shirt, Sandra stuck her head out the door to announce she had turned the refrigerator to the coldest setting and that no one was to turn it back. When she saw Starlight, she blew her a kiss, then retreated into the house to carry paintings into the laundry room.

Bradford was at the dock, preparing to take his fifty-six-foot Hatteras to a safe berth up the Miami River. He had lowered the antennae, had disconnected his water hose and his power lines, now climbed up the bridge ladder to unscrew the Bimini top. "Don't you listen to the radio?" he asked. "Someone from my office called to tell me the highways are jammed all the way to Orlando. We've been trying to get you all day."

Starlight jumped aboard, climbed up to the bridge, and kissed his weathered cheek, thinking that he looked good for a man over seventy. "It will probably turn like they all do, wobble its way to Cuba or someplace. Where's your sun hat?"

They lowered the Bimini top, screwed it back into place, then trussed it up in a weave of lines to prevent the wind from ripping the canvas. Starlight scrambled to the deck below to slip free the mooring lines while Bradford started the engines. Exhaust gurgled in the waters behind them as they pulled away from the dock and headed north for the Miami River.

"Is Grandmother making you do this?"

"It's the prudent thing to do, Starlight. I've seen too many boats in my time smashed against their docks or lifted off their moorings."

They cruised through blue-green waters past mangrove-banked estates where homeowners were nailing boards on windows, rolling down storm shutters, trimming trees and bushes, hoisting boats out of the water. Bradford waved to a man securing a tarpaulin wrap over his car while with the other hand he steered between the channel markers. "Your grandmother and I are confident that this breakup is the best thing that could have happened. We think the whole thing was premature and rushed. You haven't said otherwise, so I presume you no longer want the house."

"Why wouldn't I want it? Just because I'm not getting married doesn't mean I don't want it. I plan to go there after we get this in its slip."

"We haven't closed on the house yet, which means you have no legal right to be there, assuming you could get in. Besides, I'm opposed to you staying anywhere alone until this thing blows over."

"I'm not staying. I just want to check on it. You can bet the owner isn't doing anything to keep it from getting trashed."

Bradford turned the radio up. Someone was advising listeners to assemble their important papers, get bleach, plywood, leave the area immediately, stay off the roads, not to panic, and to caulk up their bathtubs. "If I remember, the house doesn't have all its shutters. You'll have to buy duct tape for windows that are

722

unprotected. Don't stay one minute longer than you have to. They expect this thing sometime after midnight. I certainly want you with us long before that. The house is not a living thing, Starlight. More important, the property is still the responsibility of its present owner."

Starlight put an affectionate arm around his waist and reminded him that the present owner had no interest in the historic value of the house, in fact would have razed it to the ground if Bradford had not intervened. "Besides," she added, "you're talking like a lawyer. It doesn't matter who has the deed. The house belongs to me. It's as much mine as my nose or the color of my hair."

They passed Viscaya, rounded Brickell Key, and entered the mouth of the Miami River, where Bradford was careful to avoid the shallow waters of the southern bank, one of the armada of sailboats and power craft heading for the sanctuary of the narrow, winding waterway.

When they reached the dock space north of the 12th Avenue bridge that had been reserved for Bradford at Merrill Stevens, Sandra was waiting for them in her car. A dock hand ran out to inflate the extra fenders, secure them to the craft, while Bradford and Starlight made taut the lines.

Bradford turned to his granddaughter. "I'm counting on you to be smart. And get your gas tank filled."

Starlight swung her Jeep north on Old Cutler Road and fought a steady stream of traffic to reach the old pine house on the street behind the coral rock bluff. She parked in the weed-choked driveway beneath the canopy of the banyan. Someone nearby was using a chain saw sending branches rustling through the treetops to the ground below.

Rotten avacados littered the yard. Starlight made her way behind a tangle of leggy crotons, overgrown oleander, and sweet-candy-scented acacia, then turned the knob of the kitchen door. She was glad to find it unlocked which saved her the trouble of breaking through the screen. She stepped over the splintered threshold as someone yelled to someone else in a shrubbery-shrouded cottage nearby to fill the bathtub.

The house smelled of pine and mildew, its silence broken by the creaking floorboards and the echoes of her footsteps that bounced off the cobweb-shrouded beams.

The salvagers had stripped away all they could, the fireplace mantel, the glass-fronted kitchen cabinets, the banister from the staircase, even a hand-painted panel that Bradford said had been commissioned long ago by his uncle's wife, Paula, was torn from a dining room wall, revealing mildewed tatters of an ivy-patterned wallpaper beneath. For some reason they had forgotten the cast-iron kitchen sink which, removed from its mountings, leaned against a wall.

Starlight had fleeting memories of another vacant house where people had slept on mattresses, where her mother cowered before a big, faceless man, where a sheriff's deputy had scooped her under his arm as if she were a football. She cleared her mind, pushing aside these recollections as she set her jaw and reminded herself that there was work to do.

With nothing to safeguard within the house, Starlight ran outside to close the shutters, fastening them with rusty hooks that scraped into place. A sound truck blared from the street, advising everyone east of U.S. 1 to evacuate immediately, while she crisscrossed the unprotected kitchen windows with tape, hoping that after the gummy strips had dried in the sun, she wouldn't have to scrape them off with a razor.

By the time the house was as secure as she could make it, the wind had picked up to a salty breeze. Starlight took one last look at the pine house, climbed into the Jeep, and switched on the radio. Someone was saying that Miami Beach and Key Biscayne were closed, and that most of the shelters were filled. The scent of the yellow-flowered acacia was still in her nose. She suddenly swung around, executing a hairpin U-turn that she had been advised never to make in the Jeep, and returned to the pine frame house, deciding that was where she would wait out the storm. The idea that she could not leave the house to fend for itself was irrational, yet as insistent as the acacia.

The night seemed to come in great blankets of darkening sky. Starlight sat in the corner of the living room with the only light the beam from her flashlight and the lonely glow cast by downtown Miami. The wind was stronger now, and one of the shutters began to bang. She put on her Walkman and turned to station Y-100 to listen to meteorologist Bryan Norcross advising everyone that the hurricane was packing winds of 145 m.p.h. and that it was over warm water, which meant it would likely pick up speed. Outside the kitchen window, limbs on the poinciana rose and fell like swaying tentacles.

When the relentless wind forced rainwater under the front door, Starlight began to search for a safer place to wait out the storm. She worked her way to an upstairs bathroom until the tub banged free of the wall and water from the leaking roof poured down around the medicine cabinet. She decided that she was safer below with another story to separate her from the roof.

Starlight sought the refuge of a musty, downstairs hall closet, where she sat on the floor and trained her flashlight at the darkness. Scattered about were mothballs and wire hangers and a sepia photograph of a fair-haired woman squinting in the sun while standing stiffly beside a little boy in a dress.

She glanced idly at the photograph, then noticed that some of the floorboards had sprung. She wondered if they had always been irregular or if they had been forced up by moisture seeping from below. She examined the floor more closely, wondering if it was her great-great grandfather who had first nailed down these wide planks of wood. Something glinted beneath a board in the corner. She pried up the lifted end with her sandal. There in the rocky dirt lay a rusted tin box, inside the box, a frayed leather-bound book eaten with mildew.

Starlight flipped the book open, unmindful of the muffled chaos around her — the jangle of a dozen car alarms, the sounds of shattering glass, of metal scraping across the pavement, of crashing coconuts and garbage cans. The faded, meticulously crafted entries appeared to be a diary, but they were too faint to make out in the dimly lit closet. Only the cover page was legible, revealing that the book belonged to Eulalie Coombs and that its contents were private.

The diary's owner, Starlight thought, must have been the first Eulalie, her great-great grandmother, the woman for whom her own mother was named. She wondered if the first Eulalie was the woman in the sepia photograph, when she realized that the house was groaning on its foundation. Starlight set the diary aside to listen, scarcely moving until an outside door banged open and someone yelled her name.

With only a pinpoint of flashlight to guide her, she left the shelter of the closet to feel her way along the darkened hall.

It was Pupi, his poncho soaked, water beading his black eyelashes, dripping from his face. The wind whipped behind him in the open doorway, bending palms to the ground, snapping brittle, long-limbed avocado trees in half, rattling every door, banging every shutter, hurling objects at the outer walls, the roof.

"Your grandparents called my apartment. When they couldn't get me there, they called the station. God, I was frantic. Your grandmother is wild. You've got to leave, Starlight, now! They've evacuated this whole area."

She eased her neck in a slow, side to side roll. "Not everywhere. Just east of Bayshore. This is west. Besides, this old house has been here a hundred years, so I guess it's been through a storm or two. Too bad you forgot that I'm not a candy ass like you, it would have saved you a trip."

"Why are you so stubborn? Forget about me. It's what your grandfather wants. He's really worried. Don't even think of going in your Jeep. Canvas doesn't have a prayer against everything that's flying around out there. I'll take you in my van."

Rivulets of water crept in over the top of the front door and spat through the keyhole.

"I'm not leaving," she said.

He argued that the center of the hurricane was sixty miles east of Miami, that in a few hours, when the eyewall entered southern Biscayne Bay, dispatchers were ordering all police and fire personnel off the streets. They still had time. But they had to move. "What do you expect to do here? The power is out. This is one mean storm, baby. It could go to a category five, which makes it one in a century."

They stood apart in the puddling front room, looking awkwardly at each other as the house trembled and shivered in the growling wind. Pupi scanned the creaking rafters with the beam of his flashlight. "I'm staying with you."

Starlight's ears popped from the rapidly dropping barometric pressure. She swallowed hard. "I don't want you here."

"You can't throw me out in a hurricane. Pretend I'm a stranger." The wind began to scream like a siren, a high-pitched shriek that whistled through the cracks in the ceiling, forcing water around the front door. "Norcross is telling everyone to get into a bathtub and cover themselves with a mattress. I think we need to do that," said Pupi.

"There is no mattress. And the bathtub's walking around by itself. Any other ideas?"

The attic trapdoor began to bang as the wind tried to suck it out of the house. Pupi reached to pull her back into the closet. Starlight yanked her arm away, then punched him in the shoulder. "I'm not going in there with you. What do you think you're doing?"

"Trying to save your life." He tackled her behind her knees, flinging her before him into the closet, where she huddled in anger, careful to avoid his touch, his eyes.

When the wind began to roar like a bulldozer, he leaned over and grabbed her hand, and she let him.

Bathed in sweat, they heard an enormous crash of something overhead that made the ceiling rattle and the house shudder on its foundation. Starlight didn't know if she was trembling because she was afraid, or because she shared the vibrations of the battered house. When her breath came fast, she realized that what she felt was desire.

She reached up a hand to yank his hair, pull his head close, then kissed him full on the lips and tugged off her shorts while outside the wind whistled like a freight train.

Pupi felt the closet wall bulge against his back as he jackknifed her legs, then fumbled to open his jeans. Their furious movements mimicked the urgency of the storm, their passion the electrical energy that crackled about them. They ignored the chunks of plaster that tumbled on their heads, wanting only to wrest from each other an antidote to the destruction outside. Their orgasms were swift, jolting. Half-sitting, entangled, murmuring each other's names, they remained locked together until once more erect, he lunged into the primal sea of her body.

By early morning, the winds began to slacken. They opened the closet door to find that part of the roof over the kitchen had peeled away. Daylight rushed in, the morning's first light, an eerie cobalt blue. Glittering shards of glass from an unshuttered kitchen window, some still attached to strips of duct tape, lay strewn over the floor.

Something was blocking the front door shut. They managed to shove open the back door instead and stepped outside into a sea of sludge and seaweed and fallen acacia. A gray sandy lint covered everything, even the wet leaves that plastered every surface in sight. The canvas top of the Jeep hung in soggy shreds beneath a tangle of live oak, pigeon plum, and vines, the only trees still standing a royal poinciana, a sapodilla, and a gumbo-limbo stripped of its branches and its copper red bark. When they reached the front of the house, they found the banyan, the massive plate of its roots scooped out of the earth, its branches and stolons grotesque and awkward, flung over the lawn, the front porch, and the roof in a clumsy, awkward embrace.

An invisible cloud of fiberglass hung in the air. With irritated eyes and throat, they stepped into an obstacle course of uprooted trees, tumbleweeds of tin, downed light poles, twisted chain-link fencing, a scramble of power lines, some still sparking at their frayed ends.

Shallow-rooted Australian pines and huge banyans whose only anchor had been the sandy rock lay everywhere. Neighbors wandered about their wrenched or twisted trunks dazed and stuporous in the smothering heat, looking up at roofs that were missing tar paper and shingles, poking sticks into swimming pools filthy with mud and dead mullet, sifting through the rubble of what had been their homes. Someone had spraypainted a standing piece of wall with the warning YOU LOOT, WE SHOOT.

The street was a river. Cars were overturned or buried under trees. Smashed traffic signals lay facedown on the pavement, flashing uselessly, while street signs lay hidden under heaps of rubbish. Boats from Dinner Key, driven by winds and a fourteen-foot storm surge, lay strewn in yards, in driveways, up in trees, stacked three and four deep like cordwood, some buried in the wreckage with their masts sticking out of a jumble of asphalt roofing tiles. In the bay beyond floated mattresses, cars, and the wall of a house.

Pupi said he was going to try to return to the station, did she want to come? She shook her head. She wanted to do what she could to clear the house. "We could have been killed," he said.

"No shit. What's your point?"

"We shared an experience that's supposed to bring people closer together. Did it?"

"A hurricane just cut through here like a

buzzsaw. I'm numb, Pupi. I guess I can't think of anything else."

"What about last night in the closet?"

"I was caught up in the storm. I was afraid. I don't know what I was doing."

"I do."

"That's open to question." He jumped into his van and drove over a thicket of branches and fallen vines, riding up on someone's littered walk to avoid a dangling power line.

As Starlight watched him leave, she noticed that the shade was gone, exposing the devastated landscape to lay luminous and shadowless in an extraordinary wash of daylight that hurt her eyes.

A few of her neighbors began to bustle in the sun, organizing chunks of roofing into neat piles, hauling carpets and mattresses out to dry, shoveling out their dining rooms, hammering blue plastic sheeting over the holes in their roofs. One of them offered her a machete and a candle. Starlight took both, then went to clear the debris from her Jeep.

Wearing sunglasses and an old straw hat she found in the house, she struggled to heave a hunk of banyan that lay across the front seat. When she was finally able to fling the branch aside, peculiar gray-brown objects lay spilled beneath the running board — shards of pottery, a string of beads, a bone shaped like a fishhook. She picked up the beads and slipped them around her neck, put the fishhook in her pocket, and kicked the broken pottery into a pile of rubbish.

When it was almost dark, Starlight picked her way to the back door. With no street or house lights, no glow from the city's horizon, the night was soon coal black. She entered the kitchen, looked up to see the stars shine through the hole in the ceiling, wondering for a moment if it was on a night like this that she was named.

She lit the candle and set it on a shard of glass, listening to frogs croaking, to voices in the distance, and the occasional gunfire of neighbors shooting at trees snapping under their own weight. The candle flickered lazily, once almost snuffed by the breeze while the house creaked with what seemed like familiar footsteps. She planned the next morning, decided that she would begin by cleaning up the glass, then fell asleep.

The sound of chain saws began at dawn. Heat came through the hole in the ceiling, as did the smell of rotting foliage and household garbage. Starlight opened the kitchen door and saw that all the trees and shrubbery that had been felled the day before now lay scorched and brown from the sun and salt water, that the leaves and seaweed plastered to the pink rock house next door had stained it green.

She searched the rubble, pushing aside sailcloth and siding, window screens and coconuts, until she found a broken pine branch that would do as a broom. As she swept the glass from the kitchen floor, she was glad to see that beneath the tile was a layer of linoleum, and beneath the linoleum, wood. It was still there, all of it. All she had to do was restore it.

That night, Starlight kept her machete at her side and listened to her Walkman. She decided that what she wanted most was a hot shower and a cold drink. Then she recalled the perfume that Eulalie had sprayed everywhere, as if the smell of heliotrope and rose could take away where they had been and what had happened to them. She remembered the way her mother swept her blonde silky hair back from her forehead and let it fall to her shoulders, the way she made decisions, quickly, with a snap of her fingers, or not at all. She thought of what her grandfather had told her of how Eulalie died. Your mother was an innocent bystander, he said, caught in the middle. She was just unlucky, at the wrong place at the wrong time. Starlight didn't believe that anymore. A person picked her time and place, made choices all the time. And skipping off to the Bahamas in a boat with two guys that Eulalie had to know were drug dealers was stupid. Skipping off and leaving a child behind was even stupider.

Deciding that the stupidest thing of all was to rehash the past, Starlight jumped up to look for the tin box with the diary inside. It was in the closet where she had left it. She opened the book under the light of the candle. Some of the leather binding crumbled to the floor in a reddish dust, its brief dated entries time-washed to a pale, faint brown. "I have tried to sleep but I cannot. Thomas is in the air I breathe. I know this is not just John Quincy's punishment but the Lord's." There were references to the weather, to baking without eggs and milk, and another entry: "I did not know it was possible to hate your own child. May God forgive me. When I look at the girl, I think of him, for she has his eyes, his face." One of the last: "John Quincy killed him. I have not found out how, but I know he buried his body in the Indian mound. Even though it was my husband who killed Thomas, I am the one responsible, for if not for me, Thomas would still be alive."

Starlight put down the book and imagined the writer, the first Eulalie, her grandfather's grandmother. Whoever Thomas was, she must have loved him. Possibly even had a child by him. Was it always like this, even in olden times? Did people love another, then screw each other up? Would that happen to her, to her own children, even in some unbelievably distant future, to grandchildren who would read her letters, thumb through her photographs, smile at her secrets?

She remembered what she had said to the makeup artist on the shoot about being responsible for her mother's death, then ran her fingers through her crop of hair. It felt good, the hair of a woman who had no time to fuss over her looks, who would swing a machete, make do without power and water, protect a house, make choices, forgive.

The next day brought mosquitoes, rats, fire ants, and afternoon rains. The tank top and cutoffs that Starlight had worn for three days were soaked with sweat and tree sap. She had not been dry since the night before the storm. Everything stank, an odor of insect repellant, rotting garbage, mildewing soaked furniture, the stench of bay sludge and sewage. There were new sounds, the hum of generators and of olive drab military choppers fluttering overhead.

Starlight decided that she had done all she could for the pine house. She put on the old straw hat, then went across the street to make a phone call to the television station.

While canvas tatters flapped against the roll bar, Starlight headed west on the Tamiami Trail. She drove past steel supports of billboards twisted as if they were plastic, through smoke from the thousands of tons of burning debris that stung her eyes, into the lonely landscape of the Everglades, where rotting flotsam choked the canals and a fallen regiment of downed oaks and slash pines that had snapped in half lay on the side of the road. As she drove farther west, she noticed that cypress heads, small tree islands that rose from the sawgrass, had lost their foliage, yet the sawgrass seemed unharmed. Unruffled great blue herons stalked darting killifish. Violet flowers dusted the stalks of pickerelweed, and white spider lilies glimmered in the water under flocks of ibis.

The reservation was visible from the highway. She turned onto a sandy road across a canal clogged with pigweed and water lettuce, where an otter bumped from one bank to another. At first she saw only that the palms still stood while giant Australian pines had toppled power lines. Then she noticed that most of the trailers in the encampment were destroyed, some smashed as if by a giant fist, others twisted like tinfoil shells. Many wooden structures lay in splintered ruins while buildings made of cement block remained intact, as did most of the chickees, although all were missing fronds, a few, their roofs. Surrounding everything was a wreckage of rotting pumpkins, the rusted skeleton of an old hand-cranked sewing machine, broken glass, roofing, propeller blades wrenched from their scaffolds, and waterlogged television sets.

Pupi's van was parked beside the windowless bingo hall, where two men on ladders were nailing blue plastic over the damaged roof. Starlight parked her Jeep nearby, found him standing near an open cooking fire, interviewing a gray-haired Miccosukee Indian who wore a bright patchwork jacket. She sat on a cypress log while the Miccosukee, who she realized was Ray Gopher, said that he wasn't sure when the electricity would be restored, that they had generators for some of their main buildings, and that the tribe had given out emergency funds to tribal members out of its festival fund.

Pupi asked if he had noticed what happened to the wildlife. Ray Gopher said that the panther, deer, and bobcats did all right, that he saw a bear ride out the storm on a mangrove island.

"I'm told that the Seminole tribe in Hollywood has donated bottled water and canned goods to you," said Pupi.

"We make out okay," said Ray Gopher.

"People think you can always fish."

Ray Gopher said that at one time he had gigged fish from the canal, but no more. "The hurricane is not the problem. You need a hurricane to clear away deadwood. The problem is that our land is being used for farm water runoff. Do you expect your neighbor to drink your garbage?"

"I'm sure you know, Ray Gopher, that there are plans to clean up the water."

Ray Gopher spoke low. "What I know is, the Everglades is our mother. She is dying and her care is in the hands of others." He turned to help an elderly woman lift a cook pot onto a tripod.

Pupi had twenty-five seconds until the update. He had decided to tag it out with commentary

739

when his eye was caught by legs. He didn't have to see anything more. They could only belong to one person. He hurried across the littered open space, kicking aside the lead as the cameraman ran to catch up, then bent to hold the microphone to her face. "What brings you to the Miccosukee reservation?"

"I've lost someone. I came to find him."

"What are the odds of finding him out here after a hurricane? Aren't you better off placing an ad?"

"He doesn't read the paper anymore."

"What does he look like? Maybe someone here has seen him."

"He's got dark hair that flops in his eyes, a great smile that he flashes too much. He's a cocky, macho man who's never on time, and he's short, like a *camarero*."

"*Camarone*. A *camerero* is a waiter. What makes you think you'll find this person here?"

"I'm hopeful."

"It's important not to give up hope. I know I never did." He turned to the camera. "I'm tossing it back to you, Bryan," he said, then pulled the IFB from his ear, dropped beside her on the cypress log and enveloped her in a somber embrace. They sat locked and silent beneath the hot sun while a limpkin, confusing day with night, gave its strange wailing call.

"I want to get really old with you," she said.

"You've got it."

"I threw away your salsa tapes."

He kissed her hair. "No problem. I've got more."

"What about the house?"

"If it's what you want, it's okay with me. I saw a great place for speakers. The ceiling beams. Speakers and recessed lights. We'll clean it out and start from scratch. Maybe put in Cuban tile."

"I prefer wood."

"Well, maybe just tile in the kitchen."

"We'll have to replace the banyan," she said.

"With guava and avocado."

"With grapefruit and lime." She pulled back to search his eyes. "Big Fish will cater."

"We'll be married by a priest."

"A judge."

"How about a Catholic judge?"

Ray Gopher had left the cook fire and was walking away. Pupi stood, pulled her up beside him. "I've got to talk to him. It'll just take a minute."

Ray Gopher stopped when he heard his name. He waited until they caught up. The girl was badly sunburned. He wondered why whites were so unfinished in their skin, why the women grew so tall. While Pupi thanked him, he squinted at the beads around his woman's neck, then walked slowly toward her, rolling softly from one side of his foot to the other. "Where did you get the necklace?"

"I found it under a banyan tree. It's nothing

741

much. Some of the beads are broken. I kept it because it's kicky."

"They belong to the old ones."

"Which old ones?"

"The people beyond memory." Ray Gopher looked away so as not to appear impolite, his eyes on an anhinga, feathers wet and glossy, surfacing from the murky water of the canal with a mullet wriggling on its needle-sharp beak.

Starlight fingered the shiny black beads, her eye caught by the patchwork of Ray Gopher's jacket, in one place intertwined with tattered roses that seemed to be made of silk. "Would you like to have them?" she asked.

"I'll take them," he said softly. "They will be pleased to get them back."

"How will they know? I mean, you're talking about dead people."

He shook his head slowly, then spoke into the distance, as if to the bulrush margins of the canal. "Do you know how pelicans survive a hurricane?"

"How?" said Starlight.

He turned to face her with eyes as black as obsidian. "They hug the ground."

"I don't understand. Is there some hidden message in that?"

"Nothing hidden. Open to all who see. They make themselves small. They make themselves no better than the earth."

Pupi thanked Ray Gopher, then led her away.

"He's speaking in metaphor," he said. "Who knows what he's talking about? Look, I'm almost finished. I have to check out tent city, then talk to Carrie Meek. It looks like she's going to be elected the first black member of Congress from Florida since Reconstruction. All I have to do after that is find my dad a generator."

They left in Starlight's Jeep. Pupi said that he wanted to drive, only until they were out of sight of the reservation. Starlight refused. He sat beside her, complaining about the ripped canvas that slapped him in the face, about the way she drove.

"I didn't give Ray Gopher everything I found," she said. "I still have this."

While Pupi reached over to taste the salt on her neck, she plunged her hand into the pocket of her shorts and pulled out the bone shaped like a fishhook. In the retreating Everglades behind them, hurricane-stirred bottom sediment churned unseen nutrients to shrimp and crabs in the waters above and Ray Gopher placed the thong of beads within the sanctuary of his medicine bundle.

We hope you have enjoyed this Large Print book. Other Thorndike Press or Chivers Press Large Print books are available at your library or directly from the publishers. For more information about current and upcoming titles, please call or write, without obligation, to:

Thorndike Press
P.O. Box 159
Thorndike, Maine 04986
USA
Tel. (800) 223-6121
(207) 948-2962
(in Maine and Canada, call collect)

OR

Chivers Press Limited
Windsor Bridge Road
Bath BA2 3AX
England
Tel. (0225) 335336

All our Large Print titles are designed for easy reading, and all our books are made to last.